MURDER AT
GREYSBRIDGE

Also By Andrea Carter

Death at Whitewater Church

Treacherous Strand

The Well of Ice

The Body Falls

MURDER AT
GREYSBRIDGE

AN INISHOWEN MYSTERY

ANDREA CARTER

OCEANVIEW ⟨ PUBLISHING

SARASOTA, FLORIDA

ISBN 978-1-60809-518-6

Published in the United States of America by Oceanview Publishing

Sarasota, Florida

www.oceanviewpub.com

10 9 8 7 6 5 4 3 2

PRINTED IN THE UNITED STATES OF AMERICA

*For Nikki and Owen, and Coote House,
where we were lucky enough to grow up*

Chapter One

MY EYES SHIFTED away from the skeleton. They moved to the central nervous system, up along the spinal cord to the brain, the cerebellum and pituitary gland. They pinged across to the height charts, the nutrition pyramid and the posters saying *Antibiotics won't cure your cold!* and *Baby clinic every Wednesday 1 p.m. to 3 p.m.*

I tried to relax.

God, how I hated going to the doctor. This one was particularly embarrassing.

A gravelly voice interrupted my thoughts. "He's a grand wee young fella."

"Sorry, Jim?"

The old man seated opposite me leaned across. "I said, the new doctor—he's a nice young fella." He winked. "But then you'd know that."

I sighed. Glendara, where no private life was private. Having said that, I was glad to see that Jim was looking a lot better than the last time I'd seen him, despite us both being in a doctor's waiting room. Three weeks earlier, I'd drafted his will and wondered at the time how long it would be before I was called upon to administer it. He'd had a sickly grey pallor and a hacking cough I was sure would do him in before the year was out. But now his eyes were bright and there was color in his lined cheeks. And a distinctly mischievous grin on his face.

"And sure, a few more months around here and he'll soon lose the accent," he added.

I gave in and smiled. "No doubt."

Jim returned to clicking his teeth and I reopened the three-year-old copy of *Woman's Way* I'd been reading. I wondered whose stash Harry had raided—the practice had only been open a few months.

Dr. Harry, as he'd quickly become known, had arrived in Glendara in the spring and taken over the practice of old Dr. O'Doherty—or "Needles" as he was known, his nickname derived not from the injections he administered, but because his grandmother was an obsessive knitter, never seen without her needles and a ball of wool. Harry didn't have a nickname. His mother was a local but had married a French Canadian with the relatively unusual name—in Inishowen, at least—of Dubois, which was deemed sufficient to distinguish him from the raft of Dohertys and McLaughlins in the area. But he was firmly Dr. Harry rather than Dr. Dubois, and I suspected that would not change.

He was also Leah's cousin. When he had arrived in town, my trusty legal assistant had persuaded me to help show him around, and eventually to double-date with her and her fiancé Kevin. It was casual and fun, and it was something I'd badly needed.

But the past few weeks I'd been feeling a bit off. I had a lump in my throat that came and went, and there were times when my throat felt constricted, as if it was being squeezed by an invisible hand. But if I had a glass of wine—I'd had quite a few this summer—the symptoms seemed to disappear, which convinced me that the problem was psychosomatic.

Psychosomatic or not, I'd been unable to conceal it from Leah, who had nagged me into speaking to Harry about it. And since

Harry was now Glendara's only GP, and Leah's wedding, at which I was due to read, was imminent, I was left with little choice. I'd finally caved in and had some blood tests done. Now I was back to get the results.

I looked up again from my magazine, stifling a yawn. I was distracted and tired. I'd been in Buncrana Garda Station until the early hours of the morning with a client who'd been arrested for a vicious assault in the back room of a pub called the Drunken Piglet. I hadn't managed to get to the bottom of it yet, but he was due to be brought before a special sitting of Glendara District Court at half past twelve.

I checked my watch. It was twelve o'clock. The waiting room had been full when I'd arrived. Now, at midday, nearing the end of morning surgery, only Jim and I remained. The long, narrow window that ran along the top of the front wall was open, and the screech of seagulls diving for leftovers from the lunchtime takeaway trade drifted in from the square. Despite that, the room was uncomfortably warm. It was early August and one of the hottest summers on record in Inishowen.

"Wild warm, so it is," Jim offered, reading my thoughts. He pulled a grubby-looking handkerchief from his pocket and wiped his brow with it. "It's not good for us, you know."

"No, we're not really cut out for heat in this part of the world, are we?"

Jim shook his head in agreement while using the same handkerchief to vigorously blow his nose.

The door of the waiting room opened and the receptionist stuck her head in. "Jim? The doctor is ready for you now."

Jim stuffed the hanky back into his pocket, hauled himself to his feet and shuffled towards the door, raising his right hand in salute. "Right, Solicitor. I'll be seeing you."

The door clicked shut. I massaged the muscles in my neck and tried not to think about the likely cause of my symptoms. I was pretty sure it was all in my head, and not just because a glass of wine seemed to improve it. Several months earlier, I'd survived an attempt on my life by one Luke Kirby, the man who had killed my sister. Luke was now dead. I'd thought his death would mean I could finally get on with my life, but the relief was short-lived. Sleep had been erratic and elusive over the past few months, and it was hard not to make the connection between the throat problems I was having now and almost being strangled in reality. I'd survived Kirby's attack, but the memory of his hands around my throat in a filthy boatshed in Culdaff was one I was unlikely to forget. I glanced again at the wall opposite, with its posters on nutrition and exercise, and thought how little it all meant if one didn't have peace of mind.

I was lost in these cheerful thoughts when the door opened again.

The receptionist smiled. "Ben?"

I followed her out of the waiting room, past her desk and through the door of the bright, freshly painted and very blue surgery.

Harry stood up from his desk. "Hi."

At well over six foot, he towered over me. I smiled as I remembered Jim's description of him as a "wee young fella".

"Any better?" he asked.

"Ah yeah," I lied. "It's nothing really. I'm sure it'll just go away on its own at some stage."

Harry closed the door behind me with a soft click and indicated the chair beside his desk, which I took, bag resting on my knee. He sat down, tapped at a few keys on his computer and peered at the screen. His light-blue striped shirt matched his eyes, and the walls. Not for the first time, I could see why he'd become such a hit in town, particularly with his female patients. Dr. Harry was decidedly easy on the eye.

He looked up at me, eyebrows raised. "Well, all the bloods are back, and everything seems to be clear. We've tested for thyroid, coeliac disease and infection, but all are negative. Your iron levels are good, there's no vitamin B deficiency . . ." He shook his head, looking back at the screen. "All in all, you seem pretty healthy."

"Great." I stood up to go. "So that's it?"

"Hold on," he said, motioning for me to sit back down. "I'd like to refer you on to an ENT guy in Letterkenny."

I obeyed, sinking back into the seat. "Do you think that's necessary?"

"I think it's a good idea, just to rule out anything nasty."

"Okay," I said slowly.

"It'll take a few weeks. But . . ." he hesitated, "there is also the possibility that you have something known as globus hystericus."

"What on earth's that?" I raised my eyebrows.

He crossed his arms and leaned back in his chair. "Simply put, it manifests itself as a choking sensation, or a feeling of having a lump in the throat."

"Which is what I have. Periodically," I added.

"It's certainly something similar to what you've described."

I paused. "Hang on. You said "a *feeling* of having a lump in the throat". So you mean the lump isn't really there?"

"Exactly," he said. "I'm not suggesting that the feeling isn't perfectly real to you, but it's a condition that's thought to be connected with anxiety."

I smiled suddenly, putting two and two together. "Globus hystericus. Hysteria. You mean 'lady madness'."

Harry had the grace to look uncomfortable, and then he grinned too. "Actually, I shouldn't have said that. It's not called hystericus any longer. It has the more PC term globus pharyngeus now. The good thing is, it's nothing to worry about. Have you had anything worrying you lately? Stress at work or anything?"

"Some, I suppose."

I'd have been surprised if Harry hadn't heard about the events at Christmas. News travels quickly in Inishowen, and Leah would have told him if no one else had. But he didn't mention it; just turned back to his screen.

"Look, I'll refer you to an ENT in Letterkenny anyway." He looked up. "In the meantime, there are some exercises you can do that might help. Throat stretching and exercises for your voice. They're on the net."

"Great. I'll have a look."

"Yoga and meditation might help too. The problem is, if it is globus, it's quite difficult to shift."

"I'd noticed that."

I stood again, pulling the straps of my bag onto my shoulder. Harry stood too, his hands in the pockets of his white coat. His face softened, signaling that the professional bit was over.

"Ready for Saturday?"

I smiled. "I'm reading a poem, assuming my throat holds up."

"Lovely. This will be my first Donegal wedding in a while." His eyes creased in amusement. "Are they still gigantic? I came back for another cousin's about ten years ago. I'd swear that one had about four hundred guests."

I laughed. "Leah's won't be that big. Greysbridge is too small."

Harry crossed his arms. "That's right. Greysbridge." His voice changed to a mock whisper. "My mother tells me that house is haunted. She was amazed to hear it was reopening as a hotel."

My eyes widened. "I wonder if Leah knows that."

"Maybe leave it till after the ceremony to tell her." He paused. "You sure you don't want to travel together?"

I shook my head. Handsome as he was, I sure as hell wasn't ready for that kind of public declaration. "I'm going up tomorrow night with Maeve. Your parents still aren't coming over?"

"No. My dad's not a great traveler anymore and my mother's happy to stay with him. So, I'll see you there."

He made his way over to the door and held it open for me. As I was leaving, he gave me a surprise kiss on the cheek.

★ ★ ★

I paid at the desk and walked out into the square, momentarily blinded by bright sunshine. I reached into my bag for sunglasses, put them on and checked my watch—it was twenty-five past twelve. I barreled up the street towards the courthouse.

The man I was representing was being led in in handcuffs just ahead of me. I tapped the guard accompanying him on the shoulder and asked that he be taken to the small anteroom off the main court so I could speak to him before we got started.

Once inside, I closed the door and perched on the only piece of furniture in the room, an old kitchen table with peeling green paint. My client, one Eamonn McShelley, stood in front of me, handcuffs removed, gaze firmly fixed on the wall opposite.

"How are you doing this morning?" I asked. "All right?"

He grunted something resembling an assent. He was more subdued than he had been last night, but the stench of stale booze was undeniable, his hair was greasy and his skin had a sheen that indicated he hadn't had the benefit of a shower today. I'd met Mr. McShelley for the first time at midnight the night before, after a call from the Garda station asking me to come and represent him. He'd requested me by name, I was told, but I still wasn't sure why. He was no more communicative this morning than he had been last night.

I took his charge sheet from my bag. "Okay, as you know, you've been charged under section 3 of the Non-Fatal Offences against the Person Act, which is assault causing harm. It's a serious offence. But all that will happen this morning is that the guard will give evidence of arrest, charge and caution and I will have an opportunity to apply for bail on your behalf. Do you understand?"

He nodded, still not meeting my eye. I sighed. This wasn't going to be easy. The night before, I'd been told he'd resisted arrest, but he'd refused to tell me anything then either. I recalled my exchange with the arresting guard. *What are you saying he did?* I'd asked. *Chained a guy to a radiator and then proceeded to get pissed for two hours.* I'd raised my eyebrows. *But you're charging him with assault causing harm, not false imprisonment?* The guard had narrowed his eyes. *The radiator was on. Full pelt. We have a victim in intensive care with second-degree burns.*

I crossed my arms. "As I told you last night, the guards have said they will be objecting to bail on the basis that you may interfere with witnesses. Last night you said that you didn't want me to apply for bail. Is that still your position?"

McShelley nodded again, staring at the ground with a surly expression on his face.

"Are you sure?" I paused. No further response. "Okay. That means you will be remanded in custody and taken to Castlerea prison. The case will be put back for one week." I took a blank Statement of Means from my bag. "What about your circumstances? Are you working?"

He shook his head.

I stood up. "Give me a minute and I'll come back to you."

I made my way into the courtroom. As was typical for the summer months, the heating was on and the place was like a sauna. The thought of being chained to a radiator made the skin on the back of my neck prickle.

An inspector from Letterkenny was speaking to the court clerk, but other than that the courtroom was empty. The inspector turned when he heard my footsteps and I made my way over. He nodded a good morning.

"Eamonn McShelley," I said, counting off the issues on my fingers. "No application for bail. We'll consent to a remand in custody for one week."

The inspector nodded. "In case you were considering an application for legal aid, there'll be an objection to that too."

I raised my eyebrows. "Any reason? He tells me he's unemployed."

The inspector smiled. "He might be claiming the dole, but there's a hefty pay packet coming from somewhere."

"What do you mean?"

"He's from Castleblaney. He's in a pub in Inishowen with keys to a lorry but no vehicle. And quite an amount of cash on his person." The man's tone was sarcastic. "What would you think?"

I had some ideas, but I wasn't about to suggest them to the inspector. The high rate of tax on cigarettes and alcohol meant that smuggling of those goods was rife. Red diesel used in agricultural machinery had a significantly lower rate of tax than ordinary diesel but its use in road vehicles was illegal, meaning that fuel laundering, the removal of the red dye, was pretty profitable. There were any number of offences he could have been referring to.

I shrugged. "I don't know. You'll have to tell me what you're thinking."

Unsurprisingly, the inspector wasn't prepared to share his suspicions with me either. "I think you'll have to ask your client about that."

"You do know you haven't charged him with anything in that regard? It's a straightforward Section 3."

"I'm aware of that," he said coolly. "I'm simply marking your card that that is unlikely to remain the position. What I'm saying now is that despite what he may be telling you, your client is on someone's payroll, which means we'll be rigorously objecting to any application for legal aid."

The clerk called, "All rise," and the judge walked into the courtroom.

Chapter Two

A LINE OF sweat was running down my back within seconds of leaving the courthouse; my suit was way too warm. The sun beat down and it hadn't rained for over a week, a major phenomenon in Donegal. As old Jim had remarked, we weren't really cut out for it. For the first few days people had embraced the good weather, leaving work early to go to the beach, dragging chairs from the Oak pub to drink afternoon pints outside. But now, after a month of almost solid sunshine, they were beginning to complain, sporting sunburned skin and red eyes, claiming they were too hot to sleep and that animals were suffering and plants were dying. And as I walked through the square, I saw that the flower beds, usually a blaze of color at this time of year, were a sorry sight, despite the Tidy Towns committee's attempts to water them more regularly than usual.

Crossing the road in the direction of the office, I spotted Phyllis Kettle fanning herself with a paperback in the doorway of her bookshop. She waved, and I walked towards her. Her Border collie, Fred, was flopped down beside her on the mat, tongue lolling from the side of his mouth. The bookseller hadn't made too many concessions to the heat—she was wearing an ankle-length purple linen dress with long sleeves.

She looked at me curiously as I approached. "Everything okay?" she asked.

"Fine, why?"

She nodded towards the doctor's surgery, from where she must have seen me emerge earlier. Not much escapes Phyllis. "Now I know you've been out and about with the handsome doctor, but you were in there a long time. During morning surgery. Looked more like a professional visit to me."

"I'm grand," I said, using the universal Irish response to any enquiry about health.

But her eyes narrowed as they always did when she was ferreting information, and I gave in. "I have a throat thing I can't seem to get rid of."

I took off my jacket and hooked it over my arm, and tried to remember if I had a clean shirt in the office; I'd taken to bringing one in most days.

"A paste with honey, lemon, ginger, garlic, and cayenne pepper," Phyllis pronounced. "Only thing for a throat. Tastes disgusting, but it works. Or gargle with salty water." She fanned herself again. "If it wasn't so warm, I'd suggest a hot whiskey."

"Noted," I said, bowing my head.

I hadn't the energy to explain that I'd already tried every cure I could think of the past few weeks and none of the traditional remedies had worked. Whatever I had, it was no ordinary sore throat.

"All set for Saturday?" I asked, changing the subject. "Got your inspirational words ready?"

Phyllis's face creased into a smile. "Ach, it'll be great. I can't wait."

A few months earlier, Phyllis had announced that for some reason best known to herself she'd been secretly training as a marriage celebrant, and when Leah had heard, she'd asked if she and Kevin could be her first official couple. If nothing else, Phyllis was guaranteed to bring a spot of color to the proceedings.

"The first one was always going to be special," Phyllis said, beaming. "But the fact that I know Leah and Kevin makes it all the better."

"I'm sure it will be lovely. They've been together a long time." I swallowed. I really needed a drink. "Speaking of which, I'd better get back and let the bride-to-be head off."

Phyllis looked at me curiously, screwing her face up against the sun. "Is she working today? I thought she'd be off all week."

"She starts her wedding leave this afternoon, so I'd better get back to man the phones."

I inhaled too quickly and coughed, finding it difficult to speak. But Phyllis wasn't letting me go so easily.

"When are you heading up to Greysbridge?"

"Tomorrow evening. Maeve's coming with me. There's a barbecue the night before the wedding."

"Well, make sure you get an early night tonight with that throat thing. It'll be a long weekend." Phyllis leaned down to pat Fred, who gazed up at her. "Now I'd better get this poor creature and myself something to drink before we pass out."

I walked on, relieved to be able to do the same, dropping into the Oak to pick up a sandwich and some water. Glendara's pub had been rebuilt in the spring after it was burned down at Christmas. Tony Craig, the owner, had done Trojan work and somehow managed to re-create the atmosphere of the original, triumphantly reopening for the August Bank Holiday weekend just past. The only dark spot was that his daughter Susanne had been absent, serving a nine-month sentence for arson of the same pub. But the opening had coincided with the town carnival and the square had been full of stilt walkers and strange costumes, giving the town a much-needed lift. And lots of sunburn the week after.

Armed with my takeaway lunch, I pushed open the door of O'Keeffe & Co., Solicitors. The cool interior was a relief; one of the advantages of working in an old, slightly damp terraced house. Leah was standing waiting at reception, bag and phone in hand, computer switched off. I dumped my purchases on the counter with a groan.

"Well?" she demanded.

"Remanded in custody till next week. They think he's involved in some kind of smuggling. Not that he's admitted anything to me. I can barely get two words out of him."

"I meant Dr. Harry! What did he say?"

"Oh. Blood tests were all clear, but he's referred me on to a consultant just in case."

She frowned, looking worried.

"I'll be fine," I added quickly. "I'm sure it's psychosomatic. I just need a holiday."

She regarded me doubtfully before sighing. "I know what you mean about the holiday. I'm beginning to wonder why Kevin and I didn't just elope. My mother's all stressed because his family are landing over from the island tonight. And although *she's* got used to the idea, she's not sure what they'll think of us having a civil ceremony rather than a church one. And with a female celebrant."

Leah's fiancé had grown up on a small island called Inishathair, which lay off the north coast of Inishowen. Though I'd been to other islands, such as Rathlin and Tory, I'd never been to Inishathair and, oddly, had never met anyone from there other than Kevin. I'd been told the population was less than sixty, so maybe that was why.

"Well there's not much they can do about it now, is there?" I flopped down at Leah's desk. My legs felt shaky all of a sudden. It must have been the heat.

"No," she admitted. "Except make their feelings known. Loudly. Which they are perfectly capable of doing after a few pints."

"Do you think that's likely?" I asked with a grin.

She raised her eyes to heaven. "Oh yes. God knows what Saturday is going to be like."

"Things always get a little fraught when families get together," I said soothingly. "Maybe you can get all the rows out of the way tomorrow and then Saturday will be the calm after the storm."

She grinned suddenly. "Actually, that's not such a bad idea. Maybe I'll do a bit of stirring tonight on purpose." She picked up her keys. "Anyway, I'd better get to this hair appointment or Stan will kill me. I'll see you tomorrow evening."

I gave her a hug. "Good luck. I'm sure it will all go swimmingly. And you have Greece to look forward to after it's all over."

Her face softened as she turned to go. "Is there any way I could skip straight to that bit?"

I unwrapped my sandwich, but before I could take my first bite, the phone rang. The phone was going to be the most difficult part of running the office without Leah, I realized. I took a sip of water before I answered.

"Hi." A male voice with an American accent was followed by a momentary hesitation. "Is that you, Ben?"

I glanced nervously at the door. Leah could easily come back for something. "Yes. Hello, Mitch."

"I hope you don't mind my ringing your office. I found the number online. It's easier than calling your cell."

There was a smile in his voice, but I didn't respond. He was checking up on me. I should have expected it.

"Answering your own phone—you won't have to do that over here, you know. And I'm sure you'll be glad of a bit of sunshine, won't you?"

I couldn't help but smile at that, glancing towards the window and the perfectly blue sky. "You're not going to believe it, but it's twenty-seven degrees here at the moment. And sunny."

"You're kidding. I thought it did nothing but rain over there." There was a pause. "You've been missed, you know."

"That's nice to hear."

"I have good news. We've sorted a locum for you. There's a Monaghan man who is dying to get home for a bit, would take the leave in a heartbeat." He paused as if checking something. "Castleblaney's not that far away from you, is it?"

★   ★   ★

I hung up feeling uneasy. Mitch was the managing partner of the firm I'd worked for in the States before I'd come to Inishowen. We'd stayed in touch with the odd email at Christmas and St Patrick's Day. But then, a month earlier, he'd phoned me out of the blue to say that the firm's Irish-American client base was growing, and they liked the idea of having another "real" Irish lawyer on their staff and would I be interested in being that lawyer? I'd immediately said no, but I'd been feeling low when I'd taken the call and he could hear it in my voice.

The problem was, when he rang back a week later, that hadn't changed. And Mitch knew it. Mitch was a trial attorney—he was trained to smell weakness and exploit it, even over the phone, thousands of miles away. And somehow, I'd found myself agreeing to do a few months, a year at the most, though only if I could find a locum for my practice in Donegal, which I'd thought was unlikely. I wasn't due to start until January, five months away, but I still hadn't told Leah. It seemed too much to land on her just before her wedding.

I pulled myself together, ate the sandwich at my desk and worked through lunch. The afternoon was busy. Managing the phone *and* seeing clients required a high degree of co-ordination, so when my last appointment was over, I left on the dot of half five, locking the door behind me with a sigh of relief.

The Mini was like an oven when I sat in the driver's seat, reminding me of hire cars on foreign holidays. I drove out of the car park with the window fully down, relishing the breeze, passing the Garda station, boarded up now, looking morose and unloved. It had been closed for almost six months. Garda Andy McFadden had been re-stationed in Letterkenny after a stint in rehab for his gambling addiction and I'd run into him in court a few weeks back looking a lot better than the last time I'd seen him. He'd asked after his old sergeant, but I had nothing to tell him.

Driving along the coast, inhaling the sea air, I allowed myself to think about Molloy, something I generally resisted these days. Tom Molloy, Glendara's old sergeant and my ex, had left for Cork in February, having been put on enforced leave pending an investigation into Kirby's death. At first there'd been regular texts and phone calls between us. We'd even attempted to get together on a few occasions, with some vaguely romantic notion about meeting halfway. But Cork is a six-hour drive from Inishowen, and once the investigation was concluded, clearing Molloy of any wrongdoing, he'd been stationed in Clonakilty, which is a further hour.

With his shifts and my practice, whatever we had seemed impossible to sustain. He'd sounded tired when I'd rung, and so we'd spoken less and resorted to texts. Never the most open of individuals, he'd become more and more distant, causing me to send terse replies, until eventually I'd stopped responding altogether. It was too hard. In my mind he'd been the one to pull back, again. He had saved my life and left.

And then Harry had asked me out. I'd said no at first and rung Molloy in some pathetic last-ditch attempt to retrieve whatever we'd had. I was greeted with a foreign ringtone. It was the final straw. I didn't leave a message. And I said yes to Harry. It was easy and uncomplicated and fun.

Chapter Three

THE WATER GAVE me a shock when I lowered my shoulders in at Lagg the following morning. Heatwave or not, the sea in Donegal is cold; bracing an understatement. Since the warm weather, I'd got into the habit of an early-morning dip before work. It helped my throat, although that was probably because it was all I could do to keep breathing while my heart raced in the icy water, leaving no room for other concerns.

It was still only seven, so I stayed in longer than I usually did, although, as always, within my depth and close to shore. Five Fingers Strand or Lagg as the locals call it, is not safe for swimming. For the third night running I'd had difficulty sleeping, waking at three a.m. to toss and turn for hours. At half past five I'd risen, made myself a coffee and curled up on the couch with a book and Guinness, my grouchy black tomcat. At half past six I'd grabbed a towel and swimming togs and climbed into the car.

I hauled myself out of the water and wrapped myself in the towel, standing for a moment to stare at the view that I loved: the water, the rocks, the green mystery of Glashedy Island, its beach a golden gash in the morning light.

I looked down, enjoying the sensation of the cold sand between my toes, and made myself think about the job in the States, wondering if I'd done the right thing. It wasn't as if Mitch was asking me to move there permanently—he was asking me to take a year out, do something different. Maybe that wasn't such a bad idea. I needed a break after the trauma of what had happened. But if I left, would I return? Inishowen was my home, but something had changed in the past few months. The events of Christmas had taken their toll, and Molloy's absence hadn't helped. But the notion that my happiness should be dependent on his presence or absence irritated me. Though our working relationship stretched further back, our romantic one had been short-lived and certainly not worth basing long-term decisions on.

I felt my throat close over, the effects of the swim wearing off, and I breathed in deeply. I'd followed Harry's suggestion and found some exercises on the net, so I gave them a go now. Raising my face to the sky, the gulls swooping and diving above, I rolled my head slowly from left to right, counting the beats. I felt a stretch in the muscles in my neck and it was oddly calming. When I'd finished the first exercise, I moved on to a second, called "kiss the sky". It made me feel pretty foolish, but I did it just the same.

I heard my name being called and I lowered my chin, surprised and embarrassed; I'd assumed I'd be alone on the beach at this hour. A runner was approaching in red singlet and shorts, his long strides propelling him quickly across the damp sand. It was Harry.

He reached me, breathing heavily. I said good morning and he raised his hands in silent greeting before leaning forward, hands on knees, catching his breath. After a few seconds, he straightened.

"Sorry. Trying to push myself." He looked exhausted, with dark circles under his eyes. I wondered how far he'd run. "So, you found the throat exercises?"

I grinned. "You saw me then."

"I did. I'm sorry, I hadn't realized what you were doing or I wouldn't have disturbed you. But they should help." He brushed the sweat from his forehead. "You've certainly nothing to lose by doing them."

I saluted "Okay, Doc. Will do. I'm prepared to do anything at this stage."

He glanced at the water and frowned. "Are you sure you should be swimming here? I thought this beach wasn't safe."

"It's not, but I don't think you could call what I do swimming. More of a shock immersion. I just dip myself in. I do it all year round."

He gazed at me with an amused smile. "You're quite the strange little creature, aren't you?"

I flushed. Harry had a way of looking at you that made you want to giggle idiotically. Not my style usually.

"Be careful, though, won't you?" he said, his expression suddenly sober. "Don't take any risks."

"Always am. Never do."

"Good." He wiped his face with his sleeve again. "Although I must admit, it's looking pretty attractive even to me at the moment."

I followed his gaze to the water, its deceiving Caribbean blue. "Believe me, it's still pretty chilly."

He grinned. "I'll bet." He looked up at the sky; there was heat in the sun even at this hour. "How long is it going to last, do you think—this weather?"

"Oh, it'll probably break soon. It has to," I added unconvincingly.

"I'll be glad when it does." Harry checked his watch. "Anyway, I'd better go—early surgery."

"Okay."

He turned back. "That was a nice surprise," he said, his eyes meeting mine flirtatiously. "Rather a good start to the day."

I smiled. "See you tomorrow."

"For sure."

He walked towards the dunes, stopping to stretch his muscles along the way. I waited till he had disappeared through the gap in the eroded rocks before walking on a little, intending to resume my contemplation. But I'd lost my train of thought, so I picked up my towel and headed back to the car. I'd decided on one thing at least—no decisions until after the weekend. This weekend was for Leah.

★ ★ ★

The office was quiet, and without Leah to chat with, the day fairly dragged. I finally lost momentum about four o'clock, when, conceding defeat, I made myself a coffee, grabbed a Kit Kat from the jar and a magazine from the rack and sat at Leah's desk to kill the last hour. I reckoned I'd better stay on the premises at least.

At twenty past four, having drained the last of my coffee, I heard the door open. I looked up, heart sinking; I'd been so close to escape. Two teenagers burst in, shoving one another and laughing: a girl and a boy of about fourteen. They walked down the narrow hallway shoulder to shoulder, not easy in such a limited space. When they emerged into the reception area, they looked up and stopped laughing, as if resentful of my presence. The girl was Niamh, Leah's youngest sister.

I greeted them. "Hello."

They glanced at each other uncomfortably.

Niamh spoke. "Leah left cufflinks here."

"Oh yes," I said. "She had them made up for Kevin to match her bouquet, didn't she?"

Niamh nodded.

She was not unlike Leah, pretty and clear-skinned, with smart green glasses framing blue eyes, and blonde hair in a high ponytail. She was wearing a purple hoodie, unzipped to reveal a similar-colored T-shirt and black jeans. The boy was baby-faced, with a touch of acne on his forehead, marginally taller than Niamh, with a long fringe, paint-splattered shoes and a battered rucksack on his shoulders. He looked at me, unblinking, with a defiance I found amusing, since he was the one who had entered my space rather than the other way around. There was no offer of introduction.

"I'll have a look. They're probably around here somewhere." I rummaged in a drawer without success, feeling their eyes on me.

"She said they're in with the Post-its and things," Niamh offered eventually.

I followed her suggestion and found a small blue box, which I held aloft. "Do you think this is it?"

Niamh nodded again. I handed it over and she put it into her bag.

I sat back in Leah's chair. "Are you looking forward to your bridesmaid duties tomorrow?"

Niamh smiled a little, her eyes flickering towards the boy. But before she could reply, he cut across her. "We'd better go."

Her smile faded. She nodded her thanks, and as if obeying some siren, they both could hear but I couldn't, they turned and left without a word.

When the door clicked shut, I went to the front room and the window that looked out onto the street. Holding the blind to one side, I watched as they crossed the road, arms linked, heads inclined towards one another as they talked. They stopped at two bikes locked together at a telegraph pole, still deep in chat until suddenly the boy reached for Niamh and kissed her on the lips, pushing her head back just that little bit too far. When he released her, she smiled shyly and put her hand on his shoulder. I felt oddly disconcerted as they cycled away.

★ ★ ★

When I drove back to Malin, the village a few miles from Glendara where I live, the sun was still hot, the sky a deep, clear blue. The village had a summer Friday feel to it, with people sitting outside the pubs on benches on the green, having early pints and gin and tonics. Despite the complaints, it was strange how quickly we'd become accustomed to this unaccustomed weather, when it came to outdoor drinking at least.

I waved to some neighbors I spotted, including Charlie from next door, who'd promised to feed Guinness while I was gone for the weekend. He returned the wave and came over, followed by his little corgi, Ash. Poor Ash was beginning to look his age, with greying whiskers and a touch of arthritis in his gait. Charlie was dressed in a pair of unflattering Hawaiian shorts and was rather red-faced. Whether from the sun or the pint in his hand, I couldn't be sure, but it clearly wasn't his first.

"Is it this evening you're away?" he asked as I bent down to tickle Ash's ears.

I nodded. "Heading shortly." I rooted in my bag for the spare key I'd had cut and handed it over. "Thanks for this. It makes me feel better knowing you'll be feeding him." The year before, Guinness had nearly died from poisoning, so I wasn't taking any chances.

Charlie took the key, examined it and put it in his shirt pocket. "Aye, well, I hope you have a grand weekend. Enjoy the wedding."

"Thanks, Charlie. I'll be back on Sunday evening." I walked across to my cottage, pushing open the gate and making my way up the path.

The cat in question was sunning himself on the doorstep, tail wrapped neatly around himself. I bent down to rub him, and he stretched luxuriously and rolled onto his back.

I straightened myself with a groan. "Sorry, Guinness, I haven't time for that. I'm in a hurry."

My phone buzzed in my bag. It was a text from Maeve, my friend and the local vet. *You ready to go? I can be over in half an hour.*

I texted back, *Give me forty minutes*, as the cat dragged himself to his feet and followed me in through the door.

I raced upstairs taking the steps two at a time. After my shower, I changed into jeans and sandals and a T-shirt and started to pack, something I definitely should have done the day before. Now I was doing it all in a rush, picking things up and dropping them, covering one item with another and forgetting where I'd left others. To add to the chaos, I was followed from room to room by Guinness, who could tell that I was going away. Somehow, he managed to be both clingy and stand-offish at the same time, a gift possessed only by felines. He tripped me up repeatedly, but when I attempted to rub his head, he walked away with his tail in the air and sat with his back firmly turned on me.

I hadn't reached a decision on which dress to wear to the wedding, so I put two into the bag—a red vintage one, which I loved because it had pockets, and a more simple black shift with a wrap. As an afterthought, I threw in some old jeans and boots too. I might go for a walk at some stage over the weekend, I thought.

I was chucking shampoo and shower gel into a washbag when I heard Maeve's voice from the hallway downstairs. I'd left the door open for her.

"You ready?"

"I'll be five minutes," I called down. "Make yourself a coffee if you like."

"God, no, it's too hot, thanks all the same. I'll have some water."

I heard the tap in the kitchen going as Guinness finally walked away from me in disgust and padded down the stairs. And as I threw the last few things into the bag, I heard Maeve chatting to him.

Five minutes later, we were in the Mini, a mournful-looking Guinness gazing at us reproachfully from the doorstep.

"That cat can sure do a guilt trip." Maeve laughed.

"Don't I know it," I said. "Yet he's allowed to wander off for days on end without a by-your-leave."

"That's a tomcat for you. Anyway," she rubbed her hands together, "let's get going. Road trip!"

I put the key in the ignition. "Why do I feel like Thelma and Louise?"

Maeve frowned. "Oh Jesus, don't say that—you're not intending driving us off a cliff, are you? No shortage of them up that end of Inishowen."

I started the car with a grin. "I was thinking more of the giving–Brad–Pitt–a–lift end of things."

Chapter Four

I DROVE ON up the coast, passed the turn for Lagg as if heading for Malin Head, then crossed to the east side of the peninsula. I wore sunglasses: light was streaming into the car as if it was midday rather than half past six. It was rare for Maeve to be in my car; usually we traveled in her jeep if we went somewhere together, but today I'd volunteered, since her husband was away and she was going to the wedding on her own. It didn't take long for me to question the wisdom of that decision. My old Mini doesn't have air conditioning; in fact, it barely has heat, which makes it a little like the courthouse in Glendara—freezing in winter and warm in summer. So the windows remained open for the entire journey, which didn't help Maeve's newly done hair, and though the drive was short, the road was twisty and meandering and full of potholes, which provoked regular complaints about suspension and springs.

After one particularly bumpy section, she hinged forward in some kind of yoga stretch. "How the hell do you travel in this car all the time? I'm really stiff."

"It's probably more suitable for short people," I conceded. "You're just not used to being so low to the ground."

"You're joking, aren't you? It's designed for people under five foot." She leaned back, massaging her neck.

I slowed down, but it didn't seem to help much.

"So who is going to be at this wedding?" she asked. "Who will we know?"

"I think there are about fifty coming. Leah and Kevin's families will make up the bulk of the numbers. There'll be all the islanders, of course . . ."

Maeve grinned over at me suddenly. "That's right, Kevin is from Inishathair, isn't he? I'd forgotten that."

"Yes." I was slightly distracted, glancing around me. "Keep your eyes peeled and watch out for a sign, will you? I reckon we must be nearly here."

Obediently, Maeve shielded her eyes from the sun to look. "They're a strange lot, those islanders. Keep very much to themselves."

"Kevin's the only one I've met. And he only spent a few years there in his teens after his parents died. Have you been there?"

Maeve shook her head. "I get the impression they don't really welcome visitors. Not like Rathlin or Tory. They have their own version of Irish, I've heard, that they slip in along with the English. And they like a drink. Long, dark winters with not much else to do, I guess." She grinned. "Be prepared for a hangover this weekend at the very least."

I groaned inwardly. The dryness in my throat was bad enough without a hangover. I took a gulp from the bottle of water I'd left on the dashboard. As I replaced it, I caught sight of a brown and white sign I couldn't yet read.

Maeve clocked it at the same time. "Is that it, do you think?" she asked.

"Should be," I replied, slowing down to get a closer look.

And it was. *Greysbridge House Hotel 500m*, the sign read. After the suggested half-kilometer, I slowed at a set of grey pillars framing black iron gates.

"That's a bit unusual," Maeve remarked.

I looked to where she was pointing. The pillars were like Roman columns, but each had deep cracks, one in particular traveling its whole length, making it look as if it might collapse at any moment.

"Cripes. I think I'd be inclined to remove them entirely. They look a bit precarious."

The gates were open, but I groaned when I saw the cattle grid, another obstacle for the Mini to negotiate.

"Greysbridge," Maeve said, glancing around her as we turned in. "Where's the bridge, I wonder?"

I shook my head. "No idea. I presume there's one somewhere. We'll have to ask the Greys."

Ian and Abby Grey were the Dublin couple I'd acted for in buying Greysbridge the previous year, which was how Leah had come to hear of it and choose it as her wedding venue. Although the Greys had bought it to run as a small hotel, it turned out that the house and lands had originally been owned by Ian's grandfather, who'd lost it in a card game in the thirties. I'd been impressed by the estate agent's brochure, but I hadn't seen Greysbridge in the flesh, so was looking forward to seeing it now.

The Mini managed the cattle grid, but the rough gravel drive wasn't so easy on the car's low undercarriage. And it was a long drive. A couple of hundred yards through sun-dappled ash, lime and sycamore trees, and the house still wasn't visible. Maeve groaned, her hand on the roof to steady herself as we bumped along. Then the drive took a turn to the left and a group of riders on horseback came into view.

I pulled in to allow them to pass, and the woman leading the group smiled and waved. It was Abby Grey. She came over to speak to us through the open window, leaning forward and tipping her hat.

"Hello, and welcome. I hope you have a lovely weekend."

"Thank you," I said. "I'm excited to see the house, finally."

"We're pretty excited ourselves. It's our first wedding." Abby put her hand to her mouth in a mock whisper. "I hope there are no disasters."

Maeve leaned across to say hello. "There won't be. It'll be great. Have we taken over the whole house?"

Abby nodded. "Just about. There are two extra guests who've been here a few days. But the bride very kindly said she didn't mind them staying on, as we've enough rooms to cater for everyone else." She shot us a wry look. "Which isn't a problem since some of her future in-laws decided that they'd rather sleep on their boats."

"Boats?" Maeve and I chorused in surprise.

Abby's smile hinted that there was more to that particular story than she was prepared to divulge, while Maeve shot me a sidelong look.

"I presume you're both here till Sunday?" Abby asked, and we nodded in reply. "Any interest in a ride in the morning? The wedding doesn't start till two and I was thinking of heading up to the old fort."

Before I could say anything, Maeve replied for both of us. "Aye, absolutely. Count us in. If you can supply this one with a hat, that is. I brought my own just in case."

I swiveled towards her. "This one?"

"Not a problem," Abby said with a broad smile. "We've loads of spares. I'm sure we'll find one to fit you."

"Excellent," Maeve said, giving me a nudge. "We'll look forward to it. Won't we, Ben?"

"Yes," I said reluctantly. Abby had tried to get me to come on a ride when she'd been working in a stable near Glendara, but it hadn't happened. Which meant that the last time I'd actually ridden a horse, I'd been a teenager.

"Right," Abby said, sensing the horses' impatience to get going; the large black cob she was riding had begun to paw at the ground. "Go on up to the house. Get settled in and we'll see you later." She tapped her crop on the roof of the Mini and trotted off with her group following her.

I turned to Maeve before I started the car again. "I haven't ridden in about twenty years. I'm not sure I'll be able to stay on, let alone ride up to some fort."

"Ach, you'll be grand," she grinned. "It'll all come back to you. She'll give you some quiet old mare to start you off." She nodded towards the departing group. "If the hotel's empty other than the wedding guests, who are those other riders?"

"Maybe she takes people who aren't staying here."

"She'd probably need to. Big outlay, all those horses. Especially when they're only starting out."

We drove another hundred yards through the trees before emerging at what looked like the back of a very large residence. The drive snaked to the right of the house, where a glimpse of blue was visible through the green. It seemed the place had been built to face the shore, creating a strange first impression for a hotel, as if it were turning its back on visitors. I drove on past the gable end, where a small door was almost completely hidden by a huge pear tree, laurels to our right, and azaleas flaming in cerise and orange. When they'd bought the house, the Greys had told me it had been allowed to fall into disrepair, but it seemed the garden had not. Despite the heat, it was mature and lush.

As we rounded the building, the shore came dramatically into view, the water blue and welcoming in the evening sunshine. An expansive lawn with sprinklers and flower beds of pampas grass and hydrangeas sloped down towards a little beach and a pier. Two large boats that looked like fishing trawlers were moored there—the guests' accommodation that Abby had referred to, I assumed. I stopped the car and simultaneously Maeve and I turned to look at the house.

It was an Italianate villa in cut limestone, imposing in size—a three-story central block with a balustrade, an east and a west wing and a large portico with steps leading to a red door with a fanlight. But protruding from the right gable was something exceedingly odd. It was a covered footbridge and it appeared to link the main part of the house with another, smaller building almost entirely hidden by dense rhododendron bushes. It was a strange and rather ugly addition that jarred with the rest of the house, omitted, on purpose I assumed, from the brochure I had seen.

There was no denying that Greysbridge was a fine house, but there was something still and secretive about it, something hidden, even in the bright sunshine: a sense that it was hunkering down against the world.

"What a strange place," Maeve said finally, an understatement if I ever heard one. "I'm not sure I should say this," she added, her voice low although we were alone in the car, "but I'm not entirely sure I like it."

She'd read my mind. She nudged me again. "I suppose we'd better park."

She pointed to a sign indicating guest parking. Reluctantly, I peeled my eyes away from the house and moved the Mini forward, turning into a small area where there were already about six cars. I parked in the one shaded spot that remained under the trees, and we climbed out, taking our bags from the boot and making our way back around to the front of the house and towards the main door.

"Where is everyone?" Maeve asked, echoing my thoughts as our footsteps crunched across the gravel.

I looked at my watch—it was a quarter to seven. "I don't know. Having naps before the fun starts? I thought there'd be more people around all right, the night before the wedding."

The harsh call of gulls and the sound of the waves hitting against the pier broke the silence as we walked up the steps and in through the door. The portico had a high ceiling and a stone-flagged floor with some threadbare mats and rather strange sculptures—two pairs of feet, a man's and a child's, caught my eye.

As Maeve led the way through a church-like inner door, a large barrel-chested man in shorts and a long-sleeved Elvis T-shirt came hurrying towards us, head bowed. He stopped just in time to avoid a collision and looked up in alarm.

"Ach, Jesus, sorry, wild sorry. Not looking where I'm going." He produced a big smile and an outstretched calloused hand. An unlit cigarette was cupped in the other. *"Cad é mar atá sibh?* How are ye doing? Are ye part of the wedding?"

We nodded, put our bags down and introduced ourselves.

The man pumped both of our hands enthusiastically. He was pink-skinned and ginger-haired, a slight quiff and sideburns giving him a fifties look. "That's class. Good to meet ye. I'm Fridge, the best man. I'm Kevin's cousin." He grinned. "I was rehearsing my speech in my head. Wee bit distracted."

Maeve managed to keep a straight face. "Nice to meet you, Fridge."

I'm not sure I did quite so well; I was sure I'd have remembered if Leah had told me the best man was called Fridge.

"Should be a rare old weekend anyway," he said, shoving one hand back into the pocket of his shorts now that the formalities had been dealt with. *The king is dead, long live the king* sang his T-shirt. "Some class of a house, isn't it?"

"Fantastic," I agreed.

He glanced over his shoulder before putting the cigarette-wielding hand to his mouth. "You know it's haunted? Some doll in a long dress stalks the hallways at night."

"Really?" Maeve said with a grin.

He nodded. "Keep your eyes open and your doors locked. Stories about this place would make your toes curl."

"But ghosts can get through locked doors, can't they?" Maeve said, still grinning. "Isn't that the whole idea?"

Fridge didn't look amused. "I wouldn't joke about it if I were you. This is a wild strange house." His brow furrowed suddenly and then his expression cleared. "Anyway, we'll meet up later for the barbecue?"

We nodded.

"Hope ye are hungry. We've brought a shedload of pollock and mackerel over with us and it needs to be eaten," he added before heading out into the garden.

"Ever feel as if you've just wandered into a Scooby Doo cartoon?" Maeve said as she picked up her bag again.

Chapter Five

"YOU DON'T THINK that's why they're sleeping on the boats, do you?" I asked. "Because they think the house is haunted?"

Maeve shrugged. "Maybe. Maybe they're superstitious."

We made our way into what appeared to be the reception area, a square hall with a high ceiling and a single dusty chandelier. There was a small desk with a computer where a young man of about nineteen sat tapping at keys, brow furrowed, floppy hair falling over his face. I recognized him as Abby and Ian's adopted son Ronan. I'd met him only once, about six months earlier. He'd been tall and lanky then, but he'd matured since, I noticed. His shoulders were broader, his jaw more pronounced. When he looked up, I saw that he still had the same startling blue eyes. I wondered if he'd remember me.

"Welcome to Greysbridge," he said, getting to his feet and offering his hand.

"Thank you," I said. "It's Ronan, isn't it?"

He nodded. "It is. You're Miss O'Keeffe, my parents' solicitor, aren't you? We met once in Glendara."

"I am. I'm Ben. Well done for remembering. This is Maeve."

He shook Maeve's hand in a gesture that seemed oddly formal for someone of his age.

"We should have two rooms reserved," I said. "For tonight and tomorrow. We're part of the wedding."

I gave him our full names and he tapped at the keyboard before looking up. "Would you like rooms beside one another?"

I looked at Maeve and she nodded. "Great," I said.

We looked around us while he did his work. The hall we were in led into an even larger one with a huge fireplace and enormous armchairs on either side like thrones. To the right of the fireplace was a staircase, a rather grand one from what I could see, which disappeared towards the upper floors.

"These rooms are next to each other," Ronan said as he handed us two sets of keys. "You have Lady Grey's Room, Miss O'Keeffe, and you have the Blue Room, Maeve." He pointed towards the stairs. "Turn left at the return and go through the arch. Take the left fork and your rooms are the first and second in that hallway; the names are on the doors. There's a bathroom at the end of the hall."

Clocking Maeve's expression, I realized I'd forgotten to tell her that the few en suite bedrooms were reserved for the bridal party. But she didn't seem to mind.

"No numbers," she said. "I like that. How many bedrooms are there?"

"Fourteen guest rooms," Ronan replied.

We resisted his offer of help with our bags and headed off towards the staircase. It was mahogany, with ornately carved banisters and a red runner going all the way up. The house seemed to be a bit of a maze, with corridors jutting off in all directions. There was a real sense of clutter too—paintings jostled for space on the walls, portraits and landscapes, originals and prints, and there were plants everywhere, from cut flowers in vases to exotic-looking greenery in pots. Ornaments too played their part—on a sideboard at the return I noticed a set of three porcelain figurines in eighteenth-century costume that looked as if they might be valuable.

We followed Ronan's instructions and found our rooms without too much difficulty. As I slid the key into my door and arranged to meet Maeve later, I resolved to explore the rest of the house when I got the chance—I had a particular yen to see if I could find the covered bridge from inside.

The lock turned easily enough but the door was stiff, requiring a push with my shoulder to get it to open fully inwards, as if the wood had expanded at some point and was too large for the frame. The room was dark and stuffy, the shutters on the windows closed, presumably with the intention of keeping the room cool, but it hadn't worked. A chink of evening sun streamed through a gap, casting a ray across the bed, dust motes floating in the light.

I put down my bags and crossed the room to open the shutters. When I'd done so, I opened the window too, pushing it up with difficulty and leaning out to breathe in the fresh air. I had drawn well—the room was at the front of the house and there was a view of the sea. A couple walked arm in arm along the path that crossed the lawn, heading down to the pier. I watched them as they stood looking out to sea, their silhouettes familiar—it was Leah's sister Niamh and her boyfriend.

I stood for a while listening to the gulls and looking out at the pier and the boats, silent and still, the sea lapping gently at their black and red hulls. I wondered how comfortable a fishing boat would be to sleep on, with maybe two small cabins on each. And why you would choose it over a luxury room in a hotel.

Eventually, I turned to look at the room that would be mine for two nights. A four-poster bed, mahogany furniture and an iron fireplace with embroidered screen confirmed the "luxury" part. Rich burgundy wallpaper, thick carpets and heavy bedclothes confirmed that this was a room for winter rather than summer. Even with the window open, it was still warm. Realizing I was thirsty, I was relieved to see that although there was no bathroom, there was a hand basin. I filled a glass with water and drank thirstily. Then, as a sudden wave of tiredness hit me, I climbed onto the bed and lay down, closing my eyes for a few minutes. But when I felt myself drifting off, I forced myself to move and unpack. I wanted to sleep tonight.

Making my way over to the huge wardrobe to hang up my dresses for the following day, I noticed a large green hardback on the dressing table. Curious, since it was the only book in the room, I sat down on the bed to look at it, dress on my knee.

It was a *Girl's Own Annual* from 1913. Fascinated, I turned it over in my hands. It was a little ragged; the spine was broken, showing the stitching inside, but other than that, it was pretty much intact. The cover showed a young woman by a fire in a long red skirt and blouse, reading to an older woman dressed in black with a white shawl and bonnet. Snow was visible through the open window and a cat not unlike Guinness sat on the hearth.

I opened it carefully and ran my fingers over the heavy cream pages. There were articles on nature, on identifying wild flowers; there were short stories like "The Little Princess" and "The Story of Rose" and fashion pieces on "How the Hair will be Worn this Spring" and "Fashionable Blouses". There was a problem page and a piece on "Practical Careers for Women"; suggestions were indexing and cataloguing, florist, and lady nurse—not nurse, I noticed, but lady nurse. I smiled when I came across a full page on "The Modern Girl and Matrimony" and wondered if I should copy it for Leah.

I turned to the flyleaf, interested to see if there was an inscription. And there, before the ads for Bournville Cocoa and Borwick's Baking Powder, written in very precise, small handwriting, were the words: *To Miss Louisa Grey, Christmas 1912. Do not try to be something you are not, my dear. From L. G.*

Maybe it was my modern eye, but the dedication gave me the shivers. I looked around me. This was Lady Grey's room. Was Miss Louisa Grey Lady Grey? Had she slept in the very bed I was sitting on? I wondered.

A knock on the door roused me and I put the book down. It was Maeve. She had changed into a skirt and T-shirt and even put on a little mascara, a lot more progress than I'd made.

She looked me up and down as if reading my thoughts. "Are you ready to go down?"

"Pretty much. Come on in."

She followed me in, flopped down on an armchair and surveyed her surroundings. "Nice room."

"I know. It's lovely. How's yours?"

"Great too. It overlooks the back, but I've a view of the garden and the stables."

"That'll suit you."

She nodded. "I know. I can't wait to get out tomorrow. I haven't been on a horse in ages."

I pulled off my T-shirt and replaced it with a cream linen shirt. "Your 'ages' isn't quite the same as my 'ages'."

"Ach, you'll be grand," she said dismissively. "Fancy a quick walk before we go into the fray?"

"You mean a walk to the stables?" I said with amusement.

"Well, yes, but I wouldn't mind looking round the grounds too. I can see the barbecue from my room and they're still setting up. I'd say we have fifteen minutes, easy."

I'd have preferred to have a nosy around the house, but I agreed.

★ ★ ★

Ronan had vacated his post by the time we made our way out of the main door. It was still warm; a lazy haze seemed to linger over the grounds, but the light on the water was beautiful, shimmering and silver. We turned to look up at the house and my eyes were drawn again to the covered bridge.

Maeve shielded her eyes with her hand. The sun glinted on the windows, giving a coppery glow. "It's strange, that bridge, isn't it? I've never seen anything like it in a private house. I've seen the one in Oxford, and the Bridge of Sighs in Venice, but . . ."

"It's a fairly down-market version of those," I said. "But yeah, it's a real oddity. It looks as if it was thrown up as an afterthought. Doesn't seem to match the rest of the house."

Maeve grinned. "And exactly what kind of a house *would* a bridge like that match?"

"Fair point."

She moved her hand from her eyes and squinted. "I think there's someone up there."

I followed her gaze. "Really, where?"

"On the bridge." She pointed. "Can you see? Just there through the window? About halfway across?"

She was right. There was a figure crossing from one side to the other, although with the light, it was difficult to tell if it was a man or a woman.

A noise behind us made us turn. There were voices coming from the boats, the sounds of people disembarking. As my eyes refocused, I saw a large woman being helped off one of the decks by another woman and a man.

"Let's head," Maeve said quickly. "I want to have a look around. We can meet everyone at the barbecue."

But we were too late. Once she was on dry land, the large woman moved faster than expected. She waved and walked towards us purposefully, flanked by the two people who had helped her off the boat, one of whom I saw was Fridge, the man we'd met earlier. There were a couple of people behind her too, who had emerged from the other boat. It was quite the cortège, and it was making a beeline directly for us. We were trapped. Our walk would have to wait.

The woman was truly enormous, the impression as she approached that of a ship making its way through calm seas. She walked with difficulty, exhaling with a whistle at each step. But she wore a warm smile.

"Wedding guests, I presume?" she asked, pudgy hand outstretched. We both accepted a very firm handshake.

"Yes," I said. "I work with Leah."

Her eyes widened in recognition. "Ach, you're the lawyer. I'm Belva McCreesh, Kevin's aunt. Everyone calls me Auntie Belva."

"Good to meet you, Belva. I'm Ben, and this is Maeve."

"Ben?" She wrinkled her brow, pushing out her huge cheeks.

"Short for Benedicta. She was an Italian saint," I added when she continued to look perturbed.

"Aye, I see." Her face relaxed and she leaned in. "What do you think of this civil ceremony raiméis then? I'm sure with a saint's name you'd prefer a wedding in a church?"

"I suppose it's whatever Kevin and Leah prefer that's important," I said uncomfortably. I wasn't about to dive into that particular wasps' nest, particularly after Leah's warning.

Belva pursed her lips without responding, clearly deciding to let me get away with it for the time being. She straightened herself, arms crossed underneath her huge bosom. "Still, she's a grand wee girl, Leah. I brought Kevin up when his mother died, you know. She was my sister."

I nodded. "I'd heard that."

"Although I was beginning to think they would never get round to getting married, they spent so long foostering about. Now if I could only do the same with these two." She gave a stage wink while throwing a glance at Fridge and the woman who from her dimensions had to be her daughter. The woman raised her eyes to heaven; it was clearly not the first time she'd heard this comment.

"Have you met Luther and Audrey, my son and daughter?" Belva asked.

"We met Luther earlier," I replied, deciding to run with the more traditional name rather than the household appliance. I smiled at Audrey and she returned it rather sweetly. Her features were similar to her mother's, illuminated by perfectly applied make-up.

Suddenly a loud gong sounded from the house.

"Sounds as if dinner is served," Belva remarked, uncrossing her arms and hoicking up her skirts. "Are you coming for some food?" We both nodded, and she bowed her head. "We'll away on so. See you up there."

We watched as the strange procession made its way across the lawn towards the house, Belva with her tug boats on either side.

"I hope Phyllis is prepared to defend her position on civil marriage," Maeve grinned.

"Ah, she'll be well able for her," I replied. "Now let's go for that walk before we get waylaid by someone else."

Chapter Six

WE SET OFF down a path that wound its way along the water's edge, swatting at the midges as we walked. The garden was lush. Mature ashes and oaks were an end-of-summer deep green, the flower beds were beautifully maintained, and the grounds were full of shrubs, buddleia in particular providing a splash of purple and white. With the sea on our left and the garden on our right, we were treated to a melange of scents, both salty and sweet, heavy in the evening warmth. After a short while, the house disappeared from view and we came across what looked like an old walled garden.

We peered through the gate, which was locked with a padlock. Like the rest of the garden, it was well tended, with vegetables in neat rows and to the left, along one wall, a greenhouse with a sloped roof, covered in moss.

"Augurs well for the food this weekend," Maeve remarked.

We continued on, and the path forked. One branch heading inland appeared to lead back towards the house, so we chose the left, following a route through trees that lined the shore. Gradually the wood grew dense, a gloomy canopy of alders, the forest scent strong and pungent. We walked along quietly, the evening sun dappling the ground.

"Great trees, aren't they?" Maeve remarked. "Bit of a rarity to have so many of them in this part of Inishowen."

I nodded. "Someone's taking care of them."

After a few minutes, we emerged blinking into the light again and found ourselves in a circular area with flower beds bounded by rocks. A man in a cloth cap was on his knees working, a brown mongrel dog flat out on the gravel beside him, tongue lolling. Both man and dog turned their heads, and the man stood up, trowel in hand.

"So you're the one responsible for the beautiful garden," Maeve said, walking towards him and bending down to greet the dog.

The man nodded with the merest hint of a smile. He held a half-smoked cigarette between the thumb and forefinger of his free hand. I introduced us, and he bowed his head in acknowledgement.

"I'm Rudy. You going for a walk?"

"Not a long one," I said. "Just a stroll before dinner."

He took his cap off and wiped his brow. He had a craggy out-doorsy face and, despite being mid-fifties or so by my reckoning, jet-black hair. His eyes were dark too.

"Be careful," he said, gesturing towards the path we were following. "Don't go all the way to the end. It isn't finished, and it gets dangerous especially when the tide is in. Stop when you can see the shore and come back."

We thanked him and walked on. At some point, the trees changed from deciduous to coniferous and it became consider-ably darker, until we came to another break where we emerged at the shore.

We stood and gazed out to sea for a few minutes. It was a relief to be out in the open again. The tide was out, and the rocks were glinting, the water a deep evening blue. An island was visible in the distance. It seemed larger than Glashedy, the island I was used to gazing at from Lagg beach.

"Is that . . .?" I asked Maeve.

"Inishathair?" She nodded.

The island was silhouetted against the sinking sun, a slash of black on a painting of blue and orange. It was impossible to make out any physical characteristics, although it seemed to draw you in and make you try. Reluctantly I tore my eyes away and cast my gaze along the shore. Despite what Rudy had said, the path did not come to an end, but it did become rocky and uneven as it climbed towards a small cliff. I wondered how much of what we could see was Grey land. I remembered from the conveyance that the house had come with a vastly reduced acreage from the original extent of the estate. Parcels of land had been lost in various gambling escapades, until the final fateful card game that deprived the family of the house.

Maeve followed my gaze, putting her hand up to shield her eyes again. "That path doesn't look too bad, does it? He must imagine we're real delicate flowers if he thinks we wouldn't be able to manage that."

"Maybe there's a dangerous part further on that we can't see," I said.

"Maybe."

At the top of the cliff, before the path disappeared from view, there appeared to be some kind of walled-in section. Maybe that marked the boundary, I thought.

"What do you think that wall and gate is?" I asked.

"Another vegetable garden?" Maeve said doubtfully.

"Funny place for a vegetable garden, isn't it? All this way from the house. Especially when there's already that big walled one."

She shrugged and checked her watch. "It's getting late. We'd better go back to the party. The stables will have to wait till the morning."

We turned and headed back the way we'd come. By the time we reached the clearing, Rudy and his dog had departed, leaving some freshly raked clay and newly planted blue hydrangeas. And as we approached the house again, the smell of cooking, accompanied by voices and laughter, reached us. Following both, we found our way easily to the barbecue area at the back of the house.

It had been a terrace originally, I suspected, made of huge stone flags, in grander times used for afternoon tea or pre-dinner drinks. Tonight, it had been laid out with tables and chairs, a long trestle table with a white tablecloth for drinks and glasses, and a large barbecue section with meat, breads and salads. Fairy lights were strewn in the trees, and a small crowd milled around drinking beer and wine. Among them I spotted Belva, Fridge, and Audrey, and Leah's sisters and parents. Maeve was pointing out her bedroom window above when Leah herself appeared, dressed in a long blue flowery number, with her hair pinned up in a loose bun and a large glass of white wine in her hand.

"Oh, thank God, some friendly faces who aren't family," she said, giving Maeve a hug.

Maeve grinned. "It's like that, is it?"

Leah lowered her voice. "My lot have behaved themselves so far, but Auntie Belva's just had a go at me about the civil ceremony. I hope she doesn't make a fuss tomorrow. She's lovely really but she does like to get her own way."

"I'm sure she'll be fine," I said comfortingly. "She was saying great things about you when we met her earlier."

Leah beamed. "Was she? Oh, that's good. I've never been entirely sure what she thinks of me. She can be a bit overwhelming. But she's really kind. She even made the cake for tomorrow. No marzipan, she knows I hate marzipan . . ."

"I like the hair," Maeve remarked, changing the subject. Leah seemed a little hyped, breathlessly chattering nineteen to the dozen.

She touched the bun gingerly. "Stan arranged it so it will work in the morning without my having to do anything. I just need to put a hairnet over it tonight."

While Leah was in full hair and make-up mode, I felt a tap on my shoulder and turned to see Ian Grey, Abby's husband and the other owner of Greysbridge, in jeans and an apron with the words *Keep calm and carry on cooking*. He held a large barbecue fork in his hand and he gave me a kiss on the cheek.

"Good to see you. Just a quick hello before I have to get back to the cooking."

"Smells great," I said.

He smiled. "So far it does. I have to try and not cremate everything, which is my instinct. And we have a load of bloody fish that I'm not entirely sure how to cook." He glanced over at the barbecue, where Belva was leaning dangerously over the grill. "Although I *am* being given instruction."

"So it appears," I laughed.

"I'll come over and have a proper chat later, when everyone's been fed." He turned back towards the barbecue. "And I'll send Ronan over with some drinks."

"They seem to be doing a lot of the work themselves," Maeve remarked as she watched him depart.

"They've been great," Leah agreed. "They work really hard."

"It's a great place for a wedding," I said, deciding to keep my views about the house to myself. The garden was certainly very pretty.

"I know," Leah said. "And I had no idea when you mentioned it that it was so close to Inishathair. Kevin had to show it to me on the map. That pretty much decided it for us, his family being able to take the boats here." She dropped her voice again. "You have to make it easy for them to persuade them to go anywhere. They don't travel much, any of them."

"Have you been out to the island?" Maeve asked.

Leah looked sheepish. "Two or three times, just. Not as often as I should have. Although they don't make it very easy to visit either."

At that moment Ronan appeared with a tray of drinks. As we helped ourselves to wine, there was a loud burst of laughter from a group to the right and I looked over. An overweight, balding man with glasses was bent almost double laughing at something Fridge had said. He had a glass of beer in his hand that he only just managed not to spill.

Leah and Maeve followed my gaze.

"Another islander?" I asked.

Leah shook her head. "The man laughing is one of the two guests who were staying here already. I invited them tonight because this is the only cooking going on in the house, but I've asked them tomorrow too. I thought it would be a bit odd being the only people staying who weren't involved in the wedding."

There was another laugh and I looked over at the man again. Now that he was upright, I could see his face and he really did look very drunk. He waved his arms about expansively as if telling some big story, but his face was pink and there was an unhealthy sheen to his skin.

"He looks pretty worked up about something," Maeve said.

"What about the other guest? Are they together?" I asked.

"No," Leah said. "They don't know each other. Well they didn't, although they seem to get on pretty well now. That man is Michael Burrows. He's English. I think he's researching old houses in the area, at least that's what he started out doing. Kevin said he's going to make some kind of a film." She put her hand in front of her mouth. "He's a bit boasty, to be honest—what my mother would describe as 'full of ol' big talk'."

Maeve grinned. "I know what she means."

Leah glanced around her, then pointed to a tall, dark-haired youth with a long jaw, chatting to or being chatted up by Audrey, Belva's daughter. "That's the other guest—Jay Stevenson. He's American, here on a cycling holiday. On his own at the moment, but hoping to meet up with friends. He's leaving on Sunday. He's quite sweet—he gave me a card this morning . . ." She trailed off when there was a shout from the barbecue. Ian Grey was waving at her. "Looks as if the food's ready."

I realized I was hungrier than I thought as I helped myself to halloumi, tomato and chickpea salad while Ian removed meat from the barbecue with a fork.

"Looks great," I said.

"Hopefully it tastes as good as it looks," he said with a smile, nodding at my heaped plate. "It's Rudy, the gardener, we have to thank for the salads. He's done a great job with the old walled garden."

By the time I'd filled my plate, I'd lost Maeve. But searching for a seat, I spotted one at a table with Leah's fiancé Kevin and two of Leah's sisters, Sinéad and Cara, so I made my way over to them. Kevin shunted to one side to make space and I sat down beside him.

"No Harry tonight?" he asked.

I shook my head. "He's coming tomorrow."

He smirked. "Nice fella, Harry."

My eyes narrowed. "Don't start. Did you get your cufflinks?"

He took a sip of his beer. "Oh aye. I'd be in trouble if I wasn't wearing those tomorrow. I probably won't get an "I do" until she spots them."

"Just as well Niamh was in town to pick them up. Although I could have brought them, really."

Kevin frowned. "I think Leah wanted to give her a job, to be honest. I wouldn't be surprised if she left them behind on purpose. Did Niamh have that boyfriend with her?"

I nodded. "She had a boy with her. I didn't exactly get an introduction."

He shook his head. "Doesn't surprise me. That's Finn. He doesn't say much. She's been seeing him since the beginning of the summer, but no one met him before this week. They're joined at the bloody hip—it's like they're in their own little bubble."

I took a forkful of tomato salad. It was delicious. "I suppose teenage relationships can be pretty intense."

Kevin lowered his voice so that Leah's other sisters couldn't hear. "I don't want to say too much to Leah in case I worry her, but I'm not sure I trust that young fella."

I leaned in. "Why not?" Kevin was a teacher, and his instincts when it came to teenagers were usually spot on.

He rubbed his nose, brow furrowed. "I can't put my finger on it. It's not as if he treats Niamh badly, from what I can see, and she seems happy enough. But I don't like the control he has over her."

I nodded. From fifteen minutes of observation, I knew just what he meant.

"She was always a feisty, independent kid and now she won't say a word without checking with him first," he continued. "She says they're a team but there's no doubt as to who's the captain."

He paused to concentrate on his food while I wondered whether to voice my own unease. But before I could, Sinéad leaned across to ask him something and the moment was gone.

I withdrew a little from the conversation and glanced around me while I ate. Audrey had moved on to Michael Burrows, I noticed, and Ronan was chatting with Cara under one of the trees. He'd come over to pour some wine and she'd gone back with him on the pretext of getting a clean glass, but she hadn't returned—there was a definite bit of flirting going on. When I remarked on it, Kevin told me with a smile that Cara had just broken up with her boyfriend.

"Mind if I join you?" I looked up to see Ian Grey, apron removed, glass of wine in hand.

"Absolutely." I moved over and he climbed in beside me. "Food was great, by the way. You were right about the salads. You were lucky to find Rudy."

Ian placed his glass on the table in front of him and smiled. "We inherited him with the house, as a matter of fact. He was retained by the estate agents to keep the place in some sort of shape." He put his hand in front of his mouth. "Although I don't think he was too thrilled when it was finally sold. I suspect that he was not only feeding himself from the vegetable garden but selling stuff as well."

I smiled. "Oh well, he's done a fantastic job keeping the garden alive."

"That's true," Ian agreed. "We can afford to lose a few tomatoes!"

I sat back. "So, tell me a little about the house. It's quite a place."

He smiled. "What do you want to know?"

I paused. "Well, that footbridge is pretty unusual for a start. Is that where the name Greysbridge came from?"

"No. The house gets its name from a little humpbacked bridge just outside the gates."

"Right. So not the covered footbridge then. It's rather odd, isn't it?"

Ian nodded. "It is pretty strange. It's not safe to go into at the moment, though. It's not stable."

"Oh? I thought I saw someone in there earlier on."

He shook his head. "You couldn't have. We've blocked it off." He took a sip from his glass. "We're thinking of having it removed, as a matter of fact. It's cheaply constructed and ugly, and it's not protected or anything. It was added a long time after the house was built."

"Why *was* it added?" I asked.

He frowned. "I'm not entirely sure. It was built by my great-grandfather, who was a bit eccentric by all accounts. There are stories, but it's impossible to know what to believe."

I leaned forward curiously. "What kind of stories?"

He smiled, clasping his hand to the nape of his neck and massaging it. "Michael Burrows, one of the guests, is the one to ask. He's become a bit of an expert on the history of the place."

"I heard the house was haunted," I whispered.

Ian adopted a spooky tone. "Did you hear that the ghost of Louisa Grey stalks the hallways at night when a resident of the house is about to die?"

"She's the ghost? There's a book inscribed to her in my room."

Ian grinned mischievously. "Louisa was my grandfather's sister. If there's a book inscribed to her, that means you're in her room. You'd better sleep with your eyes open."

"What happened to her?"

Ian shook his head. "She was supposed to have suffered from her nerves, whatever that means. She was fascinated by recipes and cooking but refused to eat and apparently starved herself to death. It sounds as if she may have suffered from some eating disorder, but back then they didn't know what it was or how to treat it."

"Poor girl," I said.

"Yes," he agreed. He lowered his voice with a half-amused look on his face. "People have said they've seen her walking along the corridor at night, sensed her presence in their rooms, even smelled her cooking."

"Really?" I wasn't sure how to respond to that. "Where does the bridge lead, by the way? It seems to almost disappear into those rhododendron bushes."

Ian took a sip of his wine. "There are parts of the house that we haven't had a chance to restore yet, and that section on the other side of the bridge is one of them." He sighed. "We'll get there eventually. When, or rather if, we have the money."

At that moment, Maeve and Abby appeared.

"Ah, there you are," Maeve said, taking a seat and topping up her glass from the bottle on the table. "We have another recruit for the ride in the morning—Jay is coming. Abby has an American saddle for him."

"Great."

Abby leaned affectionately on her husband's shoulder, flicking a speck of blue paint off his shirtsleeve. She was smiling but she looked tired.

Ian glanced across at me and stood up. "I'll get Michael Burrows and introduce you."

Abby took the hand he offered and went with him, while I chatted to Maeve and looked around me at the same time, people-watching being one of my favorite pastimes. Leah's parents were sitting with Belva, drinking a pot of tea; Leah and Kevin were moving about from group to group; and Ronan, I noticed, was still chatting to Cara, although Jay the American had now joined them. He appeared to be demonstrating some kind of dance move and they seemed to be having a laugh.

Attracted by the lamplight and the remains of the food, the midges had started to bite by the time Ian reappeared.

"No Michael, I'm afraid. Apparently, he's gone to bed. You'll just have to make do with my muddled account for the moment."

I smiled. "You didn't do too badly."

Ian didn't hang around this time—he was needed to help clear up, he said—and I decided to go too. Maeve said she wanted to chat horses with Abby, so I left her to it and said goodnight.

I walked around to the front of the house, realizing when I moved away from the artificial light that there was a full moon. I walked onto the lawn to have a clearer look. The dew soaked my feet, but it was worth it—the moon was huge, perfectly reflected in the sea, all glimmering and silver and eerie, and the stars were bright and clear in the inky sky. It was hard not to stay for a while just looking.

Before I went in, I stopped to take one last look at the house, bathed now in an almost blue light. But as I did so, something small and black flew low and very close, causing me to step suddenly to one side. It was a bat. When I looked up, I saw many more circling the house, warming up before heading on a long flight. It was quite the sight.

Chapter Seven

OTHER THAN SOME clearing-up noises from the kitchen, the house was quiet. Standard lamps glowed here and there, and the light was dim and low as I made my way up the stairs. I dawdled, full of curiosity, feeling privileged to have the place to myself, and stopped to have a look at a portrait I hadn't noticed halfway up, drawn in by the stern expression of its subject. It was a woman with a high collar and a cameo brooch who looked as if she might have been a governess. Beside her were some other framed photographs, old, sepia—a sort of family gallery, I assumed. In one, a man and woman and two children stood stiffly in front of a house I recognized instantly as Greysbridge. There was no footbridge, I noticed. It must not yet have been added.

I was wondering if these were Ian Grey's ancestors—if one of them was Louisa Grey herself—when suddenly out of the corner of my eye I saw a figure at the top of the stairs. I shivered, then instantly told myself off for being silly enough to be spooked by a ghost story. I leaned silently into the wall, trying not to make the floorboards creak underfoot. But the figure, barefoot and in pyjamas, hadn't seen me. He was too busy concentrating on taking something from a side table and hurrying off. Though I couldn't see his face, I was sure it was Leah's sister's boyfriend Finn.

I tiptoed the rest of the way up the stairs. When I reached where he had been, I saw that one of the little porcelain figurines I'd seen earlier was missing. There had been three and now there were only two, I was sure of it. But why would he steal something like that? I wondered.

He was gone, so I continued on to my room. On turning the key and pushing open the door, I noticed a strong, heavy scent that hadn't been there before. And when I turned on the light, I saw that a vase of blue hydrangeas had been placed on the dressing table. I wondered who had put them there—I found it hard to imagine who would have had the time. The scent was a little overpowering and the air was warm, so I opened the window before picking up my washbag and heading down the hall.

The heavy oak door groaned as I opened it. The bathroom was large, with black and while tiles and a bath large enough to fit three people. A precarious-looking shower like a telephone box was an odd addition—it looked as if it had been parachuted in in a panicked attempt to modernize. I knew which one I'd be using in the morning. I turned on the tap and waited for the ancient plumbing system to growl into life.

Back in my room, I discovered that I'd left in such a rush that I'd forgotten to bring a book. So I took the *Girl's Own Annual* to bed, propping a pillow behind my head and flicking through the pages, careful to handle them as gently as I could, conscious that the book had survived a century already. I noticed some recipes flagged and remembered what Ian Grey had said about Louisa's eating disorder. Was she the one who had marked them? Pineapple pudding and oyster soup were expected, but the lentil dhal took me by surprise; I'd thought Indian cooking was more of a modern thing. Louisa might not have eaten much herself, but her tastes were certainly eclectic.

After a few minutes I found a short story called "The Littlest Dog" and settled down to read. It was just what I needed, and when my eyes began to flutter, I put the book on my bedside locker and climbed out of bed to close the shutters before turning off the light. I was drifting off when I heard voices from outside, the islanders going back to their boats, I presumed. But they faded quickly and I turned onto my side and fell asleep.

An hour later, I woke to the sound of some kind of large vehicle on the drive and a beeping noise like a lorry reversing. A delivery for the wedding, I thought sleepily. It didn't last long and I fell back asleep.

A while later, I woke again, this time with a jolt. It felt as if I'd been asleep only minutes, but when I checked my watch, it was three a.m. My heart was racing. What had woken me? A noise again? But no, the house was quiet, and outside there was nothing but the soft sound of the waves. A bad dream? I couldn't remember. Suddenly, and with increasing disquiet, I knew what was wrong. There was someone in the room with me.

Hands trembling, I flicked on the light and my eyes darted fearfully around, from the wardrobe to the window to the hand basin. There was no one here. But there was something, I was sure of it, a presence, a sort of thickening in the air. I shook myself. I could see the entire room and there was no one. What was wrong with me? I had no belief in ghosts. I took a deep breath and a sip from my glass of water and waited for my heart rate to slow down. After a few minutes, I forced myself to turn off the light, lie down, and close my eyes.

Suddenly, I felt breath on my face and something at my neck like cold hands. I coughed and sat up, waving my arms wildly, hitting nothing but thin air. The floor creaked and I froze. Someone was walking across my bedroom.

I turned on the light. Again, there was no one in the room and the door was closed. And when I climbed out of bed to check, legs trembling, it was locked. Of course it was. I'd locked it before getting into bed. I stood there, hand on the doorknob, feeling foolish and terrified at the same time.

I heard footsteps outside and strained my ears to listen. Someone was walking slowly along the corridor, past my door, trying not to make a noise. I unlocked the door with a quiet click and opened it a fraction, oddly grateful for some human company. Because whoever it was, they hadn't been the one in my room. I looked out, but the light was dim and I just about managed to catch sight of someone disappearing towards the return and the stairs. I had a sense that my opening the door had caused them to move faster.

I wanted to ask them if they'd seen anyone, but I was wearing just a T-shirt and knickers, so I pulled on a pair of jeans before following. By the time I reached the return and looked down the stairs, whoever it was had long gone, and the house was silent and still. I didn't feel like following any further.

★ ★ ★

Despite the night-time interruptions, I woke early, about half past six, needing the bathroom. It must have been all the water I'd been drinking for my throat. I'd fallen asleep again about half four, having kept the light on to read before attempting to go back to sleep. I realized now that the person I'd seen in the hall had probably just been using the bathroom, there being so few en suites in the house. I lay in bed trying to rationalize what had happened before that, but failed miserably on that score. Eventually, I climbed out of bed and grabbed a towel.

When I returned from the bathroom, I knew I wouldn't be able to go back to sleep, so I decided to explore the rest of the house while it was still quiet. Maeve and I had only really seen the garden the night before, and I was more than a little curious about the covered bridge, especially after what Ian Grey had said about it being blocked off. I *knew* I had seen a figure, and so had Maeve. And with what had happened in my room, I had to admit I was more than a little spooked.

I got dressed and set off. I had plenty of time. It was still only seven and our ride wasn't till nine. The sun was up, beaming through a window in the hall, casting a white line across the floor as I tried to keep to the runner in the center. I thought the figure I'd seen the night before had been attempting to do the same.

My first impression was correct—the house was like a maze, with corridors branching off in all directions. So I made my way back towards the stairs and headed in the direction I thought the footbridge must be, following a narrow passage until it took an unexpected turn to the left.

I stopped dead. My way was blocked by an antique chest of drawers wedged between the two walls, with a hand-written notice tacked to the front: *Passage dangerous. Stay out.* I tried my best to peer over the chest but could see nothing, I was way too short. Ian was right—the bridge was blocked off. So how had the figure crossed? I wondered. They could have just moved the chest, if they'd been strong enough, I thought. I tried to lift it now and failed. It was way too heavy. Then I heard voices: the house was waking up.

I returned to my room and ran a brush through my hair, then made my way downstairs. En route I glanced at the porcelain figurines; the third one was still missing. I wondered if it could have been Finn I'd seen the night before, looking for something else to pilfer. I hadn't had a good enough view to see if it had been a man or a woman; only a fleeting shadow. Should I say something about the figurine? To Finn? Or to someone else?

The dining room was at the front of the house with a view similar to mine. Through a large bay window, the sea looked beautiful, the morning sun glinting on it like pewter. Leah would have a great day for her wedding. The room had been laid out with five large round tables with white linen tablecloths—two were set for breakfast, with jugs of orange juice and pottery bowls of cereal and fruit, and there was a sideboard with rashers, sausages, scrambled eggs, tomatoes and mushrooms, all in silver platters that looked as if they might have been there since Lady Louisa's time. I almost expected kidneys and kippers and a butler in tails supervising the meal.

Maeve was alone at one of the tables, dressed in jodhpurs and a T-shirt, pouring herself a coffee and eating muesli and yoghurt.

I joined her. "You on your own?"

Her mouth curled up in a smile. "I think the rest of them might have had a later night than we did."

I helped myself to some orange juice. "Did you hear any noise during the night?"

"What kind of noise?"

"Voices outside. A lorry. Footsteps along the corridor about three o'clock."

Maeve shook her head as she looked at me curiously. "I slept like a log. Must have been the three glasses of wine." She pushed her bowl away and moved on to some toast. "By the way, you were right about the ghost keeping the islanders on their boats."

"Go on."

She smothered a slice with strawberry jam. "I was chatting to Audrey and Fridge. They don't mind being here during the day, but they won't stay in the house at night." She grinned. "They reckon the gardener's dog won't even come in the door."

I said nothing, my skepticism having lost some of its edge during the night. Maybe I should ask the islanders if they had a spare berth, I thought.

The door opened and the young man who'd been pointed out to us as Jay came in, dressed in what looked like a blue cycling jersey and chinos. He shot us a smile before loping towards the sideboard and helping himself to a full plate of food. When he joined us at the table, Maeve did the introductions.

"I hear you're coming on the ride," I said.

He nodded as he buttered himself some toast. "I've been out already, a couple of days ago. It's a great way to see the coastline." His accent was a West Coast drawl. He looked at me before taking a bite. "So how was that room?"

I looked up. "Why?"

"You're in Lady Louisa's room, aren't you? Michael told me that's the spooky one. They don't normally rent it out." His eyes narrowed in amusement. "They must have thought you'd be able to handle it."

I smiled. "Maybe they just ran out of rooms."

"No strange experiences, then?" he asked again.

Maeve turned to me with a grin. "Go on, Ben. You haven't answered his question. Nothing go bump in the night?"

"No, nothing." I shook my head, concentrating hard on my coffee. I'd discovered I wasn't hungry. I told myself I was still full from the night before.

In contrast, Jay dived into his breakfast with the appetite of the young and fit. He spoke through a mouthful of food. "You know they said she didn't eat?"

"Lady Louisa?"

He nodded. "They said she starved herself to death, but there was more to it than that. That was a rumor put out to conceal how she really died."

I looked up again. "How did she die?"

He shrugged. "I'm not sure. Michael knows but he's not telling." He shoveled another forkful into his mouth.

"How old was she?" Maeve asked.

He swallowed. "Young, I think. Twenty?"

"It sounds as if Michael is a real expert on the house and family," I said.

"He is. He's been researching the Greys for years." Jay said. "He couldn't believe his luck when the house opened as a hotel and he found out he could stay here. He was their first guest and he's been here *three* times since."

★   ★   ★

It looked as if Maeve was right and people had had a late night. Certainly no one else had appeared by the time we left for the stables. At nine o'clock we walked around by the terrace where the barbecue had been and along the pathway to the stable block. Butterflies flickered around the shrubs and the morning felt fresh and cool. I wondered how long that would last.

As we approached the stables, we heard voices, a man's and a woman's, the tone of which made us stop in our tracks. It didn't sound like an exchange you wanted to walk in on. It was Abby and Ronan Grey.

Abby sounded petulant. "Why you would choose to behave like that, I don't understand. You're worth more than that."

Her son's tone was sharper. "What the hell is that supposed to mean?"

"You shouldn't be rushing into anything."

"I'm not. It's only a bit of fun. I like her."

"You have other things you should be concentrating on."

"I'm capable of doing more than one thing. I work hard here. I want to enjoy myself."

There were tears in Abby's voice. "The thought that you might throw yourself away on . . . It hurts me, surely you know that."

"Oh for God's sake. It's not about you. It's nothing to do with you."

There was a sob. "You mean I'm unimportant—that my feelings don't matter?"

Ronan sounded weary and exasperated. "No, I didn't say that."

His mother's voice became shrill and high-pitched, infused with self-pity. "So you're hurting me on purpose?"

Maeve, Jay and I looked at each other, mortified. Then, as if united in wanting to put an end to this embarrassing exchange, we moved as one through the stable gate. Ronan stormed past us, cheeks flushed, glancing at Jay as he passed and shooting him a look full of meaning.

Abby was alone in the yard with a bridle in her hand. She let it fall limply to the ground as she followed her son with her gaze, eyes dark and brimming.

"Morning," Maeve said brightly. "Great morning for it."

With an obvious effort Abby tore her eyes away from Ronan and gave us a fake smile. "Morning, all, just tacking up. Nearly there—just two more to do. Sorry I'm a little behind."

"Do you want me to do one?" Maeve offered, hand outstretched, riding hat in the other.

Abby looked relieved. "Sure, that would be great."

She handed Maeve the bridle before turning to Jay and myself and glancing approvingly at our feet. We were both wearing wellies. I'd had a pair in my car—after a number of soakings over the winter, I'd finally invested, and since then they had lived in the Mini's trunk, saving me more than once. Jay had borrowed a pair from Ronan.

"Do you two want to go and choose hats?" Abby asked, pointing us in the direction of a tack room.

The room was cool and smelled of leather. Jay and I had a laugh trying on various balding velvet-covered helmets before finding matches.

"Never thought I had a particularly big head until I came to Ireland," he grinned, attaching a strap underneath his chin.

"I thought you'd been out for a ride already? What hat did you wear then?" I asked.

He shook his head, glancing around him. "It seems to have done a disappearing trick. Someone else with a giant head must have stolen it."

"How was it?" I nodded towards the open door, through which we could see Abby tacking up a large grey. "The ride, I mean?"

"We had a great time. Lots of laughs. It was just Abby and Ronan and myself." He lowered his voice. "They were getting on better then."

"Glad to hear it." I shortened the strap on the hat I'd selected as we made our way out of the tack room. "What brought you to Donegal, by the way?"

"The hills. I'm on a cycling holiday."

"Ah."

"Nah. I'm joking really. I always wanted to come to Ireland. I've just finished first-year pre-med and I needed a break before I go back in the fall."

In the yard, Maeve and Abby were holding two horses each, and Abby called me over while Jay went to Maeve.

"Maeve tells me you haven't ridden in a while." She nodded towards the grey on her left. "This is Dixie. She's really gentle, if a little on the lazy side."

"A while?" I laughed. "Try two decades. The last time I rode, I landed on my head. Someone told me you needed to fall seven times before you were a proper rider, and I was working on that." I rubbed the mare's neck and she whickered.

Abby smiled. "I don't think you're supposed to make it a goal. Don't worry. It'll all come back to you." She linked her hands together to give me a leg-up. "Just try and relax." She tightened my girth. "How are the stirrups?"

"Bit on the long side."

"Do you think you could shorten them yourself? Can you remember how to?"

"I think so."

Five minutes later, we trooped out of the stable yard, led by Abby on the large black cob she'd been riding yesterday. It was a beautiful morning, fresh and clear, with the promise of heat later on.

We made our way down the drive towards the main gates, then turned left, trotting along the road, the sounds and smells of late summer vibrant in the morning sunshine, until we heard the rush of moving water.

"A river?" I asked as we slowed again to a walk.

Abby nodded without turning her head. "It's forded by the bridge that gives the house its name—Grey's Bridge."

As the sound of water grew louder, the road took a sudden swing to the right and we emerged at an old humpbacked bridge. I glanced down instinctively as we crossed it, and I noticed that Maeve and Abby did too. Jay was the only one who didn't; he kept his gaze fixed on the road ahead, and I wondered why. The river didn't look particularly deep, but then there hadn't been rain for over a week.

Abby remained silent as we walked along in single file: Maeve behind Abby, and then Jay and myself. We continued on the road for a short while before turning left down a rough lane, which we followed until we emerged at the shore, where Maeve and I had stopped the day before. There we turned right and began to climb, and I realized we were heading towards the walled-in area that we had spotted the evening before.

"What is that?" I asked Abby when it was just ahead.

"Oh, that was a family burial plot," she said dismissively. "It's not used anymore."

"You know who's buried there, don't you?" Jay said, his eyes narrowed mischievously. "Louisa Grey."

"Do you mind if I have a look?" I asked, as Abby shot him a look of displeasure.

"If you want to," she said reluctantly. "Although it's a bit early for a break."

"She has a snout on her like a sniffer dog, this one." Maeve grinned. "Nosy as hell."

When we arrived at the gate, I climbed off Dixie with some difficulty, legs almost giving way when I landed on the ground. Maeve laughed when she saw I was already stiff after fifteen minutes, but she took my reins while I pushed open the rusted old gate.

The plot was overgrown and unkempt, with only a couple of gravestones visible, and the ground was rough, a knot of weeds and brambles. Before I could read any inscriptions, Abby called to me to hurry up, and reluctantly I made my way back, with time only for it to strike me as an odd location for a graveyard, so far from the house.

Closing the gate, I realized with surprise that you could see Inishathair from here, far clearer than you could from the house. It was green and rocky, and I could make out cliffs I hadn't been able to see before. The island continued to be visible as we rode on along the shore, and I found myself gazing out to sea rather than concentrating on the path ahead.

After a while, Maeve hauled Abby out of her slump by chatting about the horses, and I found myself falling into step with Jay.

"Did you find her grave?" he asked.

I shook my head. "I couldn't read any of the inscriptions."

"It's there all right." His eyes narrowed; his voice lowered to a whisper. "Michael said her ghost's been seen there at night, with flowers in her hand, as if she's putting them on her own grave."

Chapter Eight

THE RUINED FORT was quite a sight, silhouetted against blue sky and sea, its grey stone imposing and stark in the bright sunshine. The horses clearly knew the place, picking their way around the ruin, choosing their footing carefully and halting suddenly here and there at a particularly sweet patch of grass. I found myself battling with Dixie more than once, and Maeve laughed as I almost toppled over her ears. Abby had fallen silent again, her row with her son still clearly on her mind. I gazed out to sea, the water a gorgeous azure blue, not a common shade for the North Atlantic.

"Ooh, I'd love a swim now," Maeve said. "Fancy a quick dip before the ceremony? Jay, are you interested?"

"I can't swim," Jay said, and we both turned to him in surprise.

"Really? A sporty young guy like you?" Maeve asked.

Jay looked down at his hands on the reins. "My dad is terrified of the water. His best friend drowned in front of him when they were kids and he's had a phobia ever since. So we were never taken to the sea or the pool."

"God," I said, wondering if that was why he'd avoided glancing down at the river. "Surely you'd be even more inclined to have your kids learn how to swim if you were afraid of it."

Jay shrugged. "He could never get over his fear of it. I'm not really afraid of the water; I just can't swim . . ."

He trailed off as Abby called suddenly from the front, suggesting that we turn back. The day was warming up and the flies
were beginning to bother both the horses and us. And we needed
to get ready for the wedding. When I looked at my watch, I was
amazed to see that it was past eleven.

We took the same route back. But when we turned into the
avenue at Greysbridge, the place felt different—there was immediately a sense that there were more people around, a real buzz
of activity. Cars lined the avenue as we trotted along, enjoying
the shade provided by the old ash trees. Twice we had to stop, to
allow a florist's van and a catering truck to pass by.

Just before we turned to go towards the stables, a large woman
bedecked in orange and red with full headdress emerged from
the side door of the house, waving enthusiastically. Phyllis could
usually stop traffic, but today she had gone all out.

She beamed. "I thought it was you. What a lovely sight. I don't
suppose you have a beast big enough to handle a passenger of my
dimensions?" she asked Abby.

"I'll have to check," Abby said with a smile, her first in a while.
"Welcome to Greysbridge."

Liam McLaughlin, Glendara's estate agent, emerged from the
same door as Phyllis. He grinned when he saw us. "Should be a
good wedding. I've just met a man named Fridge."

"He's the best man," I said.

Liam rubbed his hands together with relish. "Sounds like the
man to know."

"You're early," I remarked. "The wedding's not till one."

"Gave the priest here a lift up." Liam winked, while Phyllis
gave him a dig.

They walked alongside us as far as the stables and waited
while we dismounted. I realized my legs were like jelly—the
insides of my thighs ached as if I'd cycled a hundred miles. We

thanked Abby and said goodbye, at her insistence leaving her to untack.

As we left the stable yard, Jay stopped suddenly. "Maybe I should go back and help? It's not as if I have much changing to do."

"Do you want me to come with you?" Maeve asked.

"No. You go ahead." And with that he was gone.

"Where's the actual ceremony going to be?" I asked Phyllis as we walked back to the house. "Is it outside?"

She shook her head. "It's in the old library. They haven't finished restoring it. There's no furniture, so it's perfect, and the gardener has decorated it with flowers. I've just been in there and it looks gorgeous."

We rounded the house, where the sun was glistening on the water and a long table had been set up on the lawn with white tablecloth and glasses.

"Strange kind of a house, isn't it?" Liam said, turning towards it and gazing upwards. "Parts added on from different eras, I'd say. That footbridge is pretty quirky."

"That's one word for it all right," I said. "Any idea why someone would build it?"

"Not a clue," he said. "Never seen one outside of Venice." He turned towards the sea. "Great setting, though. They must have a deep pier to accommodate those fishing trawlers. Why are they here?"

"The islanders are sleeping on them," Maeve replied.

He raised his eyebrows. "You're kidding. Jesus, they're a wild strange lot."

We turned to make our way up the steps. Once inside the house, Phyllis asked, "Do you want to see the library?"

"Yes please," I said.

"I'll take first bath then," Maeve said. "God, it's like being ten again. Although at least we don't have to share the bathwater!"

"We hope." I laughed.

Maeve took off upstairs and Liam took the opportunity to go back outside for a cigarette on the pretext of looking for his wife, while I followed Phyllis down a hallway to the left of the staircase. The library was a fine room with carved cornices, and bookcases covering all four walls, from floor to ceiling. Although most of the shelves were empty, they had been strung with garlands of pale pink azaleas, which gave the place a rather haunting, romantic look. There were two rows of unmatched chairs, creating an aisle, and a desk at the top.

"It's perfect," I said.

Phyllis sighed, her hand to her face. "Isn't it?"

A whistling noise and heavy footsteps indicated that there was someone in the doorway behind us, and we turned to see Belva, pink-faced, hands on hips, dressed in a rather startling blue dress with an exotic bird print, and matching hat. I tried not to smile as the two large women clocked each other, firstly up and down, then eyeball to eyeball like gunslingers.

I introduced them. "Belva, this is Phyllis, the celebrant. Belva is the groom's . . ." I hesitated.

"Auntie." Belva finished the sentence for me. "And what do you mean, celebrant? You're not a priest, are you?" She breathed heavily, her hand on the door jamb as if she'd been running.

Phyllis shook her head. "No, I'm not a priest. I'm a civil celebrant," she said patiently.

Belva pursed her lips. She didn't need to say anything. Her expression said it all—it was bad enough getting married outside a church, but another thing entirely having a large Donegal woman in full African traditional dress conducting the ceremony.

But Phyllis was unfazed. "First time for me, Belva. Hope I don't cock it up. It's a special one. I'm very fond of Leah and Kevin."

And with that, Belva's face softened. "Ach, you'll be grand. Wee buns to you."

★　★　★

When Maeve and I came down at one o'clock, the room was almost full. Kevin and Fridge greeted people as they arrived, spruce in their hired grey suits, all pink and nervous and freshly shaven, while Phyllis sat at the desk looking through her notes. I was surprised to see that her brow was furrowed. Maybe she hadn't been trying to get Auntie Belva on her side. Maybe she was nervous too.

We decided to leave her alone and found a seat beside Liam and his wife. As I sat, Jay waved from across the aisle. His hair was wet and slicked, and he was wearing jeans and a yellow T-shirt, probably the best he could do with clothes he'd brought for a cycling holiday. I wondered where the other guest, Michael, was. Maybe he was hung-over; he'd looked pretty drunk the night before.

There was a tap on my shoulder accompanied by the soft scent of aftershave, and Harry smiled down at me, dressed in a light grey suit, an open-necked shirt, twinkling blue eyes and a tan.

"Are you keeping the seat for someone?"

I smiled, and he took the aisle seat, his long legs stretching out in front of him.

Liam reached over to shake his hand. "Good to see you, Doc."

"You too." Harry nudged me. "Great dress."

"Thank you," I said, pleased. I'd decided to wear the vintage dress with the pockets.

"This is some place," he whispered. "What is it with that strange footbridge?"

Before I could respond, a hush fell on the room, the music began and everyone turned.

★ ★ ★

Phyllis was surprisingly concise; the ceremony was mercifully short and Leah and Kevin looked happy. Leah was particularly striking in a turn-of-the-century-style dress that matched her surroundings beautifully. I managed to make it through my poem without screwing it up, and when the ceremony was over, we filed out onto the lawn, where I dived for a glass of iced water that I consumed in one. Then it was on to the champagne.

I found myself standing in a group with Liam, Maeve, and Harry, and within minutes we were joined by Phyllis, glass in hand. "Well, how'd I do?"

"You were the star of the show, Phyllis," Liam said, raising his glass in a toast. "Totally outshone the bride."

"That's not what I meant," she said indignantly. "Did it seem like I knew what I was doing?"

"Yes, Phyllis, you did a beautiful job," I said soothingly.

"Good." She exhaled as she looked across the lawn to where Leah was chatting to Kevin's family. "Doesn't she look gorgeous?"

"I prefer funerals," Liam snorted. "At least that's the end of the misery; a wedding's only the beginning."

This time his wife gave him a whack on the shoulder.

"I'll have no problem officiating at your funeral if that's the case," Phyllis said with a grin. Liam was all talk; it was clear to anyone that he adored his wife.

I glanced around me. Guests were scattered across the lawn and down by the pier, where the tide was in, the sun was glinting on the water and the sky was a deep blue with not a single cloud. So unlike Donegal.

"Has anyone seen Michael Burrows?" I asked suddenly.

"Who is Michael Burrows?" Harry asked, frowning.

"He's a guest who was staying here. He's an expert on the house, apparently, and I wanted to have a chat with him. Leah said she'd invited him."

"I'm going to get another drink—do you want to come with me and see if you can find him?" Phyllis asked.

Before I could reply, Jay came loping across the lawn. I smiled at him, but was surprised when he didn't respond. He didn't even look in my direction; he seemed much more interested in Harry. His eyes looked bloodshot, and I wondered how much champagne he'd had. Harry was chatting to Maeve when Jay tapped him on the shoulder. He looked up, startled, his expression changing from animation to shock. I watched as Jay whispered something to him before taking him to one side.

Phyllis took my arm and I walked with her across the lawn, glancing back. "What do you think that was about?"

Phyllis shrugged. "No idea." She twirled her empty glass in her hand. "But the new doctor certainly seems to have taken a shine to you."

I looked back again. Harry and Jay appeared to be having an intense conversation. I couldn't see their expressions, but it looked as if they knew one another. Harry glanced up, caught my eye and smiled. I smiled back.

To Phyllis, I said, "We're just having a bit of fun. It's nothing serious."

She stopped; her eyes soft. "Are you still missing the sergeant?"

"God, no, that never really got off the ground," I lied.

She looked at me, unconvinced. I didn't blame her. What had happened between Molloy and me had meant a lot to me. It still did.

"Speaking of budding romance." Phyllis's gaze switched to where Leah's sister Cara was leaning over a table where Ronan was serving drinks. She looked beautiful in her bridesmaid's dress and their heads were almost touching. "Is there something brewing there?"

"I thought so last night. Although not everyone is so thrilled about it. Watch this."

Abby had appeared with a tray of clean glasses and a face like thunder. She barked something at Ronan, Cara left, and he went back to work.

Having collected a fresh glass of champagne from a chastised Ronan, I took a stroll around the lawn but could find no sign of Michael Burrows. After a few minutes I returned to Harry and the others, and was a sip away from telling Harry about my job offer in the States when the gong went for dinner. It was just as well. Telling him would have been a really bad idea, considering I hadn't even mentioned it to Leah yet.

Liam was down at the pier, having announced that he was going to mingle with some of the islanders, so I waved to him before we trooped inside. Blinking after the bright sunlight, we filed into the dining room and took our seats. We helped ourselves to some wine and examined the menu, ate a few bread rolls.

The minutes passed.

"Where is everybody?" Phyllis asked eventually.

I looked around me. The room was only half full. Liam and his wife, who were supposed to be at our table, still hadn't arrived. Any minute now, Leah and Kevin would be making their grand entrance and there would be no one to cheer them. Just as I was about to say as much, there was a loud shout from the hallway outside.

"Help! There's someone in the water!"

Chapter Nine

RONAN APPEARED IN the doorway, his eyes wide and panicked. Harry stood and dashed out past him, the rest of us in his wake. Watching him run, it crossed my mind that doctors are never fully off duty; despite his couple of glasses of champagne, he could be called upon at any time. I was glad I was a lawyer. Racing down the steps along with everyone else, I could see people clustered together on the pier, just staring into the sea. There was someone, or maybe more than one person, in the water.

Reaching the pier, breathless, I was shocked to see that Liam was one of them. The tide was in and the water was deep. He was thrashing about in his shirtsleeves, his distressed wife calling to him to be careful, her hands clasped to her face in panic. But Liam wasn't the one in difficulty. He was trying to save someone. Trying and failing by the looks of things. With a sick feeling in my stomach, I caught a flash of yellow. It was Jay. And it looked as if he was unconscious, a dead weight that Liam was struggling desperately to keep above water. I remembered with horror what Jay had said about being unable to swim.

I watched helplessly along with everyone else as Harry ripped off his jacket and shoes and dived in after them. After a few agonizing minutes, they managed between the two of them to get Jay to land, and with Ronan's help to drag him out and lift him onto the pier. There he lay on his back, unconscious, as they climbed out after him.

Harry cleared a space and made everyone stand back while he knelt down beside Jay. Desperately he checked his pulse and his breathing, then immediately started CPR. He alternated compression with breathing—thirty compressions to two breaths, thirty compressions to two breaths. Every so often he would check Jay's heart.

"It's coming and going." He spoke under his breath, almost to himself. Fifteen compressions to two breaths, thirty compressions to two breaths, thirty to two. He shouted for someone to get his doctor's bag from his car. "There's some adrenalin in it. Quickly."

I volunteered, glad to have something to do, and he pointed urgently at his jacket lying in a heap on the pier. "My keys are in the pocket."

I picked it up, found a set of car keys in the inside pocket and held them up.

He nodded. "Car's in the car park." He gasped for breath. "The bag's in the trunk. Bring it to me."

I ran up the lawn and across the gravel to the car park in my high heels, the heat beating down, chest hurting with exertion. I found Harry's car easily enough, and his bag too. It was heavy. As I ran across the lawn, I sensed something fluttering to the ground and looked back. It was a piece of paper—it must have been stuck to the bottom of the bag. I stepped back, picked it up and shoved it into the pocket of my dress.

On the pier, Jay was still unconscious and Harry was still on his knees giving him CPR. I dropped the bag beside him.

"Here," he said. "You take over for a minute. Keep compressing while I get a line in."

Terrified, I knelt down while he told me what to do, compressing Jay's chest as instructed and doing the rescue breaths, wondering why the hell I had never taken a first aid course. Harry took the adrenalin from his bag, filled a syringe and injected it, then took over from me again.

I stood up, relieved and scared at the same time. Because there was still no heartbeat. Liam stood beside me, looking dazed. His wife had taken off her wrap and put it around his shoulders, but he was still shivering despite the heat. I caught him glancing at other people's faces, confused, as if he was in shock.

"Has someone called an ambulance?" I asked quietly.

Phyllis nodded. "They're on their way. They're coming from Letterkenny; they said there'd be someone here as soon as possible, but . . ."

Looking with horror at Jay's blue face, I knew what Phyllis was reluctant to say: that there was a distinct possibility that by the time they arrived, it would be too late. We watched as Harry tried CPR again and again without success, battling desperately to save Jay's life.

While Liam's wife comforted him, I found myself in tears for this young man, dying thousands of miles from home with strangers around him.

★   ★   ★

Half an hour later, the ambulance arrived and an exhausted Harry handed Jay over to the paramedics. Most people had drifted away by this time, and only Maeve, Liam, Phyllis, and myself remained on the pier, along with Ian. Leah and Kevin had come down to see what had happened but had left again at the urging of both their families when it was clear there was nothing they could do. I felt so sorry for them—such an awful thing to happen on their wedding day.

Those of us who remained departed when the ambulance arrived, with the exception of Harry and Ian, who stayed behind to give information. I walked up the lawn towards the house with Liam, his hair and clothes still wet, an awful reminder of what had happened. His wife had gone to seek out a change of clothes for him.

"That poor boy. You were very brave to dive in after him like that," I said. "What happened? Did he fall in?"

Liam looked pale beneath his suntan. "I don't know. I just saw him flailing about. I was on my way back to the house when I heard a shout and realized someone was in the water, so I ran back." He shook his head as if he was trying to work something out.

"What is it?" I asked.

He looked around him and lowered his voice. "Jesus, Ben, this is the last thing I'd want to say out loud, but . . ."

"Go on," I urged.

"I'd swear that some of the islanders could see him in the water, and they did nothing."

"You mean they could see he was in trouble?" I said incredulously.

He nodded. "Yes."

"And they left him to drown?"

He scratched his forehead. "Aye. That's what it looked like to me. It was obvious the kid couldn't swim. But they just stood there on the pier, drinking."

"Maybe none of them could swim either?"

"Maybe," he said doubtfully. "Although they didn't do anything else to help. It was Jay's own shouts that I heard. It was almost as if they were happy to let the sea take him."

"Who was there?"

"I can't be sure. It's all a bit of a blur. I just have this impression of people standing about."

"But you were chatting to them, weren't you? I waved at you."

"I tried, but they wouldn't be the friendliest. I had just turned away and was on my way back to the house when I heard Jay. I pushed past them to run at the water, but no one helped until the doc arrived."

I whistled. "That's some observation."

Liam looked grave. "I know. I'm not sure enough to say it out loud to anyone other than you, but that's what I thought."

"Ronan was the one who told us. He came running into the dining room."

Liam nodded. "Aye. I saw him. He heard the shouts too, at the same time as I did."

I looked down. My dress was wet in patches where I had knelt on the pier.

We fell silent as the ambulance men walked by us with a stretcher. Jay's face was covered, confirmation if any were needed that we had been too late.

★   ★   ★

Once the ambulance had pulled away, Ian and Harry joined us at the door of the house. Liam and I had caught up with Phyllis and Maeve and were standing there unsure what to do.

"What happened?" I asked quietly. "Did he slip?"

Ian's hand flew to his mouth. "He must have. Lord, I'm going to have to get that pier looked at. I had no idea it was so dangerous." He sounded upset. "What should we do? Go ahead with the meal or cancel the rest of the wedding?"

He looked at Harry as if he should have the answer, but Harry didn't seem to be listening. He was gazing into the distance, his face rigid. I placed my hand on his arm. He registered my touch and gave me a weak nod.

"I suppose people still have to eat," Liam said with a sigh. "And it's still poor Leah and Kevin's wedding day." He took a deep breath. "I'd say you should carry on."

"I agree," said Phyllis. "It was a horrible accident and an awful thing to happen, today of all days. But we should really try and carry on. For Leah. Of course, you'll have to contact the poor kid's family. He was American, wasn't he?"

Ian nodded. "We should have some details for him on the register. I'll have a look. Then I'll check with the bride and groom and see what they want to do." He looked at Liam and Harry. "And I'll find both of you some dry clothes."

★ ★ ★

It was decided to go ahead. The meal was a rather shocked affair, the speeches shorter than expected, people laughing rather unnaturally at the jokes and, from what I could see, drinking a lot more than they ate. When we'd returned from the pier, Leah had asked me what I thought they should do, and I'd said they should continue, but I wondered now if I'd done the right thing. My view had been the same as Liam's, that they had little choice. They had a house full of guests and if they postponed the meal, any future date would carry the memory of what had happened today. But there was a pall over the proceedings that couldn't be ignored.

Liam, in the clothes Ian Grey had loaned him, was particularly shaken and not his usual self. I'd been to a few weddings with Liam and he was always the life and soul. Not today.

Harry, also in borrowed clothes, was beside me but he hardly spoke for the duration of the meal. I wanted to console him, but I struggled to find the right thing to say, making me realize that I didn't know him well enough to be of any real comfort. When I sneaked a look at him during the cutting of the cake, he was barely present; he was facing the bride and groom, but his eyes were glassy, his mind elsewhere.

So when Fridge had wrapped things up with an Elvis impersonation that managed to provoke some smiles, I turned to him. "Are you okay?"

He forced a smile, but it faded as soon as it appeared.

"I suppose so." He picked up a spoon and started tapping it on the table. "I'm just so frustrated I didn't manage to save him. He was only a kid."

"I know."

He shook his head. "That water is so cold; he must have lost consciousness really quickly. He'd inhaled too much water; his lungs were already full of it. Just hoped I could get air in . . ." His voice was low and I realized he was talking to himself rather than me.

"Did you know him?" I asked.

"Know him?" He turned his head suddenly. He seemed so taken aback that I almost regretted asking.

I shrugged. "He came over to chat to you on the lawn. I wondered if you might know him somehow."

He shook his head, his shoulders slumped. "No. He was in pre-med. Someone told him I was a doctor and he asked if he might come and visit the surgery while he was here. Small-town general practice. I said that of course he could." He continued tapping the spoon, eyes glimmering. "But that won't be happening now, will it . . ."

He trailed off, his voice drowned out by guitar chords, and I realized the music had begun. A space had been cleared for dancing without my even noticing and the lights had been dimmed.

Harry's gaze switched to the dance floor. He gave a sudden weak smile. "Someone's not allowing the small matter of a drowning to ruin her evening."

I followed his gaze. Audrey had removed the cardigan she'd been wearing earlier to reveal a strappy low-cut number, and was leading a posse onto the floor. The dress showed off her considerable dimensions and a rather eclectic collection of tattoos: a rose, a rocket, and what looked like Marilyn Monroe, although I couldn't be sure since Marilyn's lower half disappeared into quivering folds of flesh as her host shimmied up and down.

I glanced over to where Leah and Kevin were sitting, sipping from glasses, not speaking.

"No bridal waltz," I said. "They must have decided not to bother."

Belva was at the same table as the bride and groom, glaring furiously at her daughter on the dance floor. Ronan Grey crossed the floor, empty glasses in hand, and Audrey grabbed him by the arm as if trying to get him to join her. But he shook her off roughly and walked on.

I wondered if Belva thought Audrey was being disrespectful. It could certainly have been interpreted that way, but in fact, she was just what was needed. She was a distraction, she could dance, and she was having fun. And she was attracting attention, male attention particularly. That was, until Fridge arrived to the table with a tray of drinks. Belva whispered something to him, and he looked over at his sister and immediately went up to join her. Her face fell visibly. Elvis fan he may have been, but he didn't have his sister's rhythm.

Harry lapsed again into silence and I continued to watch the events on the dance floor, until Ian Grey tapped me on the shoulder. He crouched down with a groan and his hand went to his stomach.

"Are you okay?" I asked

He winced. "Ah, yeah. Just a bit of stomach pain. I'll be fine." He lowered his voice. "We don't seem to have an address for Jay for some reason. He filled in the register but the only detail he gave was a mobile number."

I raised my eyebrows.

He nodded. "I know. We should have noticed. Or rather, Ronan should have noticed. He was the one who checked him in. We should have taken his passport. Have you any idea what we should do?"

"You don't even have an e-mail address?" I asked.

Ian shook his head sheepishly, hand still on his stomach.

"Have you checked his room for his passport?"

Ian nodded. "It's not anywhere obvious and I don't really want to go rummaging through his stuff. Unless I have to."

I was stumped. "Do you know where his phone is? There might be a home phone number in it—or maybe some family details in his contacts."

"We'll have a look and see if we can find it." He looked hopeful, and then his face fell suddenly. "Although it was probably on him when he went into the water. In which case . . ."

I finished his sentence. "It's gone in the ambulance with him, or it's in the sea."

"I'll have a look in his room again for his passport," he said, standing up with another groan.

Then something occurred to me. "Maybe he gave his contact details to that other guest—Michael," I suggested. "I haven't seen him all day, but from what Jay said, they chatted quite a lot."

Ian's eyes widened, while I had a sudden sad flashback to the laughs I'd had with Jay in the tack room. "Actually, that's a good idea."

"If they exchanged Facebook details or something, it might give you a way to connect with Jay's family," I added.

"Of course. Thanks for that." Ian headed off, a new purpose to his gait.

Chapter Ten

I TURNED TO speak to Harry, but he was gone. Liam looked across at me and took the opportunity to slide over to occupy the seat Harry had vacated, pint in hand. Phyllis watched us from across the table.

"How are you doing?" I asked. "You look a little better."

He tapped the pint. "This is helping, I suppose. Or at least it was, until Phyllis told me a story about Inishathair."

He looked across at the islanders, who had remained in the same corner for most of the afternoon. Belva was giving Kevin a hug, clasping him tightly to her huge bosom as her son and daughter looked on. Both wore expressions I couldn't quite read. I wondered how they had felt about their mother adopting their cousin. She certainly seemed to favor Kevin, but then maybe that was because he had lost his parents.

"Go on," I said.

Liam leaned in closer, though he couldn't have been heard over the music anyway. "Apparently, the islanders believe that if they rescue a stranger from drowning, then the sea will take one of their own to make up for it."

I exhaled loudly. "You're kidding. Is that true? Do they really believe that?"

He frowned and scratched his head. "I don't know. But something strange happened down there at that pier, I'm sure of it. I just can't figure out what it was. I keep replaying the whole thing in my head."

He glanced again at the other table. I did too—I couldn't help it.

"They don't mix a wild lot, do they?" he said. "They just talk to each other."

"Fridge was friendly enough to Maeve and me when we met yesterday," I said. "And Belva . . ."

Liam nodded, gazing into his pint. "Aye, he was to me at first, but then . . . ach, what do I know?"

I shook my head. "I don't see it, Liam. They might believe a house is haunted, but I can't believe they would have purposely left someone to die. That seems a superstition too far."

Liam sighed. "I suppose not. Maybe you're right. It's been such a weird bloody day; I don't know what to think any more."

I paused. "Although it does seem strange that no one saw what happened with all of those people so close by. That no one saw him fall in."

Liam looked up again hopefully. "Doesn't it?" he said. "I had my back to him and *I* heard him call out. Ronan heard him too. But none of the islanders did."

★ ★ ★

Fifteen minutes later, Ian reappeared. This time he asked if he could have a quick word with me outside. I put down my glass and followed him curiously, watched I knew by others at the table, especially Phyllis.

"What is it?" I asked as he closed the door of the dining room behind us, muffling the music. I realized he looked even more shocked than he had earlier, his eyes shining.

"I've just been up to Michael Burrows' room. On your suggestion."

There was a sheen of sweat on his upper lip. "Go on."

"He didn't answer when I knocked, so I opened the door." He swallowed. "He's there all right. But he's dead."

"What?" Somehow, I couldn't quite take in what he was saying.

He repeated himself. This time he added, "I think he must have had a heart attack during the night."

I tensed, reaching my hand out to the wall to steady myself. Slowly it sank in. Michael Burrows was dead. Two deaths in twenty-four hours. How was that even possible?

Before I could respond, Ian shook his head in disbelief. "It must have been all he drank last night—maybe he wasn't used to it."

"Are you sure he's dead?" I asked, knowing even as I spoke that it was a stupid question. How difficult was it to tell that someone was dead?

He nodded. "He's cold. I'd say he's been dead a good few hours." He paled further as realization hit. "We've been celebrating all day while he was lying dead in his bed upstairs."

Not all day, I thought. The celebrations had been pretty muted since Jay's death. "You'd better let Harry have a look," I said. "He'll have to certify the death."

"Of course," Ian said, his hand to his forehead. "I'd forgotten we had a doctor here. Stupid of me. I was about to call that ambulance again."

"I'll get him."

He ran his hand through his hair. "I can't believe this. Two deaths during our first ever wedding. People will say we're cursed, that the house is cursed."

As I pushed open the dining room door, I couldn't help but think that although he might be right about that, it shouldn't be his first concern on finding a guest dead in his room.

I made my way back in through the voices and the laughter and the music, all jarring against the knowledge of this latest tragedy. I was relieved to see that Harry had returned to his seat. He saw me approach and was on his feet before I reached him, as if he'd been expecting something.

"Can you come?" I said. "You're needed again, I'm afraid."

He nodded and followed me without a word. Ian was waiting for us at the door, eyes darting around in panic. As he explained what had happened, Harry's expression darkened. Whatever it was he had been expecting, it wasn't this. But he responded quickly. Again. On finding out where Burrows' room was, he made his way up the stairs, his long legs taking them two at a time, while Ian and I followed behind.

On Maeve's and my floor there was a fork. Our rooms were on the left, but now we took the considerably narrower right-hand corridor, with a long display cabinet that Harry barely missed as he rushed by, directed to the last room on the right. The door was ajar, presumably left like that by a panicked Ian Grey. Harry pushed it and went inside, followed by Ian and me, although we stopped just inside the door. I wasn't sure if we should even be here, but there was no one yet to tell us that we shouldn't be.

The room was dark, the shutters still closed, dust motes swimming in the warm air. A rather strange smell lingered, particularly around a large high bed, much like the one in my room, where a figure lay on his back. Harry was there in a flash. From where I stood, I could see a white face, a balding head on a pillow. I couldn't even be sure it was the same man who had been at the barbecue the night before—I had seen him so briefly. Ian and I watched as Harry picked up the man's wrist and felt for his heart.

I looked away, for the second time today feeling like a voyeur, and glanced around the room. It was smaller than mine, painted a deep moss green, with white skirting boards and drawings from Dickens' novels on the walls. The room had the same heavy furniture as mine, but instead of a dressing table, there was an old gentleman's desk, which was covered in papers and books.

Surprisingly, there was an en suite. The door was open, and a rather unpleasant smell emanated from within: Burrows had been sick at some stage. In fact, the room was a cacophony of smells. Underlying the ones from the bed and the bathroom was a third I couldn't identify. Something sweet.

A phone rang and made me jump. It was Ian's. I'd almost forgotten he was beside me.

He took it from his pocket and examined the screen. "I'll have to take this outside," he said apologetically. "The reception up here is terrible. I won't be long."

While he was gone, I went over to the desk. I glanced at the bed, but Harry was paying no attention to me—he was deep in thought, examining the dead man. The desk was a mess. Either Michael Burrows was an untidy man—and the rest of the room indicated the opposite: his jacket was neatly hung on the door, his shoes placed at the foot of the bed—or someone had been rummaging about in his notes. There were papers on the floor, notebooks and torn photographs scattered about the desk. I didn't touch anything, but two pictures caught my eye—one was the family portrait I'd seen on the stairs, another a man on his own.

Footsteps in the corridor sent me flying back to the door, where Ian appeared looking anxious, his hand clutching at his stomach.

"Are you okay?" I asked.

"I'm fine," he said dismissively. He looked at Harry. "Well? There's nothing to be done, is there?"

Harry finally turned to face us; his brow furrowed. He shook his head. "No, he's dead. And you're right that he's been gone for some time. At least ten hours, I'd say. But the pathologist will have to confirm that."

Ian's face fell. "Pathologist? Why would we need a pathologist? Surely it was a heart attack? Can't you certify the death?"

Harry shook his head again. "I can't assume a natural death. I've never seen this man before, so I have no way of knowing his medical history."

He stopped suddenly and made his way into the bathroom. He reappeared in seconds.

"Bloodstained vomit, signs of some kind of distress in there. By the looks of things, he struggled before he finally fell onto the bed. It doesn't look like an ordinary death to me."

Ian looked at him, confused. "What do you mean? Was it the alcohol?"

Harry took a deep breath. "I don't think so. I'm afraid we're going to have to call the guards."

★　★　★

There was no way to keep this latest tragedy from Leah and Kevin and their guests. Within half an hour, an ambulance and two gardaí had arrived, the pathologist was on his way and a real flurry of activity had begun. The two young gardaí who were unfortunate enough to be on duty when the call was made looked completely out of their depth as they asked everyone to stay downstairs. Warning people not to leave the estate until they knew what they were dealing with did very little to quell a rising sense of panic.

I went looking for Leah and found her still in the dining room. She looked distraught, trying her best to calm her mother and sisters, who were seated around one of the tables. I went to give her a hug and she stood up, mascara running.

"You poor old thing. What a way for your wedding day to turn out," I said.

She gave me a wry look. "I told you we should have eloped but I sure as hell didn't envisage this kind of disaster. Those poor men. Have their families been contacted?"

"I don't know. I think Ian Grey was going to do that. At least with Jay." I hesitated. "Although now with what's happened with Michael Burrows, that might be a matter for the guards."

Leah lowered her voice. "You don't think it was something he ate, do you? Maybe last night at the barbecue?" She looked horrified. "God, you don't think it was the fish Kevin's family brought?"

I shook my head. "I doubt it. Everyone was eating and drinking the same food and drink last night, and no one else is sick." Although even as I said it, I had an image of Ian clutching his stomach.

Leah's expression cleared a little. "That's true. But still. The poor man must only have been in his fifties. I wonder if he had a wife and children." Her eyes glittered with tears. "Isn't it awful, I never got the chance to ask him."

"It is awful," I agreed. "Awful for you and Kevin and your families too on your wedding day."

"Oh, we're okay," she said bravely. "We got to do the deed at least. Kevin's taken everyone into the bar. That'll keep them mollified."

I gave her another hug and left her to her sisters and mother, noting that the youngest, Niamh, wasn't there. Presumably with the boyfriend to whom she was joined at the hip.

When I went back into the hall, Maeve was talking to Abby Grey at the foot of the stairs. Abby looked shaken and tearful, but before I reached them, she had moved away towards the kitchen.

"Is she okay?" I asked Maeve.

"She's looking for Ronan. Wants to see him before he speaks to the guards. I assume she's afraid the hotel will be blamed for this, that people will think it's something to do with the food and drink."

"I'm sure that won't be the case," I replied. "I was just talking to Leah about it. Surely, it's significant that no one else is sick. Everyone ate the same food."

Maeve nodded. A sudden burst of laughter came from the bar, and she smiled grimly. "No one seems to be too worried about the booze anyway . . ."

She broke off to allow two medics to push past us to go up the stairs. "I feel as if I'm in the way. Shall we go outside for a bit?"

"Good idea."

It seemed strange to emerge into sunshine after the gloom of indoors. Although it seemed much later, it was still only half past seven and there was some heat left in the sun. We walked down the steps to a bench overlooking the sea, goldenrod blazing its vibrant orange on either side. The whole garden was an absolute riot of color, and as the early-evening shadows grew, the scent of the flowers was heavy in the air. It all seemed strangely at odds with what was going on inside.

We sat down, simultaneously exhaling with a groan. Maeve slipped off her high heels and rested her feet on the gravel.

"Not exactly the weekend I was expecting."

"No, me neither."

She looked up and nodded toward the pier. "He's a strange kid, isn't he?"

I squinted and made out the figures of Niamh and Finn in the same spot I'd seen them the night before. They were standing looking out to sea, back in the hoodies and jeans they'd been wearing the previous day. Finn had his arms around Niamh and his chin on her shoulder.

"Yes, he is," I agreed.

It looked like a quiet, contemplative scene until Finn spun Niamh around and I could see they were smiling. As he twisted her to one side, they almost fell, and they both laughed. There was something gleeful about them that made me uncomfortable—in the light of what had just happened.

"I suppose they're young," Maeve said, reading my thoughts. "Maybe these kind of things wash over them."

I wasn't convinced. I could remember how I'd felt at their age and was sure I would have been affected by what had happened. Jay was only a few years older than they were, after all.

"I wonder where his parents are?" she asked.

"Finn's?"

She nodded. "He's young to be allowed away for the weekend on his own, isn't he? How old is he? Fifteen?"

"I don't know. About that, I suppose."

A wave of tiredness washed over me and I closed my eyes to the sun, relishing the kaleidoscope of color. I felt as if I could sleep.

Until I was roused by something hairy brushing against my legs and Maeve's voice saying, "Hello, boy, where did you come from?"

I opened my eyes and looked down to see Maeve rubbing the
ears of a large brown dog, whose tail was slapping my calf. It was
Rudy the gardener's dog.

"Maybe you're right not to go into that house, eh, boy?"
Maeve said. "Where's your master?"

Just at that moment, the man himself appeared, emerging
from behind a large copper beech at the end of a row of flower
beds. He had his back to us. There was a shout, and I realized
he was calling to Finn and Niamh, who had moved from the
pier to the pathway leading into the woods. Finn shouted back.
I couldn't make out what he said, but when Rudy looked back
in our direction, he was scowling.

His expression softened when he saw his dog. "Come here,
Sam."

The dog looked up and trotted over to him. Rudy's eyes widened when he saw the ambulance and Garda cars outside the
house. Two more had arrived while we'd been sitting here. He
came over to us, Sam at his heels.

"What's happened?"

"One of the guests died suddenly," Maeve said.

"Two," I corrected her.

"Sorry, two. Didn't you know?"

Rudy shook his head. "I only started at three o'clock and I
went straight to work in the vegetable garden."

When we told him what had happened, his face grew grave.

Suddenly Maeve's own eyes widened as she looked towards
the house. She shielded them with her hand.

"Ben," she said urgently. "Look who's walking towards us."

I looked up, followed her gaze and swallowed. Molloy.

Chapter Eleven

MY STOMACH CHURNED as Molloy approached. He looked thinner, but those grey eyes gave me the same jolt they always had. This was the last thing I needed. What the hell was he doing back? Just when I was beginning to sort myself out, to move on. Those eyes, his expression when he saw me, brought back feelings I wanted nothing whatsoever to do with.

As soon as he saw the uniform, Rudy hightailed it back in the direction from which he had come, Sam following. I felt like going with him. Maeve too decided to abandon me and head back towards the house, greeting Molloy with a cheery "Evening, Sergeant," as she passed, and leaving me on my own to face him.

For some reason, ridiculously, I stood up, as if he were visiting royalty or something; I would be annoyed with myself for that later. I smoothed out my dress—the damp patches had dried out, I noticed.

"When did you get back?" I asked.

"Just yesterday. I've been re-stationed to Letterkenny."

"Thank you for letting me know." I sounded petulant. I didn't want to sound petulant. With two men dead, my personal hurt was hardly going to be Molloy's main priority.

His eyes narrowed. "I did try, but your phone has been off."

I shook my head. "No, it hasn't."

And then I remembered what Ian Grey had said about poor reception in the house and realized that I hadn't received a single text or call since I'd been here. I'd been expecting a call from my parents, which hadn't come.

"It happened very quickly, Ben. I didn't know myself until the last minute. I'm sorry."

I looked down.

"Who was that you were talking to just now?" he asked.

"Maeve? You've met Maeve, haven't you?" I said sarcastically.

"You know what I mean."

I looked towards the gap in the trees. "That's Rudy. He's the gardener."

"Then that's the man I need to speak to."

"Why?"

He breathed in. "We think Mr. Burrows may have been poisoned, and we're working on the possibility that he may have ingested some kind of plant. We won't know what it is until the toxicology reports are back, but the gardener might be able to give us some information in the meantime. He will know what grows here."

I scanned the lush garden with its flowers and shrubs and imagined what a considerable list that would run to. And it wasn't just what I could see—there was the wooded area too, and the walled vegetable garden. But I said nothing.

Harry appeared on the steps of the house. He looked over, caught my eye and waved. But I didn't respond; I wasn't capable. My face was on fire.

Molloy followed my gaze, then switched his back to me. "These aren't exactly the circumstances I would have chosen, but it *is* good to see you."

"So you *were* planning on contacting me then?" I wanted to bite my tongue each time I spoke. It seemed I couldn't do aloof and dignified no matter how much I wanted to.

"Look. Can we speak later?" Molloy asked. "I need to find this gardener and I have a number of other interviews I need to conduct. But I do want us to talk properly."

I bowed and stood aside to let him past. When I looked up, Harry was gone.

★   ★   ★

I made my way back to the house, high heels crunching in the gravel, mind all over the shop. So Molloy was back. Where had he been? My phone might have been out of coverage for a day or two, but surely, he'd have had more notice of his return than that. So why hadn't he contacted me? And more to the point, why did I care? I'd moved on, hadn't I?

Yes, I decided, I'd moved on. Molloy's return was not my problem.

I decided to concentrate on something else. Something like two sudden deaths on Leah's wedding day. One probably an accident and the other, what? Murder? A person didn't willingly ingest poison, unless it was suicide.

I walked up the main steps of the house. Was it possible that the two deaths were connected? Was it possible they weren't? I thought about the papers I'd seen on Burrows' desk and wondered if they had something to do with his death. Why did he have a photo of that family portrait of the Greys, for instance? Suddenly I wanted to go back up to my room, to Louisa Grey's room, have another look at her book and examine the family gallery on the way. But when I arrived into the foyer, the stairs were blocked off. There was no access upstairs.

I stood for a minute, unsure what to do. Then I followed the noise and went into the bar.

The bar was really just a drawing room, with armchairs and couches, striped and chintz, a fine marble fireplace with a gilt mirror above, and a piano and card table. I'd stuck my head in briefly the night before, when it had been empty. Now it was full to bursting, neither the room nor its furniture equipped to hold the thirty or so people that were now here. Most of the armchairs had two or three people perched on them, and the room was warm and stuffy. I wondered why no one had gone outside, until Liam told me they'd been asked to remain here until they'd been questioned. There was a small table in the corner from which a dazed-looking Ronan Grey was serving soft drinks and water. I assumed the guards had called a halt to alcohol consumption for the time being.

"I never even met that man who died. I don't know what I'll be able to tell them." Liam sounded anxious. He lowered his voice. "Do you think I should mention my concerns about the boy's death? It's been bothering me all day, and now with this happening, I don't know what to think."

"They'll ask you about both, I'm sure," I said. I paused. "Do you think they're connected?"

He shrugged. "It's a possibility, isn't it? I mean, we're assuming that boy's death was an accident. But what if it wasn't?"

"I wonder if Ian Grey managed to contact Jay's family," I said. "Michael Burrows was his best hope."

Liam nodded. "He has. He took your suggestion about Facebook. Turns out Ronan had connected with the young fella on there, so he was able to track down the parents and get a message to them. But they're from Oregon, way over the north-west of the States, so they're going to have a long and terrible journey to get here. They won't be here till Monday at least."

I looked up at Ronan, his face drawn, pouring glasses of Coke on automatic pilot. I should speak to him, I realized; he had lost a friend.

"And Michael Burrows?"

"He was English, so it was easier. And they had an address and a home phone number for him. He had a wife and adult children. I'm sure they're on their way by now."

I shook my head. "How awful for all of them."

"I know," Liam said quietly. "Ian said that Burrows' son is some bigwig film producer. They didn't think he'd be able to get away but apparently he *is* coming."

Phyllis appeared at my shoulder. "Well, it looks as if we're all here for the night," she announced.

"What?" Liam spun around.

"The guards have said no one is to leave until they speak to everyone, and with so many of us, that could easily be tomorrow. So we're all stuck here whether we want to be or not."

"I hope they have somewhere for you to sleep," I said.

Phyllis gave a wry look. "Well, I suppose they have two spare rooms now."

"Jesus!" Liam exclaimed. "Can this weekend get any worse? What about the doctor?"

"He's been excused," Phyllis said. "He told the guard he had patients back in Glendara to see in the morning, so they questioned him first. I suppose they would have anyway since he was the first medic on the scene. I think he's gone." She cast her eyes around the room to check.

I did the same, but there was no sign of him. So, he had left without saying goodbye, I thought. I wasn't sure what to feel about that.

"I suppose it's fair enough," Liam said grudgingly. "He was pretty impressive today."

"I see the sergeant is back," Phyllis said, her eyes narrowed as she examined my face. "I caught sight of him in the hallway."

I nodded.

"That's good news at least," she added. "Someone to take charge. Those two young guards looked as if they were petrified they'd be next. I wouldn't have wanted to be putting my faith in them."

Anxious to avoid a full-blown cross-examination about Molloy, I left Phyllis and Liam and made my way over to Kevin and his family, who had congregated near the fireplace. They were drinking from cans of soft drinks. They opened their circle to make room and Kevin put his hand on my shoulder.

"I'm sorry about the way things turned out. This isn't much fun for anybody."

"It's hardly your fault," I replied. "It's *your* wedding that's been ruined."

"That's what I've been saying to him," Belva said, nodding. "He's always so concerned for everybody else."

"Well, you all traipsed over here for us, didn't you? And poor old Fridge didn't even get to do his party piece." He thumped Fridge on the shoulder in a transparent attempt at false jollity.

"I have to ask," I said. "How on earth did you get the nickname Fridge?"

Fridge looked sheepish while Kevin grinned, relishing the story. "When he was a wee lad—I know that's hard to imagine—he went missing, and it turned out that he had locked himself in a fridge."

My eyes widened. "You're kidding. A working fridge?" I turned to the man in question. "How did you survive that?"

He grinned. "My father fixed kitchen appliances. The shed was always full of cookers and fridges and the like, and one day I just climbed into one and pulled the door after me. I don't think I was in there long, and it wasn't plugged in. But I've never lived it down and the name just stuck."

"Always the crazy one, so he was," Belva said. "You never quite knew what was going to happen next. Always some old shuffle going on."

"Not much has changed," Audrey added. "Isn't that right, Luther?" She gave her brother a push that wasn't entirely in jest, and I realized that it was the first time I'd heard her speak. She had a low, whispery voice that was in contrast to her considerable size.

Fridge shoved his hands in his pockets, shrugged and looked away. As he did so, the sleeve of his shirt rose up and I noticed he had quite a burn on his wrist. Before I could ask him about it, Ronan appeared behind us with an empty tray. He nodded to us, but I noticed that his hand trembled as he collected glasses from the mantelpiece and placed them onto the tray.

"Awful about that poor man," Belva said with a sigh. "Wild sore on the family."

"He was on the island, wasn't he?" I was surprised to hear Ronan speak. He held an empty Coke bottle in his hand like a truncheon.

Kevin looked as surprised as I did, although apparently for a different reason. His eyes darted quickly from his cousins to his aunt.

"I didn't know that. I thought you were all being friendly to him because he was on his own. How come you never mentioned it?"

Audrey and Fridge looked at each other and shrugged. "It never came up."

"Audrey took a bit of a shine to him, didn't you, Audrey?" Fridge added with a grin as Ronan made his way back to the bar, bottle in hand, shoulders hunched. He'd left the tray behind, I noticed.

"I did not," Audrey said indignantly. "He was married. But he was nice to talk to."

"He played some music in the pub," Fridge said. "Had a tin whistle with him. Terrible musician, but he was a bit of craic."

"What was he doing on the island?" I asked.

Fridge shook his head. "Not sure. I think he was birdwatching or something."

"He was a nice friendly wee man," Belva pronounced authoritatively, both chins wobbling. "Meant no harm to anyone." She lowered her voice. "They've said he was poisoned. Is that true?"

I nodded. "So I hear. Some kind of plant, possibly."

Since Molloy wanted to speak to Rudy about this, I knew it must be common knowledge. Not that he'd be sharing it with me if it wasn't.

"I'd say he'd be just the kind of man who'd eat the wrong berry, you know," Fridge said thoughtfully. "If he was supposed to be birdwatching, he was no expert: mistook a cormorant for a seagull one time."

What did birdwatching have to do with Burrows' interest in old houses? I wondered.

I paused. "Did any of you see what happened to poor Jay?"

"The American lad?" Belva asked, and I nodded.

"I didn't catch his name. I think he must have just cowped over. He was there one minute, and the next that auctioneer man was in the water trying to save him."

"You didn't see him fall in?" I asked, tempted to ask about Phyllis's story but not at all sure how to do it without accusing.

They all shook their heads in unison as Ian Grey came over, picked up the tray his son had left behind. and walked off again without a word.

Fridge's gaze followed him. "A wild handling for that poor man. It'll be a right wheel of days before people forget what's happened. Won't be easy for them to keep going."

"I know," I said. "But it's not their fault—hopefully people will realize that and give them a chance."

"Aye, hopefully," Fridge said unconvincingly as he took a slug from his Coke.

Chapter Twelve

HALF AN HOUR later, Molloy was asking me the same question.

"So, what do you know about the drowning?" he said. "Did you see it happen?"

We were sitting on the bench that Maeve and I had occupied earlier. It was half past nine and the sun was low, a deep coral disc hovering over the sea. Phyllis's fears had proved groundless and most of the questioning had been finished, allowing those who wanted to leave to do so. The pathologist's office had taken the body away, watched silently by those who happened to be in the hallway at the time.

Leah's wedding was over. The place was quiet, both house and garden. Only those who were already booked to stay remained, effectively family and close friends. The two young guards, named now as Boyle and Clarke, were still around, slightly surer of themselves but still looking as if they'd rather be anywhere else but here. Molloy had asked if he could have a private word, and we'd come outside.

"Liam was the only one who chose to mention it," Molloy added.

"I don't think people would have forgotten about what happened to Jay on purpose. I think Michael Burrows' death rather overshadowed it, unfortunately," I said.

Molloy examined my face. "Did you see him go in?" he asked again.

"No, I didn't—I was inside. The meal was about to begin when Ronan came in to tell us that someone was in the water and we all rushed out."

Molloy looked at me curiously. "He definitely said 'someone'? Not Jay'?"

I thought about it. It hadn't occurred to me before, but that was a little odd. "I think so."

"No one seems to have seen him fall in. A few of the guests have said they were down at the shore when it happened, but they all say they saw nothing until Liam tried to rescue him."

"I know. I've been talking to some of the islanders."

Molloy shielded his eyes from the low sun. "Where exactly did it happen?"

"Down at the pier," I said, pointing. "The other side to where the boats are moored. It looked as if he'd fallen off; that maybe he'd slipped or something."

"Can you show me?" Molloy asked.

"Of course."

We stood up and made our way across the lawn and down the pathway to the pier. My high heels and his long stride brought back memories that I immediately shook off. When we reached the shore, we walked along the short pier, and about three quarters of the way in, I pointed at the water.

"I think it was around here. The tide was in and the water was pretty deep, deeper than it is now. Liam dived in after him and he was followed by the doctor. Harry," I added.

Molloy gave me a sidelong glance but said nothing. I wondered if Harry had mentioned me when Molloy had been questioning him. The thought gave me a twinge. I didn't want to acknowledge what that twinge meant.

"Liam was in the water when I arrived," I said. "But I think it was too late even at that stage. Jay couldn't swim. He was unconscious. Harry and Liam managed to pull him out with Ronan's help."

Molloy looked around him. "And who else was down here from what you can remember? When he fell in?"

"Kevin's family mainly, I think, the islanders. Belva, her son and daughter, I'm not sure who else."

His eyes narrowed as if he was trying to picture the scene. I followed his gaze, scratching my head. The midges were plentiful down here by the water, especially in the evening, their bites like hundreds of tiny stabs. I swatted them away ineffectually.

"Do you think it might not have been an accident?" I asked.

Molloy shook his head. "Impossible to know at this stage." He looked down. "I suppose someone could have fallen in by accident, especially if they were a drinker, although I understand the young man who died was not. We've spoken to Letterkenny and they've established that there was no alcohol in his system. First thing they checked." He rubbed his shoe against the surface of the pier. "But it's not a particularly dangerous pier—it's not slippery. And it's a bit of a coincidence to say the least—two deaths in the one day."

I paused. "Did Liam tell you . . ."

"The notion of islanders not rescuing a stranger from drowning in case the sea takes one of their own instead?" Molloy nodded. "I think that story spooked him. But he can't swear to anything. It all happened very quickly, and he was pretty panicked."

"Yes, he was."

"And of course, there's also a possibility that none of the other people nearby could swim either. That's not unusual amongst islanders."

"True," I replied. "So there may be only one suspicious death." I kicked a pebble into the water and it made a splash. "As if that makes it any better—Leah's wedding is still ruined."

"The truth is, we're not certain yet that either death was murder," Molloy said. "Michael Burrows could always have eaten something by mistake."

"What makes you think it was a plant?"

"There were some leaves in his room, on his bedside locker and on the floor. We're not sure what they are, but they looked as if they'd been dried or cooked. It's the only thing we have to go on. There was nothing else in the room, not even a glass of water."

I looked up. "Was the gardener any help?"

Molloy shook his head. "Not particularly. He's rather a taciturn individual anyway, I'd say. And he felt he was under suspicion, so was even less forthcoming than usual, I suspect. But he agreed, reluctantly, to put together a list of plants."

I opened my mouth to respond and a midge flew into my mouth. I inhaled and coughed as Molloy looked at me with a mix of concern and amusement.

"Are you all right?"

I swallowed. That wasn't going to help my throat. "Fine."

I heard a voice and looked up towards the house. Maeve was at the top of the lawn, waving and heading down the hill towards us, full tilt.

She was out of breath by the time she reached us, still in her wedding outfit and high heels. She took a deep breath. "Jesus, these really are sitting-down shoes. Sorry to interrupt, but people are asking when they'll be allowed back upstairs to their rooms.

Everyone wants to change out of their wedding gear—especially Leah and her sisters. I think she's been in that wedding dress long enough, poor girl."

"They should be able to go back up now," Molloy said. "The tech bureau are finished. If the crime-scene tape is gone, then it's okay to go up; if it's still there, come back to me. Mr. Burrows' room will of course be sealed off, as will Jay Stevenson's."

"Of course," Maeve replied. "Thank you. I'll let everyone know."

As we watched her head back towards the house, I had a flashback to Niamh and Finn earlier. They had been in jeans; I was sure of it. I couldn't remember what Finn had worn to the ceremony, but Niamh had definitely been wearing a bridesmaid dress. How had *they* managed to get back into their rooms to change? I wondered.

But I didn't say anything to Molloy. Instead I said, "I'd like to do the same, if that's okay."

He nodded. "Of course. I need to get back to Letterkenny. Check on toxicology reports and some other things. The other guards can take the remaining statements. I'll be back tomorrow."

"Fine."

"And I'll be leaving Garda Boyle and Garda Clarke here for the night, to be on the safe side. The kitchen's been shut down, so there'll be food delivered in."

"Okay."

As I turned to walk back towards the house, Molloy called me back.

"Don't shut me out, Ben, please. I'd like a chance to explain things. I don't have the time at the moment, but—"

I cut across him. "I won't, and you'll get it and I understand."

And as I turned away again, another midge went up my nose.

★ ★ ★

Ian Grey glanced up from the reception desk. He looked awful: he seemed to have aged ten years in the past twenty-four hours, and his grey hair was sticking up as if he'd put his finger in a socket.

"What's wrong?" I asked, realizing as soon as I did that I should have changed my question to "What's wrong now?"

He ran his hand through his hair. "Michael Burrows' family will be here tomorrow. His wife and both sons."

"I know it won't be easy," I replied. "But the sooner the better, surely?"

He shook his head in disbelief. "I'd hoped his son would come here at some stage, but Lord, I didn't think it would be under these circumstances . . . What on earth am I going to say to them? The guards have shut down the kitchen. They'll think we poisoned him."

"But you didn't, Ian—that's just a precaution," I said comfortingly. "And they'll know that too. The guards will tell them. As soon as they find out what happened, you'll be able to reopen. It's not your fault; none of this is your fault."

"I'm not sure everyone will agree with you." He sighed. "We have to order from the damn chipper if anyone wants anything to eat this evening. It's the only place that's open." He gave a wry smile. "Not exactly the look we were going for."

"People won't feel much like eating, I don't think," I replied.

"But it's the same for breakfast. All that food we bought in for the guests. It's just going to go bad in the kitchen. We're going to take a huge hit."

And with that, I gave in; there was no soothing him. "That *is* awful, Ian. I'm sorry. It's rotten luck for your first big event, it really is."

"Our first and last, I suspect," he said gloomily.

Maybe he was right. There was no bright side to this and there wasn't much point in my looking for one. I changed the subject.

"How's your stomach, by the way?"

"Ulcer. Had it for years, but it flares up every so often." He smiled grimly. "Stress doesn't help."

As I made my way upstairs, I remembered what Liam had said about Michael Burrows' son being a film producer, and I wondered if that was part of Ian's concern; if maybe he'd hoped to have the big name as a guest someday. But I decided I wasn't doing him justice. Things couldn't be easy for him at the moment. Greysbridge had only been open a few months.

As I passed the family gallery on the stairs, one picture caught my eye and I stopped to take a closer look. It was one of the photos I had seen on Michael Burrows' desk: a portrait of a man, a rather formal sepia photograph. Dressed in a dark suit, with long hair and sideburns and a rather self-satisfied air, he had the pose of a member of the judiciary. But he didn't appear to be a judge—although he was wearing a gown and holding a scroll, he didn't have a wig or tabs. There was a caption below the picture—*The Honourable Linus Grey, Baronet of Greysbridge, Donegal, 1911.* I remembered the inscription in the book in my room, the one to Louisa Grey. It had been signed *L. G.* Was Linus Grey her father? I examined his face. There was a slight resemblance to Ian; they had similar eyes and eyebrows.

I looked at the other pictures. Along with the governess, Linus Grey, and the family portrait in front of the house, there was one of a young woman, Lady Louisa Grey herself perhaps, looking thin and wan, eyes huge and liquid in her small face. It made me think of what Ian had said about her not eating. I wondered if she was also the little girl with ribbons in the family portrait.

She'd looked considerably happier then. Beside her was a younger boy in short trousers, her brother, I presumed. They were alike, the two children– the same dark hair and eyes. Was the boy Ian Grey's grandfather? The grandfather who had lost the house in a card game?

I continued on up the stairs, pausing for a moment where the corridors split, unable to resist a glance down the hallway to Michael Burrows' room. I would have liked to have another look at his desk, but I knew it would be guarded. Strangely unsated, I headed on back towards my own room.

I changed into a pair of jeans and a light shirt. I was tempted to have a shower but decided it could wait. My mind was dancing around the issue of Molloy's return and the last thing I wanted was to settle on it. I needed a distraction. So I pulled on a pair of flat sandals—a relief to get out of the high heels—washed my face in the hand basin and put on some moisturizer. A lick and a polish, as my mother used to call it, which reminded me to check my phone. There was one bar, which meant limited reception, but there were no messages. I made a mental note to ring my parents before the day was out.

Before then, I needed some fresh air. I decided to visit the old family graveyard again. I was curious about Louisa Grey, but it seemed not insignificant that Michael Burrows had died at Greysbridge, the house he had been researching, with photographs of the family on his desk. I was keen to find out what he had discovered.

As I left my room, I heard Maeve's voice next door. She was on the phone. I made my way downstairs as quietly as I could, wanting to be alone for a while. The house was silent, even the bar, everyone having retreated to their rooms and boats. The door to the library where the ceremony had taken place was open, so I went inside. It was deserted and bare: chairs neatly stacked along one wall, the desk Phyllis had used moved to the side, flowers taken down from the bookcases.

I wandered about looking at the few books that had been placed on the shelves, floorboards creaking beneath my feet. They were a mixed bunch: *Guide to Practical Philosophy*, *The Game of Billiards*, a few old Crime Club hardbacks. I took one or two down to see if they had inscriptions, but most were stamped *Withdrawn from stock*. The Greys must have bought a job lot from the library to fill the shelves. Disappointed, I was about to give up and go back outside when I saw a small row of books on a shelf by my feet that I hadn't yet looked at. I kneeled down and took a couple of them out.

The first was a small red hardback entitled *Practical Mathematics*. I opened the cover. The name inside was inscribed in a childish hand: *Evan Grey*. Louisa's brother and Ian's grandfather? I wondered. The boy I'd seen earlier in the family portrait? So, he learned math while his sister was encouraged to sew and cook. A product of the time. I opened a couple of others—considerably heavier tomes. With titles such as *Outlines of Human Physiology*, *Philosophy of the Human Mind* and *Electrotherapy and Neurological Practice*, they all bore the same inscription—*L. G.*

Chapter Thirteen

I PICKED UP a few more volumes and flicked through them, all demanding scientific tomes relating to physical or mental health. Linus Grey was a learned man by the looks of things. I wondered if he had been a doctor, if the portrait with the gown had been a conferring of some medical degree? I replaced the books and went back out into the hall just as Maeve was coming down the stairs. Like me, she had changed out of her wedding outfit and into jeans and sandals.

"Is the sergeant gone?" she asked, glancing towards the door from which I'd just emerged, as if she half expected him to come out after me.

I nodded. "Back to Letterkenny for the night. He'll be back in the morning."

She leaned against the banister on the bottom step, stretching her calves. "Phyllis and Liam are gone too. They left while you were with Molloy. They *won't* be back in the morning." She gave a wry smile. "Although I suspect Phyllis would like to be. Her curiosity levels are off the scale."

"I'll bet."

She descended the last step and we walked together out onto the lawn. Ian Grey had finally left his post, I saw, hopefully to get some rest.

The light was very different now; the vibrant pink sky had been replaced by a muted orangey brown. It was dusk, and the air was considerably cooler, which was a relief. I said as much to Maeve as we strolled along the lawn.

"I was just checking in with the clinic and they tell me the weather is to break next week," she replied. "There's a storm coming, apparently, Wednesday or Thursday." She sighed. "Just what we need."

"Might be good to have an end to this heat, though."

"True." She paused. "Although a heavy storm at this time of year will wreck some of the crops." She stopped to pick up a large stone from the grass and chuck it onto the gravel. "That was a bit of a turn-up for the books, wasn't it? Molloy appearing like that. Is he back for good?"

"I'm not sure. He says he's been re-stationed in Letterkenny. I don't know for how long."

Maeve clapped her hands together to brush the clay off. "He's probably looking for an inspector's position. He'd make a good inspector."

"Maybe you're right."

That was something that hadn't occurred to me. Molloy had been a sergeant for a long time, and while the investigation after Luke's death had undoubtedly held him back, that wasn't a consideration now. But I shook my head. I didn't want to think about Molloy. I found myself shifting from one foot to the other, looking down, anxious to be off, uneasy.

Maeve looked at me suspiciously. "What's wrong? You seem distracted. You're like a hen on a hot griddle."

I shrugged. "I thought I'd go for a walk, get a bit of fresh air. It feels as if we've been penned up here for a long time."

"No, you're right. I feel the same—cabin fever. It's hard to imagine the ceremony was only this afternoon; it seems like a week ago. Where were you thinking of going?"

"Up along the shore, where we went with the horses. I was thinking of having another look at that old graveyard."

Her eyes narrowed. "Any particular reason?"

I shrugged. "Just curious really. I wouldn't mind knowing a bit more about the family."

"Couldn't you just ask Ian Grey if you're curious?"

I avoided her eye. "I have but I don't think he knows very much. He said Michael Burrows was the real expert. But I didn't get a chance to ask him."

She straightened herself, putting her shoulders back. "Okay, I'll bite. It'll be nice to have a walk along the shore. And I didn't go into the graveyard the last time, so I wouldn't mind having a nosy there myself."

We set off across the grass. It felt good to stretch the legs—mine were still stiff after the ride this morning.

"God, I could do with heading home myself, to be honest." Maeve sighed. "I probably should have got a lift with Liam. I just didn't think of it in time."

"Sorry," I said sheepishly. "I can't drive till tomorrow. Too many glasses of champagne earlier."

"Sure, I know," she grinned. "It was shaping up to be a really good wedding. Maybe we could have a glass of wine later, when we come back from our walk. I feel like I need another drink after this day."

"You're on," I agreed. "I'm sure the kitchen ban doesn't extend to bottles of wine."

She gave me a slightly guilty look. "As a matter of fact, I have a bottle of champagne in my bag. If it does, we could drink that."

I laughed. "You're kidding."

"Nope. I was intending giving it to Leah before the ceremony, but I didn't get the chance." She paused. "Doesn't the sea look beautiful?" She looked out towards the shore, then stopped suddenly in her tracks.

"What?" I asked, following her gaze but seeing nothing of any significance other than that the sun was sinking. We'd need to get a move on if we were to get to the graveyard and back before darkness fell.

"The boats," she said, pointing towards the pier. "The islanders' boats. They're gone."

I looked. She was right. The pier was clear and empty—not a trace of its earlier occupants. "They must have left while we were inside."

"Did they say anything to you? Any tearful goodbyes?" she asked with a crooked smile.

"Nope."

"Me neither. Maybe they didn't expect two deaths at a wedding," she said ruefully.

We continued along the path through the trees, taking the same route that we'd taken on our first walk. It was darker now, the scents stronger, the wind rustling the branches above. We walked briskly until we reached the clearing where we'd seen Rudy and his dog the night before.

This time, I was the one who spotted something different. The flowers Rudy had planted had been dug up. There was a section of freshly turned soil in the midst of other plants. I said as much to Maeve.

"Now why would he do that?" she asked, looking down. "Plant them and then remove them?"

"Assuming it was he who removed them," I said. My eyes narrowed. "Can you remember what they were?" I asked.

Maeve stood with her hands on her hips. "God, no. I'm hopeless when it comes to cultivated plants. Much better on the wild ones, Give me a cowslip or a dandelion any day."

"Me too." I knelt down to check, but there was no trace of the earlier plants. All that remained was soil. "I can't even remember what they looked like, can you?"

Maeve shook her head. "Haven't a clue. Why do you want to know?"

I paused. "Because apparently there's a possibility that Michael Burrows died from ingesting some kind of poisonous plant."

Her eyes widened. "That's right. Liam told me."

I shook my head. "I'd better text Molloy when I get back."

When I stood up, Maeve was looking at me with an exasperated expression on her face.

"What?" I asked.

She shook her head disbelievingly. "Don't tell me that's why we're schlepping up to the old graveyard. So you can do your amateur sleuth act again."

"What do you mean?" I said innocently.

"Have you forgotten that it nearly got you killed a few months ago?"

Straight away I saw red. "Of course, I haven't forgotten. It was eight months ago. And it wasn't my "amateur sleuth act" that nearly got me killed, it was Luke Kirby. He'd have come after me no matter what I'd done."

The second I finished speaking, I regretted it. Maeve had been a good friend to me since I'd been in Inishowen. Her concern was no reason to snap.

"Sorry," I said.

She nodded in acknowledgement, but there was a stubborn expression on her face that I knew well. We walked on, and she glanced across at me.

"How do you feel about him being back?" she asked. "Really?"

"Molloy?" I shrugged.

Never mind discussing the events of last winter, I definitely wasn't ready to have this conversation. I had no idea how I felt about it, other than extremely pissed off.

Maeve narrowed her eyes. "Because I thought you and the new doctor were getting on swimmingly."

"Rather unfortunate choice of word in the circumstances, Maeve."

"What? Oh yes, sorry." She gave me a wry look. "But I did."

"We are," I said.

"Good."

We emerged at the shore and began to make our way up the rocky path to the old graveyard. Behind me, I heard Maeve take a breath, and sensed she was about to press me again.

I turned. "Look, do you mind if we change the subject? Why is it that married people always want other people to settle down? Is it so awful you want everyone to suffer it?" I smiled to show I was joking.

"That's probably it." Maeve grinned and I knew I was forgiven. "Okay, I'll keep my trap shut from now on."

The climb seemed considerably steeper without a horse, and we arrived at the top of the cliff feeling slightly out of breath. I stood for a few seconds looking across to the island, silhouetted now against the evening sky. As the sky darkened, it was disappearing from view, merging with the horizon and the sea.

Maeve stood beside me. "Do you think they're home yet?"

"I wonder. How far away is it?"

She shrugged. "Five miles maybe? I'm not sure. Ian might know."

I turned towards the graveyard and unhooked the latch, and the gate swung inwards with a high-pitched whine. It needed oiling. Maeve followed me in and I shut it behind us.

The gate wasn't the only thing that needed tending. The little graveyard was terribly overgrown. I'd noticed it the last time, but today, having grown familiar with the rest of the beautifully kept grounds, it seemed in huge contrast. Nettles and brambles were everywhere, tangled together in a mass of threatening green, the fading light casting shadows on the walls. Was this place not part of Rudy's responsibilities? I wondered. He hadn't seemed too keen on us coming up here the first night.

With no Abby Grey waiting for me, I decided to take my time and examine the graves methodically, starting with the one at the front. I felt an inexplicable jolt when I saw it was Louisa Grey's— I'd expected to have to hunt a bit. It was oddly positioned in the center of the graveyard, almost as if it were pointing towards the island, or maybe that was just a flight of fancy on my part.

I was startled when I saw that there were fresh flowers on it, shivering when I recalled what Jay had said about Louisa's ghost placing flowers on her own grave. They were blue hydrangeas, the same as those that had been left in my room. Then I remembered: it had been hydrangeas that Rudy had planted in the bed in the trees, I was sure of it. I bent down to take a closer look. These flowers had not been cut; they had been pulled up by their roots. Were they the same plants?

I must have made a noise, because Maeve called to me and asked me if I was okay.

"I'm fine," I replied, feeling slightly foolish.

I glanced over at her. She was at the back wall, high-stepping, trying to avoid being stung or scratched by marauding nettles and briars. She looked as if she was searching for something at her feet.

I knelt down to examine Louisa's gravestone. Despite the flowers, her grave was overgrown with moss and long grass, and the stone was ravaged by time and weather and mottled with lichen. With difficulty I made out the inscription: *In memory of Louisa Grey, born 24th July 1893, died 15th January 1914. Every Eve shall I think of her.*

I sat back on my haunches. It was odd. There were none of the usual references to parents or other family members that were traditional on gravestones even now, and "Eve" was written with a capital letter. I took a picture on my phone.

I moved to look at the grave immediately behind Louisa's, stepping over the weeds. This one had a stone that was smaller and more modern, although the inscription was equally stark: *Susan Grey, born 13th August 1870, died 24th July 1914.* Was this Louisa's mother, I wondered, the woman in the family portrait? If so, she had died only six months after her daughter, on what would have been Louisa's twenty-first birthday.

I stepped across Susan's grave and my clothes caught on a bramble. As I struggled to disentangle myself, I noticed tiny green blackberries, reminding me that despite the unusually warm weather, autumn wasn't far away.

By the time I was free, I realized that I was standing on a much smaller grave with a small stone. I moved quickly aside and crouched down to see if I could read an inscription. But there was none, at least none that I could make out. If there had been, it had faded with time—the stone was completely smooth. I wondered if this was a baby's grave, a baby who hadn't lived long enough to be named. Perhaps Susan Grey's baby, a sibling to Louisa and Evan who had not survived. Had Louisa's mother died in childbirth? The nameless grave seemed so sad.

I realized I was getting pulled into the story of a family who had lived a hundred years ago and wondered if that was what had happened to Michael Burrows.

I stood up and moved to look at the other graves, but was surprised that I could find none. Maeve was making her way over to me, having come to the same conclusion.

"Strange, isn't it—a graveyard this big for two graves."

"Three," I said, pointing to the little one I'd found.

She made her way over to look. "A baby?" she asked. "Unbaptized?"

"Maybe. Are we sure there are no other graves?" I looked around me. "Maybe there are stones hidden underneath all the briars. It's a bit of a mess."

"Certain," Maeve said firmly. "I've searched. The ground is actually very even underneath. There aren't any more graves here, unless they're very deep and completely unmarked."

I rubbed my face. "That's odd."

"Maybe they intended using it as a family graveyard and then changed their minds."

"But why would they do that?" I asked. "Why isn't Louisa Grey's father buried here, for instance? Why was Susan buried with her daughter but not her husband? Her gravestone looks newish, as if she was moved here quite recently."

Maeve shook her head. "I don't know. Maybe the father died at sea or something."

"Maybe," I said doubtfully. "But there was a son, too. Evan. I saw him in the portraits at the top of the stairs. This is only half the family."

"The women," Maeve added darkly. "I wonder if the baby was a girl."

We left the graveyard and closed the gate behind us. Neither of us said much on the way back. It was clear we had both been struck by the strangeness of the place. Why had Louisa Grey been buried here alone with her mother? It didn't make sense. And it certainly wasn't the family graveyard we had been told it was.

I gazed again at Inishathair as we made our way back down the path towards the wood. It had almost disappeared from view now, absorbed into the inky blue of the horizon, but I wondered again if there was any significance to the usually clear view of the island from the graveyard.

And I remembered that Michael Burrows, who had been researching Greysbridge and the Greys, had visited Inishathair.

Chapter Fourteen

"Shh," Maeve hissed suddenly as we walked back through the woods.

"What is it?" I whispered.

It was almost dark now and I could barely see in front of me, but Maeve's eyesight had always been better than mine.

"Just over there, under the tree. Quick, let's go past quickly before they notice us."

They turned out to be Ronan Grey and Leah's sister Cara; as we sneaked by quickly, I caught a glimpse of them. They were kissing under one of the old alders. Maeve was right about leaving them to their privacy, but from what I could see, they were so engrossed in each other they wouldn't have noticed us if we'd burst into song.

"At least this wedding's been good for someone." Maeve smiled as we finally emerged from the woods.

"I'm not sure Abby would agree with you," I said. "She didn't seem too thrilled about the whole thing at the stables this morning."

"God." Maeve looked at me in astonishment. "Was that only this morning?"

"Seems incredible, doesn't it?" I agreed.

Poor Leah and Kevin, I thought, everything had seemed so hopeful back then—a beautiful day, a lovely setting; it seemed certain that all would go so well. Who could have foreseen what was about to happen?

"Bloody clingy mothers," Maeve said as we made our way across the lawn, the dew wetting our feet. "She tried to bring the subject of Ronan up on the ride, thinking I would understand, being a mother of boys. I made the right noises, but honestly, I thought she was being a bit weird. I mean the kid's nineteen or something."

I nodded. "Nearly, I think."

"She didn't like his friendship with Jay either, but she couldn't say much with him there."

"Were they close?" I asked. "Ronan and Jay?"

"Abby seemed to think so. But she was pretty paranoid and jealous from what I could see. Who knows how skewed her judgement was? She was afraid Jay would encourage Ronan to go back to the States with him."

I stopped in my tracks. "Really? Was that a possibility? Jay didn't mention it."

Maeve shrugged. "I have no idea. She said Ronan has money of his own—it seemed to drive her nuts that she couldn't control him that way. He's independent."

I knew that Ronan's birth parents had both died, his father from natural causes while serving a sentence for eco-terrorism, while his mother had been murdered by Luke Kirby, the man who had killed my sister. Although Ronan hadn't known either of them, he had inherited, since his adoption by the Greys had been unofficial to say the least.

We reached the top of the lawn, the lights of the house sur-prisingly welcoming despite what had happened there over the past few hours. Once inside, we heard voices coming from the bar, although far fewer than earlier on. I suspected it was mostly Leah's family now that the islanders had left.

"Do you want to go in?" Maeve asked doubtfully as we stood at the bottom of the stairs.

"Would it be very unsociable not to? I'm pretty wrecked."

"Absolutely not." She looked relieved. "Let's have that bottle of champagne in my room. We'll need some glasses and ice, though."

"I'll have a look in the kitchen and meet you up there."

Maeve took the stairs in her usual fashion, two at a time, while I made my way down to the kitchen. I pushed open the heavy fire door with difficulty, and switched on the light to find myself in a large room with high ceilings, stainless-steel worktops and industrial-size appliances. I suspected this had been the original kitchen of the house but upgraded to satisfy the health and safety requirements of a modern hotel. An expensive job, I would have thought. And now it was closed down until further notice, silent save for the low buzz of a blue-lit fly-zapper.

I stood there surveying cookers, dishwashers and cooking implements and tried to figure out where I might find glasses and ice. Then I spotted a door leading to a back kitchen, where I found plates, cups and glasses and an industrial fridge from which I managed to extract some ice. It did occur to me that maybe I shouldn't be in here, but then the area wasn't closed off, so I presumed it had been thoroughly searched. It appeared that the guards didn't really suspect the food—they were just being careful.

I closed the fridge door and returned to the main kitchen with my loot. I was just about to leave when the door opened inwards. I looked up guiltily, clutching my bowl of ice and two borrowed glasses. But Abby didn't notice my takings—she had something else on her mind.

"Have you seen Ronan?" she asked, her hand on the door, her small face pinched with anxiety.

I was torn. Should I tell her and have her tear off into the woods to break up Ronan and Cara's tryst, or should I stay quiet and have her worry unnecessarily about her son on a day when two men had met their deaths?

I paused for too long and she looked away, her mouth turned down unattractively at the edges.

"I know he's gone off with that girl again," she said. "Just when I need him, as usual."

And that was enough for me. Decision made.

I shook my head. "I'm sorry, Abby. I haven't seen him, I'm afraid."

I wasn't going to deprive Ronan of some comfort on a day when he had lost a friend. Abby closed the door and left without a word.

Seconds later, I pulled it open and made my way back towards the stairs. As I passed the bar, the door opened and Leah and Kevin emerged looking shattered. I stopped.

"How are you two doing?" I asked.

Leah gave me a wan smile. "Oh, we're all right." I was glad to see that she'd finally changed out of her wedding dress into a summer skirt and top. "As well as can be expected, I suppose."

"We've decided to head off on honeymoon in the morning as planned," Kevin said. "So that's given us a bit of a boost. There didn't seem to be any reason to stay, and the guards have said it's okay."

"I'm glad," I said. "There's nothing you can do, I'm sure."

"We'll stay and meet that poor man's family before we go, of course. They're due here first thing." Leah crossed her arms protectively in front of her. She looked as if she was cold.

We walked up the stairs together, and I took my leave of them at the top, passing one of the young guards on my way to Maeve's room: Clarke or Boyle, I wasn't sure which. He smiled wearily and I nodded back. I understood the sense of having a Garda presence in the house tonight, but I wasn't entirely sure what these two nervous young men would be able to do if there was a homicidal maniac roaming the premises.

I knocked on Maeve's door and she let me in. She was in bare feet and had a strange expression on her face.

"Are you all right?" I asked. "You look as if you've had a shock."

She closed the door quietly, her voice hushed. "Have you had anything weird happen while you've been here?"

Uh-oh, I thought. Not Maeve too. Sensible, scientific Maeve the vet. "Like what?"

"Knocking on the wall? A kind of rustling noise?" She looked embarrassed. "Like a dress."

"Coming from where?"

"Your room, I think. You didn't go back in there, did you, just now?"

"No," I said slowly. I placed the glasses and ice on an old writing desk. "Although . . ." I hesitated.

Her eyes widened. "What?"

"I did have a rather strange experience myself in the middle of the night."

She rubbed her nose nervously. "Go on."

"Well, I thought there was someone in the room with me. I felt a presence of some sort, breath on my face. And then I heard footsteps. But when I turned the light on, there was no one there and the door was still locked, just as I'd left it."

Her eyes widened. "Shit. Why didn't you tell me? Do you think the islanders are right about the house being haunted?"

I shook my head definitively. "No. I don't. I think once you're told somewhere is haunted then you're more likely to experience it. It's the power of suggestion—that's all."

"Right," she said firmly. "That makes sense. Okay, let's get this bottle open. I definitely need a drink now."

She pulled the champagne out of her bag, popped the cork and poured out two glasses, throwing a couple of ice cubes into each one.

"Sacrilege," she said as she took a sip, "but I really don't care. I'm feeling a bit freaked out."

I joined her, the sharp tang of the alcohol refreshing on my throat. I realized how tense I'd felt for the past few hours.

"Is that the first time you've heard knocking?" I asked.

She shook her head. "I heard it earlier today when I came up to change for the wedding. I knew you weren't in there, so I thought maybe it was water pipes or something. But then it happened again just now, while you were downstairs. I don't believe in ghosts in the slightest. But if you had something similar happen . . ."

"Then at least we're both losing it." I smiled and wandered slowly across to the window, glass in hand. "I'd say it's that tiny grave in the graveyard that has us spooked."

"It's a strange house, isn't it?" Maeve said, flopping down on the bed with her glass. "Haunted or not."

I looked around me, taking in the room. It was larger than mine and more masculine. The wardrobe was bigger, and instead of a dressing table there was the writing desk I'd put the glasses on, which was similar to the one in Burrows' room. I wondered if this was Louisa's brother's room. I looked out of the window and saw that it was almost dark. There were lights on in the stables.

I nodded. "It has an odd atmosphere, as if something unhappy happened here. That footbridge is a weird addition. I wish I knew what it was for."

"Where does it lead to? Do you know?"

I sat down on a red and cream striped armchair. "I've been trying to work it out. There's an extra piece of the house that I can't seem to get to. I thought it might be beside the kitchens, but they don't stretch back that far. It's obviously separated by the bridge."

Maeve pulled her feet up onto the bed. "I wonder what it was like to live here back when Louisa Grey and her family were here. They're ancestors of Ian's, aren't they?"

I nodded. "They are. Although the house was out of family hands for a long time. I assume since there are family portraits and rooms named after them that Louisa's family were the last Greys to live here."

"Until now," Maeve said.

"Until now," I agreed.

Maeve gazed towards the window. "It's quite lonely here, isn't it? The family must only have had each other for company. I don't think I'd have liked that."

"The father's name was Linus," I said. "There's a portrait of him on the stairs. The Honorable Linus Grey."

Maeve's eyes widened. "Really? I've heard of him. I think he was a TD, or MP it would have been back then, wouldn't it?"

"Right." So that was Linus Grey's story, I thought. "Although he was probably a member of the House of Lords if he was a baronet. Which means he'd have been away in London quite a bit, leaving his wife and son and daughter alone in this big house."

Maeve grinned. "Apart from all their servants."

"True. With a house this size, they probably had a big staff." I took another sip of my champagne. "And they'd have had books. There are some in the library that belonged to Linus and Evan. I wonder how they survived."

"Abby told me they found a load of stuff in the attic when they moved in," Maeve said. "The previous owners mustn't have been interested and just chucked it all up there. Ian and she dragged it down, went through it and kept whatever they thought might be of value. Cleaned up the pictures and books and put them around the house, thinking that guests might like them."

"You might be interested in some of Linus's books actually," I said. "They're medical. *Philosophy of the Human Mind, Outlines of Human Physiology*, that kind of thing."

"I'd say it was all pretty mad stuff if it was published in the early nineteen hundreds. I'll take a look, though."

The champagne was beginning to have its effect and I could feel the tension releasing from my shoulders and the rest of my body. I stood and picked up the bottle.

As Maeve held her glass out for a refill, she looked at me mischievously. "Shall we see if we can find out where the covered footbridge goes?"

"I've tried. It's blocked off."

"Let's go and have a look anyway."

We put down our glasses and left the room, making our way as quietly as possible to the corridor I had found before. At the entrance to the bridge, the chest of drawers was still in place.

"See? It's blocked off," I said.

"Not very effectively," Maeve said. "We can move that if we take all the drawers out."

She started removing them one by one and placing them on the ground. Then she tried to lift the end of the chest, and managed to shunt it to one side, creating enough of a gap to fit through. I peered in but could see nothing. There were no lights.

"Shall we have a look?" I said.

Suddenly Maeve was doubtful. "It does say it's not safe. Maybe we've had too many accidents today already. What if we fall through?"

But my curiosity and the champagne got the better of me.

I grinned. "I'm only little—I should be all right."

Maeve continued to look concerned as I squeezed in through the gap and made my way slowly onto the bridge. It was filthy, the windows on either side opaque with dirt, blue paint peeling off in strips. I placed one foot in front of the other as gingerly as I could, but it seemed sturdy enough. I felt about ten years old again, doing something I'd been told I couldn't do, with my little sister as lookout. The thought gave me a pang.

The bridge was only fifteen or twenty feet long, but I was relieved when I reached the end of it.

Maeve called out in a loud whisper, "Are you okay?"

"Fine. Just give me a few minutes. Stay there, will you?"

"Of course." Her voice echoed as it traveled along the bridge. "You'll need someone to call the ambulance when you go through the floor."

"Don't say that!"

On the other side of the footbridge was a tiny room with no windows that seemed to exist only as a landing. There was a narrow winding staircase, which I made my way down, with just enough light from the hall where Maeve was standing to guide me. When I reached the bottom, I stood for a minute, my eyes adjusting to the gloom.

I was in a small octagonal room with no furniture, and bars at the windows. I searched for a light switch, but there didn't seem to be one. The only illumination came from the moonlight outside, weak and pale through the rhododendrons. Branches scratched against the windows as if trying to gain entry. It was eerie.

I looked for a door, but there was none, and with a sickening feeling I realized that the only way out was via the staircase and bridge. This room was completely cut off from the rest of the house, and even in the daytime there must have been very little light.

On the floor I spotted something poking out from beneath a large piece of peeling paint. I went over cautiously, wondering if it was a dead mouse or something, and lifted the dried paint. It was a leather strap.

Chapter Fifteen

"WHY DON'T THEY use it?" Maeve asked when we'd collapsed in her room like a pair of teenagers. A noise from downstairs had caused us to hurry back before we were caught, once I'd climbed the stairs and made my way back across the bridge. "I mean, it could be a bedroom or something, couldn't it?"

"I suppose," I said, brushing dirt and cobwebs off my clothes. Flecks of blue paint had attached themselves to the back of my shirt. "Although it is difficult to get to. The only access is from that bridge."

"But surely they can't afford to just not use one full room? I mean, it's a hotel. Space is money. They could sell it as a room for couples or something, connect it with the main house properly."

"With no bathroom? And it's spooky. You think the rest of the house has a strange atmosphere; you should go down there. It's freezing, despite being close to the kitchens."

"No thanks." She shuddered. "I think I'm ready to go back to my nice modern house with no personality."

"So, what do you think this could have been used for?" I held up the leather strap again.

Maeve shrugged. "A dog collar or something?"

"Maybe. Anyway," I yawned, "I know what you mean. I'm looking forward to getting back to my cottage and my cat. I think I'll head off to bed. Enough for one day."

"Fair point. Actually, I forgot to say. Do you want to come for another ride in the morning? Abby said if we were interested, to come to the stables at nine."

I opened my mouth to say no, and then stopped myself. "Actually, a bit of fresh air might be good. You're on."

★   ★   ★

Despite being completely exhausted, I found it difficult to get to sleep, my brain turning over the events of the day. Molloy's return, too, disturbed my peace of mind. I eventually fell asleep about two and didn't wake properly until eight, when I climbed out of bed, pulled on a pair of jeans and, after a cursory wash at the end of the hall, made my way downstairs. It was another warm and sunny day. Sunlight poured in through the main door and cast a spotlight across the stone flags. The weather certainly didn't look as if it was ready to break yet.

Ian Grey was back at his desk in the hall, looking considerably better than he had the day before. Maybe, against all odds, he'd managed a good night's sleep. The closure of the kitchen had at least meant that they hadn't had to cook the night before, so they could retire earlier.

He looked up from what he was doing with a smile, his grey hair neatly combed in contrast to yesterday's thatch. "Good morning. There are croissants, coffee and tea in the dining room, and some fruit. All brought in fresh this morning. Best we can do since the Garda ban—no cooked breakfasts, I'm afraid. Your friend is in there already."

"That sounds great, thank you."

"You'd better be quick, though: those two young gardaí have mowed their way through quite a few of the pastries already."

"I'll bet. They've probably been up all night." I paused. "You look better this morning."

He smiled. "You just have to get on with it, don't you? Maybe all isn't lost after all."

I hoped he was right, but I had my doubts. I paused. "I wanted to ask you about the family gallery at the top of the stairs. I've been trying to figure out who everybody is. Since I'm in Louisa's room, I'm curious."

He sat back in his chair, arms crossed. "Oh yes, you are. I'd forgotten. Any bumps in the night?"

"I must have been lucky." I decided to leave it at that. "Was Linus Grey your great-grandfather then?"

Ian nodded. "He was. The Honorable Linus Grey. His son Evan was my grandfather and his daughter Louisa was my great-aunt."

"Ah, that makes sense. So Evan was . . ."

"The one who gambled away the family inheritance and lost the house? Yes, that was him. A feckless sort of an individual by all accounts. I never knew him. He was dead a long time before I came along. I think he died soon after my father was born; Dad certainly never had a relationship with him. He was a drinker as well as a gambler, I believe—my grandfather, that is, not my father." He smiled. "My father was a different kettle of fish."

"Did your father ever live here at Greysbridge?"

He shook his head. "No. The house was lost in the 1930s and my father was born in 1940. Evan died soon after. The family had moved to Dublin by that stage."

"And . . ." I hesitated, "the little graveyard on the top of the cliff? We passed it on our ride yesterday morning." I decided not to mention that Maeve and I had gone poking about the day before too. "I noticed that Louisa and her mother are buried up there."

"Yes, Susan Grey was my great-grandmother, Linus's wife. It's a strange little spot, isn't it? I believe Susan was buried elsewhere, then disinterred and moved up there to be with her daughter. I'm not sure why." He smiled. "Maybe they thought Louisa would be lonely. She had problems, Louisa. I think I mentioned that. Psychiatric problems. She was even committed at one stage, I think."

"Really?" I said, surprised. "I thought most people who were committed back then didn't get out again."

Ian nodded. "I know. I thought the same. Maybe her father pulled some strings. He was certainly a powerful enough individual. She came home, but she died very young, so I don't know if she ever actually recovered." His brow furrowed. 'People back then were afraid of mental illness. The servants were probably scared of going in there, and that's how the room came to be thought of as haunted." He smiled. "That's my theory anyway. For what it's worth."

"No, you're probably right. Where are your grandfather and great-grandfather buried?"

"My grandfather was buried in Dublin, where he was living. He died before I came along. Linus is buried in the local church graveyard. It's a turn to the left just after the bridge, up an old laneway. I presume that's where Susan was buried too, before she was moved."

I raised my eyebrows, and he nodded. "It is odd, I agree. There's certainly a story in it somewhere that's worth telling. Poor Michael spotted it."

"And what about the smaller grave—the one that has no inscription . . ." I stopped suddenly, aware that the questions I was asking were intrusive. "Sorry, this seems really nosy. You don't have to tell me if you don't want to. It is your family, after all."

He smiled wryly. "It's fine. It's quite pleasant to have a conversation about something other than the events of the weekend, to be honest. And as far as disclosing family secrets is concerned, it's not as if I ever knew any of them, I never even met my grand-father or my great-aunt. So ask away. I'm just not sure how much I can tell you."

"I was just thinking that the small grave—it looks like a baby's."

He nodded, scratching absently at the indentations on the desk. "Yes, it does. But I've no idea who it is, I'm afraid. I assume, given the way the graves are arranged, that the baby was my great-grandmother's and that she died in childbirth, or shortly afterwards."

The phone rang, and he gave me an apologetic look before he answered it. I left him to it and went into the dining room. It was empty—no Maeve. Only one table was set. There was one large empty plate in the center, containing nothing but crumbs, and a second heaped with pastries of all kinds and a net to keep the flies off. There was also a huge full fruit bowl. Despite Ian's concern about the lack of a cooked breakfast, I wasn't about to starve.

I sat down, helped myself to a banana and a pain au chocolat and poured myself some coffee. I wondered if there was a way of finding out more about the baby—a search in births, marriages and deaths, perhaps. But if the baby hadn't been named before he died, it was likely that the birth hadn't even been registered. It wouldn't have been a priority back then.

I was shaken out of my contemplation by Maeve's return.

She flopped down beside me. "Morning."

"Morning. Where have you been?"

She raised her eyes to heaven. "Abby wanted a word. She's in the kitchen."

"Ronan again?"

She nodded. "I don't know why she's decided I'm the parenting guru. Maybe it's because I've got two boys. But then mine are ten and eight. Not eighteen. I wouldn't have a bull's notion of how to handle an eighteen-year-old."

"Surely that's the point," I replied through a mouthful of pastry. "That she shouldn't be 'handling' an eighteen-year-old at all."

Maeve grinned. "That seems to be Ronan's view, and Ian's too come to that—who does seem to have a rather hands-off style of parenting, by the way. I think I'd fall somewhere between the two. But Abby insists that she knows what's best for her son and there's no talking to her. I've told her she's going to lose him if she keeps going the way she has been." She pulled the coffee pot towards her. "And that seems to be exactly what's happening."

"Why?" As I asked the question, I realized I'd forgotten to ring my own parents the night before. I made a mental note to do so later when I got the chance.

"He's threatening to leave. Go to London to fill his gap year instead of staying here."

"Maybe he'd be better off," I said, taking another bite from my pastry. It was good, soft and flaky and warm. I wondered where Ian had got them.

"I honestly think he would," Maeve said. "I think it would be better for the pair of them. But what's really driving Abby up the wall is that he wants to go with Cara."

"Leah's sister? God, that's a relationship that's moving at breakneck speed. Didn't they only meet this weekend?"

"You see, I'm not sure about that," Maeve said, taking a sip of her coffee. "I think they may have met when Leah was planning the wedding. I just don't think Abby knew about it."

"Still," I said, "it is fast. I thought he was thinking of leaving with Jay up until yesterday."

"The fickle nature of youth. Maybe he's just determined to escape. I wouldn't blame him." Maeve closed her eyes. "The ridiculous thing is that Abby's taking it so personally. It's not personal in the least. I keep trying to tell her that." She broke off suddenly as Ian came bursting into the room.

He was breathless and red-faced. "Leah's sister is missing."

Maeve and I looked at each other. "Cara?" I asked. Had she and Ronan taken matters into their own hands and just left after all?

Ian shook his head. "No, Niamh, the young teenager. She and her boyfriend Finn. Their beds haven't been slept in, so God knows how long they've been gone. Leah's parents are frantic; she's only fifteen . . ."

"Oh no!" Maeve said, getting to her feet. "Jesus, that's all they need."

"So neither of you have any idea . . .?" Ian didn't finish his sentence. He didn't need to.

We shook our heads in unison. "No." I stood up too.

"Lord, can anything else possibly go wrong this weekend?" Ian raised his hands to the ceiling and left the room.

"I suppose we'd better . . ." I said.

Maeve nodded, and we trooped out of the dining room just as Kevin and Leah were coming down the stairs, looking relieved.

Kevin was signing off from a phone call and nodding his head. "No, that's grand. I just thank Christ they're all right. Thanks for ringing. I'll give you a shout later on when we work out what to do." He pressed the end call button while we stood at the bottom of the stairs expectantly.

"They're on the island," Leah said with a sigh. "They snuck off on one of the boats yesterday evening."

I remembered Niamh and Finn having changed out of their wedding clothes before anyone else was allowed back up to their rooms. They must have planned this escapade in advance and stashed their bags on the boat. It was possible Finn had done it during the ceremony. I had no memory of seeing him there. Had they known that the islanders would be leaving last night?

"I feel so stupid," Leah said, her hand on her cheek. "We didn't even miss them last night."

"It's hardly your fault," I said. "With everything going on."

"Niamh said she was going to bed early and we thought that's what she did." She shook her head. "The oldest trick in the book—she put clothes in her bed to make it look like she was there, so Cara, who was sharing a room with her, didn't even notice she was gone."

Maeve shot me a sidelong glance. I knew what she was thinking: there was a distinct possibility that Cara had never made it to bed herself. But neither of us said anything.

"That was Fridge on the phone," Kevin added. "They found them this morning—freezing, still on the boat, bloody idiots." He shook his head. "As if we hadn't enough to worry about this weekend."

"And now we have to meet this poor man's family." Leah looked tearful and he put his arm around her.

"When are they due to arrive?" he asked Ian.

Ian looked at his watch. "They're getting the first flight into Belfast. So, an hour or so, I reckon." He looked brighter again; the latest crisis averted.

"Right, let's get some breakfast then," Kevin said firmly, and Leah nodded.

"We have to meet Abby at the stables at nine, Ben," Maeve said. "We'd better go."

I followed her out of the door and down the steps, slightly reluctantly. With all this going on, I wasn't sure if I wanted to spend an hour with Abby.

But I was saved by Molloy, coming up the steps to meet us.

Chapter Sixteen

FLANKED BY TWO other guards and with a squad car at the bottom of the steps, Molloy meant business.

"Good morning," he said, addressing both of us. He looked solemn as he said something to the two guards before they headed into the house. "Have you a minute?" he asked, directing this last question to me.

I looked at Maeve and she nodded. "It's grand. Go ahead. I'll explain it to Abby. Text in the next few minutes if you still want to come and we'll wait for you."

"Thanks, Maeve," I said gratefully.

Molloy looked at Maeve's departing figure striding towards the stables. "Have I kept you from something?"

"No, it's fine." I looked down. I was finding it difficult to meet his eyes. His presence made me uncomfortable, unsure of my ground. Especially since we hadn't yet properly talked. "What did you want to speak to me about?"

"Let's go for a quick stroll."

His arm brushed against mine as we set off, and I felt a quiver. The attraction was still there, not that there'd been any doubt about that; it was everything else that was the problem. I stepped to one side, creating a wider gap between us as we started around the perimeter of the lawn, keeping the house in sight.

"You've been here all weekend, so I wanted to let you know about some developments and see if you'd noticed anything no one else did. Or that no one else wants to tell me," Molloy said. "You're usually pretty observant."

"So you want me to be your spy?"

"Not quite."

"You know I acted for the Greys when they bought this place? So I'm not exactly independent."

He nodded. "Yes, I did know that. They told me. But I also know you'll do the right thing if called on."

"Thanks," I said sarcastically.

He ignored my tone. "The thing is, there's a possibility we may have two murders on our hands, not one. And if so, they're linked."

That got my attention. "You're kidding."

He shook his head. "I wish I was."

"You think Jay was murdered? I thought it was impossible to tell since no one saw him go in the water."

Molloy shoved his hands into his pockets and took a deep breath. "The initial assumption was that he had fallen in and drowned because he couldn't swim. Tragic but straightforward. But because of the proximity of the two deaths, it was decided to carry out similar tests on both deceased." He paused. "Just as well, as it turns out."

I discovered I was holding my breath. "Go on."

"Initial blood tests show traces of the same substance in Jay Stevenson's system as in Michael Burrows". But either Stevenson took it later, so it hadn't taken full effect by the time he fell, or he took less of it."

"What was the substance?" I said impatiently.

"Cyanide."

I stopped dead. "Cyanide? But I thought you said Michael Burrows ingested some kind of poisonous plant?"

Molloy stopped too. "He still may have. We found dried hydrangea leaves in both Jay Stevenson's and Michael Burrows' rooms."

My eyes widened. Hydrangeas were becoming a bit of a theme. "That's what they were? The leaves on the floor of Burrows' room? Hydrangeas?"

Molloy nodded. "Only a few scattered around in his room. There were more in Stevenson's. A neat bowlful, in fact, on his bedside locker. They looked as if they'd been dried out on purpose, in an oven or something."

We set off again, strolling along the path that circled the lawn.

"But what's the connection with cyanide?" I asked.

"Many plants produce cyanide—it occurs naturally in a variety of seeds and pits; peach, apple, apricot for instance." We passed a flower bed, and this time it was Molloy who stopped. He looked down. "But also in hydrangeas."

I followed his gaze. The bed was full of luscious blue ball-shaped flowers. An image popped into my head of the same flowers on Louisa Grey's grave, followed by those on my dressing table, and suddenly I felt a little faint.

"You mean they *ate* the plant? Michael and Jay. Or were fed it?"

Molloy shook his head. "The plant is highly toxic, all parts of it—root, leaves, flowers. But you'd have to eat a lot for it to be fatal. The poison would have to be extracted by someone who knew what they were doing, and it would need to be highly concentrated."

"I see."

"We don't know that it was hydrangea that caused Michael Burrows' death. In fact, it seems unlikely. But it's a coincidence.

Cyanide in both men's blood, dried hydrangea leaves in both bedrooms. Hydrangea is a cyanide-producing plant . . ."

"Do you think it's possible that someone put cyanide in their food or drink?" I asked.

Molloy shook his head again. "We're not sure. With Burrows, the amount in his system was enough to kill him. Stevenson also showed traces of cyanide but in a much lower quantity, enough to incapacitate him but that's all."

I tried to absorb all of this. "So someone could have given Jay some of this stuff and pushed him in the water?"

"Possibly. It could make you appear drunk or stoned, flushed, giddy, cause you to lose coordination. A stronger dose would produce nausea, stomach pain, vomiting, sweating. Convulsions causing death within hours."

I remembered Molloy's training in science before he joined the guards.

"Michael Burrows had definitely been sick," I said. "You could smell it from his bathroom. And he'd struggled." I thought for a second. "But then that would have been the case with any poison, I suppose."

Molloy sighed as we rounded the path that ran parallel to the shore. "We haven't yet established how it was administered in either case. All we have is its presence in the blood and some dried leaves. Leaves that would require a huge quantity, and quite an amount of processing, to kill."

"But less to incapacitate?"

Molloy nodded. "Especially if the Stevenson boy made the mistake of telling the wrong person that he couldn't swim."

I remembered the ride up to the fort the morning before. "That's very possible. He told us yesterday when we took the horses out. He said he'd never learned because his father had been terrified of water."

Molloy stopped dead. "Who heard him say this? Who was on the ride?"

"There were four of us. Jay, Maeve, Abby and myself."

With Molloy deep in thought, I glanced down at another flower bed. Pampus grass and hydrangeas. "Jesus. They're all over the garden."

"Now you can see why I need to speak to the gardener," Molloy said with a sigh. "I wonder where he is."

I looked around the garden, the colorful shrubs and plants taking on a considerably more threatening aspect. Where *was* Rudy?

The sound of a car made us both look towards the house. A taxi pulled up at the steps and a woman and two men got out. The taller of the men put his arm around the woman as Ian Grey came running down to meet them.

"It looks as if the gardener will have to wait," Molloy said.

He made his way towards the house, striding across the lawn. I finally allowed myself to look at him, now that he had his back to me. Where exactly had he been these past few months, and what had he been doing? I knew he hadn't been in Cork the whole time—the foreign ringtone had told me that. I watched him take a call before he reached the steps, and he stopped, then paced up and down on the gravel, brow furrowed. I knew how I still felt about him, but I'd learned how to be without him over the past few months and I was in control, a state of affairs I valued. And, I kept having to remind myself, there was Harry.

I decided to take the long way around to get back to the house. The Greys, Leah and Kevin, and Molloy all wanted to speak to the Burrows family and I'd only be in the way. Thankfully there was a breeze for the first time in a week and the air was considerably cooler. Maybe Maeve was right about the weather breaking. But who knew? I gazed across at the lush flower beds in the bright sunshine and thought again about the threats that lie in nature.

As I walked along the pathway by the shore, heading towards the pier, I realized there was someone there on the pier itself, looking out to sea. It was Ronan Grey. He cut a lonely figure; his shoulders hunched as if he was carrying some great weight. My footsteps crunched on the gravel, and he heard me and turned, arms crossed over his chest. When he saw me, he managed a smile

I walked up the little pier towards him. Despite the breeze, the sea was sapphire, an incredible blue for Donegal.

"Gorgeous, isn't it?" I said.

He nodded and turned back towards the horizon. "You know you can see seals from here sometimes? And there are whales and dolphins if you go a bit further out. There's a man up the coast at Malin Head who takes people whale-watching in his boat."

"So I've heard." Still playing the hoteliers' son, I thought, suggesting days out to the guests. His parents should be proud of him.

I paused. "Do you ever miss Dublin?"

He shrugged and shook his head. "Not really. I'll be back in a year anyway, unless I go to college in England."

"What do you want to study?"

"Chemistry probably—something sciency. It depends on my results."

Unbidden, an image of Ronan in a white coat extracting cyanide from hydrangea plants came into my head, but I pushed it away.

"Oh, that's right—they're due out soon, aren't they." The results of the Leaving Certificate, the end-of-school examination, came out mid-August. "Good luck."

"Thanks." He looked up towards the house. "Have Mr. Burrows' family arrived? I thought I saw a taxi."

I nodded. "Just now. I thought I'd give them all some space."

"I know what you mean." He closed his eyes, looking drained.

I bit the bullet. "Is everything okay? You were friendly with Jay, weren't you? This must be very difficult for you."

He crossed his arms again as if he didn't know how to respond. He looked away, but before he did, I saw tears. He shook them away.

"It's a shock when someone so young dies suddenly like that," I added.

"He was a good guy." His voice sounded hollow.

"Yes, I liked him too."

There was silence between us for a few seconds.

Ronan sighed and gazed up at the house. "I thought it would be different."

"What would? Being here? Working with your parents?"

He nodded, a guilty expression on his face. "I'm supposed to be here for the year. I know it makes me sound ungrateful, but I don't think I'm going to be able to stick it much longer."

I looked down. "I see."

"You know I'm adopted?"

I nodded.

"Yes. I thought since you were my parents' solicitor, they'd have told you all right." An edge entered his tone. "You probably knew before I did."

I didn't respond, although I knew this to be the case.

He hesitated; the edge replaced by something like guilt. "And they've been great, don't get me wrong. It's not that I'm not grateful for everything they've done for me."

I smiled. "I don't think they expect you to be grateful. They're your parents."

"I know all that. That wasn't really what I meant."

He frowned, and it made him look younger somehow. More vulnerable. Just because he had the physique of a man, it didn't mean he was one. God, I thought, I was beginning to sound like Abby.

"I think it's all this family history," he said eventually. "Coming back to the Grey ancestral home and so on. Dad's so bloody fascinated by it all, especially with the prospect of a film."

"This is the film Michael Burrows was talking about?" I remembered suddenly what Leah had said the night of the barbecue.

Ronan nodded towards the house. "I bet Dad's up there now, licking the arse of the big film producer son while pretending to be sorry about his father."

He flushed as if regretting his crudeness. I didn't react, and when he spoke again a few moments later, his tone was softer. "I mean, all this stuff about the Greys, it's not my family, is it? Not genetically."

"Genetics isn't everything. Family is about more than that."

"I know." He nodded again. "But it plays a part—being here has brought that home to me. I feel as if I want to find my own place in life. After all, I had another family once."

"You mean your birth parents?"

He gazed out to sea again. "Mum and Dad told me everything a few months ago. Finally. Although I think Mum would have kept it from me if she could."

"It can't have been easy to hear. She probably just wanted to protect you," I said.

"That's what she says." His eyes flashed suddenly. "But I'm nearly fucking nineteen. And telling me the truth seems to have made her so possessive. I don't think I can stick it any more. And, I don't know . . ." He shook his head, eyes welling again. "Jay's death changed something for me. It made me realize that I have to live my own life, not the life my parents have decided for me, even if they do have my best interests at heart."

"I'm sure they'll understand if you talk to them about it."

"I wish." He brushed away a tear. "Jay was only two years older than me and he was on a trip on his own, eight thousand miles from home. At the moment, my mother will barely let me go to Dublin without wanting me to ring her every five minutes."

I looked at him but chose not to remind him that Jay's adventure had led to a very untimely end. He seemed sharply enough aware of that.

"And then all this," he spread his arms, "this weekend, is hardly likely to help."

He looked up and his expression softened. He waved to someone and I followed his gaze. Leah's sister Cara was coming across the lawn, dressed in a long, colorful summer skirt.

Chapter Seventeen

I PASSED CARA on my way back to the house and she smiled. Leah's sister was warm and kind; I didn't know what Abby's objection to her could possibly be. But then I expected that anyone who took Ronan away from his mother would be a problem. She would need to get over that; he was an adult and it was going to happen whether she liked it or not.

I hesitated at the main door, unsure whether to go in. I felt in the way, knowing what was going on inside, and wondered if I should have gone for the ride after all. Maeve's words resounded in my head. These deaths were none of my business. Although, in a way, Molloy had now enlisted my help.

But I wanted to give Cara and Ronan their space too, so I made my way up the steps. There were voices coming from the bar: Molloy's, Ian Grey's and some English accents. I walked past to the bathroom in the lower hall, beside the kitchens.

When I pushed open the door, there was a woman there: middle-aged, with short grey hair and glasses. She was in tears, hands gripping the sink. With a jolt, I realized she must be Michael Burrows' wife. Or widow now, I supposed, her new status thrust upon her so brutally and without warning.

She looked up at the sound of the door, her face streaked with tears. I stood for a second frozen, unsure what to do, and then in an utterly uncharacteristic gesture on my part, surprising even myself, I stepped forward and put my arms out to her. I was surprised too at her response: she collapsed into my arms, sobbing. When finally we pulled apart, I told her my name.

"I'm Kate Burrows, Michael's wife," she said as she blew her nose with a length of toilet roll. Her accent was English, northern, I thought. She smiled weakly. "But I presume you've guessed that."

I nodded and said how sorry I was.

"Thanks. Do you work here, or are you a guest?" she asked.

"A guest. I was at the wedding yesterday."

She shook her head with sudden anger. "Michael told me there was a wedding and I told him to come home. I couldn't understand why he wanted to stay. I don't know why the hell he had to come to this godforsaken place at all. No offence."

I smiled. "None taken."

She dabbed at her eyes with the tissue. "He was so bloody fascinated by this house and the family that lived here."

I decided to dive in and give voice to an idea that had occurred to me in the graveyard. I knew the dates didn't match up, but it was worth a shot. "Had Michael any connection with this area, do you know?"

Kate Burrows looked up. "What do you mean?"

"Well, he wasn't adopted by any chance, was he?" My chat with Ronan Grey was also on my mind. I was getting obsessed with parentage.

She shook her head, frowning. "No, why?"

"Well, at a certain stage in our history, babies were born and illegally adopted across the water. On both sides. The US too. It was very traumatic for the people who were affected by it and some have come back looking for their roots. I thought maybe

that was why your husband was so interested in the Grey family."
I shrugged. "It was just an idea."

Kate nodded; her shoulders slumped. "Oh, I see. No, Michael
was born and bred in Manchester. Lived there all his life. *We*
lived there all our lives." She sighed. He was a librarian, but he
was very interested in old houses. He'd been here in Inishowen
as a child, remembered this house, and wanted to visit it again.
Knew it had belonged to that strange peer."

"Linus Grey," I contributed.

"Yes. So we all came here a couple of years ago, for a holiday."
The words were spilling out of her like water. "Of course, the
house was empty then and very run down. But Michael was
fascinated by it. He decided he wanted to write a book about it.
Greysbridge," she spat the word out, "seemed to get under his
skin. After that holiday he came back here on his own, and he
kept coming back. Couldn't believe it when it opened as a hotel
and he could stay here. I think he was their first guest."

"And he stayed here more than once?"

She nodded. "He loved staying here." She shook her head in
disbelief. "He even bought into all the ghostly stuff. I mean, he
was a librarian, for God's sake."

"What do you mean, ghostly stuff?"

"You've heard the rumors about the house being haunted?"
I nodded.

She spread her palms, stringy tissue still in her left. "Well,
Michael was convinced of it. He had stories of a grey misty shape,
knocking on walls, a figure in his room at night . . ."

"A figure?"

She shook her head. "I can't remember the details, because it
was all nonsense. I used to get very frustrated with him. But this
place really seemed to get to him."

"And he *was* writing a book?"

"So he said." She smiled sadly. "He was a bit of a novelist manqué, Michael. Said he'd uncovered something in the history of the family that would make a great story, the reason why it was haunted . . ." She trailed off; her hand clenched into a fist. "I know it sounds awful, but I *hate* this bloody place. I *hate* the fact that Michael became so obsessed with it. I *hate* that it took him away from me and the boys." Her voice broke and the tears welled again. "Permanently this time."

I placed my hand on her shoulder and handed her a clean tissue. "Did he talk to you about what he had discovered? What he thought would be worth writing a book about?"

She shook her head and turned towards the mirror. "I'm ashamed to say that I didn't show much interest. I thought he should give up and get back to what he was good at. Being a librarian. Spend time with his own family and drop this obsession with the Greys and this bloody house." She gazed at her reflection sadly. "But Michael never really achieved what he wanted to. He attempted various novels over the years—had been trying to get published all his life. He thought he'd finally found the story that would make his name." She turned. "Our son is very successful, and I think he wanted some of that. I wish he'd been more content."

"You have two boys?"

She smiled through the tears. "Two men now. I don't know what I'd do without them. They've been wonderful." She wiped her nose again. "When we were told first, I thought that Michael had eaten something by mistake. Picked some poisonous berries or something. Although that wouldn't be like him. He loved his food, but he wouldn't take a risk like that." She smiled. "He was more of a cake and biscuit man." The smile faded. "But that policeman has just told me that he was poisoned on purpose. That someone killed him."

I looked down. "So I believe."

Her eyes welled again, the tears running freely down her cheeks. "Why would anyone want to hurt Michael? He was the most harmless, inoffensive individual. He got excited about things sometimes, thought his big success was just around the corner, but what's wrong with that?" She brushed the tears away. "Don't we all need a bit of optimism in our lives?"

I hesitated. "Have you any idea why he visited Inishathair?"

She frowned. "Where? Inis . . ." She attempted to pronounce it and failed.

"Inishathair, it's an island not too far from here."

She shook her head, eyes glistening. "He never spoke about an island. How do you know he was there?"

"Someone mentioned it. There were some islanders at the wedding."

She examined my face, seeking answers. "What the hell was he mixed up in?"

But I had none to give her. I shook my head helplessly. "I'm so sorry."

She sighed. "We can't even take his things with us. They need them for evidence."

"You should get them eventually. When they've done what they need to do."

I fell silent. I seemed to have run out of things to say. So had Kate Burrows, it seemed. We stood there in the bathroom, confessor and confessant, unsure what to do next.

Eventually Kate spoke. "My boys are out there on their own. I suppose I'd better pull myself together and get back." She straightened up, smoothed her hair down, and checked herself out in the mirror. She looked at me gratefully. "Thank you."

"I did nothing," I said, embarrassed.

"You listened. And gave me a shoulder to cry on." She attempted a watery smile. "Literally."

I paused, unsure for a second, and then reached into my pocket. She looked alarmed until I produced a business card, which I handed to her.

She looked at it in surprise. "You're a solicitor?"

I nodded. "I know giving you a card makes me look like an ambulance chaser, but I don't mean it that way. I just want you to have my contact details in case you need someone to talk to while you're here. Not professionally." I gave her a small smile. "My mobile number is on there."

"Well then, I'll take it in the spirit in which it was given. Thank you." She placed it in her bag and left the bathroom.

★   ★   ★

I gave Kate Burrows a few minutes, and by the time I followed her out, she'd gone back into the bar and the door was closed. In the entrance hall, I was forced to step to one side suddenly as Abby rushed by looking anxious. She didn't speak, just made a beeline for the bar, pushed open the door and walked in, pulling it closed behind her. She and Maeve must have finished their ride early.

I went out to the front steps, where Kevin and Leah were standing on their own, surrounded by bags and suitcases. The same taxi that had dropped the Burrows family off was waiting there, without a driver.

"Are you leaving?" I asked.

"Cephalonia here we come," Leah said with a weak fist pump and an even weaker smile.

I gave her a hug. "It's just what you need. A bit of time together, just the two of you."

"I know. But God, that poor family. They've had such a shock," Leah said, looking back towards the house. "And Jay's family still have to get here. Who could have imagined that our wedding would be such carnage?"

The taxi driver emerged from the house and started taking bags down the steps. Kevin went to help him.

I put my hand on Leah's arm. "It's not much consolation, I know, but it had nothing to do with your wedding. It was just a horrible coincidence that it all happened the same weekend."

She nodded. "I know." She bit at the nail of her thumb, a habit she had in the office when she was particularly stressed. "Cara and Ronan have said they'll go to Inishathair to collect the runaways, by the way."

"That's good," I said, wondering if Abby had heard that particular news. "Is there a regular boat that goes there?"

Kevin heard me, coming back up the steps for another bag. "Goes from Malin Head. It's a longer trip than from here, but it's a reliable ferry service." He raised his eyes to heaven. "Or it's supposed to be . . ."

"They can be completely cut off during the winter or when the seas are rough," Leah added. "And Inishathair people tend to live by their own rules. If they don't want visitors, they don't have visitors."

I smiled. "Well, they have two visitors at the moment that they haven't invited!"

Kevin and the driver hauled bags into the boot until Kevin called, "Okay, we're ready," from the bottom of the steps, last bag in hand.

"We've said our other goodbyes inside," Leah said quietly. "We didn't want a big send-off in the circumstances. Everyone is leaving shortly anyway,"

Kevin came back up the stairs to give me a kiss, then I gave Leah a last hug and watched as they climbed into the taxi and headed off, disappearing around the corner of the house.

As I turned to go back inside, I spotted Rudy's dog Sam lying on the gravel. Flat out with his chin on his paws, he was looking towards the house, ears pricked. I remembered the story about him refusing to come into the house and wondered how much of that was because he wasn't allowed in. I walked down the steps and walked over to him.

"Hi, Sam, what are you doing on your own? Are you waiting for someone?"

He lifted his head and gazed up at me with wet, mournful eyes while I looked around for his master. But there was no sign.

As I made my way back up the steps, I heard voices; it sounded as if the Burrows family were leaving. I wondered if they would have to go to Letterkenny to see the body, or if that wasn't possible yet. A horrible journey to have to make; even worse not to be able to. They came through the foyer with Molloy and Ian Grey, Abby trailing in their wake. I stood to one side. Mrs. Burrows gave me a smile as they passed, arm linked with one of her sons. The other, an impressive-looking man in his thirties with a short beard, walked alongside Ian, Ian doing most of the talking. I wondered if he was the film-maker.

Once they'd gone out onto the steps, I headed back upstairs intending to pack. But when I reached the return, I heard footsteps coming from the hallway where Michael Burrows' room was. I assumed it was one of the guards—Burrows' room had been guarded since the body had been discovered. Curiosity getting the better of me, I turned in that direction.

There was a guard in front of Burrows' door and a guard at the one opposite. They looked up at my approach. I was about to turn back, pretend I'd taken a wrong turn, when a door opened on my left and made me jump. Rudy came out of what appeared to be a bathroom.

"Oh, hi," I said.

He nodded mutely and walked by me without a word. I followed him, intending to go to my room and expecting him to go downstairs. But he didn't—he took the hallway towards the covered bridge. I followed him at a distance. I'd never seen him in the house before now.

He stopped when he reached the bridge and I hung back, watching him kneel down to pick up some tools. When he stood up again, I realized that the chest of drawers had been moved to one side and that Rudy was in the process of putting up what looked like a wooden barrier. I was mortified, remembering what Maeve and I had done the night before.

I shifted position, causing an unintended creak, and Rudy turned to face me with a mouthful of nails, hammer in hand.

"Sorry." I stepped forward, deciding to come clean. "I'm just being nosy. Is that the bridge you can see from outside?"

He spat out some nails. "It's not safe, needs to be blocked off."

"I see."

He turned back to the job at hand. "They should knock it down completely. If I had my way, I'd just borrow a bulldozer . . ."

I leaned against the wall with my arms crossed. "It's a strange-looking thing," I said. "Why was it put there, do you know?"

He turned to me, eyes blazing. "So that old bastard could keep an eye on her, that's why." The vehemence in his voice surprised me. I'd barely heard him speak up till now.

I straightened myself. "Her? Do you mean Louisa Grey?"

He nodded. "He could go in there whenever he wanted, and she couldn't get out."

"You mean her father kept her there? In that strange room downstairs?" I asked, realizing too late that I'd confessed to having crossed the bridge.

But Rudy just nodded.

"God. Why did he do that?"

"She was supposed to have been mad. They said she wouldn't eat. That she starved herself."

"Was he trying to force-feed her or something?"

He shook his head. "I reckon she wasn't mad at all. I reckon it was being locked up in this house, and that bastard of a father, the poor craitur. There's stories that he used home-made medicines on her. Experimented on her with all sorts of strange herbs."

I shivered, remembering that two men had just been poisoned with a plant in this same house.

Rudy's voice hardened. "It's no wonder she haunts this place, the suffering that she went through here. It wasn't the poor wee girl that was mad—it was her father. All that at the hands of her own clan."

"How do you know all this?" I asked.

He looked at me, his eyes wide and intense. "My great-grandfather used to work here. The old bastard would buy seeds from far away, have them sent here, make my great-grandfather grow 'em. That's what I've been told."

I thought of the books I'd found in the library. Linus Grey's medical books. "So he was the gardener here too? Your great-grandfather?"

He nodded his head in the direction of the window, as if his great-grandfather was just outside in the garden.

I found myself following his gaze. "And your father and grand-father?" I wondered if it was a family role, handed down from father to son. Was that why the estate agent had employed Rudy to take care of the house while it remained unsold?

But he shook his head. "They both worked in the fish factory. Wouldn't set foot in this place if you paid them."

Chapter Eighteen

AFTER MY CONVERSATION with Rudy, I made my way back to my room. Hearing voices coming from the floor above, I walked out and stood on the stairs at the return. It was Ian and Abby. They were standing on the upper landing and they were having a row. Though their voices were hushed, it sounded vicious, on Ian's part at least.

"Why the hell would you do that?" he hissed. "Scupper it? It's our last chance."

"Oh, for God's sake, where's your pride?"

"You're the one who needs to face reality, do you know that?"

But there was no reply from Abby, just the sound of footsteps coming towards me down the steps, causing me to flee back to my room.

★ ★ ★

It was impossible not to remember that this room had once been Louisa Grey's, especially after what Rudy had said. Had she ever returned to it, I wondered, or had she died in that horrible blocked-off chamber, at the mercy of her family, cut off from the rest of the world? And how exactly had she died? Had she starved herself, as rumor had it, or had her own father been responsible for her death in some way? I shivered at the thought, and as I stood there, I felt the walls closing in as if the past was returning, its presence frighteningly real.

I pulled myself together and went for a shower down the hall. Despite the precarious-looking contraption I was forced to wash in, wetting my hair and scrubbing the rest of me helped—the water way hotter than needed. As I passed Maeve's room on the way back to mine, I heard her moving about. She was back from her ride, although Abby must have left her to untack. It sounded as if she was packing. There was something comforting about the notion of preparing to leave this house.

Back in my own room, I did the same. I opened the window to let in some air and started to gather my belongings and fold my clothes. I was almost finished when I noticed a packet of throat lozenges that I'd left on my bedside locker. I reached for them clumsily and somehow managed to trip on the edge of the mat by the bed. As I reached for the dressing table to rebalance, it shifted, and I knocked the *Girl's Own Annual* onto the floor.

The book fell face down and I frowned at my own carelessness. I picked it up carefully, not wanting to damage the spine any more than it was already. An advertisement on the bottom left of the page it had fallen open on caught my eye. *Chlorodyne*, it trumpeted, *best and surest remedy for coughs, colds and bronchitis. Acts like a charm on diarrhoea, cholera and dysentery. An effective medicine!* It sure was, if it could cure all of those ailments, I thought with a smile. *Effectually cuts short all attacks of spasms, hysteria and palpitation!* I could do with some myself.

As I turned the page to close the book, I noticed that it felt heavy, thicker somehow than the rest. I ran my finger over it and realized there were two pages sealed together. I took the book to the window for a closer look in natural light, and saw that there was something concealed between the two pages. I ran my finger along the bottom edge, trying to avoid a paper cut. The action separated the pages a little, and I used my nail to gently do the rest. I peered into the gap; there was a slip of paper inside.

I extracted it carefully using the tips of my fingernails. It was a picture, on paper that was flimsy and thin. I placed it on the dressing table, not wanting to handle it any more than necessary. But when I looked at it, I almost cried out. It was an old photograph, tiny, full-length, of a young woman who was pregnant. It was Louisa Grey. Somehow I wasn't entirely surprised; I'd had my suspicions since visiting the graveyard that the baby might have been hers. But what I found most shocking about the picture was that she looked happy. More than happy, she was beaming with joy and pride. Because Louisa Grey was still Grey when she died, so she mustn't have married, which would have meant a pregnancy would be a source of shame to an aristocratic family like hers.

I stared down at the little picture and wondered who had taken it. Photography had become popular in the early part of the nineteen hundreds, though it was surely the preserve of the wealthy classes as a hobby. Her father? It seemed unlikely. The pregnancy it evidenced cast Rudy's story about Linus Grey's treatment of his daughter in an even more disturbing light. Maybe it wasn't her hysteria he was trying to cure, but her pregnancy. Ian had said Louisa had been in a lunatic asylum. Was that to conceal the pregnancy? It happened to girls in those days, didn't it? Had Linus taken his daughter out because he was convinced he could make her miscarry with his "strange herbs" and plants? Was that why she had been shut up in that horrible room?

I remembered the piece of leather strap I had found down there and shivered. Had Louisa been the one who had died in childbirth, and not her mother? And if so, who was the father of her baby?

I looked at the dedication on the annual again. *To Miss Louisa Grey, Christmas 1912. Do not try to be something you are not, my dear. From L. G.* I checked the date of Louisa's death from the picture of the gravestone on my phone—15th January 1914. She had died aged twenty, a year or so after she had been given this book. Which meant she would have been nineteen when she received it, and pregnant not long after. The annual seemed young for a nineteen-year-old, particularly one who was soon to be a mother. Had her father been trying to keep his daughter a little girl?

I took a photograph of both the picture and the dedication with my phone, replaced the picture carefully between the pages, and put the book back where it had been. Then I gathered up my bags and left the room, giving it one last look before I closed the door. Relieved.

In the hall, I knocked on Maeve's door and said that I'd wait for her downstairs, and she called back.

Molloy was waiting for me at the bottom of the stairs. "You're heading home?" He glanced at my bags.

I nodded. "Finally."

"It looks as if I'll be here for a while. Can I give you a shout when I'm free?"

I replied without looking him in the eye. "Sure."

A noise from behind indicated that Maeve was struggling down the stairs with her wheelie bag. Molloy climbed a few steps to give her a hand.

She smiled her thanks. "You're a gentleman, Sergeant."

★   ★   ★

We took our leave of the Greys, Ian gracious and apologetic, Abby clearly distracted, her small face pinched with anxiety. Ian was still furious with her; as we waved goodbye, she put her hand on his arm and he shook it off. A huge contrast to the happy and tactile couple we'd seen on Friday night.

We loaded up the Mini, and as we drove over the clanging cattle grid and out of the gates, Maeve took a deep breath. "Phew, I can't say I'm not glad to leave there. What a weekend."

"I know."

"I'm not surprised the Greys look worried. It's a hell of a start to their wedding business—two deaths." She rolled down the window. "You don't think it's something to do with the house, do you?"

"What do you mean?"

She put her elbow out and gazed out at the sea as we drove back down the peninsula. "I don't know. But there's definitely something dark about that place."

I told her about my conversation with Rudy, although I didn't mention the photograph in my room. I wasn't sure why.

"Jesus, I hope they don't know it was us poking about up there." She looked over at me. "We probably shouldn't have had that extra dose of champagne."

I shook my head. "Rudy didn't mention it. But it's a horrible story, isn't it? Imagine that poor girl trapped down there. Her father able to visit her whenever he wanted over that horrible bridge, and she unable to get out." I paused as I took the turn for Glendara. "Remember that piece of leather strap that I found?"

Maeve shuddered. "God, now that's creepy. But you see what I mean, don't you? Some houses are like that. Bad things happened there, so bad things will continue happening there. It's as if the house has absorbed what happened in the past, like a sound recording or something, and it's influenced the atmosphere of the place."

"That doesn't sound very scientific for a medic," I teased.

"No, it's probably not." She shivered. "But you can't deny there's a very strange feeling about that house."

"No," I said. "I can't deny that."

There was silence between us for a few seconds, each of us absorbed in our own thoughts.

Then Maeve spoke. "Can you remember the titles of those medical books you found? The ones belonging to Linus Grey? I never got around to having a look at them."

I tried to think. "Em, *Outlines of Human Physiology, Philosophy of the Human Mind* and *Electrotherapy and Neurological Practice*, I think. Why?"

She clicked her fingers. "Electrotherapy. There you go. That's your leather strap."

"What the hell is electrotherapy?" I asked.

"Inducing seizures to treat psychiatric disorders. Electroconvulsive therapy, or ECT—what used to be called electric shock treatment. That's what your baronet was up to. Using his own quackery to treat his daughter."

"Jesus." I almost stopped the car. "Was that around back then, in the early part of the nineteen hundreds?"

The wind whipped Maeve's hair about. She nodded. "It sure was. I remember reading somewhere that Benjamin Franklin said that an electrostatic machine could cure a woman of hysterical fits. A woman, you'll note."

I swallowed, thinking of my own globus hystericus. "So that's what he was up to."

Maeve brushed her hair back from her face. "Sure, that boy could have been up to all sorts back then and no one would have stopped him. He was too important."

"That poor girl. She was his own personal guinea pig."

We were both quiet for a moment.

"Right." Maeve straightened herself and hit her head on the roof of the car. "On to more cheerful things. Let's leave that house behind us. Weren't you thinking of going away this week, now that the office is closed?"

"I was," I said slowly.

She picked up something in my tone and looked over at me. "Ah, Ben, don't tell me you've changed your mind."

I kept my eyes on the road. "I haven't. I just haven't made any particular plans as yet. And I have to be around for a court appearance on Thursday anyway." That bit was true. I'd suddenly remembered my assault case. "I might go after that."

"Maybe you should take Harry with you." She grinned, then held her hands up in surrender when she saw my expression. "Okay, okay, I'll back off."

★   ★   ★

Back in Glendara, I dropped Maeve at the veterinary clinic, where her husband had arranged to collect her on the way back from his trip, and called into the supermarket to pick up some milk and bread. I knew Guinness would have consumed any milk I'd left over the weekend. It was only two o'clock in the afternoon, but it felt much later when I drove out along the shore road. I was exhausted, and my throat was dry and sore. I hadn't done the exercises Harry had suggested since Friday morning, and I'd had plenty of booze over the weekend, which hadn't helped. What I needed was a long night of undisturbed sleep.

I crossed the bridge and pulled into the green in Malin, heaving a deep sigh as I slid the key from the ignition. Guinness strolled lazily down the path to meet me, something he rarely did—usually he waited for me on the doorstep.

"Hello, old fella, how are you?" I climbed out of the car and bent down to scratch his ears, dropping my bag onto the footpath.

The cat rolled over on his back and stretched luxuriously. As I rubbed his furry stomach, I thought about my American trip. I'd planned to leave Guinness with my parents—they'd volunteered for a previous trip that hadn't happened—but now the prospect gave me a pinched feeling in my stomach. Had I been thinking clearly when I'd made the decision to go?

I unlocked the door and walked into my cottage, cat trailing behind me, and realized how glad I was to be back in my own space. I dumped my bag on the table, made myself a pot of tea and took it out the back, where for the next hour I sat on a deckchair concerned only with the latest Ian Rankin and the cat. Although I did ring my parents. As usual, I got their answering machine, so I left a message.

I dithered about going for a walk or a swim but couldn't bring myself to do either. It was only when I felt hunger pangs that I forced myself to move inside to the kitchen. Rooting around for something for dinner and finding nothing but cat food, I made myself some toast and another pot of tea. And gave Guinness the cat food.

★ ★ ★

I was woken the next morning by a text. I'd slept the sleep of the dead in my own bed, and it was a few minutes before I could extract myself sufficiently from my stupor to take my phone from my bedside locker. I was surprised to see Leah's name pop up—I was sure she'd be incommunicado until the end of her honeymoon. Groggily I opened it—it was a one-liner saying she'd sent me an email from an internet café.

Fully awake now, I sat up and opened my emails on my phone. The heading on Leah's was "Favor for a newly-wed!?"

Skimming through the first few lines, I gathered that the essence was that the two kids, Niamh and Finn, had gone missing again, but there was less worry this time because everyone was certain they were still on the island. They hadn't taken the ferry to Malin Head, and no other boat had left since they'd been there. Anyone with a boat, fishing or otherwise, had been warned to check for them.

My first thought was to wonder why the families had bothered Kevin and Leah with this, but then it occurred to me that maybe Leah's parents hadn't been told that the kids had gone missing again. When I read on, I saw that was the case.

We haven't told my parents. After this disastrous weekend we don't want to worry them any more than necessary.

It was at that point that I guessed the favor Leah was asking of me.

I hate to ask, but I know the office is closed this week and I thought you might be at a loose end.

If I hadn't known Leah so well—and conceded that she was right—I'd have bridled at that.

We're pretty sure they're okay—they left a note saying not to
worry—but . . . is there any chance you could go over and help Cara
and Ronan, maybe have a word with the kids, scare them a bit? Let me
know if you can.

I lay back on my pillow, craving a coffee but without the
energy to get up and make one. The whole thing was a little
odd. I hardly knew Niamh and Finn. I accepted that Cara and
Ronan were young and might need some support, but surely
Kevin's family could deal with it? They would know where the
kids might be likely to hide, and Belva—unlike me—would
certainly have the moral authority to deal with two wayward
teenagers, and wouldn't shy away from using it.

I suspected the truth was that Leah simply wanted someone
she knew and trusted on the spot—someone to take the worry
away from her so she could finally enjoy her holiday. And it was
on that basis that I couldn't say no to her, particularly after this
awful weekend. So I emailed her back and said that of course
I would go to the island, that it would be good to see it, apart
from anything else.

She responded straight away, as if she had been waiting for my
reply. She was grateful, but suggested that I leave it for a day in
case Niamh and Finn turned up. If they did not, she said, there
was a ferry at nine on Tuesday morning from Malin Head that
I could take. She'd text me and let me know. She said again that
she thought I might have more authority than Cara and Ronan.

I wasn't convinced.

Chapter Nineteen

WHILE I WAS in the shower, it occurred to me that if I was going to take a trip to Inishathair, I could also find out what Michael Burrows had been doing there. I could see if there was any connection between the Greys and the island, in particular Louisa Grey. I couldn't shake the notion that there was some significance in the location of her grave, with its perfect view of Inishathair, especially now that I knew she had been pregnant. And Burrows going there strengthened that idea. He had to have been on the trail of something connected to the house and family, although it was odd that his wife hadn't known he'd been over to the island.

But by the time I was dressed and downstairs, I'd realized that I should have more sense than to involve myself in a situation like this again. Not to mention that if I did, it would bring me into further contact with Molloy, which was the last thing I needed at the moment. I would do what Leah had asked of me and no more. I'd help find the teenagers then come home.

Unsurprisingly, since I lived alone, the food situation hadn't improved since the night before. So after I fed Guinness, I decided to drive into Glendara. Coffee and a pastry in the Oak would do me just fine.

★ ★ ★

I drove the few miles along the coast with the windows down, the smell of the sea reviving and fresh. It occurred to me that whatever I did about the American job, I would have to live close to the sea. I'd become too used to it now to give it up. And I certainly didn't want to live in a city again. The job was in Tampa, Florida, so I might be able to work that out. Although wherever I lived I'd have a longer commute than the one I had now, which was ten minutes at the most, unless I came across a tractor or a flock of sheep.

I parked the car across from the office and walked up to the square. Phyllis and Liam were sitting at a table on the footpath outside the Oak—a temporary arrangement that Tony Craig, the proprietor, was getting away with only *because* it was temporary. The sunshine this summer was an oddity to say the least, but the council was bound to be on his case if it lasted much longer. The pair of them waved me over enthusiastically. I suspected they were dying to hear what had happened at Greysbridge since they'd left.

"So, you're back." Liam stated the obvious, leaning back in his chair, arms crossed expectantly.

"We've been keeping an eye out for you," Phyllis said, patting the seat beside her. "Sit and spill."

"Let me get a coffee at least," I pleaded. "I haven't had any breakfast."

The scent of freshly ground coffee inside the pub was nearly as reviving as the sea air. I ordered a cappuccino, a Danish and some fruit salad from Tony and headed back out to the sunshine. The eager faces as they removed their sunglasses made me smile, until I remembered what I had to relate. I wondered if it would make Liam feel any better knowing that there was probably very little he could have done to save Jay with cyanide in his system.

Taking my seat and a grateful sip of my coffee, I gave them a brief outline of what had happened since they had left; that which was public at any rate. Including the dried hydrangea leaves that had been found in the rooms.

When I had finished, Phyllis exhaled and leaned back in her chair. "God, two murders over the same weekend, in the same place."

"*Possibly* two murders," I corrected her.

She sat forward again. "Have they any idea who did it? Was it the same person who murdered both?" she asked, completely ignoring what I had just said.

I shook my head. "The investigation has only just started."

"Well that's the last time I touch the hydrangeas in our garden without gloves on," Liam sniffed.

I grinned. I couldn't imagine Liam gardening, unless he was looking for a golf ball. "They don't know anything yet, really. Just that leaves were found in both bedrooms and that hydrangeas are a possible source of cyanide."

"And they were definitely dried leaves?" Liam said. "They couldn't just have fallen off some flowers that happened to be in the room?"

I shook my head, still picturing the flowers that had been left on my dressing table. "I don't think so. They'd been dried out in an oven or something."

Phyllis looked at Liam and lowered her voice. "That gardener who was knocking around the place was a strange fish."

"I'd be more inclined to look towards those islanders," Liam muttered darkly.

I nabbed a bite of my Danish while I could.

Phyllis tapped her fingers on the table. "It's a strange house, isn't it?"

"You'll get no argument here," I said through a mouthful of pastry.

"I looked up the man that owned the place, Linus Grey. He was a pretty weird dude himself, you know. There's a Wikipedia page on him."

"Oh?" I said with interest. There had been so little reception at Greysbridge that it hadn't even occurred to me to check the internet, but *of course* there would be information about someone like him online.

Phyllis leaned forward eagerly. "He got up to some very unsavory things in London, I can tell you. I wonder if his wife and children back in Donegal knew about it . . ."

"What kind of things?" I asked, wondering what Phyllis had discovered.

"Well, for a start he was a Freemason, which is probably why he got away with so much—plenty of powerful people to protect him."

Liam grunted disapprovingly.

"Go on," I urged.

"He frequented brothels . . ."

"Oh?" Liam's eyebrows were raised.

"Not for the reason you think," Phyllis said. "He fancied himself as a bit of a homeopath, thought he could cure the women of their evil ways."

"I'll bet," Liam snorted. "No mention of curing the men?"

"No mention of that, funnily enough. He made up concoctions from plants and herbs and brought them into the brothels. I'm sure the women thought he was a bit of a crackpot. But there was a sinister side to him, a suspicion that if they didn't co-operate, he'd use certain means to persuade them."

"What means?" I asked.

Phyllis leaned forward again. "Some of the women went missing. Of course, back then, those kinds of women went missing all the time and nothing was said about it. They were the dregs of society, lived chaotic lives, no one missed them, and no one cared. But it *was* noticed when more than one woman went missing from the same establishment that Linus Grey frequented." She scoffed. "Probably because there was a loss in income."

I shuddered. "Did they ever reappear?"

Phyllis nodded. "One did, alleging all sorts of things against Grey, but of course she wasn't believed. He was a member of the House of Lords and she was a prostitute." She waved her hand dismissively. "She was assumed to be a lunatic." She sat back, arms crossed. "None of this was on the Wikipedia page; it was all in articles there were links to at the bottom."

"What did she say he did?" Liam asked, his eyes wide with curiosity.

"Apparently," Phyllis looked around her, "he'd graduated from his strange plants and herbal remedies . . ."

Liam cut across her. "Maybe concluding that they didn't work."

Phyllis looked at him impatiently before continuing. ". . . and moved on to electric shock treatment. The woman who reappeared claimed he'd brought her to his flat, where he'd strapped her down to a bed and held her prisoner."

Liam raised his eyebrows, while I had a flashback to that strange octagonal room.

"Of course," Phyllis added, "she thought he intended something else entirely. She said that as it turned out, that would have been the lesser of two evils."

"What did he do?" I realized that both Liam and I were leaning in, elbows on the table, holding our breath.

"He gave her an electric shock every hour for two days. Didn't feed her, just kept her there tied to the bed. And then when he decided she was cured, he released her." Phyllis clicked her fingers. "Just like that. I'd say her poor head was fried."

Liam looked up suddenly, his eyes on something over my shoulder. "And here's Dr. Harry for his morning coffee."

I sat up. I hadn't heard from Harry since Saturday evening, when he'd seen me talking to Molloy. I realized that was a little odd, but then I hadn't contacted him either. Maybe I should have. Maybe I owed him an explanation of some sort. The three of us watched as he crossed the street, hands in his pockets, slightly stooped. He seemed distracted until Liam called out a greeting; when he spotted us, he smiled and came over.

"Mind if I join you?"

Liam pulled out a chair in response.

"Anyone want anything?" Harry asked, pushing his sunglasses up onto his forehead.

There were two takers for coffee; I still hadn't finished with mine. Harry disappeared into the pub and reappeared a few minutes later with a tray. He sat, distributed the coffees, removed the sunglasses from his forehead and placed them on the table before taking a sip of his espresso and emitting a deep sigh.

"I've been thinking about that all morning. I must get a decent coffee machine for the surgery."

He looked tired and drawn. I realized he'd looked tired since I'd seen him on the beach on Friday morning, so it couldn't be my fault.

Liam leaned forward. "Ben's just been telling us that the two deaths at the weekend might both be murders."

"Really?" He took another sip of his coffee.

"It appears so," I said.

"Poison?" he asked.

"You knew?" Liam said.

Harry rubbed his nose. "I suspected with Mr. Burrows—that was his name, wasn't it? Only because there was something about the odor in the room . . ."

Phyllis was shifting in her seat as if she was bursting to say something.

"What's wrong, Phyllis?" I asked.

"I meant to say," she blurted. "Do you know who that man's son is?"

"Michael Burrows? He had two. One of them is involved in films, isn't he?"

"That's right!" Liam got to his feet and pulled a newspaper from the pocket of his jacket, which was hanging on Phyllis's chair.

As he went searching through it, battling with a sudden breeze, Phyllis said eagerly, "He's Don Burrows. You know, *Don* Burrows."

The name *was* familiar. Liam found what he was looking for and handed me the paper, an English tabloid daily, pointing to a small piece at the bottom of an inside page.

The headline was *Don Burrows' father dies*. I read on. *It has been announced that the father of film-maker Don Burrows has died suddenly in Donegal, Ireland. Cause of death has not yet been established. Mr. Burrows is the producer of feature films such as* The Ripper *and* Nebulous *and the drama series* The Monarch. The piece was short, but the news was clearly significant enough to make the national papers.

"I loved *The Monarch*," Phyllis said with a sigh. "The costumes were magical."

Phyllis's eclectic taste always amused me. She could be working her way through a book on French philosophy while simultaneously devouring the latest Marian Keyes. And she was similar with her viewing habits.

The same couldn't be said for Liam, despite his otherwise live-and-let-live approach. "Complete rubbish," he remarked. "Although *The Ripper* was good," he conceded reluctantly.

I offered the paper to Harry, who looked down and shook his head. "I've seen it. One of my patients showed it to me earlier."

I folded it and handed it back to Liam. I realized that Harry had been avoiding my eye since he sat down.

"Sorry," I said to him. "You were saying? About the poison."

"It was just . . . well, there was something about that young guy too."

Liam looked at him, listening attentively now. "What do you mean?"

"Well, it occurred to me that he might have taken something. Maybe weed."

"Can you tell that even when someone's unconscious?" Liam asked.

Harry shook his head and glanced across at me, the first time he had looked in my direction. "I was chatting to him earlier on at the wedding. His eyes were bloodshot and I didn't think he'd been drinking." As he spoke, I remembered noticing something similar.

"Could that have been what happened?" Phyllis asked. "He was stoned, and he fell in?"

"I suppose that's up to the guards to figure out," Harry said, taking another sip of his coffee and leaning back in his chair. "I must admit, it's not what I expected when I moved back to Inishowen. Two deaths over one weekend at my poor cousin's wedding."

"I've been meaning to ask you, why *did* you move back?" Phyllis asked with interest, hands clasped in front of her bosom. "You were, what, eight when your parents moved out to Vancouver?"

Harry looked at her, eyes widened in surprise. "You have a good memory. I was nine, if you want to be exact."

Liam grinned and tapped his nose. "You'll have to get used to small-town nosiness. Everyone knowing your business. It's not like the big city here, you know."

Harry smiled. "I know. And I like it. As a matter of fact, it's one of the reasons I moved back. Family. I liked the idea of getting to know my cousins again. Felt the pull."

Phyllis narrowed her eyes. "But your parents are still in Canada, aren't they?"

He bowed his head in acknowledgement. "They are, and they want to stay there. They have my sister and their grandkids. I did ask them if they fancied coming back with me, but there was no contest." He added. "I'm single and childless so I hold no interest for them."

Phyllis shot me a look Harry couldn't possibly have missed, and I flushed. But he didn't react.

"What about you two?" he asked. "Never had any hankering to leave Inishowen, either of you? I think I remember your father, Phyllis . . . And your dad owned the fish factory, didn't he, Liam?"

Neither Phyllis nor Liam responded, which amused me. Phyllis traveled widely and would usually be happy to share stories, but Harry's approach was too direct. It takes time to find your place in a small town, and although Harry wasn't a complete outsider, while they were happy to interview him, he would need to earn his position before they were forthcoming with information in return.

But they exchanged such knowing smiles when he offered to walk me back to my car that I knew their reticence would not last long. I was surprised that he did.

"How's the throat?" he asked as we turned off the square.

"Not too bad. The exercises seem to be helping. Although I need to do them more often."

"Some time off is really what you need. Especially after this weekend."

We stopped outside my office. "Lucky I have some coming up then, isn't it?" I pointed towards the sign in the window indicating that we were closed for the week.

He smiled. "So does that mean you have some free time on your hands? For a drink or dinner during the week, perhaps?" He exaggerated his Canadian accent. "From that conversation, it seems I'm still a stranger in town. I need minding."

I laughed. "You're not a stranger. Your roots are here. That makes you less of a stranger than I am, no matter how many years I've spent here."

He bowed his head. "Point taken. So, what about dinner?"

"Would you mind if I come back to you on it? Leah's asked me to go to Inishathair to chase up Niamh and Finn."

He raised his eyebrows.

"They've run off, but keep that to yourself. I don't think Leah's parents know. Leah's not particularly worried, I don't think—she knows they're somewhere on the island."

"Okay," he said slowly. "Will you let me know what happens?"

"Of course."

He kissed me on the cheek, but it was awkward. We still weren't meeting each other's eye. Not properly. I turned the key in the door of the office. I hadn't intended going in, but suddenly I needed a refuge, to close a door both physically and metaphorically on the outside world. Why was I pulling back from Harry? Was it Molloy? Neither of us had mentioned him, but . . . I shook my head. I didn't want to think about it.

There was some post on the mat, which I picked up and took into reception, not bothering to open it. With Maeve's words ringing in my ears, I sat at Leah's desk, turned on her computer and opened up a few holiday websites. But scrolling through the last-minute offers, I realized I had no interest in a city break with a load of sightseeing, nor tramping up mountains with a bunch of "like-minded" people. I didn't even fancy a few days at the beach. I had my favorite beach in the world right here, so why would I leave it? And for once there was sunshine too. Suddenly I felt reluctant to leave Inishowen at all.

I closed down the holiday sites and began a search for something that actually interested me: Linus Grey and Greysbridge. I found the Wikipedia site Phyllis had mentioned easily enough, recognizing the portrait from the family gallery on the stairs. I remembered the long hair and sideburns and the gown. The intensity in his eyes and the determined set of his mouth took on a new meaning now that I knew more about his less savory practices. I read through the text. *Linus Grey was an Irish peer and a member of the British House of Lords from 1896–1915. Family seat: Greysbridge, Co. Donegal. Spouse: Susan; children: Louisa and Evan.* It went on to provide details of his political career, bills that he had voted on, campaigns that he had been involved in.

It was all pretty dry stuff until I got to the bottom of the page. There I discovered the myriad footnotes that Phyllis had mentioned with links to all sorts of other articles. The first was an academic piece for an online periodical called *Historical Architecture*. It was a comparison between "the big house" in Ireland and the equivalent landlords' houses in the UK. In it there was a brief mention of Greysbridge and its gardens—by all accounts they had always been significant—followed by a couple of lines about Linus Grey's interest in exotic herbs and plants, which he used to "cure" people. It implied that he saw himself as something of a medic, professing to have a knowledge and ability he probably didn't have. A later, more salacious piece referenced Grey's dubious behavior towards the ladies of the night, but again it was only a line or two.

After reading through five or six articles, I realized that there was very little of actual substance. It was mostly rumor and gossip, with no evidence to back it up. Only one mentioned an eyewitness account—Phyllis's prostitute who wasn't believed. It seemed that Maeve had been right. Linus Grey had been left to do whatever he wanted.

Before I went home, I returned to the original search once more to see if there was anything I'd missed. But this time I was stopped in my tracks. A WordPress site called Jay's Blog mentioned Greysbridge. I clicked on it, hands trembling. A cheerful-looking website opened up before me with photographs of Dublin and Inishowen. It was a blog Jay Stevenson had set up to document his travels. Sligo and Galway were next on his itinerary. My stomach twisted, knowing that he wouldn't make it any further than Donegal.

I scrolled down looking for the reference to Greysbridge and found it below a picture of the footbridge he must have taken with his phone, illustrating a post entitled "Hollywood comes to Donegal?" I read on.

First there was Psycho—*Anthony Perkins and his mother in a creepy house on a hill. Will Greysbridge, the house where I have been staying, be next for the Hollywood treatment? One of my fellow guests (my only fellow guest in this spooky house) sure believes so. He has uncovered a story so shocking, so compelling that it simply must be made into a movie. Watch this space! More next week, friends . . .*

I checked the date. The post had been uploaded on the Thursday before the wedding. Two days after he'd posted it, Jay was dead. What the hell did it mean? And did it have anything to do with his death? I sat staring at the screen, the words blurring in front of my eyes, until I eventually switched it off and stood up, rubbing the back of my neck. My head was beginning to hurt. I needed to think, and I couldn't do it here. It was time for a walk on the beach.

Before I left, I took a look at the post. Only two were envelopes; the rest was advertising and marketing rubbish, which I tossed in the recycling. The first was from the Land Registry: completion of an application for first registration for a client. The second was a bank envelope with a window. I ripped it open with the dagger letter-opener Molloy had given me for Christmas, and unfolded the page. It was marked *Urgent*.

The reference at the top of the letter was *Mortgagors: Ian and Abby Grey. Property: Greysbridge, Inishowen, Co. Donegal.* I scanned the contents anxiously. The bank wanted me to return the deeds to the house as soon as possible. They were threatening to force a sale and wanted to ensure that their mortgage had been registered.

It appeared that the Greys were seriously in arrears. In fact, they hadn't made a single payment since they'd bought the place.

Chapter Twenty

I KNEW I was in trouble when I turned off the road to Lagg and saw that the lane leading down to the beach was lined with cars. I should have turned the car around right then and returned to the house and my lazy spot in the back yard, but I was far too tempted by the glimpse of the azure sea I caught between the dunes. And then by a parking space that opened up beside me.

I pulled in, climbed out, put my sunglasses on and made my way down to the sand, where there was a beautiful cooling breeze coming in from the sea. The beach was packed with families and kids and picnics and dogs, and Harry's comment about being single and childless returned to me, along with Phyllis's embarrassing glance. As I walked along the shore watching parents take toddlers for a paddle, I tried to imagine myself in that position, and found it difficult.

I shook these thoughts off. That wasn't why I was here. Instead I looked out to sea, to Glashedy Island, with its cliffs and its beach and its green grassy roof. Though uninhabited and considerably smaller, it made me think about Inishathair. What would I find there when I visited tomorrow? I wondered. My reason for going was to help look for Niamh and Finn, but I knew I would find myself wondering what Michael Burrows had been doing there, and probably, despite myself, asking about it. I thought about Jay's blog post and what it had meant. It was youthful

exaggeration, but had there been something in it? Kate Burrows had told me that her husband had uncovered something he
thought would make a good book. Had Michael told Jay what
that was? I thought too about the Greys and their precarious
financial position. I should ring them and let them know about
the letter. Although I suspected they had received something
similar—I knew how banks worked.

As I walked further on up the beach, moving away from the
families and the picnics, I passed a group of young lads sitting in
a clump, almost hidden in the dunes. Lagg has spectacular dunes,
amongst the highest in Europe. I sometimes think the beach
looks as if it has been sliced from a golden cake of sand topped
with green icing. Possibly by the giant of the five fingers, the
protruding rocks that give the place its name.

Two of the lads were clients of mine, and they waved uneasily
when I glanced at them, their expressions giving them away. It
wasn't until I saw the joint that I realized why they looked so shifty.

As I came to the end of the beach, rounded the shore along by
the mudflats and walked back towards the road, I remembered
what Harry had said about suspecting Jay was stoned. Surely the
guards would have found traces of dope in his belongings and in
his system if that were the case? But all they'd found were dried
leaves. It was then that something occurred to me that almost
made me run to get back to the car.

★   ★   ★

Ten minutes later, I raced in through the door of the house and
flopped down onto the sofa, laptop on my knee. On the beach,
I'd remembered coming across something about a wild plant
called jimsonweed that had killed some young people in the

States after they'd taken it as a hallucinogenic. I wondered if it was possible that something similar had happened at Greysbridge with Jay. With all those plants at his disposal, he may have been curious, especially since he was pre-med.

I found what I was looking for initially without too much trouble. There were a number of articles on the dangers of jimsonweed and its abuse by teenagers. But it didn't seem to fit what had happened to Jay—the effects of jimsonweed were extreme and it was far more common in the States than here. I wasn't even sure if it grew here. But then Jay was American.

Then I did a search for hydrangea, which had been found in both rooms, and bingo! In a piece in the *Telegraph* online, I found just what I was looking for. Under the headline *French hydrangea thieves search for the high life*, there was an account of a spate of hydrangea thefts in northern France that had been blamed on "cash-strapped thieves looking for a cheap alternative to cannabis". Further websites confirmed that the leaves of the hydrangea plant (and buds and petals) could be dried and smoked when mixed with tobacco. When I searched further, there was even a video giving instructions as to how to go about it. The article on the thefts said that a local pharmacist had "confirmed the hallucinogenic and euphoria-inducing effects of the plant". But there was also a warning about it producing hydrogen cyanide.

I sat back to think, running my hands through my hair. Had Jay smoked the dried hydrangea leaves? Was that what had incapacitated him in the water? There was mention online of smoking the plant resulting in dizziness and light-headedness, and I remembered again Jay's bloodshot eyes when he'd came over to chat to Harry at the wedding. Hydrangea was a source of cyanide and Jay had had cyanide in his system when he died. And dried leaves in a bowl in his room.

Before I could give it any more thought, my email notification pinged. There was a short message from Leah confirming that the teens hadn't yet appeared and asking again if I would go to the island. I responded immediately by saying that of course I would and that I would get the nine o'clock ferry in the morning.

★　★　★

I was throwing some things into a bag, on the assumption that I would have to stay at least one night on the island, when there was a knock at the front door and I went to answer it. It was Molloy in sunglasses and shirtsleeves. He had the grace to look marginally ill at ease.

I raised my eyebrows at him. "Front door? Formal visit then, is it?" Molloy always came to the back door, but that had been when we had been trying to keep our relationship a secret. And now we didn't have one.

He removed his sunglasses. "Have you time for a chat?"

I turned and let him follow me into the kitchen.

"Coffee?"

"Sure."

While I took down some mugs, he chatted to Guinness, who had appeared from the sitting room to rub himself against the visitor's legs. Cat and cop had always been mates. I listened to Molloy's voice and Guinness's purr, keeping my back to them until I'd finished scooping coffee into a pot and putting the kettle on to boil.

Then I turned, resting my back against the units, needing the security of something solid to lean on.

Molloy straightened himself. "I've just come from meeting that young lad's parents."

"I'd say that wasn't easy."

"No. It wasn't. They're shocked and bewildered, to say the least."

"What are they like?"

"An ordinary family. Wealthy, I'd say—they had a son in college who could afford to go on a cycling holiday to Europe. They have some Irish connections if you go back far enough. Perhaps that's why he chose to come here." He shook his head as he placed his sunglasses on the edge of the table. "They're just broken-hearted and baffled as to what happened. Distraught at the fact that he never learned how to swim."

"Would that have saved him?"

"Possibly. Probably not."

I crossed my arms. "They must be feeling guilty about that, his father particularly. Apparently, Jay's dad saw his friend drown when he was a child and developed a fear of the water that he passed on to his kids. That's why Jay never learned."

Molloy raised his eyebrows. "Is that what he told you?"

I nodded. "Why?"

"Because his parents told a different story. They said Jay himself saw his friend drown in a river when he was about ten, and that made him afraid of water."

"God," I said thoughtfully. "Why would he lie about something like that?"

"No idea." Molloy gave it some thought too. "Maybe he blocked it out. If he was shocked enough, he might have. Convinced himself that there was some other reason he couldn't swim."

"Maybe."

"Awful way for him to die though, if he had a fear of the water, wherever he got it from."

"Yes." I heard the kettle switch off behind me. "Have you established how the cyanide got into his system yet?"

Molloy looked at me curiously. "Why?"

I told him what I'd discovered online.

Molloy nodded. "As it happens, that's exactly what our lot think: that he may have smoked it. As you said, there's no short-age of hydrangea plants at Greysbridge. We examined his stom-ach contents and there was no trace, but we did find roll-up papers and tobacco in his room, though his parents say he wasn't a smoker."

"They wouldn't necessarily know. Parents usually don't. I suppose it's a cheap way of getting high."

"Except that you also risk consuming hydrogen cyanide in the process."

I shook my head. "Why would you smoke cyanide? It seems crazy. I mean, the kid was a med student."

Molloy gave me a wry look. "Even ordinary cigarettes produce some level of hydrogen cyanide. Anyway, you met him. Did it seem like the kind of thing he might do?"

I shrugged. "Maybe. He was young. Possibly a bit of a thrill-seeker. He was on a cycling holiday on his own." I paused and looked down. "He was a nice kid, with his whole life ahead of him."

Molloy was quiet for a moment.

"So you think that's what happened?" I asked. "He'd been smoking and fell into the water? An accident, then?"

"I don't know. It still seems too much of a coincidence. An accident and a murder within a day of each other, both involving the same poison, but unconnected."

"I know what you mean." I paused. "Jay might have been smoking hydrangea joints, but Michael Burrows was unlikely to have been, surely?"

Molloy took a deep breath. "We know now that the cyanide in Burrows' system was ingested. He consumed a substance called amygdalin, which releases cyanide into the gut."

"So Burrows swallowed his cyanide while Jay smoked his. On its own? Was the . . . What was it called again? Amygdalin?"

Molloy nodded.

"Was it hidden in something?" I asked

Molloy shook his head. "We don't know yet. We're awaiting the full post-mortem results. There was no trace of anything edible in his room, nothing but those few dried leaves. And it wasn't possible for him to have consumed enough of them to kill him."

"So how did they get there, do you think? The leaves?"

"Someone must have dropped them. They were scattered on the carpet as if they had fallen out of someone's pocket. Jay's were neatly in a bowl."

"Maybe Jay dropped them," I said. "Michael Burrows and Jay used to talk, apparently. I get the impression they were the only guests at Greysbridge for a few days. Maybe he was in Burrows' room." I told Molloy about Jay's blog.

"Okay," Molloy said slowly, taking out a notebook. "I'd hope our tech people would have found that, but you never know. These things can be missed."

As he took a note of the blog address, I turned to heat the pot and spoon some coffee in. I'd left the kettle too long and had to re-boil it.

"You know Michael Burrows was doing some research on the house?" I said, my back still to Molloy. "He was writing a book."

"His wife told us," he replied. "As did Ian Grey. We've taken all the papers we found in his room. Copious handwritten notes. A lot of it indecipherable, unfortunately."

I filled the coffee pot and put it on the table along with two mugs and a jug of milk. "Jay was friendly with Ronan Grey too, Ian and Abby's son. Maybe they were smoking buddies . . . It might be worth asking him."

I sat down. Molloy joined me at the table while Guinness sat watching us from the floor, tail twitching. "I don't like to think that the killer was one of the guests at Leah's wedding," I said. "That's a pretty horrible thought."

"Yes, it is."

I poured out two mugs and slid one over to Molloy. He thanked me, added some milk. And then there was silence, an uncomfortable one, while we both sipped our drinks. We'd run out of safe territory. If discussing a murder could be considered safe territory.

Until Molloy looked up. Finally. "I know you're angry with me."

I looked him in the eye. "And why would that be, do you think?"

"Because you think I pulled back again."

"Oh, is that what you did?" My sarcasm was back. I couldn't help it. He made me so angry. "Because you see I wouldn't have known that, because you didn't tell me. You just contacted me less frequently."

"I didn't know what was going to happen," he said helplessly. "Whether I was ever going to be moved back here. Whether I would be able to . . ." He trailed off.

I pounced. "What do you mean? Whether you would be able to what?"

But immediately he clammed up. It was vintage Molloy. He looked down, stirring his coffee unnecessarily; he didn't even take sugar. I watched him, waiting for him to say something. It didn't happen.

"I rang you and I got a foreign ringtone," I said eventually.

He looked up. "When? I didn't get a message."

"I didn't leave one. I didn't see the point if you didn't want to stay in touch."

He looked away. "I couldn't. There was nothing I could do."

"Why couldn't you?"

"I was sent abroad. Suddenly. There was a while when I couldn't contact you."

"Where were you sent?"

"I can't tell you."

I shook my head angrily.

He met my gaze. "I already tell you too much, you know that. Even about this . . ." He waved his hand at his notebook still sitting on the table between us. "But what you are asking me about is something else. The stakes are too high. Just accept that it was work. An ongoing investigation."

"Into what?" I insisted. "Just give me an idea. How can you expect me to trust you if . . ." I stopped when I saw his expression.

He was glaring at me. "*You* trust *me*?" he said.

He looked away. I swallowed uneasily.

He took a sip of his coffee, his eyes fixed on the table. "Money laundering, smuggling, drug-trafficking. Among other things. A large criminal network we've been following . . . A money trail."

I took a breath. "Gangland stuff?"

"Not quite. There were some people I knew when I was younger in Cork. I'm one of the few people who can recognize them. I was asked to do something and it's why I haven't been able to come back, why I haven't been in touch for a while. That's all I can tell you. Even that is too much."

There was a loud scratching noise and I looked down. Guinness was at the back door, wanting to be let out. I didn't blame him. He can sense tension. I stood up and opened the door for him.

When I sat back down, Molloy went on, still avoiding my eye. "Your business was here—at the other end of the country. I didn't want you to be tied to someone you never saw. Someone who might get hurt. You've had enough of that already."

Molloy's paternalism had always infuriated me, but this was too much. It wasn't up to him to make decisions for me.

"That was my choice," I snapped. "You didn't even discuss it with me. Surely you owed me that? Even if you couldn't tell me the details, you could at least have . . ."

He looked down. "I'm sorry. That was my mistake. I thought it would be easier on you. I did intend speaking to you, but I just kept putting it off. I couldn't tell you exactly what was happening, and I didn't think you'd tolerate that."

"You didn't give me much credit."

Suddenly his eyes flashed. "Oh really?" Now *he* was being sarcastic. "But I was right, wasn't I?"

My stomach churned. But something made me pull the pin and throw the grenade. "What do you mean?"

"I mean, you've moved on, haven't you? I don't remember you telling me you were going to do that."

My heart sank and I flushed. So Harry had told him about us. Of course, he had. He'd been interviewed by Molloy right after the discovery of the body. He'd have mentioned that he was at the wedding with me.

Molloy sat back, hurt in his grey eyes. "I didn't change my number. You could have told me."

His expression was like a punch in the stomach. I stared into my coffee. I had to accept the truth in what he said. When his texts and calls had become less frequent, a certain stubbornness on my part had set in and I had cut him off in my head until I had stopped contacting him entirely. It was too hard otherwise. I missed him too much. With a jolt, I realized that was what he had meant, about it being easier on me. Maybe he had been right.

He steeled himself. "The problem is that I didn't want a short-term relationship with you . . ." He trailed off as if losing his nerve, and then started again. "I knew I wouldn't be happy with that. I wanted something permanent. I knew that when you were in danger last year, and all I wanted to do was protect you. I've probably always known it." He paused and looked down.

I struggled to digest all of this. Upset that the main thing I'd heard was his use of the past tense. I tried to respond. "Firstly, you didn't contact me for over a month. Secondly, I don't need protecting."

He didn't bother to say that the events of the winter before had shown that that was patently untrue. His expression said it for him.

"Things have changed," I insisted. "Luke Kirby is dead. Are you saying that if you can't have a guarantee of permanence, you don't want anything at all? Do you know how idiotic that sounds?"

I was deflecting, I knew I was.

Molloy shook his head. "Of course, I'm not saying that. Although I don't see how any of this is relevant now. It's obviously not something you want. You've clearly moved on."

I didn't know what to say. I felt trapped. A rat in a trap. So, I lashed out. "Well maybe we should just leave it, then."

He got to his feet. "I think *we've* already done that, don't you?"

At the door, he turned. I thought he was going to say something, but . . .

"That client of yours, McShelley?"

I looked at him blankly for a second, then clicked back into professional mode. "Eamonn McShelley. He's back up in court in Glendara on Thursday."

"We found his vehicle. Burned out. A petrol tanker."

"Right." I was struggling to think clearly. "So he was driving an oil lorry."

"Carrying laundered diesel. Collecting it from somewhere and delivering it to garages here and in the north, we suspect. There'll be additional charges."

"Right."

Molloy looked at me. It hurt. "Be careful, Ben. McShelley's part of something . . ." He sighed. "They're nasty people." He shook his head and turned to go.

I closed the door on him, my heart breaking. I knew I loved him, more than I had ever loved anyone. But he hadn't even said he loved me—just that he *had* wanted something permanent. It was time to pull back.

I didn't sleep well, and when I awoke, I had that horrible sinking feeling that I'd just made a huge mistake. But I couldn't take it back. It was out of my hands now. I knew Molloy.

I needed a distraction. Something like a trip to an island. I got up at seven, giving myself plenty of time to finish the packing I hadn't been able to face the night before.

I'd decided to take a rucksack rather than the bag I had taken to Greysbridge. I stuffed in a couple of shirts and pairs of jeans and then went looking for my washbag, realizing when there was no sign that it was still in the other bag.

The dress I'd worn to the wedding was still in there too, badly needing a clean. I took it out and shook it, checking the pockets so I could take it to the dry-cleaner's later in the week. A piece of paper fluttered to the ground. Then I remembered—it was the paper from Harry's car. I'd meant to give it back to him, but with everything that had happened, I'd forgotten. I smoothed it out. It was a page ripped from a notebook: a handwritten phone number with Jay Stevenson's name underneath.

I sank down on the bed. Harry had lied to me. He had known Jay before he met him at the wedding, or at least had some contact with him.

I headed downstairs to the kitchen, feeling dazed, moving mechanically around the room trying to work out why Harry would lie. While I was feeding Guinness, my phone rang on the counter and I picked it up. I didn't recognize the number—it was a UK mobile—so I answered cautiously.

"Hello." The voice was hesitant. "This is Kate Burrows." She paused, as if she were checking something. I assumed it was the card I had given her. "Is that Ben O'Keeffe?"

"Yes, it is. Hello, Kate. How are you doing?"

"Oh, you know. Not great."

"No. I can imagine."

She let out a breath. "I've been given a load of papers belonging to Michael. It's all the research that was on his desk in his room when he . . ."

"Okay," I said slowly, wondering where this was going.

"Your police kept the originals and gave me copies. But I can't make head nor tail of them. My first instinct was to destroy them, but I couldn't bring myself to do that, and then I was thinking of giving them to the Greys because it seems to be mostly about their family." She spoke quickly, all in a rush. "But I didn't want to do that either, leave them back in that horrible house." Finally, she paused for breath. "God, I loathe that place."

I smiled at the other end of the phone. "It's probably an acquired taste even at the best of times."

"Yes. The thing is, I wondered if you would take a look at them before I decide what to do with them."

I hesitated. My curiosity said yes, but my gut instinct said no, stay the hell out of it—it's none of your business. Especially with what had happened with Molloy.

But when she spoke again, there was a tremble in her voice that convinced me otherwise. "If you have time, that is. I'm sure you're very busy, but you did say if there was anything you could do to help . . ."

"No. Of course I will," I said, without hesitation this time.

"Oh, thank you." The relief in her voice told me I was doing the right thing. "I'd be very grateful. I know they meant something to Michael and I'd like to find out if there's anything in them that I should know. That Michael would have wanted me to know."

"I understand."

"The police will look through them, of course, but they'll be looking for a connection to his death. Of course I want to know that too," she added quickly, "but I thought you might see something else . . . I just can't face it yet and neither can the boys. The papers are in a bit of a mess, but I can drop them over to you today if you like."

I glanced at my watch. "I'm leaving in an hour but probably just for the night. Where are you?"

"We're staying in a hotel in Derry. How far away are you?"

"Derry is about half an hour from Glendara—I could meet you there, at my office, in about forty minutes? The address is on the card I gave you. It's easy enough to find; Glendara isn't a big place."

"Perfect. I'll see you then. Don will drive me. We have a hire car now." Her voice broke. "We're hoping they'll release Michael's body tomorrow . . ."

She rang off suddenly as if unable to continue.

As I pressed the end call button, I remembered that I needed to ring the Greys to tell them about the letter from their bank. But I dialed all three of their numbers with no answer.

After that, I had a very fast breakfast, called in to Charlie next door to beg his services again in case I had to stay longer, and drove on into Glendara, rucksack in the car, ready to turn around and head straight to Malin Head after my meeting with Kate Burrows.

I was a few minutes early, so I dropped into Stoop's newsagents to buy the local newspaper. I couldn't face going into the office again, so I sat in the car where I could see Kate arrive and while I waited had a look at the paper. I didn't make it past the front page.

Two guests die in double food poisoning at new hotel! screamed the headline. Below was the large color photograph of Greysbridge that I recognized from the brochure, tweaked to make it look more like a Hitchcock house than a Donegal hotel.

I skimmed through the article. It referenced the Garda inquiry, the drowning and Michael Burrows' death, all the while implying heavily that it was the food at Greysbridge that had killed the two men. How any hotel could survive that kind of publicity, particularly one that was just starting out, was beyond me. And if the letter from the bank was anything to go by, the Greys were already in trouble.

Suddenly there was a knock on the passenger window and I looked up. Kate Burrows was standing on the footpath with two large plastic folders in her hand.

Hurriedly, I shoved the newspaper into the glove compartment, hoping she hadn't seen it, opened the door of the car and climbed out. She greeted me with a sad smile and instinctively I hugged her again. God, I thought, I'm turning into a hugger.

She handed me the folders with a wry look. "Michael's pride and joy."

"Thank you. I'll go through them carefully." I opened the car door and placed them on the passenger seat.

As I straightened, I spotted a silver Ford Focus parked just in front—a typical hire car. The son with the beard who I'd seen at Greysbridge was at the wheel. He gave me a small wave.

I waved back, and Kate followed my gaze. "That's our son Don. He's a producer. Film and TV."

"Yes. I've heard lots about him." I smiled. "You must be very proud of him."

Despite her grief, her pride showed in her face. It was the first softening I'd seen. "He's very successful."

She gestured towards the folders on the seat of the car. "Michael was trying to rope him in to what he was doing at that horrible house. Claimed that what he'd discovered would make a great feature film." She shook her head. "But I don't know if it would have ever happened."

"I see."

"The only thing is, Michael seems to have given the impression to the man who owns the hotel that it was a dead cert." I caught the edge in her voice.

"Ian Grey?"

She nodded. "He could be a bit like that, Michael—a tad over-enthusiastic. But that man was really pushy on Sunday, insisting that we stay for a few days, me and the boys. Luckily, his wife seemed less keen. As if I'd sleep a single night in that place."

Chapter Twenty-One

I MADE IT to the ferry with ten minutes to spare. Kate Burrows hadn't hung about. Before she left, I'd asked if her husband had ever mentioned Jay Stevenson, but while she knew he was the boy who had died the same day as her husband, she was baffled as to any further connection. She didn't think Michael had mentioned him, although she did promise to go through any emails or texts her husband had sent while he was in Ireland, to see if she had missed anything. She said the guards had already asked for them.

After she was driven away by her son, I stuffed the plastic folders into my rucksack and headed on up to Malin Head. I drove back through Malin town, keeping the shore on my left, past the mudflats and the wildlife sanctuary and the turn-off for Lagg beach with its beautiful white church. Crossing the Keenagh River, I veered right past the Crossroads Inn and, with the sea now on my right, passed the signs for Farren's Bar and the Seaview Tavern. Immediately before the coastguard station I took a right turn and drove down the hill, where Portmore pier appeared in front of me.

I parked on the road and walked down. The sea was a deep blue, with small rocky islets dotted here and there and Inishathair itself further out in the distance. For the first time in a few weeks there were clouds overhead, although the sun was making a valiant effort to peer through. The sea breeze was cool; the waterproof jacket I was wearing flapped in the wind like a sail. As I made my way down onto the pier, I checked my phone to see if there was a last-minute email from Leah saying that the teens had been found, but there wasn't. So I turned it off and slipped it back into my pocket.

I put my rucksack down and looked around me. There was a fiberglass boat with a large open-backed deck, which I assumed was the ferry, moored to the pier, but there wasn't a soul about. There was even a chain across the gangplank. On the way here, I'd wondered if I should have booked a ticket in advance, but that didn't appear to be an issue. It seemed that Inishathair wasn't exactly a day trippers' paradise.

A familiar voice startled me. "Now isn't this a coincidence?"

Molloy. Absolutely the last person on earth I wanted to see. He must have been walking behind me onto the pier, but I'd been so distracted by my phone I hadn't noticed. Rookie mistake. He was wearing a civvy jacket and jeans and there was a female garda in uniform with him, carrying a file. She gave me a brief smile, then turned towards the sea while we talked. I wondered if she knew something of our history. I suspected not—Molloy certainly wouldn't have said anything.

"What are you doing here?" I asked. After our conversation the night before, it was hard to meet his eye.

He raised his eyebrows. "Investigating what's possibly a double murder. And you?"

"Leah asked me," I said defiantly. "Her sister and her boyfriend are on the island. They ran away, snuck off on one of the boats going back from Greysbridge."

"Ah yes. I knew that. But why exactly are you going?"

"Because they've run off again. Ronan Grey and Cara, Leah's other sister, went over after them, but they haven't been able to find them."

Molloy frowned. "Have they been reported missing?"

I shook my head. "They're not really missing. The family knows they're somewhere on the island. Leah thought I might be able to help."

In fairness to Molloy, he refrained from making any of the comments I would have made in the circumstances. Instead he asked me to let him know if they weren't found by the evening and wished me a good trip before turning back to his companion. She was pretty, I noticed resentfully, then immediately berated myself for being both shallow *and* a dog in the manger.

Thankfully, just at that moment, there was a shout from the ferry captain, who had now appeared, and the chain was removed, allowing us to make our way up the gangplank and onto the boat.

"What's the craic?" the captain greeted me as he took the money for the ticket and stuffed it in the pocket of his grubby fluorescent jacket. "Good day for it so far." He looked up at the sky and scratched his cheek. "Long as it holds."

Molloy and the other guard were ahead of me, and when I saw them go out on deck, I decided to sit on one of the few hard benches available inside. A strong salt and petrol smell hit me as the door swung open. There was room for about ten people, I noticed, with bright orange life jackets piled up beneath the seats. After a few minutes, the engine roared and cranked into life, and we set off, pulling slowly away from the pier.

I stood to look out and saw gannets and gulls, and seawater turning green and foaming in our wake. But as land disappeared, I took my seat and tried my best to concentrate on the book I had brought. I was tempted to have a look at the papers Kate Burrows had given me, but I couldn't risk Molloy catching me at it. Plus, there was a breeze coming in through the door that was bound to cause me trouble with loose pages. So I scanned my crime novel without taking in a word, constantly glancing out of the window to the deck, where I could see Molloy deep in conversation with his colleague.

Thoughts crowded my mind with the rolling motion of the boat, confused, unclear, unregulated. My emotions were all over the place. I squirmed when I imagined how Molloy had felt when Harry had told him about us, however he had chosen to paint it. I was irritated with myself for the pangs of unreasonable jealousy I felt watching Molloy have a laugh with a colleague. And of course, Molloy would have discovered that Michael Burrows had been to Inishathair. How ridiculous that it had never occurred to me that he would.

The journey took about forty minutes. When we were finally approaching land, I snuck outside on deck to have a look, being careful to keep some distance from Molloy and his friend. The island looked different to the way it had appeared from Greysbridge. From there it had seemed green and rocky, with a cliff facing the mainland. But we had shifted course around the headland and were approaching it now from the eastern side, which also had rocks, but a pier and a beach too. The smell of petrol from the boat, mixed with the salty smell of the sea, was strong as the boat turned in between the gaps in the rocks and eased its way into the pier, seagulls diving and screeching and swooping and fighting above us. There was salt on my lips when I licked them.

When the boat was secured, I grabbed my bag and waited to go ashore, Molloy and his colleague again just ahead. The captain held the chain as I stood at the top of the gangplank.

"Have a good day," he said, his eyes half closed and lined in his weather-beaten face. He nodded at my rucksack. "Are you doing some walking?"

I said yes, and he looked up at the sky. "Hope the weather holds, although I wouldn't bet on it with that sky."

I looked up too. The clouds I'd seen from the mainland had taken on a considerably greyer aspect. I hoped the storm Maeve had mentioned wasn't imminent.

"I'll probably need somewhere to stay tonight—have you any idea where I could get a room?" I asked.

The captain raised bushy eyebrows. "Are you sure you need to? There's not really anywhere to stay." He put a callused hand in front of his mouth. "Or any reason to, for that matter."

I wasn't about to go into the reasons for my visit—I was happy to let him think I was part of the happy hiker brigade. "Nowhere?" I asked again. "Not even a B and B?"

He scratched his chin. "Mrs. Brady might give you a room. She'll generally do it for anyone who gets stuck. She's up beside the pub; just walk up that hill."

He pointed towards the tiny village at the end of the pier. I could see both ends from where I was standing, and there was a road dissecting it that led to a collection of buildings just above.

"She's a little odd, mind," he said. "Mother died a few years back—was supposed to be a hundred and two."

"Thanks." I hoisted my rucksack onto my back and made my way down the gangplank onto the pier. It was a busy pier for an island with a population as small as Inishathair, I thought as I recognized the two boats that had been at Greysbridge.

Molloy was still there. He'd been watching and waiting for me. I wasn't sure how I felt about that.

"Everything okay?" he asked.

"Fine," I said shortly.

"Are you staying the night?"

He'd been listening too, I thought. I was tempted to snap but I resisted.

"Yes. Are you?" I tried to direct my question to both him and the other guard in a chatty, we're-all-friends-here kind of way.

He shook his head. "Flying visit. We'll be on the evening ferry."

"Well, have a good day," I said, and turned on my heel to head for the hill.

It was one steep hill. The pull in my calves as I plodded up the narrow tarmac road had me promising myself a return to some kind of exercise. About halfway up, I spotted a long single-story white building like a community hall with a tarmacked space out front. A sign saying *McLaughlin's Bar* with the distinctive Guinness disc confirmed this must be the pub Michael Burrows had played music in. There didn't seem to be another one. In a further text the night before, Leah had asked me to meet Ronan and Cara here at ten.

I looked at my watch; I had ten minutes to spare. I should try and find a bed while I had the chance. I spotted a large three-story house down a laneway to one side of the pub as the most likely candidate and made my way down. Plain, white-washed and not particularly attractive, it was brightened by a number of colorful window boxes bursting with flowers. What looked like a greenhouse protruded from the back.

I knocked at the front door. There was no bell, so I waited for a few minutes before knocking again, and eventually the door was opened by a tiny bird-like woman with a heavily lined face. She must have been eighty at least. She smiled broadly.

"Can I help you?" Her accent was strong, but her voice was soft.

"I was wondering if you'd have a room for the night? The ferryman said . . ."

"Of course," she said. "Come away in."

She opened the door wide and shooed me into a small hallway at the bottom of a staircase. Then she closed the door with a slam and without saying another word walked past me and started to climb the stairs. Assuming I was expected to follow, I did so, arriving just behind her onto a first-floor landing where she showed me into a simple, bright double room that looked out over the sea. There was even a kettle and some instant coffee.

"Will this be okay?" she asked.

"This is perfect, thank you." I checked my watch. I was late already. "I have to go and meet someone in the pub. Is it okay if I leave my bag here and come back later?"

"Of course." She narrowed her eyes. "Are you here about those two young ones?"

I nodded. "You've heard about them."

"Oh aye. Not much happens here I don't hear about. I had to search the house. Young Luther was here asking if I'd seen them. I hope they turn up. I'm sure their families are worried." She smiled. "I was told to expect someone, so I suppose you must be it."

★ ★ ★

As I walked back down towards the pub, it occurred to me that if Mrs. Brady's was the only accommodation on the island, then it was likely that Michael Burrows had stayed there too. Which meant that Molloy would want to speak to her at some stage. So much for giving each other a wide berth.

McLaughlin's pub looked, both inside and out, as if it hadn't changed since the seventies: pebble-dashed, with a flat roof and double doors leading into a lounge that boasted brown lino, faux-leather banquettes and Formica-topped tables. Save for a single barman and a table occupied by Cara, Ronan and a large man who even from the back I recognized as Fridge, the bar was deserted.

Fridge stood up while Ronan and Cara stayed seated: Auntie Belva's training, I suspected. He was back in his Elvis T-shirt, or maybe he had a few of them.

"Good of you to come over," he said, pumping my hand enthusiastically. "What would you like to drink?"

I noticed he had a pint of Guinness in front of him, as did Ronan, while Cara was drinking a clear liquid that could have been gin, 7 Up, or water. It was a bit early for me.

"I'll have a fizzy water, please. Thank you."

I couldn't bring myself to use the Fridge moniker, but Luther didn't seem to fit so I ended up using neither, although he didn't seem to mind. He took himself off to the bar while I sat down to join the other two. I noticed that along with the drinks, there were three phones on the table.

"Thanks for coming," Cara said. "I know Leah's very grateful."

She looked tired. The wedding alone would have been sufficient to create those shadows under her eyes, I thought, without this added grief.

"Not at all," I replied. "I'm not sure what I'll be able to do that you two haven't already done, but I'm happy to give you a hand however you need it."

"We just can't seem to find them," Ronan said, shaking his head. "They're giving us the slip. They've taken a load of food with them, stolen from Fridge's family . . ."

"Which they're going to run out of soon," Cara added.

She looked worried. Ronan, on the other hand, looked irritated, I thought.

"Ach, we'll find them." Fridge returned from the bar and handed me a glass and a bottle. No ice, I noticed. He sat down and took a deep slug of his pint, leaving a moustache of white on his top lip. "It's only a matter of time. And if not, they'll turn up when they get hungry."

"Why did they run away in the first place?" I asked, relishing the cool tang of the fizzy water on my throat. "Did they offer any explanation when they were found the last time?"

"Not a word," Cara said. "I'd say they thought they'd get further than here, but they didn't think things through." She gave me a wry look. "I don't think they saw themselves trapped on an island in the North Atlantic."

"It was just a skite that got out of hand," Fridge said, taking another drink. "Typical teenaged stuff. And now their pride won't let them give it up."

"I don't know." Cara looked concerned. "My parents blame Finn—they think they made a mistake letting Niamh have a boyfriend so young. But I don't see what they could have done. They didn't even know he existed until she asked to bring him to the wedding."

"He's a strange kid," Ronan said hesitantly, tapping his phone on the table.

"Why do you say that?" Cara whirled around to face him. "You've never said that before."

Ronan looked uncomfortable. "I caught him nicking some stuff at the house. Just some ornaments and things."

Cara looked at him in alarm, her voice shrill. "Why didn't you say so?"

Ronan shook his head. His face was drawn. "I didn't want to get him into trouble. He was only a kid, so I just warned him off. I should have told you, I'm sorry."

"Actually . . ." I paused, "I saw him do something similar with a little porcelain figure. I should have said something too, but with everything else that happened, I just forgot. I'm so sorry."

Cara ran her hand through her hair.

Fridge shrugged and put his hand on her shoulder. "Ach, I wouldn't let that worry you. He probably thought he could make a bit of cash selling them, if he's planned this skite all along. They're still not going to get off this island without our knowing it."

"You don't think he'd hurt her, do you?" Cara said suddenly.

Chapter Twenty-Two

I LEARNED THAT Cara, Ronan, Fridge and his family had already searched most of the island, but they thought various areas should be searched again. There were deserted cottages and old cowsheds, so no shortage of places where Finn and Niamh could be spending the night, and they could give everyone the slip if they moved each night.

"How long have they been missing?" I asked as Fridge returned from the bar with a second round of drinks. I'd discovered that Cara was drinking water like myself, and Ronan had switched to Coke in anticipation of his afternoon of searching. Fridge was sticking to stout.

"Two nights now," Cara said. "Fridge found them on Sunday morning on the boat." She looked over at Kevin's cousin for confirmation, and he nodded. "But they did a runner on Sunday evening again, just before we got here. They knew we were on our way."

"So you haven't seen them at all?" I asked.

"Not since the mainland," Cara replied.

Ronan was staring wide-eyed into his Coke. He'd seemed distracted and disconnected since he'd mentioned Finn's stealing. I noticed now that there were dark purple shadows under his eyes.

"How big is the island?" I asked.

"Two miles long and one mile wide," Fridge said. "Fifty-eight inhabitants." He sniffed. "We're not one of those islands whose population doubles during the summer."

"Can we get anyone else involved in the search?" I asked.

Fridge nodded. "Already have, and I can round up a few more heads this afternoon. Everyone's involved one way or another— we all stick together here." He touched Cara lightly on the shoulder. "Don't worry. With everyone looking, we'll find them in no time. They won't get off the island."

"I hope so." She picked at a fingernail. There was a rumble of thunder outside that made her look up. "God knows, my little sister drives me mental at times, but I don't want her out in that."

★   ★   ★

Shortly afterwards, we gathered ourselves together and set off. On Fridge's instructions, Cara and I took the road towards the cliffs that I'd spotted from Greysbridge, while Ronan left with Fridge in a rusted old car that belched out white exhaust fumes. No National Car Test on the island, I presumed. Fridge had mentioned going back to the house to see guards from the mainland about the deaths at Greysbridge, a matter that seemed very much secondary to the missing teens. The arrangement was that when they'd finished with Molloy, Ronan and Fridge would gather up some extras, who would divide up the rest of the island between them, and we would all meet up later at the pub.

Cara and I set off along a steep and winding tarmacked road that ran parallel to the shore, with low stone walls on either side and a line of grass in the center.

"There are some old cottages up here," she said, pointing towards the right. "We searched them when we arrived, but

I keep coming back to them in my head—they seem the most likely place to shelter. There's not much cover on the rest of the island unless they've broken into someone's house, which I really hope they haven't."

"What about outbuildings, sheds, barns, that kind of thing?" I asked. "There are plenty of farms, aren't there?" In the distance, I could see a number of large sheds I thought would be obvious places to search.

"They're all inhabited, or used, and people are keeping an eye out. Fridge is making sure everywhere is searched."

We pushed our way up the hill against a gentle easterly wind, small wispy trees quivering in the fields.

Cara shook her head suddenly. "Whatever the men say, I don't understand how they've managed to give us the slip these past few days." Her brow furrowed. "I'm really worried. I mean, what if they weren't running away?" She swallowed. "You hear of teenagers making these pacts, don't you?"

I stopped in my tracks. "You don't think they might do something stupid?"

She nodded miserably, her arms crossed, shoulders hunched as if she were cold, reminding me of Leah. "That's what I'm afraid of. What if they went into the sea somewhere? I mean, it would be easy enough here, wouldn't it? On an island."

"But you'd have found their stuff, Cara. They'd have left bags behind on a beach or wherever. I don't think it's likely, to be honest."

She looked at me hopefully.

"Finn stealing is a good sign," I added. "Fridge is right—he was probably trying to raise money to run away. And you'd have picked up on it if they were planning on doing something drastic, surely? Niamh's never shown any indication of that, has she?"

Cara shook her head. "I hope you're right. You just never know, though. She might not have said anything to us . . . And she has changed since she met Finn."

We continued along in silence, each immersed in our own thoughts. There were few trees now but low hedgerows on either side, binding sheep and cattle in fields full of clover and gorse. What worried me was that the weather was changing. The sky was clouding over and in the distance the sea looked unsettled. It seemed likely that a storm was imminent.

Though the wind was increasing, the silence between us became oppressive and I decided to change the subject.

"Things seem to be going well with you and Ronan," I said brightly. "I'm sure you're glad he's here."

She smiled. "I thought so, but . . ."

I looked at her. Her smile was sad. "Is there something wrong?"

"I'm beginning to think I'm nothing more than a means to an end for Ronan Grey."

"What do you mean?"

She shrugged. "Oh, I don't know. I wonder if maybe he grabbed the first vaguely appealing female that passed his way just to get away from his mother." She laughed. But it was a laugh lacking in mirth.

"I did notice she's a bit on the clingy side."

"Clingy?" Cara raised her eyebrows. "She's psychotic. He told me that she was jealous of Jay. Accused Ronan of caring more about his friends than he did her. I saw her with Jay before he died—she was horrible to him, and he was a guest."

"That is a bit weird all right."

"It's so hard to say anything, though. I think Ro realizes he made a mistake taking a year out to work with them—he should have gone straight to college. His mother was possessive before this, but he says since they moved to Greysbridge, she's become increasingly strange." Though we were miles away from anyone, she lowered her voice. "Don't say I said this, but I don't think he'll go back."

"From here?"

She nodded. "I think he'll go straight to Dublin or Belfast when we get back to the mainland and then just take off traveling somewhere. He wanted to do that with Jay, but then . . ." Cara trailed off.

"And what about you?" I asked.

She shook her head. "I'm not sure I figure in Ronan's plans. And anyway, I'm going back to college myself next month."

We had arrived at the brow of the hill. The edge of the cliffs was not far away, maybe a couple of hundred meters or so across the fields. To our right was a collection of ruined stone cottages, some with corrugated-iron roofs, some without, all covered in brambles and nettles. It didn't look particularly welcoming to me, but then I supposed it would provide some shelter.

Cara pushed open an old iron gate and we went in, picking our way across the dried mud. There were only two cottages with any kind of covering left, and we each took one, bending low to search inside. It didn't take long—they had only one room each. When we had finished, we met in what must have once been a communal yard. There was something haunting about this place and the realization that these sad buildings had once been family homes.

Cara climbed on top of a low stone wall for a better view, and I joined her, pushing aside the nettles at its base.

"You can see what I mean," she said. "The island is very open, with not many trees. Very few places to hide other than houses and farm buildings."

From our vantage point, you could see much of the island. Beyond rocky fields the sea was visible in both directions, looking greener and greyer by the minute. Cara was right—there was very little coverage: stone walls, the odd small tree, and then farms and houses.

"And you've asked people to look out for them?" I said. "Let people know that they're missing?"

Cara nodded. "On Sunday night in the pub Fridge made an announcement and we showed people pictures of the two of them on our phones. Hardly necessary really. They don't get many visitors here. People notice strangers. But everyone said they'd keep an eye out for them."

"Is that a lighthouse?" I asked suddenly, pointing towards a flashing light in the distance.

"Yes. We looked there yesterday. It's not manned, but we've searched it completely. We should look again, I suppose."

With that, there was a sudden gust of wind, so strong it made me unbalance. I reached out to one of the houses to steady myself. "Maybe we should, before this weather comes."

We jumped off the wall and set off up the road again, passing a small lake choked with rushes. Turning a corner, I spotted a large barn or slatted shed across the fields. I pointed it out to Cara.

"What about that building over there?"

She followed my gaze. "Oh, that belongs to Fridge's family. It's used to keep old farm machinery or something. Fridge says he uses it to tinker about with engines. It's been searched already."

"Okay." I remembered Fridge's story about how he'd got his nickname and wondered if this was where his father had worked too. If in fact the very fridge was still in there. "Should we have a look anyway? While we're here?"

Cara looked unsure, but when we reached the turn, we took it and made our way down.

A tractor and trailer was parked outside, and there was a smell of petrol as we approached. The building had an open front, and just as Cara had said, it was filled with engines of all sorts, old fridges and cookers, washing machines, pipes, compressors and wires. So this was where Fridge spent his time, I thought, working with engines and household appliances like his father. There was a stack of wooden pallets and a shelf lined with bottles; I examined them but could read only one label: *Ether.*

Then I saw that bales of straw had been stacked along the back, and suddenly it seemed the perfect place for two teenagers to hide out. Especially when I noticed that one of the bales had been pulled down, the straw spread out and flattened in one corner like a bed.

I nudged Cara, and her eyes widened. We called out Niamh and Finn's names, but there was no response.

"God," she said. "Do you think they were here?"

"Looks as if they might have been, doesn't it?"

I walked around the large space. A tipper truck in the corner was leaking something purple and sludge-like. And then, stopping me in my tracks, I spotted a glint of silver on the ground. I bent down. It was a Kit Kat chocolate wrapping. Beside it were some peach stones. I called Cara over.

"I think we should find out exactly what the kids took from Belva's cupboards, don't you?"

I put the foil and the stones in my pocket while Cara called her sister's name again, to no avail.

When I looked around me again and took in the space, I realized we weren't seeing the full extent of the shed. The wall of straw was blocking off the back section— we were only in the front. I said as much to Cara, and we went outside to check, walking around the perimeter of the shed. Sure enough, there seemed to be a second entrance to the rear part. It was large enough for a vehicle to pass through, but it was locked.

Cara's eyes were wide and frightened. "You don't think they got in there and got trapped, do you?"

We banged on the door and called their names, but there was no reply. We went back into the front part of the shed and climbed onto the bales, peering over as best we could. From what we could see, there was nothing but machinery on the other side. More of the same—plastic containers, pipes, hoses and bags of what looked like cement. No wayward teenagers.

"We need a key," I said.

★   ★   ★

A call to Fridge's mobile produced only voicemail, so we headed back to the pub. It was fast becoming clear that McLaughlin's was used for more than just food and drink on the island. It was the focal point, where meetings were held and decisions made, a real community space. I looked at the sky before we went in, and worryingly, it seemed to me we had only a couple of hours left before the weather turned nasty.

As I pushed open the door, my phone rang. I recognized the number as the district court office and knew I'd have to take it. I said as much to Cara and told her to speak to Fridge about the shed, before closing the door behind her and heading around the side of the pub. I sat on a low wall and tapped the call answer button.

"Hello?"

"Hi, Ben. It's Sally. Just a quick call. You have a case that's remanded into Thursday—an Eamonn McShelley?"

"Yes, Sally?"

"Well, the judge has a funeral to go to, so he wants court to start at nine rather than half ten. Is that okay with you?"

"That's fine," I said, relieved it was nothing more serious. "Thanks for letting me know."

As I shoved my phone into my pocket and stood up to go inside, I heard whispered angry voices coming from the front of the pub. I only caught one sentence.

"I don't care how you do it, just find 'em to fuck, or I'm a dead man. You understand?"

I came around the side of the pub just in time to see Fridge heading inside with two other men. It was Fridge's voice I'd heard.

★   ★   ★

In contrast to earlier, the pub was full. The barman had laid on sandwiches, and a group of men were seated at a table with a map of the island spread out in front of them. Fridge walked over to join them, and before I could catch him, I was waylaid by Belva, who clasped me to her bosom in a rather unexpected hug. Audrey was with her.

"You're wild good to come. Have you somewhere to stay? Because you'll not get back to the mainland tonight, you know."

I disentangled myself with difficulty. "I'm staying with Mrs. Brady, thanks."

"She's a strange one, but she'll feed you well enough." Belva winked just as the door opened and everyone looked up.

Molloy walked in. Alone, I noticed.

Belva sighed audibly. "Ach, is he still here? I thought he'd finished with us."

"Maybe he can help with the search," Audrey said, looking him up and down appraisingly.

Belva's eyes flashed as she glared at her daughter. "We can manage this ourselves."

"Actually, we might have . . ." Before I could finish my sentence, Molloy came over and Belva and Audrey moved off simultaneously, Audrey more reluctantly than her mother, I noticed.

"Any sign of them?" Molloy asked.

"Not yet," I replied. "Although I think we might have discovered where they've been, even if they're not there now. We just need to get Fridge to unlock his shed . . ." I glanced over to see Cara speaking to Fridge. "Hopefully we'll find them before the storm breaks. Where is your colleague?"

"She took the two o'clock ferry back—something came up."

"I didn't know there was a two o'clock."

He smiled. "There isn't. Special request."

"But you're still here?" I asked.

"There's someone else I want to speak to before I go."

"I see. Well I'd better go and join this lot and see what's happening."

Molloy walked towards the restrooms while I joined Cara at the map. Instructions were being given for the afternoon's search, with Fridge assigning various routes.

"Did you ask him about the shed?" I whispered to Cara.

She nodded. "He said he checked it from top to bottom last night, but he'll have another look now just in case."

"Okay."

"Shall we stick together in the search?" she asked.

I nodded. "Good idea. You have a feel for the place since you've been here a couple of days." I paused. Something had been bothering me and I drew Cara to one side. "What about Finn's parents? Have they been contacted? Surely they were expecting him back from the wedding by now?"

Cara looked embarrassed. "I know this sounds appalling, but we don't have any contact details for them. Finn must have given my mother a false number, because it's not connecting." She shook her head. "We tried the school for contact details, but they're still on holidays."

"But that's awful. They must be frantic."

She wrung her hands. "I know. We don't even know where he lives. Niamh only asked last week if he could come to the wedding, and Leah said yes, as long as our parents were okay with it and he had a room to himself—it turned out there was a box room the Greys said he could have . . ." She trailed off.

"And they haven't been in touch, looking for him?"

She shook her head again. "Odd, isn't it?"

"It only means he lied to his parents as well. Although I'm surprised they haven't contacted the guards at this stage." I lowered my voice. "Shouldn't *you* talk to Molloy? I'm sure he presumes Finn's parents know what's happening."

She looked uncomfortable. "Please, not yet. I'd much rather we found them first. Let's wait till this evening at least. The islanders won't want hordes of people here—they're sure they'll find Niamh and Finn far quicker than the guards."

I didn't agree. Finn was a missing minor. It was too serious. And it seemed impossible that his parents hadn't called the guards if they knew he'd been at a wedding at which two people had died. He must have lied to them about where he was going to be.

I decided I'd talk to Molloy as soon as I got an opportunity, whether Cara liked it or not. While waiting for him to reappear, I made my way over to the bar and helped myself to a cup of watery coffee and a sandwich, which I wolfed down on my feet. I was pulling my waterproof jacket back on when there was a shout. It was Molloy's voice.

I turned along with everyone else.

"Are these what you're looking for?"

He was standing in the doorway with a hunched figure on either side of him. Niamh and Finn.

Chapter Twenty-Three

THERE WAS A collective intake of breath before everyone began speaking at once. Cara was the first to move, rushing to her sister and flinging her arms around her. Very quickly the two teenagers were surrounded. They looked embarrassed and uncomfortable, as if they'd rather be anywhere else but here. Finn in particular was almost in a fetal position, his arms wrapped around himself. He was coughing, a wheezing, racking kind of cough that seemed out of place during the summer.

"Where did you find them?" Fridge's question to Molloy carried above everyone else's.

"They were in the cellar," he replied. "They'd made a nice little nest for themselves behind a load of beer barrels. All sorted, weren't you?" He looked at them. "Food they could steal during the night, restrooms—everything they needed, in fact."

Fridge turned and looked accusingly at the barman. "How did you not find them? I thought you said you searched the place?"

"I did," the barman said sheepishly. "On Sunday night. But I was so wrecked after the night before, I must have missed them. Ye were all here too," he said plaintively.

"Yes, having a meeting about trying to find these two." Fridge transferred his glare to the two kids. "Do you know how much time we've wasted looking for you pair?"

Finn rubbed at his eyes and both kids looked sulkily at the ground, neither of them responding.

"The important thing is that they've been found. And they will be delivered safely back to their families before they run off again," Molloy said. He turned towards us. "Cara, is it?"

Cara nodded.

"Will you take your sister? I'm just going to have a little chat with Finn here."

★   ★   ★

An hour later, I found myself alone with Molloy, taking him up the laneway to Mrs. Brady's. It turned out I'd been correct, that Michael Burrows *had* stayed with her, and she was the final person Molloy wanted to speak with on the island. Belva had pointed him in my direction when he'd asked the way, happy to wash her hands of him if she could. Molloy told me that he still hoped to get back to the mainland that evening, taking the runaways with him.

"Finn doesn't look well," I said.

"No, I agree. I'd like to get him back as soon as possible. There's no doctor or nurse on the island." He shook his head. "God knows how they survive here. They're so cut off most of the time." He frowned, as if there was something he was trying to work out.

"Did you manage to contact Finn's parents?" I asked.

He nodded. "I rang his mother before leaving the pub. She thought he was with a friend at a holiday house in Glenveigh for the full week. Because that's what he'd told her."

"Right." I looked down at my feet. There must have been something in my tone.

"I know. He's been gone for four days; you'd think his parents would have expected some contact. Or tried to ring him themselves at least." He paused. "From what I can gather, they're divorcing. I'm sure they wouldn't admit it, but they seemed to be happy to have Finn out of their hair for a few days. They said he's been "difficult"."

I felt a sudden wave of sympathy for the surly teenager. "Poor kid. He was in the way. No wonder he was trying to get the hell out of Dodge."

"From what I can gather, I think Niamh is his only friend . . . He changed schools just before the holidays. He certainly seems a bit lost."

"Jesus, being young isn't easy, is it?" I said, pausing as we reached Mrs. Brady's house.

"No."

"Speaking of which, did you talk to Ronan?"

Molloy put his hand up to ring the doorbell and then stopped. "I did, and you were right. He and Jay befriended each other, were bored, and when they couldn't get dope, Jay suggested hydrangea leaves. Some of his mates in the States had tried it, and there being no shortage of the damn things in Greysbridge, they gave it a go."

"So he admitted it?"

"Yes. I think in a way he was relieved to."

"And that's why the leaves were in a bowl in Jay's room. Is that how they got into Michael Burrows' room then? Did Jay drop them? Out of his pocket or something?"

"Possibly." Molloy sighed. "It was hard to get much out of Ronan after that. I think he is carrying a fair bit of guilt. He knows the joint must have caused Jay to be incapacitated in the water and was possibly the reason why he fell in in the first place."

"It's hardly his fault, especially if it was Jay's idea."

"No, but he was the one who survived. That's not an easy role." Molloy looked at me and our eyes met.

I glanced away. Molloy knew way too much about me, especially now we weren't together. The admission of that, the starkness of it with him beside me, gave me a pang. But he was right: I did know how Ronan felt.

I changed the subject. "Did you see the piece in the newspaper, by the way, about Greysbridge?"

Molloy nodded. "I did. It's not exactly helpful."

"It certainly isn't to the Greys."

"No."

While Molloy finally rang the doorbell, I realized there was no reason for me to stay the night on the island now that we'd found Niamh and Finn. I could go back on the ferry, with Molloy and the teenagers, and presumably Ronan and Cara too. I said as much to Molloy as he knocked when there was no response to the bell. I had a key, but it seemed wrong to use it if I wasn't staying.

Eventually the door was answered, Mrs. Brady's thin eyebrows raised when she saw Molloy's uniform. "Goodness, I am busy today."

When Molloy explained that he didn't want a room but merely to ask some questions, her expression changed to one of concern. But she directed him into the lounge, where they could have a chat. Having explained that the teenagers had been found and that I wouldn't now be staying, I went upstairs to my room to collect my things.

Once there, I decided to ring Leah and let her know what had happened, although I was sure Cara would have told her. There was no reply, so I left a message and sent a text.

I sat at the dressing table and gazed out of the window at the greenish sea and the pier. The room darkened suddenly. There was no denying that the weather was changing: clouds were gathering, the wind increasing. I was glad the search for Niamh and Finn was over and hoped the crossing wouldn't be too rough. I checked my watch and saw that it wasn't yet four, which meant I had an hour to kill. I decided to have a look at Michael Burrows' notes. I undid my rucksack, took out the two plastic folders and distributed the papers across the bed.

Standing, I scanned the pages in front of me. Everything was photocopied, the guards having held onto the originals. There were sheets torn out of spiral notebooks, photographs, graphs, Post-its, all covered in what I presumed was Burrows' spidery handwriting. Kate was right. They were a mess—they weren't going to be easy to decipher. What I couldn't tell was whether Burrows had left his own notes in disarray or whether the gardaí had returned the copies to his widow like this. Or if whoever had poisoned him had interfered with them. That was a possibility too. I wondered if there was anything missing. Looking at what was in front of me, it would be impossible to tell.

I perched on the edge of the bed and moved the papers about like pieces of a jigsaw puzzle, glancing at each as I did so. I couldn't see any way in, so I chose a sheet at random and was startled by the coincidence. It was a page torn from a notebook, dated a week before Leah's wedding, and it was a diagram of some sort, with names and arrows and question marks, like a family tree. And the name Brady was mentioned.

I took off my sandals and pulled my legs up in front of me, sitting cross-legged on the bed, to take a closer look. But I was disappointed. Apart from the name Brady, the writing was illegible, no matter how hard I tried to decipher it. I leaned against the

wall, putting a pillow at my back. Burrows' widow had insisted
her husband wasn't looking for relatives of his own, so was this
family tree connected with Greysbridge and the Greys? Had he,
like me, thought there was some connection between the Greys
and Inishathair? Had he thought there was some connection
between the Brady family and the Greys?

There was a noise against the window and I looked up, startled. It had begun to rain. I gazed out for a few seconds at the
blackened sky before returning to the notes. But Burrows' handwriting was impossible. What had he discovered? I wondered.
What had he thought worthy of a book or a film? An idea had
been lurking at the back of my mind, but I wasn't sure how to
find out if I was right.

I looked up again as the noise from outside became more
intrusive. The rain was lashing now against the window with
the force of hailstones. I tried to ignore it, picking up another
sheet, but before I could tackle it, there was a knock on the door.
I climbed off the bed and answered it, in my bare feet.

It was Molloy, looking uncomfortable. I couldn't blame him.
It was a while since he'd stood in my bedroom doorway.

"Sorry—Mrs. Brady told me this was your room."

"It's fine," I said impatiently, wanting to get back to my reading. "What's up?"

"I thought you might want to walk to the ferry with me. That
is if you're coming?"

I looked at my watch—a quarter to five. "Oh shit, is it that
late? Hang on. I'll be two minutes." I sped back to the bed to
gather everything up.

Molloy looked past me into the room. "What's that you're
reading?"

I reddened. "Oh, nothing—just some notes."

He stayed where he was, but his gaze was fixed on the bed. "Michael Burrows' notes, by any chance?"

I didn't reply.

"I recognize them, Ben—there are photographs I remember. How did you get hold of them?"

I bristled. "I didn't 'get hold of them', as you put it. Kate Burrows asked me if I'd have a look through them. I'm doing her a favor. And," I added defensively, "I'm not doing anything wrong. Your lot held onto the originals and gave her copies, and she gave them to me. Loaned them," I corrected myself. "I have no intention of holding onto them."

Molloy put his hands up. "Okay, okay. Point taken. Knock yourself out."

I gathered up the sheets, put them back into the folders, put the folders back into my rucksack, and we set off towards the stairs in stony silence.

At the top, Molloy stopped. "Okay, I'm sorry. Just promise me you'll let me know if you find anything."

"Of course. I've only just started looking."

I walked down ahead of him to find Mrs. Brady at the bottom looking up. I wondered how much of our conversation she'd heard.

"I don't think you'll be going anywhere till tomorrow," she said as, perfectly on cue, a loud clap of thunder sounded from outside. "There's a storm brewing so the ferry's not going. The ferryman just called me in case I had anyone who was wanting to get it."

As Molloy and I looked at each other, she smiled. "Would you like a cup of tea? I've made some cake."

Chapter Twenty-Four

MOLLOY OPENED THE front door to confirm what Mrs. Brady had said, somewhat unnecessarily I thought; the noise of the rain battering against the walls and roof was sufficient evidence for me. I suppressed a grin when he was nearly blown off his feet—the rain was coming down in sheets. He closed it again just as quickly.

"The five o'clock ferry," he said, brow furrowed, hand still on the door. "Is that the last one?"

"Sometimes he'll go later, but not tonight," the old lady replied, her eyes still startlingly blue despite her lined face. "He's on the mainland and says he's not venturing out again until the morning; the forecast is too bad. It's awful you've been left in the lurch, but we're to have lightning tonight, and it wouldn't be safe to take the boat out."

She hugged her cardigan around her. "We'll be lucky if we hold onto our power. The electricity goes off fairly regular here even when there's no storm." She smiled. "Now what about that cake?"

Molloy sighed. It was clear that we had no choice but to go with it. He bowed his head. "Sounds good, thank you."

Mrs. Brady led us down the hall and into a sitting room with a roaring fire. It seemed strange for August, but with the sound of the rain pelting fiercely against the walls and windows, I wasn't about to complain. Chintz-covered armchairs, a sofa, and bookshelves filled with old hardbacks made the room seem cozy. I spotted an edition of Kipling's *Jungle Book* I'd owned as a child. On the coffee table in front of the sofa was a pot of tea, china cups and saucers, and a plate containing the largest coffee cake I'd ever seen.

Molloy turned to the old lady once she'd closed the door, and it was all I could do not to laugh. There was at least a foot and a half height difference between them—I'm no giant, but they looked like different species.

"If there's no ferry tonight, I suppose I'd better ask you if you have a room to spare," he said.

Mrs. Brady grinned. "As it happens, I do. I'll sort you out once we've had our tea."

She sat herself delicately on the couch, smoothing down her dress. We took an armchair either side while she poured tea and began to cut slices of cake. There was no asking if we wanted any; it seemed to be assumed that we did.

"Great fire," I said, leaning back from the heat after she'd handed me a cup. I noticed a combination of turf and logs in the grate. I wondered where the logs came from. As Cara had pointed out, trees weren't exactly plentiful on the island.

The old lady beamed. "Oh aye, my son fills up the shed whenever he comes back so I'm always set up. He piles it just out there in the yard where it's easy for me to get to." She pointed to a window looking out the back of the house through which I could see a fuel shed and the large greenhouse I'd spotted from the front. "Fills up the skip before he goes too, of course." She indicated a large wicker basket to one side of the fireplace.

"How many children do you have?" I asked. I couldn't shake the notion that Michael Burrows had found some connection between the Greys and this woman.

The old lady shook her head. "Just the one son. I wasn't blessed with any more, unfortunately, although I'd have loved a big family." She handed me a plate with a huge slice of cake before passing Molloy an even larger one.

She leaned forward with her hands on her knees. "I've been thinking about what you were asking me earlier, Sergeant."

Suddenly I felt uncomfortable—this woman seemed to assume that Molloy and I were together, and that anything she said she could say in front of me too. Surprisingly, Molloy didn't correct her, maybe realizing that he might get more information if there were another female present.

"Go on," he said.

"Well, I know I said I didn't know anything, and it's true, I don't. But I'm really very sad about that man who died so I want to do whatever I can to help."

Molloy took a sip of his tea. "Well, as I said, we're very anxious to find out what happened to him, and in particular what he was doing here on the island. So if there's anything you remember that might be of some use to us, we'd be very grateful."

She nodded solemnly. "I'm trying. He stayed here for three days, you know. I've never had anyone stay that long before. I don't really take guests. Just when people are stuck." She smiled indulgently as Molloy took a bite of his cake. "Mr. Burrows loved my cake too. Maybe that's why he stayed on."

"So you're not really a B and B?" I asked.

She shook her head again. "Oh goodness no. That would be frowned upon, I think."

"What do you mean?"

"Oh, just that . . ." She seemed a bit vague all of a sudden. "Well, we don't want the island overrun with tourists, now do we? But I have the room, so I do it when people can't get back to the mainland."

"Like now." I smiled. "For which we're grateful."

"Yes, like now." She smiled too and looked relieved. "And it's nice to have the company."

"I understand Mr. Burrows was interested in old houses," I said, throwing caution and my fragile truce with Molloy to the wind. "In particular Greysbridge. Did he mention that house to you by any chance?" I avoided Molloy's eye.

The old lady took a sip of her tea and placed her cup delicately back on its saucer. "He did, you know. He seemed to be very interested in the family that lived there. That house used to belong to an MP, did you know that?"

I nodded, deciding not to point out the difference between the House of Lords and the House of Commons. I had a suspicion she might not care.

She looked over at Molloy as if he wouldn't know this, as if his Cork accent meant that he was from another jurisdiction. "Back then we sent MPs over to Westminster—we didn't have our own government in Dublin yet." She gave a mischievous grin. "Not that it's made much difference now that we have. That shower in Dublin don't care about what happens to us in Donegal. And even less about the islands."

"But why was Mr. Burrows here if it was Greysbridge he was so interested in?" Molloy asked, anxious to regain control of this conversation.

"He thought there might be some connection between that MP's family and the island," she said. "What was his name again?"

"Linus Grey," I offered.

"That's it. I don't know why, but he seemed convinced of it. As I said to you earlier," she looked at Molloy, "he asked a lot of questions."

"What kind of questions?" I said.

"Questions about people here on the island, the families, people's connections." She counted them off on her bony fingers. "I wondered first if maybe he was looking for his own family; if he'd ended up in one of those terrible mother-and-baby homes or something. But he didn't say, and I didn't like to ask. Then he started asking about the Greys, so I figured I had it wrong." She smiled. "It wasn't too difficult to answer his questions anyway—there aren't many of us here anymore. We'd have known if there was a connection."

"Did he ask you about your family?" I asked.

She nodded. "He did. That was even easier. There was only me and my husband and son. My mother died two years ago, at the age of a hundred and two. I was her only child too." She smiled. "We're not big procreators in my family."

"Have you lived on the island all your life?" I asked, realizing that Molloy was sitting back in his chair now, listening and giving me free rein.

Mrs. Brady looked at me over her teacup. "Me? No." She shook her head. "I was born here and went to school here, when there was a school, that is. There isn't any more." She shrugged. "No children, so no need for one."

"There are no children on the island at all?"

"No." She closed her eyes and took a sip of her tea. "We have great peace. As you get older, you appreciate that."

"What did you do when you left school?"

"I got a job in a library on the mainland, met Rodney, married him and lived there all my life. That man Mr. Burrows was a librarian too, did you know?"

Molloy and I both nodded, and she smiled. "We had some good chats. I only came back here when my husband died. I bought this place, thought I'd run it as a B and B, as a way to support myself and have a bit of company." She looked a little sad for a moment and then brightened. "But as it turned out, I didn't need to. And of course, my mother was on her own at that stage—my father was long dead—so she moved in with me until she died."

"Your mother was an islander?" I asked.

"She was." There was a clap of thunder outside and the old lady glanced at the window, a distant look in her eyes. "She spent all her life on this island—never left it, not once, not even to have me. I don't know how she did it." She looked back at me. "People used to say she was scared to, that the island was where she felt safe. She wouldn't be the only one. There's many that say that once you settle on an island, you never leave it." She smiled. "I left, but I came back."

"Do you think that was true, about your mother?" I asked, glancing at *The Jungle Book* on the shelf. It occurred to me that there were similarities between this woman's tale and Mowgli's reluctance to return to the man village, feeling safe in the jungle with his friends.

She nodded. "I do. I tried to take her on trips in her last few years, but she refused point blank. Said she'd always had everything she needed right here and that wasn't about to change." She smiled. "And it never did. She died here, perfectly happy. I cared for her right up to the end."

The room suddenly brightened, causing us all to look up. I'd been so engrossed in Mrs. Brady's story that I hadn't noticed the rain stopping. Strange-looking watery sunlight streamed in through the window.

"Do you think the weather has cleared?" Molloy asked hopefully.

Mrs. Brady shook her head. "That's only temporary. The real storm is coming later. If there's one thing I do know, it's the weather on this island."

Molloy stood up, brushing cake crumbs from his trousers. "Is there a shop?"

The old lady nodded. "Of course—there's one down by the pier. You can't see it from where you get off the boat, but if you head to the right along the shore, you can't miss it." She checked her watch, a tiny gold face on her slim wrist. "It's open till seven, so you should be okay."

Molloy gave me a look that indicated I should follow him. The stubborn part of me wanted to resist, but once he had been given a room and we'd thanked our hostess for the tea and cake, I pulled on my waterproof jacket and we left the house.

The atmosphere outside was peculiar, the light almost blue white. A watery rainbow arched over the pier like a tent and I saw there were two extra fishing trawlers that hadn't been there earlier. Molloy noticed them too. He shaded his eyes with his hand for a clearer look, his brow furrowed. I wondered how many fishermen were on the island. Fridge tinkered about with engines, so presumably he wasn't one of them.

"So much for a rainbow signaling an end to the rain," I remarked. "If what Mrs. Brady says is true, we've only seen the start."

"What was all that about her family?" Molloy demanded, cutting across me. "Her mother, her son . . ."

"I was interested," I said stubbornly. "Weren't you?"

"What's going on, Ben? Why all those questions?"

I was about to tell him, then thought better of it. "I'll explain once it's clear in my head."

He gave me an exasperated look. "I hope this shop sells tooth-brushes," he muttered.

"I assume this isn't the first time someone has been trapped here because of the weather." I watched my footing as the water ran in streams down the hill.

"Unfortunately though, it's not very convenient in the middle of a murder investigation. And I'm anxious to get Finn back to see a doctor." Molloy's phone pinged in his pocket and he took it out to look.

"At least we still have coverage," I said.

He didn't respond; he was looking at his screen, reading something.

"What's up?" I asked.

He put his phone away. "It's the post-mortem report. Both post-mortem reports. The pathologist has just emailed them. I'll have a look at them later."

In the past I would have asked him what they contained even if I knew he wouldn't tell me. Now though, I didn't, especially after the exchange we'd just had. I wasn't at all sure how to deal with Molloy at the moment. He seemed to be taking me into his confidence as he had in the past, but was that only because I might be of use?

Before either of us could say anything further, a shout came from the direction of the pier. Fridge and Ronan Grey were striding up the hill towards us. We met them halfway, Fridge breathing heavily, cheeks pink from the exertion. He was wear-ing a checked donkey jacket over his Elvis T-shirt.

Ronan looked anxious. "There's no ferry," he said breath-lessly. "Probably won't be till tomorrow morning according to the barman." His phone buzzed in his hand, but he ignored it.

"We know," I said. "Our landlady had a call from the ferryman."

Ronan waved towards the pier. "Not a soul about to give any bloody information either."

"I've told you," Fridge said patiently, "they don't know. They can't make any decisions until they know what the storm is going to do. Everything is dependent on the weather when you live on an island. You just have to get used to it."

Ronan sighed loudly as his phone rang again. This time he answered it, impatiently, walking back down towards the pier.

Fridge looked after him, hands shoved in the pockets of his jeans, a pitying look on his face. "That poor young fella, His mother won't leave him alone. You'd think he was twelve."

"Is that her on the phone?" I asked

"I'd say so. She was going to meet him at the ferry and now she's going nuts. As if there's anything he can do about it." He snorted. "I'd say she'd swim here if she could, she's that anxious to see him."

It occurred to me then that Fridge would have known the ferry wouldn't be sailing—they wouldn't have had to ask the barman. He could at least have guessed, with a storm forecast. Also, weren't Cara, Niamh, and Finn going too? And then I remembered what Cara had said about Ronan not returning to Greysbridge and wondered if it had been some other route off the island they'd been checking out—a boat that would dock somewhere other than Malin Head so Ronan could give his mother the slip. There must be many islanders with their own boats, and I wouldn't have put it past Fridge to help him.

I wondered what Molloy would think about people leaving the jurisdiction in the middle of his murder investigation, assuming that was Ronan's intention.

"Anyway," Fridge said, rubbing his hands together in anticipation, "it looks as though you're here for the night, so my mother says I'm to ask ye all up to the house. She's making a big pot of stew, just in case the power goes. There'll be enough for twenty. Even you." He grinned, looking at Molloy.

"Thank you," Molloy said with a half-smile, "I think. I'll see how I'm fixed."

"About eight," Fridge said, pointing up a road to the right along the shore. "We're half a mile up that way. It's the only house up there. Red gate with pillars. Lions on the pillars. My mother's idea of posh."

"Thanks."

He waved goodbye and strode off, gesturing to Ronan on the way. Ronan waved at him to go ahead, and if the tractor-like exhaust we could hear on the road below us was anything to go by, he did.

Chapter Twenty-Five

BY THE TIME we got down to the pier, there was a serious wind building up. Our jackets flapped and snapped, and the sea already looked rough, a deep emerald green and white, while the sky was an angry shade of yellow and grey. The trawlers were solid and imposing, with hulls of green and red and black. From where I stood, I could see fishing nets in the sterns of the new additions. I wrapped my jacket tighter around me. It was months since I'd felt so chilly.

"Let's find this shop," Molloy said, noticing my discomfort.

About thirty yards along the road, following Mrs. Brady's directions, we found a single-story building with a corrugated roof and a rusted Player's Cigarettes sign that must have been there for fifty years. There was a small porch where I waited while Molloy went into the shop, taking the opportunity to check my phone. There was no signal. I obviously needed to be higher up.

I stood to one side to let Ronan Grey into the shop, hunched, tense, his face like the developing storm. He emerged within minutes with a pack of cigarettes and a lighter. Molloy was either taking his time choosing his toothbrush or, more likely, quizzing the shopkeeper.

Ronan stopped outside for a cigarette—I could see him through the window. I left the porch and went to join him. He neither smiled nor voiced any objection when I perched beside him on the sill. But he tore the cellophane off his packet of Silk Cut with a viciousness that made me flinch, then snatched out the silver paper and offered me one.

I shook my head. "Fridge said that was your mother on the phone. How is she doing?"

He looked down, lighting the cigarette behind his hand with difficulty in the salty wind. It was the first time I'd seen him smoke. He inhaled deeply and blew the smoke to one side.

"She wants me to come back so I can meet Jay's family. They're staying at the house for a few days while they make arrangements."

"And you don't want to?"

He shook his head. "Talking to them isn't going to bring him back—they don't know me from Adam. And anyway, it's only an excuse on her part."

"What do you mean?"

"She just wants me back where she can control me." He picked a thread of tobacco from his lip. "She showed no interest in Jay before this, said she'd be glad when he finally left."

"She didn't like him then?"

He flicked ash on the ground. "She caught us having a joint together. You'd think he'd given me heroin."

I looked down. "Cara said that you were thinking of heading off traveling with Jay when he left. You must have been close."

Ronan nodded. "It was good to have someone nearer my own age around. It felt as if I'd been on my own the whole summer, with just *them*." There was no affection in the tone he used to refer to his parents. "I'd even found a bike I could borrow . . ."

"But?"

"Jay said he didn't want company. He said he had something to do. Someone to find. It was as if he was on some kind of a mission."

A wave of nausea washed over me when I thought about the paper with Jay's phone number in Harry's car. The unease I'd felt since I'd found it had been festering away inside me.

"What sort of mission?"

Ronan looked at me. "I don't know." His eyes flickered towards the shop. "That guard asked me that too. I wondered if maybe . . ."

"Maybe what?"

He clenched his jaw. "If that's what happened. If maybe someone came after him. The someone he wanted to find."

My eyes widened. "Is that what you think? That someone pushed him?"

He shrugged and looked away. The wall was up again.

"What about Michael Burrows?" I asked. "It's quite a coincidence that they died within a few hours of each other. They got on, didn't they, he and Jay?"

Ronan nodded, taking another drag of his cigarette, kicking at the ash on the wet ground as it dissolved and created a grey paste. "They talked a lot. There wasn't much else to do. Although Michael was always asking questions about the house, and the family." He smiled for the first time. "He'd been at Greysbridge three times, you know. First guest. The parents were thrilled at first that he came back, but I think he was beginning to drive Dad a bit demented. You know he was writing a book?"

"Yes, I'd heard."

"He'd said there'd be a film too, but even Dad was beginning to wonder about that. There was a lot of talk about his son. But the son never appeared until Sunday."

"What was he asking about? Can you remember?"

Ronan shrugged. "I dunno. He was fascinated by that weird bridge and he used to snoop around the old graveyard."

I paused. "Why did he come here, to the island, do you know?"

He flicked his cigarette and looked down. "Birdwatching, I think."

There was the birdwatching thing again. It did seem unlikely with what I'd heard since. I wondered who had told Ronan this—Fridge, perhaps?

I decided to try something else. "Have you any idea where Jay was planning to go when he left Greysbridge?" I asked.

Ronan shook his head, taking a last drag from his now burned-down cigarette. "Only that he was originally going to leave earlier than he did. He'd intended to leave on Thursday but then he changed his mind. I couldn't understand why, with the wedding happening, but I was pleased he did." His eyes welled suddenly, and he brushed at them angrily. "If he'd gone when he planned to, he'd be alive now."

"I'm sorry," I said, wondering if Harry was the reason Jay had stayed for the wedding and feeling ill at the thought of it. "It's hard to lose a friend like that."

"You don't understand." He shook his head. "It's my fault he's dead. All my fucking fault."

"How could it be your fault?" I asked.

But he didn't respond, just dropped his cigarette butt on the tarmac and ground it under his heel with the same viciousness with which he'd opened the pack.

I heard a noise from inside the shop, voices, a door opening, and I stood up. "Why don't you talk to the sergeant, Ronan?"

But he shook his head again and wiped his eyes. "I have to go." He stood up and walked away, head hunched.

Molloy emerged from the shop with a small paper bag, glancing up at a sky that was looking darker and more threatening by the minute.

He sighed, a deep sigh of frustration. "Well *she* wasn't exactly helpful. These people have become too used to no police presence on the island. They're behaving as if the murders happened in a different jurisdiction and it's nothing to do with them."

I grinned.

"Anyway, I've exhausted all the people I need to talk to. Both literally and figuratively. Looks as if there's not a lot we can do here, until our stew party."

"No, I suppose not," I said.

He glanced up the hill towards the pub, where the lights were on even though it was still only five o'clock. In the gloom, it looked warm and welcoming.

"Fancy a drink?" he suggested.

Surprised, I agreed. "Okay."

As we walked back up the hill, I told him about my conversation with Ronan Grey. I felt conflicted. I had acted for Ronan's parents in buying the house, but I felt an obligation to Kate Burrows, too, to find out anything I could that would help answer her questions. I had also liked Jay very much, which left me confused about Harry. Not for the first time, I was beginning to regret becoming involved.

Molloy nodded. "He said something of the sort to me."

"All of it?"

"About Jay Stevenson being on some kind of a mission and the person he was looking for coming after him."

"You don't believe him?"

"I think Ronan knows more than he's saying."

"About Jay?"

"About this whole business. He was central to that hotel. Took bookings, took cups of tea up to the rooms. I'm sure he saw things."

I drew a breath. "Why do you think he's not speaking?"

"Maybe it's loyalty to his parents. He's afraid if he says what he knows it will jeopardize the business?" He paused. "Or maybe he just doesn't want to rock the boat, so he can get away. Not unusual for an eighteen-year-old. Especially one with a clingy mother."

★ ★ ★

It felt strange to be sitting with Molloy over a drink. I chose a beer—it seemed the most sensible option in a pub with laminate tables and sticky floors—while Molloy had a Guinness. I'd never seen him drink a pint before. I realized how odd that was. But we'd never been out for a drink together in public, just the two of us. We'd moved from being friends and colleagues to Molloy coming around to my cottage and staying the night. Then the whole Luke Kirby incident and Molloy just, well, moving away and not coming back. Until now. Only people like Maeve and Phyllis knew we had been involved. Although others might have suspected, we had never formally come out with our relationship.

It was all such a mess; I was beginning to wonder if maybe Molloy was right to want some structure on things. To have *wanted* some structure. It was too late now.

It didn't stop me feeling a flutter in my stomach when I looked at him across the table. Followed by a pang of guilt about Harry. I didn't want to acknowledge either feeling, so I looked down into my drink. Far better to talk about something else.

"What about Ronan's comment about Jay's death being his fault?" I asked. "What do you think he meant?"

Molloy took a gulp of his pint, leaving a white line above his lip which he licked off. "It may be what I mentioned earlier, his guilt at being the one who survived. He must know that what he and Jay were smoking could have had something to do with his death. He's admitted that they were smoking that morning, before the ceremony."

"But Ronan seemed okay. Not stoned or anything. He was working."

"It can have different effects on different people, I assume. Ronan Grey is heavier than Jay Stevenson was."

"I suppose. What about Michael Burrows?" I asked. "Any developments as to how the cyanide came to be in his system? You said he'd ingested it. Was it some kind of food?"

Molloy's expression was hidden.

I persisted. "Was Greysbridge at fault after all?"

He relented, shaking his head. "We checked the kitchens and there's no trace of anything. But examination of his stomach contents showed he'd eaten some kind of cake. Marzipan. Marzipan would have concealed the amygdalin because it has an almond smell." He paused. "There wasn't a cake at the barbecue, was there?"

"No. And even if there was, it wouldn't have been marzipan. Leah hates marzipan."

"Not even marzipan icing? Amygdalin crystals could have been concealed in a single slice, beneath the icing."

"Definitely not." I said. "I think she might even be allergic to almonds. There was a cake at the wedding, of course, but that would have been too late. That was made by Belva, and I know it had no marzipan on either. Where did the amygdalin come from?"

Molloy sighed. "Any number of possibilities. A plant, maybe. Or the seeds of a plant. It can be extracted fairly easily using readily available chemicals. It's a simple enough way to poison someone."

"So, we're back to plants. Not hydrangea leaves, though?"

He shook his head. "No, you'd have needed too many plants to extract enough to kill someone. It wouldn't be practical."

I tried to absorb what he'd said. Molloy had a degree in science so this all came easily to him. My brain worked rather differently.

"So we have a slice of cake, which no one else ate, consumed by Mr. Burrows. Possibly in his room?"

Molloy nodded.

"So did he bring it up there himself, or was it delivered to him?" I paused and looked up. "Abby or Ian? Or Ronan?"

"He certainly consumed it late at night. Cyanide fades after twelve hours or so, so we were lucky to get traces of it."

Suddenly, I remembered the figure I had heard and seen in the corridor outside my room on the night of the barbecue. I had been so distracted by the "ghost" that I had put it out of my mind. I told Molloy now. I expected him to be annoyed that it had taken me this long, but he wasn't. He simply took a notebook from his pocket.

"What time was that?"

"About three a.m."

He gave it some thought. "According to the pathologist, he was poisoned a couple of hours earlier. Any idea who it was?"

"I haven't a clue," I said honestly. "And I didn't give it much thought at the time because a lot of the rooms don't have en suites so I just assumed it was someone using the bathroom at the end of the hall."

"Maybe it was. Could whoever it was have been heading to Burrows' room?"

"Michael Burrows' room was along a different corridor to mine; it branched off. But we shared the same access from the stairs."

"Right." Molloy wrote something and put the notebook back.

"But why would anyone want to kill him?" I asked. "Who would gain from his death?"

"We know he was researching the Grey family. Maybe he found out something someone didn't want revealed?" Molloy looked skeptical even as he suggested it.

I tended to agree with him. "Enough to kill for? Enough to kill two people for?" I corrected myself.

"Assuming both deaths were murder," Molloy said. "The question with Jay is, how did he end up in the water?"

"Did he fall or was he pushed?" I found discussing Jay's death made me edgy. I was concealing something from Molloy by not telling him about Harry.

"Exactly."

"But apart from the cyanide in their systems when they died, the only thing Michael Burrows and Jay Stevenson had in common was Greysbridge," I insisted.

Molloy drained his pint and sat back. "And hydrangea leaves in both rooms."

"Jay and Burrows didn't even know each other before coming to Greysbridge," I said. "Yet by Saturday evening they were both dead. The house has to be the connection."

Molloy's phone rang, and he answered it, immediately getting to his feet. He frowned and went outside, leaving me to sit and mull. I could tell he wasn't convinced there was a link between Greysbridge and the deaths. He was humoring me. There was something else he was considering, something he wasn't prepared to share. I wondered if he'd have shared it with me in the past.

He came back in within a few minutes, looking frustrated. "I've lost connection. It must be the storm."

"Everything okay?"

He looked at his phone again and tipped it to and fro as if that would restore the connection. "No. It's not. I was about to get some important information."

"About what we were talking about? Or something else?"

He gave me a look.

I put my hands up. "Okay, okay. None of my business."

He sat down; his voice lowered. "I've told you there's something I'm involved in."

"The reason you were abroad?" I whispered. "Is it still going on? The investigation?"

He looked at me without responding and it hurt. I glanced away.

"Mrs. Burrows is heartbroken," I said, changing the subject. "I wish there was something I could do for her."

Molloy straightened. "I haven't had a chance to look at Michael Burrows' notes—there's someone at the station doing that." He paused. "Since you have copies, maybe we could look at them together. Then this overnight wouldn't be a complete waste."

Grudgingly I agreed. "Okay." I looked down. We'd both finished our drinks. "Do you want another?" I asked.

I wanted one, I realized. Before his call, I'd felt more relaxed with Molloy than I had since he'd reappeared, and I wanted to get that back. The trick was to stop before we started talking about anything personal.

Molloy nodded. "Okay. Just the one."

I waved at the barman, who was behind the counter playing with his phone; the same man who'd been here all day. He nodded and moved to the taps straight away, as if glad of something to do. A few minutes later he brought over our drinks.

"Do you have reception?" Molloy asked. "My phone has just lost it."

The barman shook his head as he placed the glasses on two beer mats. "Nah. Haven't since that gale started. I'm just playing a game. Stuck here for the night, are ye?"

"It appears so." Despite my protests, Molloy rooted out a banknote and handed it to him. "Thanks."

The barman crossed his arms, "Staying with Mrs. Brady, are ye?"

I nodded.

He grinned. "She's a grand lady. I wonder will she live as long as her mother? She had a party here in the pub for her hundredth, you know."

Since he was in a chatty mood, I took a chance. "Do you remember a fellow that was here on the island a few weeks ago? English. He played music in here, I think."

The barman pulled up a stool from a neighboring table and sat, taking my question as an invitation to join us. I didn't blame him. The pub was still deserted.

He leaned in curiously. "That fella died, I hear. Food poisoning or something?"

"Something like that," Molloy said.

"Aye, he was in here a fair bit. Chatted to everyone. He was going to make us all stars, so he was." He laughed.

'What do you mean?'

'Ach, he was writing some story about some feckin' thing. Reckoned he was going to be making it into a film and we'd all have parts." He grinned. "There's them that would take notice of that kind of thing, but not me. Full of ol' big talk he was."

I smiled. There was Leah's mother's expression again.

"Did he say what it was about, this story?"

"Said he didn't want to give away the twist." The barman laughed again. "A load of nonsense. Played the tin whistle though. Not too badly for an English fellow. Came in here a few times with Fridge and Audrey. We don't get many visitors here, but they seemed to get on well." He scratched his forehead. "I did see Audrey and him up at the graveyard one day. I thought maybe they were . . ." He gave an exaggerated wink. "Now there's someone who'd have liked to be in his film. Maybe she was auditioning for a part."

"The graveyard," I said. "Is that where Mrs. Brady's mother is buried, by any chance?"

Molloy gave me an odd look.

"Aye, of course," the barman said with a grin. "Only the one graveyard on the island. No religious divisions here—we're all thrun in together. And that lady, well, she'd never leave the island while she was alive, so she wasn't likely to leave it when she was dead. None of us would have done it to her."

"Where is it?" I asked. "The graveyard."

"Just beside Belva's . . . Aren't you heading up there later for the *céilí*?"

Molloy nodded, his eyebrows raised. It seemed everything was common knowledge on this island. Glendara multiplied by fifty.

The barman picked up our empty glasses before walking back to the bar. "Wouldn't live beside a graveyard myself, but they don't seem to mind it."

Chapter Twenty-Six

MOLLOY DRAINED HIS pint and stood up. "Right then. Let's go back and have a look at Burrows" notes."

We'd drunk our second drink more quickly than the first, both of us eager to get to work.

"Can we go and have a look at the graveyard first?" I asked as I pulled on my jacket.

"Any particular reason?"

"I'll tell you when we get there."

Molloy looked at me curiously. "Surely it would make more sense to go on the way to this dinner, wouldn't it? Didn't the barman say it was just beside the house?"

Reluctantly I agreed, and we left the pub, both of us deep in thought. The wind was up. It wasn't yet raining, but there was a strange wintry feeling abroad, as if darkness was falling despite it being only six o'clock. We made our way back down the lane, a sensible gap between us.

There was no sign of Mrs. Brady, so this time we used our keys to let ourselves into the house.

"My room or yours?" Molloy asked when we arrived on the first-floor landing. "I'd rather not take the papers down to the sitting room if that's okay."

I nodded. "Everything's already in mine, so let's go in there."

It was unnerving having Molloy in my room. The second beer didn't help. I wondered suddenly if Harry knew about Molloy and me, if Leah had told him. And then I remembered I'd been supposed to let Harry know that the teenagers had been found. I plugged in the kettle, and while I waited for it to boil, I drafted a quick text saying I'd call when I got a chance, realizing even as I sent it that that probably wasn't true. I'd wait until I could speak to him face to face so I could ask him why he'd had Jay's number.

I made two cups of instant coffee and handed Molloy one while he opened the folders and laid the papers back out on the bed. I stood at the edge to watch, to see if he did anything different to what I'd done earlier.

"I haven't been able to put them in any kind of order," I said. "Not yet anyway." I reached for the sheet I'd been looking at with the family tree and handed it to him. "Have you seen this?"

He examined it. "Brady?" He raised his eyebrows. "Our sweet landlady? What's this about?"

"I have an idea," I said. "But the graveyard will confirm it. Or not." I heard a door close downstairs. "Actually, Mrs. Brady herself might be able to confirm it. All I really need is a name. I should have asked her earlier, but I hadn't put two and two together at that stage."

I ran back downstairs, but there was no sign of her. I looked in the kitchen and the sitting room we'd been in earlier, but the fire had gone out, nothing but burning embers. The woman moved quickly for someone who looked so frail.

Molloy looked up from what he was doing when I went back upstairs.

I shook my head. "I don't know where she's gone."

"Well, you were right. Burrows was certainly very interested in the Grey family," he said, pushing a sheet over to me. "Look at this."

I picked it up and examined it. It was a printout of a search from the Registry of Births, Marriages and Deaths from 1914; a search under the name Grey. But there were no results. Whatever he had been looking for either hadn't been registered or had been lost.

Then I remembered. "Of course," I said. "The Customs House fire." The IRA had occupied and burned the Customs House in Dublin in 1921, and many government records had been destroyed.

I sank down onto the bed. Results or not, the very fact that Michael Burrows had carried out this search confirmed what I had been thinking, and confirmed that Burrows had been thinking what I had. I didn't want to wait any longer to make sure.

"I think I know what he was looking for," I said, picking up the sheet with the family tree and putting it in my back pocket. "Let's go up to the graveyard and check."

Molloy raised his eyebrows.

"I want to see Mrs. Brady's mother's grave," I explained. "Come on. While it's still light and before the storm gets going properly again."

Molloy looked at his watch. "I suppose we might as well. It's almost time to head anyway."

★ ★ ★

The pier looked different from how it had earlier. It took me a few seconds to figure out that there were no lights. The electricity must have gone, just as Mrs. Brady had predicted. And when I turned to look at the house, it was in darkness too. The power must have failed just as we'd left.

To my surprise, Molloy produced a small torch from the pocket of his jacket. "Purchased from the shop an hour ago."

"Boy Scout," I teased him.

He smiled, and it made my stomach flip. That wasn't good.

It was still only dusk, but the atmosphere was dark and ominous as we made our way down the hill, the trawlers almost spectral in the strange light. The odd clatter as the wind blew over an empty barrel or fish box didn't help.

When we reached the pier, we turned right in the direction Fridge had driven when we'd first arrived, the opposite way to the route I'd taken with Cara. And after a blustery twenty-minute walk along a narrow country road, during which we met not a soul, we came across a tiny church silhouetted against the grey sky.

"I suppose this must be it," I said. "The graveyard must be at the back."

Molloy gestured towards a house a little further on. "It must be. Pillars with lions on top."

We pushed open the gate. The church was surprisingly modern, surrounded by stunted trees blown into strange shapes by the wind, but there were no lights here either. A sudden gust blew the paper with the indecipherable family tree out of my hand. I chased after it and caught it just in time.

By now, the build-up to this storm was giving me the heebie-jeebies. The wind was coming and going, one moment threatening to develop into a full-blown gale, the next balmy and calm. The sky was peculiar in color and mood, a harbinger of what was to come. There was rain in the air, but it had been

that way for hours now, since the last shower. Part of me wished
it would just get on with it.

Molloy and I walked around to the back of the church, where
there were fifty or so graves. I wasn't cold, but I pulled my jacket
tighter. The gravestones were stark and simple, but eerie against
the weird sky. I stopped suddenly when I realized we were not
alone. A large figure dressed in a long waterproof coat was kneel-
ing at one of the graves. It took me a few seconds to recognize
Audrey, Fridge's sister.

She heard us and stood up, clearly just as surprised as we were
to find herself in company. She came over. Her cheeks were
flushed, and she looked as if she might have been crying. She was
wearing a brightly colored scarf that suited her skin.

"Are you looking for something?" she asked, directing her
question firmly at Molloy.

He deferred to me, and when I asked, she pointed us in the
direction of Mrs. Brady's mother's grave. She seemed unsurprised
at the question and I remembered what the barman had said
about her being here with Michael Burrows.

"Look for McSweeney," she said. "That was Ann Marie
Brady's maiden name."

I thanked her, and as an afterthought admired her scarf, which
gleaned me a surprised smile.

Despite her directions, it took us a little while, but we split up
and eventually Molloy called out and I made my way over to
him. Unlike the graveyard at Greysbridge, this was a carefully
tended grave, the inscription on the stone, clean and clear. *Here
lies Eve Louisa McSweeney, born 1914, died 22nd June 2016, much
loved wife of Charles McSweeney, mother of Ann Marie.*

I breathed out. Eve Louisa McSweeney. No exact date of birth,
just a year: 1914. I took my phone out of my pocket and checked

the photograph I'd taken of Louisa Grey's grave at Greysbridge. She had died on 15th January 1914 and her gravestone had said: *Every Eve shall I think of her.* When I had seen it first, I had assumed it referred to Louisa herself, that it was a message from her family that they would remember her every evening. But in fact, it was a reference to a person: Eve, her baby daughter. Mrs. Brady's mother had been Lady Louisa Grey's daughter.

I wondered if Louisa had ever met her daughter, or if she had died giving birth. Even if she had, they couldn't have had long together. Louisa had died on 15th January, so even if Eve was born on the 1st, she'd only have had two weeks with her. I wondered if she knew that her baby was to be taken here to the island and asked to be buried with a view of where she would be—*Every Eve shall I think of her.*

I touched the gravestone, running my fingers along the inscription as the wind whipped my hair. This meant that the tiny grave on the mainland was empty; it was there to create the impression that the baby had died, if anyone had asked. Although it was clear they didn't want to draw attention to it. The Greys hadn't wanted the baby and hadn't wanted any connection with her. She had been taken to this island, brought up here by Mrs. Brady's grandparents, whoever they were, and spent the rest of her life here, never wanting to leave. Fearful of leaving, perhaps.

I realized Molloy was staring at me and remembered there was no reason for him to understand the significance of what I was seeing. So under the strange sky, with the wind and the sound of the sea in the distance, I explained it all. The little graveyard at Greysbridge and the strange arrangement of the graves there; what Michael Burrows must have worked out and how he had followed the trail here.

He whistled. "What exactly happened to Eve's mother?" he asked. "Louisa, you said she was called?"

I told him everything I knew about Linus Grey and the disturbing room on the other side of the footbridge. He placed his thumb and index finger on either side of the bridge of his nose to think.

"So this Linus Grey may have been responsible for the death of his own daughter. You think maybe his attempts to end the pregnancy went wrong and the baby survived but his daughter didn't?"

"The baby obviously wasn't wanted if she ended up here after her mother died rather than being taken care of by the Greys."

I shuddered, an image of that room returning. Maybe Jay was right, that the story of Louisa starving herself was put out by the family to conceal what had really happened.

Molloy took a deep breath. "Well, that establishes a connection between Greysbridge and Inishathair. We know now what Michael Burrows was doing here."

I nodded. "This must have been the story he was writing. Linus Grey, respected peer and member of the House of Lords, attempts to cure his "mad" pregnant daughter. She dies, but against the odds, her baby survives. The baby is brought from Greysbridge to this island, where she spends the rest of her life, falling in love, having a family and living to be a hundred and two."

"Despite her grandfather trying to ensure she never existed." Molloy was impressed. "That's some story all right."

"And it *would* make a great film. Michael Burrows was convinced there might be a movie in it, his son being a film-maker."

Molloy scratched his chin. "I wonder if the present-day Greys know?"

"Ian Grey knew Burrows was writing a book and talked about a film being made." I gave Molloy a wry look. "We now know he talked *a lot* about a film being made. But I don't know if Ian knew about *this*."

"Well, Michael Burrows obviously upset someone with what he was doing."

"Yes."

Lightning flashed suddenly in the distance. I remembered how as children we used to count the seconds between lightning and thunder to guess how far away the storm was. There had been no thunder as yet.

Molloy reached out and touched the gravestone. "It's a sad story."

"With a happy ending for Eve, if not for her mother," I said.

I looked again at the grave, my gaze moving to one just beside it. *Charles McSweeney, died 14th August 2003.* Her husband, I presumed. She'd outlived him by quite a bit, but they'd had a long marriage.

"So Ian's great-grandfather might have murdered his great-aunt," I said. "The Greys couldn't really want that to get out, surely?"

Molloy folded his arms. "I don't know. It's a long time ago. A very old skeleton."

"They *are* trying to establish a business. I can't imagine a story like that would help."

Molloy looked at me. "Neither does two public poisonings. The details splashed all over the paper alongside an ad for Greysbridge as a beautiful wedding venue."

"Fair point."

A voice from the other side of the graveyard made us look up. Audrey was leaving and was calling to remind us about dinner in her mother's house. We waved, saying we'd follow her, and made our way back around to the front of the church.

"How did you put all this together?" Molloy asked.

"I presumed Michael Burrows was following the trail of Louisa Grey's baby, especially when I saw the family tree. Somehow he must have discovered or suspected that there was no baby in that grave and worked out that this was where she ended up. It makes sense now that Lady Louisa was buried where she was—she must have known this was where Eve was to be taken and asked to be buried where she could see her child."

"I wonder who organized the inscription on the grave," Molloy said. "With the 'Eve' link?"

I shook my head. "I don't know. It's touching though. Mother over there and daughter here. Forever a link between the two, even if there wasn't one in life."

Molloy pushed open the gate. The seagulls screamed above us, disturbed by the impending storm. He stopped suddenly, his hand still on the bolt. "Would Eve have had inheritance rights over Greysbridge?"

"Maybe," I shrugged. "Depends on wills. But any rights she had would have elapsed long since, I'd have thought. I wonder if Mrs. Brady knows . . ."

I was interrupted by a flash of lightning, followed by a loud crash of thunder and immediately it started to rain. I was about to get my wish. The storm was unleashed.

Chapter Twenty-Seven

DESPITE THE LACK of electricity, Belva's house was warm and welcoming. We dashed from the church to her front door with our coats over our heads, and despite the rain that threatened to engulf us, managed to make it without getting completely soaked. The door was opened before we even had to knock, as if Audrey had told them to expect us.

The ruddy-faced man in the checked shirt who let us in shook our hands firmly but didn't introduce himself, merely pointed us towards a room to the right. Following his directions, we made our way through a narrow candlelit hallway into a large sitting-cum-dining room filled with the smell of cooking meat. The light was dim and the chat was loud. The house was full of people—eating at a long table, lounging on couches and armchairs and on cushions on the floor, drinking from cans of Guinness. It seemed as if half the islanders had gathered here. Three cauldrons of stew were being kept warm on the hearth in front of a huge turf fire.

The mystery of where Mrs. Brady had disappeared to was solved when I spotted her in an armchair by the fire with a woman perched on the arm chatting to her. She gave me a wave, which I returned, determined after what we'd discovered to talk to her later.

As if she sensed our presence, Belva appeared, handed us two plates and pointed us towards cutlery and drinks before returning to whatever it was she was doing in the kitchen. After we'd helped ourselves to food, I discarded Molloy, leaving him to chat to Audrey, who made a beeline for him as soon as my back was turned. I smiled at him as I walked away, and he widened his eyes in mock panic.

Plate in hand, I negotiated my way to Leah's sister Cara, who was alone on a window seat looking a bit lost. I glanced around for Ronan and spied him through the door into the hall, laughing and joking with Fridge.

"Is everything okay?" I asked as Cara shunted over to give me some room.

She nodded silently. I sat down and took a forkful of stew, plate resting on my knee. It was full of flavor, with chunky vegetables and potatoes and lots of herbs and spices. I thought I could taste some Guinness in there too. I noticed a theme developing.

"I bet you're dying to get back," I said after I'd swallowed the first mouthful. "It's been a long old wedding for you."

She gave me a weak smile. "It'll be good to get Niamh back."

"Where are they? Herself and Finn?" I cast my eyes around the room, but there was no sign.

"They've gone to bed. I think they've had very little sleep these last few nights. Like the rest of us." She yawned and took a sip of her water.

"I can't imagine that cellar or the boat were too comfortable. How is Finn?"

"Not great. He seems to have picked up a wheeze and he has some weird eye irritation." She looked up to see Belva plotting a course across the floor with three plates balanced on her arms. "Although Belva's been great. She's given him eye drops and an inhaler, which seem to be helping. She's like a nurse."

"She does seem to be able to tackle anything. Kind of the island's mother. How's Niamh doing?"

"Niamh seems all right, physically at least, although she has a bit of a cold. I'm not surprised about that—a night on a boat and another night in a damp pub cellar will do that to you, even during the summer." She shook her head. "Pair of idiots."

"I suppose they're just kids."

Cara lowered her voice. "Hopefully Finn's parents will pay more attention to him now. He was the one who persuaded Niamh to do what they did. But his parents were so wrapped up in their own concerns they were hardly even aware he'd gone. He was probably looking for someone to notice him."

I smiled. "That's the thing with teenagers. They're inherently self-obsessed. I know I was."

"But God, anything could have happened to him." She caught herself. "Anything could have happened to *either* of them. There I am criticizing Finn's parents, but we're just as much at fault."

"I suppose everyone was a little distracted." I paused. "And there's no danger of them . . .?"

I didn't need to finish the sentence. Cara assured me that the window in the room Finn was in was locked, and that there was only one way out of the house and that was through the packed room we were in.

To copper-fasten things, the storm was raging outside, the rain battering against the roof and windows with a wild fury, the wind howling down the chimney and making the flames of the fire quiver. It felt good to be inside, although I did wonder how we would get back to Mrs. Brady's when the time came. There wasn't much possibility of Fridge dropping us back, given the speed with which he was disposing of those cans. I'd watched him make regular trips to the kitchen from the hall, emerging with a fresh six-pack each time. They must have cleared the pub of its entire stock.

"Harry says he'll take a look at them," Cara said, bringing my attention back. "Finn's parents are happy for him to do that. They're going to meet us in Glendara."

"You've been in contact with Harry?" I realized he hadn't responded to my text.

She nodded. "I rang when we found them, to be on the safe side. Just to see if there was anything we should be doing." She smiled. "He asked after you."

I flushed, realizing that was considerably before I'd sent him my text. Hours, in fact. "Must be handy to have a doctor in the family."

She raised her eyes to heaven. "Oh, sure they're all convinced they'll get free medical advice for the foreseeable. Everyone's mad about him."

"Did you know him when you were younger?" I asked. "He said he was nine when he left."

She shook her head. "He's a lot older than me. I don't remember him. They didn't come home very often, my uncle and aunt. They're on the far side of Canada, so it's a long journey . . ." She trailed off as Ronan appeared with a steaming plate in his hand.

He stood over us, shoveling stew into his mouth. "Food's great, isn't it? Maybe we should give Belva a job in the kitchen at Greysbridge."

"I doubt she'd take it," Cara said sharply. "Especially now."

Things obviously hadn't improved between herself and Ronan.

Ronan looked stung, but he didn't argue. "You're probably right."

He put his plate down and moved closer to Cara, touching her on the shoulder. It was a clumsy gesture and she shrank back.

Rejected, he picked up his plate again, then froze suddenly, a peculiar expression on his face. After a few seconds he put the plate back down and strode off. I realized he was a little drunk.

"Is everything okay between you two?" I asked.

Before Cara could reply, Belva appeared, shuffling over with two heaped bowls of dessert. "Some plum fool, ladies?" she offered. "The ice cream is a wee bit melted since the freezer is defrosting, but sure who minds that?"

"Lovely," I said, taking a bowl. Belva struck me as someone you didn't say no to.

"You're very kind to feed everyone," Cara said, taking one too.

Belva clamped her hands onto her considerable hips. "Ach, it's no bother. Everyone brought food that was going to spoil, so we've just pooled it all. We might well stick together till the storm passes and save on the candles at least." She smiled as Cara took a mouthful of dessert. "Those were stewed from last year. That greenhouse of Mrs. Brady's just keeps on giving."

There was a sudden gust down the chimney that caused the fire to gutter.

"How long do you think the storm is going to last?" I asked.

Belva pursed her lips. "That's the question, isn't it? It's blowing a grand gale out there now, but I'd say it's as bad as it's going to get. It'll probably have blown itself out by lunchtime tomorrow." She winked. "You'll be able to take that guard back on the afternoon ferry. Or even the morning one; get him out of our hair."

I looked over at Molloy, who was sitting with Mrs. Brady on the couch. I wondered what they were chatting about; Molloy was rarely off duty. But she was smiling broadly, so whatever he was doing was working.

Cara followed my gaze. "Is that your landlady?"

I nodded. "That's Mrs. Brady."

Belva smiled indulgently at the old lady, who was tucking into an even larger bowl of dessert than mine. "Ach, I hope she's with us as long as her mother was."

"I hear she was over a hundred," I said, taking another mouthful of plum fool.

"That's right. Although I don't think anyone was entirely sure exactly what old Eve's birth date was, Eve included. But we had a grand party at the pub anyway, organized by her grandson." She put her hand in front of her mouth. "A man with his own problems and a nasty temper, but he'd have done anything for that wee woman."

"That would be Mrs. Brady's son?" I asked.

Belva nodded, both chins wobbling. "Aye. Rudy. You've met him. He's the gardener at Greysbridge. Though God knows why he would want to work there."

I inhaled sharply, but before I could say anything, we were interrupted by angry shouting coming from the hallway.

Belva frowned. "Now what's going on?"

Through the door to the hall I could see some sort of altercation taking place between Ronan and Fridge. Ronan took a wild swing at the other man, who laughed at him and held his arm aloft, making Ronan even angrier.

The younger man's voice traveled easily across the room. "You bastard."

He looked as if he was about to hit Fridge again when Molloy dived in and held him back, getting in between the two of them and talking to Ronan quietly. Belva made her way towards her son, her huge bulk clearing a path across the room.

While Molloy took Ronan along the hall and out of sight, Fridge went into the kitchen with his mother. I glanced at Cara, whose expression was one of exasperation.

"I don't know what's wrong with him," she said. "He keeps losing it with me too, over the least little thing." She shook her head. "I've had enough of him, to be honest."

"He's had a rough few days, I suppose."

"We all have. I just want to get my sister home and forget all of this ever happened." She stood up purposefully. "Want me to take that?" She gestured towards my bowl.

I nodded and handed it to her, watching her head off towards the kitchen before making my way back out into the hall. Molloy was there on his own, checking his phone yet again.

"What was that all about?" I asked.

He looked up. "It's not terribly clear. From what I can tell, it started with Fridge slagging Grey about the piece in the paper. About his family poisoning their guests."

"I thought they were getting on well?" I said. "They've certainly been buddying up here."

Molloy closed one eye. "I'm more and more convinced there's something that young fella's not telling us."

Chapter Twenty-Eight

I WAS INCLINED to think that Molloy was correct. It seemed to me that Ronan Grey's state of mind had been declining steadily since the day of the wedding, as if the loss of his friend was only beginning to sink in. He'd lost both parents but maybe he had never grieved properly since he hadn't known them. Perhaps this loss had compounded the others and he was struggling under the weight of all three.

The strains of "Love Me Tender" drifted in from the sitting room accompanied by much laughter and cheering. I recognized the voice as Fridge's.

"He doesn't seem to be unduly concerned anyway," Molloy remarked.

"At least he'll keep everyone entertained." I paused, lowering my voice though it was unlikely to be heard over the singing. "Did you know that Rudy, the gardener at Greysbridge, is Mrs. Brady's son?"

Molloy nodded. "Yes, I did."

"I can't believe I didn't figure it out before. But then I never knew his surname."

"I only made the connection recently. Rudy didn't mention he was from here," Molloy said. "He stays on the mainland most of the week so that was the address he gave us. It was only when I saw that our landlady had the same surname that I asked. He was named after Rudyard Kipling apparently, his father's favorite."

I remembered the copy of *The Jungle Book* in the sitting room.

"I wonder if *he* knows he's related to the Greys," I said. "They'd be cousins. Mrs. Brady's grandmother and Ian Grey's grandfather were brother and sister. The grandfather—Evan—was the one who lost the house in a card game. With a father like Linus, it's not surprising he had issues. Although at least *he* survived."

"Unlike his sister, Louisa."

I nodded.

"So it turns out that Rudy is related to his employer," Molloy said. "He works at a house that under different circumstances he might have owned."

I considered it. "Well, yes, I suppose so. Although Ian and Abby bought the house in an arm's-length transaction. It hadn't been in the family for generations. But I wonder if Rudy knows who his grandmother was."

Molloy looked skeptical. "Revenge, you think? Sabotage the new hotel? For a wrong done a hundred years ago?"

I shrugged. "People have borne grudges for less. He is a gardener. He grows hydrangeas, and other plants; there is a greenhouse both here at his mother's house and at Greysbridge. And I never got the impression he was much of a fan of the Greys."

I cast my mind back to the conversation I'd had with Rudy at the footbridge, the day after the wedding. He'd known a lot about Louisa Grey. Was it possible he'd known she was his great-grandmother? He'd said that his great-grandfather was the gardener at Greysbridge and had been forced to grow strange plants for Linus Grey. Was he the one who had brought Louisa's baby to the island?

"But surely what happened to Rudy's grandmother wasn't Ian Grey's fault," Molloy said. "Linus Grey was an ancestor to both of them."

I was mulling this over when Audrey blustered into the hallway breathing heavily. She was wheezing like her mother and her hair was wet as if she'd been outside.

"What's wrong?" I asked.

"Ronan's gone out in the storm," she said breathlessly. "I'm afraid he's going to do something stupid. I'm going to get Fridge. He's the only one who can swim."

"Where has he gone?" Molloy said urgently.

Audrey had one foot inside the sitting room door. It sounded as if "Heartbreak Hotel" was next on the playlist. "The beach, he's gone to the beach, the one below the lighthouse."

Molloy and I grabbed our jackets and dashed for the door, pulling our hoods up as we went.

Audrey called after us, waving frantically to the left. "Go that way. There's a lane that cuts across and links the two roads."

The storm engulfed us on the doorstep, almost blowing us back inside. Molloy closed the door with difficulty and set off.

'I know where it is," I panted as we ran along the road in the pelting rain, staggering in the wind. "I was heading to the lighthouse with Cara earlier."

Molloy produced the torch and we were glad of it. Without electricity, there were no lights, the trees looked skeletal and sinister, and the rain was as hard as hail. We dragged ourselves along, struggling to catch our breath. It was properly dark now, although the lighthouse, doing its job, was visible up ahead. It must have worked on a generator.

We took the turn directed by Audrey and reached the road I'd been on earlier with Cara. There was a track down to the left that was easy to miss, but with the help of Molloy's torch, we found it. It led down to an inlet with a stony beach. We made our way to the shore, the wind and rain battering us like a gang of violent thugs, and a figure appeared in the torchlight. Ronan Grey was standing with his back to us in tar-like water up to his waist. Rocks towered on either side, leading to cliffs.

"Shit. He's in the sea—look!" I wiped the rain from my face to get a clearer view, but it just kept coming.

I stood on the shore, shivering, while Molloy waded in after him and the waves smashed against the rocks and the beach. The torchlight made Ronan turn, but only briefly. And after a short hesitation, I followed Molloy, the ice-cold water soaking my jeans and legs.

Molloy shouted at him. "Ronan! Don't do this. Come back, please."

Ronan glanced back again but kept on going. He was making his way out to sea.

"Come back and talk to us," Molloy said, his voice carrying on the wind. "We need your help to find out what happened to your friend."

Ronan's shoulders slumped, and he finally stopped moving. "I can tell you what happened to him." His voice was dull, barely audible.

"Tell me," Molloy urged.

Ronan kept his back to us. "I killed him. I killed them both."

Molloy kept moving forward, slowly reducing the gap between them. "Why would you think that?"

Ronan again shook his head. "I don't think it. I'm sure of it."

"Jay died because he fell in the water," Molloy said. "He died because he couldn't swim."

Ronan spun around, his eyes streaming. "His death was my fault."

"No, it wasn't. He was an adult. You may think what you were smoking contributed." Molloy spread his hands calmly. "I'm going to be honest and say that is a possibility. But he made the decision to smoke himself. His death may very well have been an accident."

Ronan shook his head. "It wasn't an accident."

"How can you be so sure? Ronan?"

Ronan sank to his knees, his legs finally giving way beneath him, the water now up to his shoulders. "I don't even know if he got to do what he needed to do. I don't even know . . ."

"Be careful!" I shouted to Molloy.

It was still raining heavily, and the sea was rough. If Ronan lost his balance now, he would go under, just like Jay had. I realized how drunk he was, his mind all over the place. I wondered if he'd smoked something this evening too.

"Why do you think it wasn't an accident, Ronan?" Molloy was keeping him talking, only a few meters away from him now.

"Was it anything to do with the house?" I offered. "Did Michael Burrows tell Jay things he'd discovered about your family?"

Ronan's eyes flashed. "They're not my family!"

I wondered again about his anger about this, but at least he was talking.

"How many times do I have to say it? They're not my fucking family." He roared it into the wind. "I was the one who sent the tip-off to the newspaper. I have no fucking interest in the Greys. Fucking Ian and Abby and . . ." He closed his eyes and fell forward as if giving himself up to the sea.

Molloy dived for him, grabbed him by the shoulders and pulled him to his feet, and Ronan let him.

Ronan staggered, Molloy's hand still on his neck, and rubbed his face with his sleeve. Suddenly he looked very young. "I hate them both. I'm never going back there."

"It's okay," Molloy said soothingly. "You're an adult, no one can force you."

He led Ronan gently out of the water just as a shout rang out and Fridge's ancient jalopy was driven on the beach.

Chapter Twenty-Nine

"WE NEED TO speak to Jay's family," I said as Molloy and I walked back down the road to Belva's house, the wind moaning and keening but the rain less heavy.

Ronan had gone back in the car with Fridge and Audrey, Audrey driving due to the quantity of Guinness her brother had consumed. But the car was small and the rain had eased, so Molloy and I had opted to walk back. There was the promise of another car to collect us, but I'd been told there were only three on the island, and I wondered who would be sober enough to drive one.

Molloy raised his eyebrows in response to what I had said. "We?"

"You. You know what I mean," I snapped.

Audrey had swapped her dry coat for my soaked one, but I wasn't in the best of moods. The coat was huge and it dragged on the ground like a dead weight while I stung and froze inside it. My shoes squelched along the wet tarmac, my legs chafing painfully in my wet jeans.

"We need to know why he really came to Ireland. Who he wanted to speak to. You heard what Ronan said about him getting to do what he needed to do. What if that person he wanted to find was really a threat?" I knew I should tell Molloy about Harry, that Harry was the most likely possibility, but I still wanted to ask him about it first.

"Assuming that wasn't all in Ronan's head," Molloy replied. "He wasn't making a whole lot of sense. Anyway, don't you think I've already asked the Stevensons what they know? As far as they were concerned, Jay came to Europe on a cycling holiday. They thought he was to meet some other friends in Munich, although that's turned out not to be true. He was on his own."

My mind raced ahead. "What about the reason he couldn't swim? His telling me something different from what his parents told you. Could it have been something to do with that? Maybe he blamed someone for his friend's death?"

"Maybe," Molloy said doubtfully.

"Poor Ronan," I said quietly. "He's so lost."

"Yes," Molloy said. "He certainly is."

We walked along in silence. The rain had finally stopped, much earlier than predicted, and the moon and stars emerged from a black sky. There was so little light pollution here. I wondered how much damage had been done after the storm. Debris was strewn all over the road and sheep huddled together in the fields, cold and wet. There was something about the strange light, the sky, Harry, my cold feet and my throat starting to hurt again that made me feel sad. And then suddenly my trip to America entered my head and I felt overwhelmed. I missed Inishowen even though I was still here, I missed Molloy even though he was beside me, and I started to cry. Molloy heard me and put his arms around me. He held me close: two drowned rats on a lonely road on an island in the North Atlantic. It would have been romantic if it hadn't been so pathetic.

Then something occurred to me and I pulled back. "I've just remembered."

Molloy released me, a half-smile on his face.

"Ronan said he killed them both."

His smile disappeared.

"That means he thinks he had some involvement in Burrows' death too. The cake!" I said suddenly. "He must have been the one who delivered the slice of cake that killed him. We thought it could have been him or Abby or Ian. What if it wasn't Jay who dropped the dried leaves? What if it was Ronan? Maybe they fell out of his pocket?"

"You mean he poisoned Burrows?"

"Maybe he didn't know the cake was poisoned. He was just delivering it, doing room service or whatever. It's a possibility, isn't it? That's why he feels so guilty."

"But why wouldn't he tell us?"

"It depends who he thinks the cake was from. Who poisoned it. Maybe he's protecting somebody."

Even as I said this, I remembered Ian Grey holding his stomach when he came to ask me about Jay's family. He'd claimed it was an ulcer, but what if it wasn't? Despite what he said about them, was Ronan Grey protecting his parents?

I looked up and saw that we were passing the lane that led to Fridge's huge shed, the one I'd searched earlier with Cara. I glanced over, the moon suspended above it like a clock. To lighten the mood, I told Molloy the story of where Fridge had got his name. I expected him to at least smile, but he didn't. He looked at the shed with an odd expression on his face.

I was surprised when he started walking towards it. I followed him and watched as he crouched down on his hunkers beside a puddle just outside. There was a rainbow pattern in the water. He dipped his finger in and sniffed it.

He turned suddenly at the sound of a car. I felt the tension leach out of me. A lift, thank God. It was a lift.

★   ★   ★

I sighed and closed my eyes. Radiant sun streamed through the window of Mrs. Brady's dining room onto her pristine white tablecloth. It was quiet. For the moment I was the only one here, and that made me exceedingly happy. I needed time to think.

After our welcome lift back from Audrey the night before, I'd gone straight to my room to peel off my soaking clothes. I'd intended having a mull over the day's events, but after I had taken a hot shower, the power mercifully having returned, something odd had happened. Toweling my hair, I'd made my way to the window to close the curtains. As I took a last glance at the pier, I noticed a light on one of the trawlers. Not an electric one, I didn't think; it was more like a torch, its beam moving from place to place. I'd thought nothing of it, had assumed it was a fisherman ensuring there had been no storm damage to his boat. Until half an hour later, when I'd heard Molloy return to his room. He must have left again while I was in the shower.

Which was why I was glad of a few minutes before he appeared. What had he been doing on the trawler? Should I ask him? Would he even tell me if I did?

The door opened slowly with a creak and Mrs. Brady came in with a tray. She looked so small that I stood up to help her. But she smiled up at me. "No need, pet. Stronger than I look, I'm told."

I sat back down and watched as she moved the items one by one from tray to table: a plate with eggs and bacon, a rack of toast and a pot of tea.

"Hope you like it strong."

"I do, thanks." I poured myself a cup straight away and took a sip. I was thirsty. "How did you get back last night?" I asked her.

"Oh, the same way as everybody else. Poor Audrey was ferrying everyone here and there and everywhere. Just as well that girl doesn't drink." She winked. "Although she eats enough to make up for it. She's a sweet girl, but it's not going to help her find a man, which seems to be her one aim in life."

I helped myself to a slice of toast. "She took a shine to Michael Burrows, I'm told."

The old lady beamed in amusement. "Oh, she did at that. Was mad about him, but ach, sure the man was married. Had no interest in her other than what she could tell him. My Rudy told her that more than once, but she wouldn't listen. Thought he was going to make her a star, she did."

"Really?"

"Aye, the silly wee girl. Rudy got on well with Michael too. But *he* knew the man was after information, not a lifelong friendship."

"About Greysbridge?" I asked.

"Aye." She clasped the tray to her chest. "Rudy working there meant he was the right person to ask. Although I think in truth Michael knew more than he did. Rudy knows about the gardens rather than the house. Thinks more about plants than people."

Did she know about her own connection to Greysbridge? I wondered. Did Rudy? Had Burrows told them what he'd discovered?

"Try some of the apricot jam," she said, sliding a jar towards me. "It's Belva's. I give her all my fruit, and she gives me back jam and chutney and all sorts of lovely things in return."

"Thanks. Have you ever been to Greysbridge?" I asked as I spread some butter on my toast.

She shook her head. "No, I'm not so bad as my mother, but I'm perfectly content where I am now. Those big houses have no interest for me. I listen to Rudy when he talks about his job, of course, but I hope that someday he'll come back here for good. I've often thought that maybe he and Audrey might . . ." She grinned mischievously, then sighed. "If only she'd lose a bit of weight."

She didn't know, I thought. Maybe it was just as well. The door opened, and Molloy came in.

"Morning, Sergeant," Mrs. Brady trilled. "Full Irish and a nice pot of tea?"

Molloy joined me at the table. "That would be lovely, thank you."

"I'll bring you your own pot," she said, nodding towards mine, which was nearly finished despite my having not yet eaten anything.

As the door closed behind her, my phone buzzed and I took it out of my pocket. Harry. He'd finally responded to my text. But it was a formal one: he had an appointment for an ENT and wanted me to call in.

Molloy glanced at my phone but didn't comment. "Sleep all right?"

"Like a log. You?" I asked, although the answer was pretty obvious. He had dark shadows under his eyes.

"I've slept better," he admitted. "Are you willing to share your tea? I'll give you some of mine when it arrives."

"Go on then, there might be a drop left in it."

He glanced out of the window as he poured, squeezing half a cup from the pot. "We should be able to get the morning ferry, with a bit of luck. Did you ask our landlady if it's sailing?"

"Not yet."

"I can't see why it wouldn't." He paused. "Would you like to come to Greysbridge with me, by the way? I'm going to call in on my way back to Letterkenny. Jay's parents are still there."

I was surprised. "Yes, I would, thank you."

"Good. There's a possibility you may notice something that I don't, since you were there all last weekend. Or it might trigger something you've forgotten." He took a sip of his tea, his eyes still on my face. "Plus, it means I can keep an eye on you. If I don't bring you with me, I have a feeling you might sneak up there by yourself."

It was then that I wondered if he wanted me there in an official capacity, as the Greys' solicitor.

★ ★ ★

The ferry was running at ten o'clock. Once we'd eaten, we paid Mrs. Brady and made our way down to the pier. My jacket had thankfully dried out; I'd hung it on the radiator after Audrey and I had swapped back in the car. I put my hand in the pocket and felt the Kit Kat wrapping and stone I'd picked up when we'd been searching for the teenagers. I glanced around for a bin but there was none. I'd have to wait till we got back to the mainland.

With the windless sky you'd never have known there'd been a storm the day before. But the aftermath could be seen on the pier. It was a mess, with fish crates and pallets strewn about and seaweed and driftwood washed up on the shore. But it was a relief to see the water calm again, the sea's fury abated.

As we crossed the road at the bottom of the hill, we were nearly run over by Fridge's jalopy heading for the pier, exhaust fumes belching out the back.

"Jesus Christ!" Molloy exclaimed, stepping back suddenly. "I'm sorely tempted to ask that man for his tax and insurance."

"You're not serious, are you? You know he won't have any."

Molloy sighed. "No, I'm not serious. What would be the point? He'd only get it up and running again as soon as I was out

of sight." He shook his head. "That's the problem with islands.
They're impossible to fully police."

I grinned, nodding towards where Fridge had pulled in. "It
looks as if we'll have company on the boat."

We watched as Ronan and Cara and the other two young
people clambered out of Fridge's car, dragging their bags behind
them. Finn and Niamh looked quiet and pale, and Finn's rucksack was open at the back until Cara pointed it out to him and
he zipped it back up. Things seemed better between Ronan and
Cara—he helped her lift her bag onto her shoulders—but there
was no communication between him and Fridge. That bromance
was over.

We crossed the road to the pier as the car turned and came back
in our direction. Fridge rolled down the window as he passed.
"Safe home now, the two of you. Don't forget to come back and
see us sometime, will you?"

Before we could even respond, he sped off.

"Ever get the feeling that someone is glad to see the back of
you?" I asked.

"All the time," Molloy said with a half-smile. "Anyway, let's
get going. We don't want to miss this ferry."

It was cooler than it had been; the storm had finally broken the
unnaturally warm weather. As we made our way onto the pier,
I spotted two glistening charcoal heads in the water. I nudged
Molloy and he smiled. "Seals."

"You can see why they want to keep it for themselves can't
you?" I said. "This morning, anyway."

Molloy nodded. He put his hand up to shield his eyes from the
sun, gazing at the horizon. Land was visible far in the distance.

"What do you think that is?"

I looked, tried to work out the geography in my head. "I suppose it must be Portrush, in Antrim. And over there, Scotland."

Molloy frowned. "So they'd have a pretty clear run to the north and south from here. Access to both borders by sea." He was speaking almost under his breath.

I looked at him curiously. "I suppose so. Why?"

An engine started to rumble and we looked towards the ferry. It was ready to depart.

"We'd better get a move on," Molloy said.

When we made our way up the gangplank, the other four were already on board and had taken seats inside.

The captain greeted me with a grin. "So how did you get on with Mrs. Brady?"

"Great," I said.

"Good job the son wasn't there, with that storm." He winked. "He's a wild strange one, that boy. He'd have been howling at the moon, most like."

★ ★ ★

The ferry set off, the seagulls swooping and diving and screeching above us. I took one last look at the island as we departed, wondering if I would ever be back, suspecting I wouldn't. I'd got the definite impression these islanders didn't welcome visitors.

I left Molloy on deck to make phone calls and made my way inside to Leah's sister and her companions. They'd made a little fort with their bags and were slumped in their seats. Ronan looked hung-over, arms crossed, almost folded in on himself. He avoided catching my eye. I knew Molloy wanted to speak to him further but was happy to leave it till the mainland, so I left him alone too. Instead, I sat beside Cara a few seats away. She looked up with a smile.

"All ready to get back to some kind of normality?" I asked.

She nodded. "We're going to see Harry when we get back. Finn's mother is meeting us in Glendara. Although they're both much better."

I looked over at them. Niamh and Finn were sitting together but not speaking. Although Finn was no longer coughing, they both looked exhausted and grubby. Niamh had a purple stain on her jeans.

"How are you getting there?" I asked.

"We weren't sure what time the ferry would leave, so I have to ring Dad when we arrive. Not looking forward to that, to be honest." Her jaw tightened.

"Do you want a lift?" I asked on impulse. It seemed the least I could do for Leah was give her two sisters a lift back. I hadn't been much help otherwise.

The tension in Cara's face eased. "Oh, that would be great. It'll save Dad from coming up. We've had to make up a story about these two, so it would help if we could go to Harry first and meet Dad in Glendara. I don't want to worry him."

I wanted to speak to Harry too before I mentioned him to Molloy. We might not have a great future ahead of us, Harry and me, but at least I owed him that.

When I went back out on deck, Molloy was still on the phone. His brow was furrowed and he was writing something in his notebook, struggling a little in the wind. I waited for him to finish, and when he did, I told him that I was going to Glendara first but would return to Greysbridge.

He gave me an odd look but agreed to meet me later. He had something to do himself, he said, before he went to Greysbridge. Something he needed to check out.

Chapter Thirty

At Malin Head, Molloy and I both offered Ronan a lift, but he insisted he wasn't going back to Greysbridge. When Molloy asked where he was going, he said he hadn't yet decided. After Fridge's remarks, I was surprised his mother wasn't on the pier to collect him.

I looked at his pale, tired face, his bag at his feet, and my heart went out to him. I'd have thought there was nothing either of us could do to force the issue, that we'd have no choice but to leave him alone on the pier, but Molloy said something to him quietly that seemed to change his mind, and I was surprised to see Ronan accompany him up the road and climb obediently into his car. I wondered where Molloy was taking him.

The Mini was a bit of a squash with Cara, Niamh, Finn and all their bags. But I was glad to see it had survived despite being left to the mercy of the elements. The storm had hit the mainland too; there were branches strewn across the road as I drove back down to Glendara. The day was bright and cool, a far more typical Donegal summer's day.

Cara chatted the whole way, but the teenagers were quiet: at one stage I thought they had both fallen asleep, but when I checked in the mirror, they were staring morosely out of separate windows.

★   ★   ★

I dropped all three at the surgery on my way through town and parked in the county council car park, deciding to kill some time with a coffee in the Oak before speaking to Harry once they were finished.

When I got out of the car, I reached into the back to take my wallet from my bag and noticed something on the floor below the back seat, on the side where Finn had been sitting. It looked like a small piece of red cardboard, and I leaned in to pick it up. It was a book of matches. It hadn't been there before the teen-agers had been in the car, I was sure of it. It must have fallen out of Finn's rucksack. Or maybe it was in his pocket. Whichever it was, it was further evidence of his magpie habit of picking things up that didn't belong to him. The matches were from a pub in Buncrana called the Drunken Piglet—Finn couldn't have bought them himself.

It wasn't the first time I'd come across that pub in the last couple of weeks. It was mentioned on a charge sheet I had in the office as the location of that assault listed for court tomorrow. So where had Finn got the matches? Ronan Grey? No, he'd had a lighter. I remembered him buying one at the shop on the island. Although maybe he'd had to buy a lighter because Finn had taken his matches. Rudy? He was a smoker. Fridge? He'd had an unlit cigarette in his hand when we'd met first him, in the doorway at Greysbridge. But then he rarely left the island.

I slipped the matches into my wallet and walked out of the car park. There was a definite cooling in the air, a return to more normal temperatures and a breeze, as I made my way to the square and headed straight for the Oak. On the way, I met my old buddy from the doctor's surgery, dressed in his winter coat.

"Afternoon, Jim. How are you doing?"

"Foundered I am," he shivered. "That's a lazy wind, that is. It won't go around you; it'll go through you." He grinned, pleased with his own joke.

Despite Jim's complaints about the cold, I sat outside the pub; there wouldn't be many more opportunities, I suspected. I finished my coffee far too quickly and was trying to work out whether to go into the office for a while, when Phyllis appeared, blustering up the street, looking agitated. Her eyes widened when she saw me.

"Ach, I'm so glad you're here. There's something I want to talk to you about." She beckoned. "Come down to the shop with me."

I stood up. "Okay."

Phyllis took me by the arm, linking mine to hers as we walked down the street to her shop. She unlocked the door, and the bell tinkled when she pushed it open. She must be seriously troubled about something to close up, I thought; she was too much of a businesswoman.

As usual, books were piled on the floor and in boxes, awaiting unpacking. Phyllis's dog Fred came down the staircase from the flat above, yawning widely. He padded over to Phyllis and nuzzled her. She rubbed his head distractedly while I shut the door behind me.

"Go on. I'm listening," I said.

Phyllis took a deep breath. "Well, I don't know if this means anything, but I've just found out that that young lad Jay was coming here to Glendara. I was going to ring you."

My stomach flipped. Harry. He must have been coming to see Harry. This was exactly what I'd been afraid of. "How do you know?"

"He was booked to stay with Mary; you know, the wee woman that runs the guest house. She told me on Sunday evening that one of her guests hadn't turned up. No phone call or anything. She was annoyed because she could have rented that room out five times over at this time of year. But when she saw the paper on Monday, she realized what had happened. She's in shock. Her guest didn't turn up because he was dead."

Harry's surgery was visible through the bookshop window. I sank down onto a stool by a display of crime novels. Harry had had Jay's number. It had to be him that Jay was coming to see. That was why Jay had decided to stay longer at Greysbridge; somehow, he'd discovered that Harry would be coming to the wedding. Suddenly I changed my mind about tackling Harry on my own.

"I'll ring Molloy and tell him."

"Good idea," Phyllis said quietly as she played with Fred's silky ears.

I stood to dial his number. Luckily, I got him. It sounded as if he was beside the sea; I could hear waves crashing in the distance. I told him what Phyllis had said, and he said he would ring the Stevensons at Greysbridge and call me straight back.

As we waited, Phyllis looked at me and I looked at her and eventually she took off up the stairs to make a pot of tea, a blend of Earl Grey and Barry's, her solution to all ills.

While she was gone, Molloy rang back.

"Okay," he said. "I told them that we'd received some information about where their son was intending to travel once he'd left Greysbridge . . ."

"And?"

"They'd never heard of Glendara before they saw a signpost for it on their way from the airport. Jay certainly didn't mention it."

"Oh." I sank onto the stool behind me. "Did you ask them if they knew of anyone their son wanted to see in Donegal? About the possibility of it being connected with what happened when he was a boy?" I knew I was making considerable leaps, but I couldn't help it.

Molloy's voice was calm. "His mother confirmed again that Jay's friend had died when he was a child, about ten years ago, and that was why he had never learned to swim. She said it was an accident but that there was a doctor there who had tried to save his friend. She said something about the child dying hours later—I'm not really sure what she meant. It sounded as if there was something a little odd about it."

He had me at the word doctor. There it was, the connection with Harry. My stomach had fallen through the floor. "Doctor?" I repeated.

"Yes, a trainee doctor. I asked if they could remember his name, but they couldn't. He left the area soon after. He was Canadian."

"Shit."

"What are you thinking?" Molloy asked.

"Jay came up to speak to Harry at the wedding. It looked as if they knew each other, but Harry denied it," I said quietly.

There was a pause. It was the first time either of us had mentioned Harry by name since the immediate aftermath of the deaths. "You think he could be the person Jay was after?"

"Maybe. I'm wondering if he was the doctor who failed to save Jay's friend. If Jay was able to track him down from some international doctors' register or something." I paused. "If maybe he held a grudge against him."

"He'd get him on Google if he needed to," Molloy said. "Although it's a long time to hold a grudge. On the other hand, it's quite the coincidence. Another drowning. If this Harry was the doctor involved in the original one . . ."

"What if Jay was going to reveal something?" I couldn't bring myself to say it. *What if Harry had failed to save him on purpose?*

Molloy was silent, thinking.

"Harry sent me a text this morning," I said. "He's made an appointment for me with an ENT in Letterkenny."

"What's that about? Are you sick?" Molloy sounded concerned. In the midst of all of this, it gave me a pang.

"Oh, it's nothing. But it does mean I could go and see him now. I'm in Phyllis's, just across the road. Cara and the kids are still with him."

Molloy snapped, "Oh, for God's sake, Ben. Who do you think you are? Don't speak to him until I get there. I'm serious."

"Well?" Phyllis asked as I hung up, her eyes wide with curiosity.

★　★　★

I hadn't intended ignoring Molloy's request, but when I looked out of the window again, Harry was emerging from his surgery. He crossed the road, heading for the Oak.

"I'll see you later, Phyllis," I said as I bounded out the door.

Harry looked up. "Back from your travels? How was the island?"

"Interesting."

He smiled. "I'll bet. Well, you tracked down Niamh and her friend. I suppose that's the main thing."

"Yes. All home safely. How are they?"

He nodded. "Good. Whoever took care of them knew what they were doing. Someone gave Finn an inhaler and some anti-inflammatory eye drops—just what I would have done in the circumstances. He was exposed to something nasty, but he's on the mend." He shook his head. "Strange kid."

"That's good." I paused. "I got your text, by the way."

"Oh yes, your ENT appointment." He scratched his forehead. "Did I give you the date?"

"No. You said to give you a shout."

"Have you time now? Come over with me to the surgery and I'll give it to you."

★ ★ ★

Harry's surgery was closed for lunch. As he turned his key in the door, I had a sudden flash of doubt. What if he *was* the person Jay had been after? Liam had felt there was something strange about Jay's death—what if Harry had been the problem and not the islanders?

Questions zipped through my mind while Harry flicked on a light and made his way over to the reception desk. He took a seat at the computer and switched it on, tapping at a few keys until he found what he was looking for. I hovered close to the door, my throat feeling dry, wishing I had followed Molloy's instructions.

"The first of December, ten a.m.," he said, looking up. "A fair while away, unfortunately."

"I suppose it's good if they don't think it's urgent."

"I think it's more to do with a lack of resources, to be honest," he said wryly. "Too many patients, too few consultants. Do you want me to write it down for you?"

I shook my head. "I'll remember." I paused, my hand on the door handle; swallowed. "I'm sure things are a lot better in Canada."

He nodded. "They are." He turned off the computer and stood up, hands in his pockets. "Are you free for lunch? Sandwich in the

Oak?" He smiled. "Unfortunately, I don't have time for anything more adventurous."

I licked my lips, my mouth dry too. "Did you train over there? In Canada?"

He shook his head, surprised. "I trained in the States, as a matter of fact."

I heard my breath catch. "Where?"

He took a step towards me, palms outstretched. "Why all the questions, Ben?"

I steeled myself, tried to steady my voice. "You knew Jay Stevenson, didn't you? Before the wedding, I mean. Even though you told me you didn't."

A flicker of panic crossed his face, but he shook his head. "No, I told you—"

I cut across him. "I found his number in the boot of your car, when I went to get your doctor's bag. To help you save him."

Harry paled and sank back against the wall.

"Was that what you were trying to do? Save him?" Then, quieter because I didn't want to utter the words out loud, "Or were you only pretending to?"

He flinched. "I should have said something."

I swallowed. I'd wanted to be wrong. "Why didn't you?"

He took a deep breath. "I received an email from Jay a few weeks ago saying that he wanted to meet. He said he was studying medicine and wanted the chance to talk to a GP in a small town. We were supposed to meet this week."

"So, it wasn't fully a lie what you told me then?"

Harry looked down at his feet, shaking his head in disbelief. "The name seemed familiar, but I didn't pay much attention at first—I thought I'd deal with it when I got back from the wedding." He detached himself from the wall and walked over to the desk again, sinking into the seat. "Then I got another email telling me where he was staying and the real reason he wanted to see me."

"And did you? See him?"

Harry sighed. "No. I didn't want him coming here to the surgery, so I arranged to meet him at the wedding. It was sheer coincidence he was staying in Greysbridge."

"Why did he want to see you?"

A pause, while I waited for an answer. Nothing. Harry scratched at the indentations in the desk.

I closed my eyes. "According to his parents, Jay lost a friend in a drowning accident when he was a child. It was the reason he never learned how to swim. Apparently, there was a trainee doctor on the scene." I opened them again. "Was that you?"

Harry looked up, his face drawn with guilt and regret. He nodded. "Yes. It was about ten years ago, in Oregon, where I did my training. I came across two boys at a river, in the Cascades. They'd been swinging on a tire. One of them was in the water, in trouble. I pulled him out, resuscitated him, and he seemed okay. The two of them went home."

I was confused. "So what went wrong?"

His eyes glistened. "He died later that night. It's called secondary drowning, or delayed drowning. Water gets into the lungs and builds up over time, causing difficulty in breathing. I made a huge mistake in not sending him to hospital. I should have known. I heard what happened, but the boys didn't know my name, or who I was, so I returned to Canada with no comeback." His voice was hollow. "I saved that little boy and then sent him home to die. And got away with it."

I took a deep breath. "So how did Jay find you?"

"I gave a lecture at a medical conference in Canada about a year ago and Jay came across my picture online. He looked me up and found out where I was, where I was practicing."

He put his hand through his hair. "I've never forgotten what happened and I've never forgiven myself for it. So when Jay told me he was the other boy on the riverbank, I thought he blamed me. I was terrified. I didn't know what he intended to do."

"Was that why he came looking for you? Some kind of revenge?"

Harry shook his head. "That's what I thought at first. I thought that now that he had some medical training, he knew the error I'd made." He smiled sadly. "But I was wrong. We had a chance to speak when he came over to me at the wedding. It was he who felt guilty. He'd felt guilty all his life. He'd teased his friend into jumping into the river, though neither of them could swim. He wasn't sure if he would make a good doctor. He thought talking to me would help."

He put his head in his hands, his voice wretched. "And then I couldn't save him either—it was horrible."

I pictured his desperation in trying to resuscitate Jay, his frantic and hopeless forty minutes of CPR. And I believed him. But I had one more question.

"Why didn't you tell the guards that you knew him?"

His voice finally broke. "Because I was ashamed. I'd failed to save either of those two boys. What kind of a doctor does that make me?"

Chapter Thirty-One

THERE WERE FIVE missed calls from Molloy when I left Harry's surgery. Plus one text message saying that something had come up, that he wouldn't be in Glendara for an hour, and warning me not to speak to the doctor in the meantime, under any circumstances.

I rang him back and left a message. He returned the call within seconds and I filled him in. He wasn't happy. He asked me if I believed Harry's story, and after a slight hesitation, I said I did. I wasn't sure how much weight he would give my opinion, especially of a man he knew I'd been seeing. But in truth, he seemed distracted by something else. He still sounded as if he was at the coast. I wondered if Ronan Grey was with him.

"He should have been straight with us from the beginning," he said finally. "I'll send someone to take a statement from him."

"Do you still want me to come to Greysbridge?" I asked hesitantly.

Molloy was clipped. "The Greys are your clients, aren't they? I think you'd better."

★ ★ ★

I drove up the coast wondering what he meant. Molloy knew
more than I did, that was becoming clear—as of course he should.
I suspected I was only seeing part of the picture, and had been for
some time. The calls he'd been taking, his search of the trawler
on Inishathair late at night; I couldn't but think there was some
connection between the case he'd been working on—the reason he'd been sent abroad—and what had been happening here.
There was an iceberg feel about this whole thing, and I could
only see the tip.

When I reached Greysbridge, Molloy was turning into the
avenue ahead of me. He saw me in his rear-view mirror and
waved. There was a figure beside him in the passenger seat:
Ronan Grey.

As soon as I rounded the house, I could tell there was something wrong. It was impossible to miss. It looked as if one wall
had collapsed. It was only when I stopped the car and climbed out
that I realized that it was the footbridge that was missing. It had
been tumbled completely, along with the strange octagonal room
with which it connected. There was nothing left but a pile of
rubble and broken glass, and a huge hole in the wall of the main
house. And some pretty wrecked-looking rhododendron bushes.

A bulldozer was parked in front. There was dust in the air,
and I coughed. Whatever had happened, it was recent. A voice
penetrated my consciousness and I looked around to see Ian Grey
on the steps of the house, roaring at someone, his body rigid with
rage. I had never seen him lose his temper before.

"What the hell are you doing, you bloody lunatic?"

It was only then that I saw Rudy the gardener standing half
hidden by the door of the bulldozer, hand resting on the handle
as if he had just climbed out of the cab. He took a box of cigarettes from his shirt pocket, lit one, and casually flicked the match

onto the ground. "You said you wanted rid of it. I'm doing you a favor."

"I wanted it done by a professional. Someone with a qualification. Not a fucking fruitcake gardener with a grudge." Ian was apoplectic, his eyes flashing, spit appearing on his lower lip.

Rudy smiled, an odd, distant kind of smile.

Molloy was ahead of me, having climbed out of his car at the same time as I had, and he stepped in. From the corner of my eye, I saw Ronan get out of the passenger seat and walk off in the other direction, head bowed. Disassociating himself from the whole thing.

"What's going on?" Molloy demanded.

Ian waved at the gardener. "This nutcase is knocking down my house."

"I'm not knocking down his house," Rudy said calmly. "I'm removing a part of the house that is an eyesore, that was added some time after the original structure and is completely at odds with the character of the rest of the building."

"Who told you that?" Grey demanded.

"Our late guest, Michael Burrows," Rudy said. He took a drag of his cigarette and exhaled luxuriously. "And do you know what else he told me? That you and I are cousins. What do you think of that?"

"You're drunk—either that or you've been smoking some of your own weed again," Ian spat before storming back into the house.

Molloy managed to drag Rudy away from the bulldozer and talk to him quietly while I followed Ian Grey inside. As I walked through the reception hall, a couple emerged from the bar looking dazed, clearly wondering what the commotion was. The man looked startlingly like an older Jay Stevenson.

On seeing them, Ian seemed to pull himself together. "I'm so sorry about the noise," he said. "We're having a bit of difficulty with one of our employees. But the guards are here now, so there's nothing to worry about."

I raised my eyebrows but said nothing. He made it sound as if he had called Molloy himself. But the couple returned to the bar without a word, while Ian slumped into the seat at reception, head in his hands.

"Why the hell did I ever buy this place? I should have had my head examined. Those islanders were right. It's bloody well jinxed."

I perched on the desk beside him. "Is that what they said?"

He nodded. "I mean, they're all bloody nuts, but in this instance, they're right. I'm going to sell it as soon as I can. Assuming anyone will buy it." He looked up. "You'll act for me again, won't you?"

"Of course," I replied. I realized I hadn't told him about the letter from the bank and I did so now. He wasn't surprised and he didn't seem to care particularly; he'd received something similar, he said. It was as if this last encounter with Rudy had sapped all his remaining energy. I felt sorry for him. "But you've put so much work into it. Are you sure you want to give up?"

Grey narrowed his eyes in disbelief. "You can't be serious? Two murders, a hatchet job of an article in the local newspaper, Ronan gone missing, and now half the house is knocked down by some maniac who's supposed to work for me . . ."

I nodded. "Fair enough. Maybe selling it is the right thing to do. Although Ronan is outside."

He glared at me. "What?"

"He was on the island—he came back with Sergeant Molloy just now. Why did you think he'd gone missing?"

Ian waved his hand dismissively. "Just something Abby said. Never mind. She panics." He stood up, running his hand through his hair. "I should go out and talk to him."

I put my hand on his arm. "Before you go, I want to tell you a couple of things. Firstly, Rudy was right about one thing. He *is* related to you."

He blinked. "What?"

"It looks as if Louisa Grey had a baby. That baby ended up on Inishathair and was brought up there—she was Rudy's grandmother."

He looked at me in surprise. "Rudy's from Inishathair?"

"Didn't you know?" The fact that he was more startled by Rudy's islander status than Louisa Grey's baby took me by surprise, considering his earlier denials that he knew anything.

He shook his head, his hands splayed on the desk. "I never asked. I just assumed he was from around here." He looked at me defensively. "I never interviewed him, remember—he came with the house."

Grey spoke about Rudy as if he was a piece of furniture. I realized he'd done that before, but I hadn't picked up on it.

"So you *did* know that Louisa Grey had a baby?"

He nodded. "Burrows told me. He turned out to be a right little ferret. I suspect he told that gombeen gardener as well. He certainly wouldn't have had the brains to work it out for himself."

So, Grey knew more than he'd admitted to, I thought. What else had he lied about?

He slumped back down on the seat. "Burrows convinced me he'd be making a film about the whole story, said his son would have the clout to do it. That there's all sorts of finance available for films made in this part of the world, rural development grants and that kind of thing. So I thought, great, a bit of publicity for the place. Finally, we might actually be able to get off our knees."

I paused. "So did Michael Burrows think Linus Grey was responsible for his daughter's death? Was that part of the story?"

Grey shrugged. "If that was the story he wanted to peddle, it was no skin off my nose. True or not, it would have made a great film. It could have been the making of us—especially with the ghost story. We sure as hell needed it." He clutched his stomach.

"Are you all right?"

"Bloody ulcer getting worse." He winced as he stood up again. "Look, I'd better find Ronan. He needs to speak to the Stevensons. He's not getting out of all his duties. Life's not that easy."

I stood aside to let him past and he set off towards the main door. Before he reached it, his footsteps slowed and he stopped. He turned around; his eyes narrowed.

"I hope that gardener isn't looking for some kind of inheritance. Because I think he'll find he's a couple of generations too late. I had to pay through the nose to get this place back in Grey hands."

"No. He was here before you, remember? I don't think he knew the connection himself until Michael Burrows told him."

Grey shook his head. "Michael bloody Burrows. Seems to have been incapable of keeping his mouth shut, that man. Abby said he was all talk, that there would never be a film. But he went on and on about his son, what his son had done, how this was just the type of story he'd be interested in. How it would put Greysbridge on the map. And I was so bloody stupid, I believed him. Made a right fool of myself."

"What do you mean?"

Suddenly I remembered the flecks of blue paint on his shirt that Abby had flicked off the night of the barbecue. And the peeling blue paint on the interior of the footbridge. Had it been Ian Grey on the bridge? In my room? But he just shrugged. I wanted to shake him. For some reason I wanted him to take Louisa Grey's story seriously.

"Do *you* believe that Linus Grey had something to do with his daughter's death?"

He laughed derisively. "Women died in childbirth all the time back then. The rumor was that the gardener was the father of her baby, did you know that? He was from the island, so if that's where she ended up, then she was brought up by her own father. Everything worked out for the best."

I said nothing. No mention of the fact that his own ancestor had rejected the baby, tried to kill her. I watched him leave, and with him my theory that the Greys would not want their sordid family history exposed. Ian Grey couldn't care less as long as he could make some money from it.

Chapter Thirty-Two

I STOOD THERE, in that huge reception hall, feeling defeated and disappointed. Grey's comfortable denial of any family wrongdoing irritated me. He wasn't responsible for the actions of his great-grandfather, but his ability to wash his hands was hard to stomach. When I'd acted for Ian and Abby in buying Greysbridge, they'd had a clear idea of what they wanted. They'd acknowledged that they needed to make a living out of the place, but for them it wasn't about money; it was about bringing the old house back to life.

But clearly things had changed. I looked around me at the dusty chandelier, the grand staircase and the strange sculptures, and I wondered if this house had just eaten away at them and made them desperate.

I decided to track Molloy down and tell him what I knew. When I made my way down the steps, I saw that a Garda car had arrived and Rudy was sitting in the back, staring straight ahead, a stormy expression on his face. Molloy was talking to a guard standing by the driver's door.

I raised my eyebrows as I approached.

"Criminal damage," he said before I had a chance to say anything. "I had no choice. He said that if I didn't arrest him, he would just finish the job. How's his employer? Any calmer?"

The other guard nodded to Molloy, climbed into the driver's seat and started the engine.

"A bit, I think." We watched the squad car disappear around the gable of the house. "Have you figured out how much Rudy knew?"

Molloy crossed his arms. "He found out about his family history from Michael Burrows. If his mother knew, she certainly never told him—probably the wisest course of action considering what's just happened. He wouldn't be the most stable of individuals, that man."

I glanced at the pile of rubble he'd left behind and tended to agree with Molloy. "You don't suspect he was involved in either of the deaths, do you?"

Molloy sighed. "At the moment, I suspect a lot but have proof of very little." He paused. "Did you notice any activity at night while you were staying here, by the way? Apart from what you've told me."

I looked at him curiously. "You mean inside the house or out?"

"Outside."

I thought for a second and then remembered the lorry I'd heard during the night before the wedding. I told him, and he nodded, almost as if he'd expected it.

"Hang on," I said, putting my hand up. "There's a connection, isn't there? Between what's happening here and whatever it is you were investigating. That's the reason you came back. You said you were following a trail when you went abroad. But that's what you're doing here too, isn't it? Following a trail."

Molloy didn't respond. He watched me as if waiting for me to say something more. To guess something.

"Where did you take Ronan?" I asked.

Molloy took a long breath. "I wanted to show him something; I wanted him to see the damage that certain activities can cause."

"What kind of activities?" I demanded.

Molloy looked at me. "I think your clients have been allowing their property to be used for something. I'm giving them an opportunity to admit it."

"What do you mean?"

Molloy looked towards the shore. "Their pier. They may claim it was being done without their consent, but I suspect they were aware of it. They may have thought it was an easy way to make money, but these are people you don't want to get involved with."

"Jesus, Molloy," I said, frustrated. "Are we playing some kind of guessing game?"

"I can't tell you anything more yet. Just speak to them."

"All right." I looked around me. "Where's Ronan?"

"Hijacked by his mother." Molloy gestured towards the center of the lawn, where Abby had Ronan by the arm—she looked as if she was pleading with him. As I watched, Ian appeared, striding towards them.

"Did you speak to him?" I asked. "Find out whatever you think he's hiding?"

"Not completely. Ronan *thinks* he knows something. Which is not the same thing as knowing. But if one of them doesn't speak to me soon . . ."

I looked over to where the three of them were now in a huddle. "May I?"

He nodded. "Knock yourself out."

I could tell they were arguing long before I reached them. Ronan was looking down, shaking his head, while Abby was still pleading with him. Ian was shouting at both of them or the world in general, the dying embers of his earlier fury easily stoked. All three looked up at my approach, the antithesis of a happy family. Abby, in particular, looked terrible, dark patches under her eyes making it appear as if she hadn't slept in a week.

"Anything I can do?" I asked, palms outstretched.

Abby swallowed. "I'm going to tell her," she said to the other two.

"Are you crazy?" Ian blustered. "You might as well tell the guards. She won't be able to represent you if you admit it, you know that."

"I don't care anymore," Abby said, her voice hollow. "What have we got to lose? We've no business left, despite your crazy ideas." She waved dismissively at Ian. "Our son hates us. What else is there?"

Ian and Ronan were both silent. Neither appeared to offer any further objection. I looked at Abby expectantly and she looked down. When she finally spoke, it all came out in a rush.

"I pushed Jay in. I pushed him as I was going past with a tray of drinks and I didn't look back. It wasn't an accident. I did it on purpose, but I didn't mean to kill him. I thought he'd just climb out. I didn't know he couldn't swim."

There was quiet for a moment, nothing but the sound of the seagulls on the pier.

"It's true," Ronan said quietly, looking away.

"Did you see her do it?" I asked him.

"No. I was told."

"By whom?" I asked, but he didn't respond, just looked down. "Did you know this?" I asked Ian.

He shook his head, his anger finally abated, leaving him slackened and exhausted. "I've only just heard."

"Why didn't you say so sooner?" I asked, glancing from Ronan to Abby. "Either of you?"

Abby's voice broke. "If I'd known that Ronan knew, if I'd known he was trying to protect me, I would have."

"But why did you do it at all?" I asked, although I already knew the answer.

"I knew Ronan was planning on leaving with Jay and I was afraid he wouldn't come back. Jay told me when he came to help at the stables that morning. He'd told Ronan no, first of all, but he said he'd changed his mind and was going to ask him to come." Her eyes welled, and she rubbed at them with her sleeve. "I was jealous and angry. It was pure unadulterated malice and I'm horrified with myself. But at that very moment I hated that boy, and I wasn't thinking straight. I didn't want to kill him. I just pushed him on impulse."

She shot her son an imploring look, but he avoided her gaze.

★   ★   ★

Molloy watched with me as the second Garda car pulled away. It was half an hour later and we were back on the steps of the house. The entire Grey family were on their way to be interviewed at Letterkenny Garda Station. I had offered to go with them, but they declined and called another solicitor. It was probably just as well. I couldn't represent them any longer. I knew too much. There would be a clear conflict.

"God, I'm gathering them up rightly this afternoon." He sighed. "Although I suspect I'm just cutting the heads off the Hydra. Chop one off and two more will grow back."

I raised my eyebrows. "At least we know what Ronan was hiding. He was protecting his mother."

"I don't think that's all of it," Molloy said. "He didn't see his mother push Jay. So how did he know she had?" He paused. "You didn't mention the pier?"

I shook my head. "Not once I realized I couldn't represent them."

Molloy looked at me, frustrated.

"What are you thinking?" I asked. "Blackmail? Is someone blackmailing them? Is that what you meant about them allowing their property to be used for something illegal?"

Before he could respond, or rather before he could avoid responding, a guard emerged from the house. It was one of the pair who had been there the first night, Boyle or Clarke, I wasn't sure which. He nodded to me and I gave him a smile.

"Finished?" Molloy asked him.

He nodded, patting his breast pocket. "I've put up a barrier where the gap in the wall is and I've taken some pictures. There's a builder coming later to make it safe. The Stevensons are about to leave. Boyle will lock up after them and bring the keys to the station."

"Good man. Right," Molloy said, turning to me, "we're off. If I don't speak to you beforehand, I'll see you tomorrow."

I raised my eyebrows. "Tomorrow?"

"I've been assigned court duties in Glendara. I'm doing the remand of your assault client. Rudy's going to be brought to court in the morning too, so I've been asked to do the two."

"Oh, right." I had completely forgotten I was due in court in the morning.

Molloy opened the door of his car. "In the meantime, let's see what the Grey family have to tell us."

★   ★   ★

Before I got to my own car, my phone rang, and I answered it. It was Kate Burrows. She and her sons were returning to England earlier than expected and she wanted to arrange to take back her husband's papers if I'd finished with them. I agreed to meet her in Glendara the following morning before court, thinking I could have one last look before then.

I was about to hang up when I had a sudden thought, triggered by Molloy's mention of blackmail.

"Do you mind me asking you something?" I said hesitantly, as I walked the last few steps across the gravel to the Mini. "You mentioned that Ian Grey was anxious for you to stay and was quite pushy about the film that Michael wanted to have made?"

"Yes, that's true."

"But his wife was less so?"

"Yes, that's also true." She paused. "Even though he wasn't keen while Michael was alive, on the plane over to Belfast Don said he might go ahead and make the film in memory of his father." She took a breath as though getting it straight in her head. "It was the day after Michael had died and I think it was grief and guilt talking, to be honest. Certainly not the time to be making decisions. But when he mentioned it to Ian, Abby said no, put her foot down completely, said that she couldn't allow the house to be used."

"Really?" I said, remembering Abby rushing past me to join Ian and the Burrowses in the bar.

"Yes. It was a bit of a surprise, to say the least. From what Michael had said when he was trying to get Don on board, both Greys were well up for it. But she obviously changed her mind."

"I expect Ian wasn't too pleased about that," I said.

There was a smile in her voice. "No, he wasn't; in fact, I think he was furious. But I was relieved, and I think Don was too. It put the kibosh on it. He couldn't make the film without the house, so that was the end of it."

I hung up the phone, leaned on the roof of the Mini and gazed at the house, utterly broken now with half its side bulldozed away. With its grey stone facade dark and still and secretive, its windows shuttered and its door closed, it looked like a Victorian orphanage, a place of sadness and cruelty. I tried to imagine what it must have been like to live here back when Louisa Grey and her family had been here; how lonely and isolated it must have been.

Why would Abby have changed her mind? I wondered. She and Ian still had the same money problems, which a movie about Greysbridge could resolve. Michael's death hadn't changed that; if anything, it had made things worse. Was she being blackmailed? Had someone seen her push Jay in? Someone who did not want Greysbridge being used in a film? Was that why Michael Burrows had been killed? Were we back to the notion of Burrows stepping on toes by digging into the past?

I couldn't help but think that the secret to everything that had happened was here, at this strange house. I knew I should go back to Glendara, but the opportunity to have a look around the house and gardens again now that it was almost deserted seemed too good to pass up. Was there some secret Greysbridge would finally give up if I looked hard enough?

Chapter Thirty-Three

I LOCKED THE car and set off to walk along the path that Maeve and I had taken that first night. A leaf fluttered down from above. With the drop in temperature, it was beginning to feel very much like autumn. It was hard to believe that two men had died here in sweltering summer temperatures only the weekend before.

I followed the route we had taken that night, passing the gate of the old walled garden. The padlock was gone, so this time I pushed the gate open and went inside. I made my way over to the greenhouse and opened the door, heat hitting me like a blast, emphasizing the now cooler weather outside.

Stepping inside, it was the scent that was overpowering, sweet and pungent. There were fruit trees of all sorts—plums, apples, pears—and rows of strawberry plants and raspberry bushes. Being August, some fruits were just ripening, not yet ready for picking. But one shrub in particular caught my eye: a small tree with a dense spreading canopy of dark green leaves, branches laden down with small orange fruit. It was an apricot tree, bearing hundreds and hundreds of apricots.

A notion flashed across my brain, and feeling in my pocket, I touched the chocolate wrapper and the fruit stone I'd found in Fridge's shed. I took it out, the stone I'd thought was a peach pit. But I realized now it was too small. I held it, my fingers running along the tiny ridges. It was an apricot stone. Molloy had mentioned apricots, but in what context? And then it came to me like a bolt. Like hydrangea leaves, apricot seeds were a source of cyanide. The hydrangeas had not been a possible culprit for poisoning, requiring too many leaves to do any serious harm. But—and my stomach flipped at the thought—what if apricots were different? What if it was possible to poison someone with cyanide extracted from apricot seeds? I recalled Mrs. Brady's greenhouse on the island, and with a sickening feeling I remembered the old lady pushing a jar towards me at breakfast. A jar of apricot jam, made by Belva.

I leaned my hand against the frame of the greenhouse, thoughts coming thick and fast. Was Rudy the poisoner? Or Mrs. Brady? Or Belva? But why? Why would they do something like that? Why would they kill Michael Burrows?

Then I thought about what Molloy had said, the questions he'd asked, the implication that there was a bigger picture than the one I was seeing. I stood in the greenhouse with the heat and the white light and the sweat trickling down my back and suddenly I felt very claustrophobic.

I heard a click. The door had closed. Panicked, I raced to it, expecting to find it locked. But it wasn't—it moved easily when I pushed it open. It must have been the wind. I kept forgetting we were back to normal Inishowen weather. I heaved a sigh of relief, stepped through the door and closed it behind me, making a beeline for the gate. Then I heard a rustling behind me and my heart skipped again. Someone was following me.

I turned around slowly, taking my courage in both hands, and heaved a huge sigh of relief. It was Sam, Rudy's dog. He gazed up at me with sad eyes. I said his name and he came to me and licked my hand. It must have been Sam who had nudged the door of the greenhouse.

I rubbed his head. "Well, boy, we'd better find someone to feed you while your master is otherwise occupied, hadn't we?"

I made my way back to the house, walking quickly, with the dog trotting along behind me. I wondered if the remaining guard was still here, if he'd keep an eye on Sam for a while. After a slight hesitation—part of me just wanted to get into the Mini and speed away in a cloud of dust—I climbed the steps and tried the front door.

It was unlocked, which was good. It meant that someone must still be here. But the house was silent. I could have shouted, but part of me wanted to have a sneaky look around inside. I wouldn't be long, I decided, and if I was caught, I had my excuse ready. I'd left my car keys behind when I'd been in earlier speaking to Ian.

Something had been bothering me since the island. If the poison, possibly from apricot seeds, had been concealed in a slice of cake as Molloy had suggested, then where had the cake come from? It wasn't the wedding cake—that cake had been intact when Kevin and Leah had cut it; there'd been no cake served the night of the barbecue and no trace in Burrows' room. But since the night of the storm, there was an image I couldn't shake: Ronan, in Belva's house, staring at a plate as if he'd seen a ghost. I made my way now into the back kitchen where I'd found glasses and ice, hoping it would jog something. As I stood looking at the vast array of cups and bowls and plates, finally something clicked.

The plates in here were all white. In fact, every piece of china I'd eaten on here was white. But Belva's plates were pink. That was why Ronan had been staring at it. Ronan *was* the one who'd brought up the cake that had poisoned Michael Burrows. It explained why he'd said, "I killed them both". He didn't say anything initially because he was protecting his parents. But what I had witnessed was the moment when he realized that the plate he'd delivered the cake on had been not one of Greysbridge's but one of Belva's. So why had he continued to say nothing? Was he being blackmailed too?

I hurried out of the room and made my way back out to the hall, nearly jumping out of my skin when I heard a voice, even though it was the very person I was supposed to be looking for.

"Hello! Can I help you?"

It was Boyle.

*   *   *

My head was fried by the time I left the house. Thankfully Boyle turned out to be a dog-lover so was happy to take Sam home with him until his future was determined. I was still trying to work things through in my head when I drove out of the gates. I thought about what I'd discovered and what Molloy had said. What was the connection?

I turned a corner and my heart nearly stopped. Coming towards me, at a frightening speed, was a huge petrol tanker, looming above me like something from a horror film. My mouth was dry. The road was only wide enough for one of us. And it wasn't my little Mini. I stamped on the brake and made for the ditch, twisting the wheel as far as it would go. I managed somehow to get out of the way, my heart beating way faster than it should have been, and the Mini juddered to a halt as the monster drove by, barely acknowledging my presence.

I sat there, bullied into the side of the road in my little car, as my breathing slowly returned to normal. Something wasn't right. Why was there a fuel lorry in this part of the peninsula?

There was no petrol station here. And then I remembered Molloy asking about disturbances outside Greysbridge late at night, and his reaction when I told him about the lorry.

Images crowded my mind: the trawlers on the pier at Greysbridge; the lorry at night; Fridge's huge shed; purple sludge seeping from a tipper truck; Molloy checking out the boats on the island. And things finally started to make sense.

★　★　★

I walked in the door of my cottage, dumped my bag on the mat and went straight to my laptop. Guinness leapt up on the sofa beside me, but kept his distance. Maybe he could smell dog.

I opened Google and did a search on how to extract cyanide from apricot stones. It was a surprisingly simple process. Take a few hundred apricot stones, crack them and extract the kernels, dry them, boil in ethanol, and once it evaporates off, add ether. Dry them off on filter paper and you end up with tiny white crystals—amygdalin. Even though I knew about amygdalin from Molloy, I looked it up and there it was in black and white on Wikipedia. *Eating amygdalin will cause it to release cyanide into the human body and may lead to cyanide poisoning.*

I sat back, Guinness seizing the opportunity to leap onto my knee and sharpen his claws on my jeans. I rubbed his furry head and read through the extraction process again. This time, one word stood out as if in flashing lights. Ether. A further search revealed that ether was used for lubricating old engines, as a starter fluid.

I had seen ether in Fridge's shed. What had he been using it for? Tinkering with engines, or extracting cyanide? Or both.

Chapter Thirty-Four

THE NEXT MORNING I woke with forty questions in my head, the same tumble of questions that had kept me awake till the early hours. Was it Fridge who had poisoned Burrows, and if so, why? Was Burrows' death connected with whatever it was that Molloy was investigating? Was it Fridge who had been blackmailing Abby and Ronan?

Everything I'd discovered confirmed my suspicions, but I still hadn't figured out what it all meant. Given time, I knew I could put it together—but I didn't have time. Not this morning, anyway. I was due in court at nine o'clock. I rolled out of bed feeling groggy, showered and dressed, putting on a suit for the first time in nearly a week.

A full pot of coffee later and I was on my way to Glendara, the papers I needed for court piled up on the passenger seat. We were still in summer vacation, so it wasn't a full sitting of the district court. As with the previous week, it had been scheduled specifically to deal with the criminal matters that had arisen in the last ten days.

As far as I was aware, there were only two cases listed: my pub assault case and Rudy's criminal damage. I was not acting in Rudy's case—I couldn't, since I was a witness—so I assumed another solicitor had been instructed. Both cases were likely to be further remanded. Nothing of substance would happen today.

But the matchbox from the Drunken Piglet was in my bag, waiting for me to figure out its significance in the whole mess.

Molloy was waiting for me on the steps of my office. Just like old times.

I turned the key in the lock and he followed me in. The office was cool, almost chilly. I dropped the files on the desk. "What's up?" I asked.

"I have your client's new charge sheets." He pulled them out of a file and handed them over along with a precis and some witness statements.

I took a quick look. "He's been charged under the Theft and Fraud Offences Act?"

"Right. We found some cloned fuel cards on him."

This was a new one on me. "What are cloned fuel cards?"

"Details are copied from the strip of a legitimate fuel card . . ."

I interrupted him. "Like a credit card?"

Molloy nodded. ". . . and a new card is produced. Except these cards don't even need to look the part, because they're not shown to a shop assistant. They're only used on automated fuel pumps."

I leaned back against the desk, sheet in hand. "Did you not say that there was laundered fuel in the oil tanker he was driving? I thought the new charges would relate to that."

"They're coming. Your man's been using cloned fuel cards to steal agricultural diesel from legitimate garages, delivering it to wherever it's being bleached and then reselling it to garages as fully taxed white diesel. A nice little earner."

"I see. So that's the allegation."

Molloy picked up his files to go. "You could tell him that any information he chooses to share with us will, of course, help his position."

I looked up from the statements.

"He's not doing this on his own, Ben," Molloy said. "As I said to you a few days ago, he's a small cog in a much larger wheel. Which means, of course, he might be afraid to share any information, but there are ways in which we can help him."

"Even with the assault charge?"

He bowed his head. "Yet to be determined."

"But why would a big criminal operation be involved in diesel laundering?" I asked, crossing my arms. "Surely that's small local stuff? I know there's money to be made, but . . ."

"It's just one of the many things they're involved in, believe me. I suspect smaller operations like diesel laundering help them keep in touch with what's happening on the ground, enable them to recruit."

There was something about the way he said the word "recruit" that made me think he was going to reveal something more. But he obviously thought better of it.

"Anyway, I'd better get to court." He straightened himself. "I'll see you there."

I was on my way out the door myself when Kate Burrows appeared, crossing the road with a wave. I'd forgotten she was coming. She followed me back into reception and I handed over the papers.

"Did you find anything?" she asked, clasping the files to her chest.

"Possibly," I said slowly. "I just have to figure out what it means. But I'll let you know when I do."

Her eyes widened. "Really? Well, I'll look forward to hearing from you. Thanks for looking at them."

I picked up my own file for court and walked her to the door. "When are you leaving?"

"Tomorrow. They're releasing Michael's body and we're bringing him back with us." She cleared her throat, her eyes watering. "And then we can put Greysbridge and Michael's book and his bloody film out of our minds forever."

I followed her through the door, locking it behind me, and set off towards the courthouse on foot. Walking through the square, I passed Liam and Harry having a chat in the street, while Liam affixed sale brochures in his estate agent's window. I waved and they both reciprocated, Harry's greeting considerably more muted and lacking Liam's smile. Was there anything left for us? I wondered. Did I even want there to be?

Liam's brochures reminded me that Greysbridge would soon be for sale again, having lost its last chance to succeed with the demise of Michael Burrows' film.

As I opened the gate to the courthouse, I wondered again why anyone would want to scupper a film about Greysbridge. Then, with a jolt, I realized how stupid I'd been. I'd been looking at things the wrong way around. Any film about the story of Louisa Grey and her baby would have to include Inishathair. It was Inishathair that someone didn't want included in the film, not Greysbridge. And I knew why. I remembered the purple marks on Niamh's jeans, Finn's wheezing cough and itchy eyes, and Belva knowing just what to do. On an island that was unwelcoming to visitors.

Without the usual crowd of punters smoking in the doorway, the courthouse felt odd, the courtroom itself almost empty. It even smelled different. I wondered if it had been cleaned,

although it didn't look as though it had been. I was surprised
to see Mrs. Brady sitting with Fridge on one of the benches at
the side. And then I remembered: she was here to support her
son. Fridge must have brought her over from the island. She
gave me a little wave and I waved back, thinking of nothing
but apricot jam.

Molloy wasn't here yet, but the clerk was at her place in front
of the bench, sifting through papers. She beckoned me over,
lowering her voice.

"Are you still acting for Eamonn McShelley?"

I nodded. "Why?"

She gave me a strange look and then picked up a sheet. "No
reason. Did the sergeant speak to you about the new charges?"

"He did."

I sat back down. There was a creak as the door opened and
Molloy appeared at the back of the court. He made his way
up the aisle and slid along the bench beside me. "Everything
okay?"

I took a breath, then leaned over to him, my voice a hissed
whisper, conscious of our little audience at the side of the court.
"It's diesel laundering, isn't it? There's a diesel laundering factory on the island. On Inishathair. It's part of what you've been
investigating."

Molloy tapped his fingers on the table, his voice as low as mine.
"Yes, I think so. A couple of guards have gone over this morning
with a search warrant for that shed. So we'll know soon enough."

"You might find something more than fuel laundering equip-
ment." I told him about the apricot stone and the plate.

His eyes widened. "Do you still have it?"

"What?"

"The stone," he said urgently.

"Oh, yes." I rooted it from my bag, where I'd left it in a tissue, as a kerfuffle at the back of the court told me that the men in custody had arrived.

"Shit. I'd better go and speak to this guy before the judge gets here," I said, standing up and shoving the balled-up tissue at Molloy.

I pushed open the door to the custody area to find Eamonn McShelley in the company of a tall, grey-haired man in a slick-looking pinstriped suit. Another solicitor. I recognized him from the rare occasions I'd been in court in Derry, but couldn't remember his name.

"Why are you talking to my client?" I demanded.

The man turned and held out his hand. There was something slimy about him. Two rings, one wedding, one pinky signet ring with a purple stone.

"William Shaw, solicitor, Derry. You must be Miss O'Keeffe. Mr. McShelley has expressed a desire to change solicitor."

"Let me guess. To you." I looked at McShelley. "Is that true?" McShelley nodded wordlessly.

"Fine," I said. "I'll make an application to come off record." I looked at Shaw. "You do know that it's procedure to wait until that's done before you take instructions?"

Mr. Slimy's mask slipped for a second and he looked me up and down with contempt before bowing ostentatiously. "I do, Miss O'Keeffe, and I'm most sorry."

When I returned to court, Molloy was reading a file at his end of the bench. I slid back up to him. "Well, it appears I'm not representing anyone this morning. I've been sacked."

"McShelley?"

I nodded.

"I'm not surprised, to be honest. Shaw?"

I nodded again as there was a cry of "All rise!" and the judge appeared.

I needed to stay in court to come formally off record in McShelley's case and hand over his file, so I sat there, arms crossed, feeling redundant and watching the proceedings. Rudy's case was called first. He walked into the courtroom and stood quietly with his head bowed. He wasn't represented, but evidence of arrest, charge and caution was given and there was consent to bail on the part of the state, which meant he was free to go until the next court date. He was advised to have a solicitor on that occasion.

While Rudy went to the back of the court to sign his bail bond, McShelley's case was called. He emerged from the custody area, head bowed also, the custody guard instructing him where to stand. But when the judge spoke his name, he looked up and glanced around the court. His eyes found Fridge and Mrs. Brady, the only members of the public in the room. They rested on Fridge and a look was exchanged that was unmistakable. They knew each other. And not in a good way. The look on Fridge's face was fear. I hadn't seen it before.

I put my hand in my bag and fingered the matchbook. The Drunken Piglet. Had Finn stolen the matches from Fridge? Had Fridge been in that pub the night of the assault? I remembered a burn I'd seen on his arm the night of the wedding. Had he been involved?

Fifteen minutes later, the court was adjourned and the judge headed off to his funeral. Molloy gathered up his files and we walked out together. The prison van carrying McShelley passed us as we made our way out the gate and onto the footpath. Mrs. Brady, Fridge, and Rudy were walking up the road ahead of us.

I watched Fridge gently take Mrs. Brady's arm. She seemed to have aged exponentially since Rudy's arrest, although her own son didn't seem to have noticed. He slouched on ahead, cigarette in hand, his shoulders hunched. I suspected that if I could see his face, it would be dressed in its usually surly mask.

"Are you going to arrest him?" I asked, referring to Fridge.

Molloy nodded. "I'm waiting for a call from the guards on the island. Hopefully, I can arrest him under the Waste Management Act while we check everything else out. And then question him about the murder." He checked his phone. "We've a number of sites being raided this morning as part of a broader investigation. But we need key players."

A rumble in the distance caused us both to turn. Seconds later, a white van with Northern Ireland plates roared by, at twice the legal speed limit. Molloy turned with me and together we looked on in horror as the van mounted the footpath behind Mrs. Brady and Fridge. Fridge spun around and shoved the old lady roughly out of the way. She stumbled towards the window of Liam's office, falling painfully to her knees. There was a devastating thump as the van hit Fridge full on and a sickening crunch as he fell to the ground and rolled into the road. Molloy and I ran towards him as the van tore off.

Chapter Thirty-Five

Ten days later

"That is good news!" Leah exclaimed, scratching at a patch of sunburn on her nose. "We could sure do with some."

I descended the last two steps as she hung up the phone and dropped a stack of files on the reception desk.

She looked up. "Are they for the licensing court?"

I nodded. There were three weeks until the annual court in September that was set aside for pub licensing, and it was always hectic. Especially for Leah, since there was a huge amount of paperwork involved.

"Who was that?" I asked, nodding towards the phone.

She smiled. "Phyllis, thanking us for the present we brought her back from Greece. A thank-you-for-marrying-us present."

The local newspaper, with ads that needed to be placed before the court, was spread out in front of her, and she ran her finger down one of the columns, checking the contents.

"And the good news?" I asked.

She looked up again and narrowed her eyes to think. "Oh, yes. Glendara Garda Station is reopening."

As if on cue, the door opened and Molloy appeared, head bent, brow furrowed, the weight of the world on his shoulders. Not a glimmer of a smile.

"We've just heard the good news," I said.

"Oh yes, the Garda station. I presume people will be pleased."

"Will you be running it?" Leah asked, her chin resting on her hands.

"I'm not sure." Molloy looked at me. "Can we have a chat?"

He followed me up the stairs to my office, closing the door behind him. I perched on the desk and he stood at the window, pushing aside one of the blinds. He seemed distracted.

"Well?" I prompted. "Any developments?"

With an obvious effort, he focused. What was wrong with him? "Yes. Fridge has regained consciousness and he's talking. I'm not sure if he'll ever walk again, but at least there's no brain damage."

"That's good. And?"

"We've arrested him for the murder of Michael Burrows. He's admitted it."

I exhaled. "I was afraid of that." I walked back around my desk and sank down into the chair. "I'm assuming he did it because he didn't want attention on the island due to the diesel laundering?"

Molloy nodded. "Partly. The last thing he needed was a film being made and the island overrun with people. That was their reason for doing it in the first place—the islanders thought they'd found a way to support themselves while keeping the island private, but they didn't realize the damage they were doing, the toxic waste that laundering produces."

"So they all knew?"

"The whole island knew and took some benefit from it. It was a neat operation. Adapted trawlers delivering fuel to and from the mainland. Tanks concealed underneath fishing nets. Using different piers to avert suspicion."

"Piers like Greysbridge?"

"Exactly. Rudy was facilitating that. Grey didn't know." He paused. "They had an arrangement with a few different garages on the mainland. It worked perfectly. The last thing they needed was for Hollywood to come calling."

I was still struggling with this. "But surely, they'd have made money from the film too, even if it meant more tourists? Was keeping the island to themselves really worth killing for?" I pictured Fridge gently taking Mrs. Brady's arm and then saving her life, and found it hard to see him as a killer.

Molloy crossed his arms. "Unfortunately, what Fridge didn't tell the other islanders was that he'd recently got into bed with some bigger players."

I leaned back, realization dawning. Finally. "The big players you're investigating?"

He nodded. "Fridge had been doing business with them for a while. But then someone took the trouble to look at a map and see where his island was located, and realized what kind of strategic advantage it had. Way into the North Atlantic, with access both north and south. Sure, there are a hundred reasons apart from diesel laundering to use Inishathair. Even more so with Brexit looming."

"So Fridge was under pressure from *them* to keep the island below the radar?"

Molloy nodded again. "Especially when he made the mistake of mentioning Burrows' film, thinking they'd laugh. Fridge isn't the sharpest tool in the box."

I smiled. "He did lock himself in a fridge."

"Yes. Well, they didn't laugh. Ordered him to put an end to it."

I remembered the matches from the Drunken Piglet and mentioned them now to Molloy.

He nodded. "That was his warning. He was brought there and forced to watch what happened to that poor guy chained to the radiator. See what happens to people who don't do what they're told."

I winced, picturing the scene. "So that's why he killed Michael Burrows."

"That's right. He probably didn't need to, but after that he got scared and panicked. Burrows had stayed with Mrs. Brady and he liked cake. An idea formulates in Fridge's head. He brings over a slice of cake laced with cyanide and leaves it with a note in the kitchen asking Ronan to take it up to Burrows. Ronan does. Burrows is drunk; he eats it, and is dead within minutes."

"So I was right about the plate then?"

"Yes. It was one of Belva's. Fridge had to retrieve it, or it would have been recognized. That's where he was when Jay went into the water. He'd gone into the house to get the plate from Burrows' room, I presume because you'd interrupted him the night before."

"So the islanders didn't let Jay drown on purpose, then?"

Molloy shook his head. "Fridge was the only one who could swim, and he wasn't there. I presume they didn't want to draw attention to his absence, whatever they thought he was doing. But Abby was seen pushing Jay, and Fridge blackmailed her to scupper the film in case Burrows' son decided to still make it. He also warned Ronan to keep quiet about the plate when he recognized it at Belva's. Told him what Abby had done."

Something occurred to me. "Where did you take Ronan when we came back from the island? You said you wanted to show him something."

"I wanted to show him the harm the by-product from diesel laundering can do to the environment. There's a dump of it up the coast and it's appalling. Damage to seabirds, to fish. I knew he was interested in science, so I thought it might make him talk. And it did. Or at least it made him talk to Abby, which made her admit what she'd done."

I smiled. "One scientist to another."

"Something like that."

I sighed. "Poor Michael Burrows."

Molloy nodded. "His only mistake was getting drunk on the island and telling everyone that Hollywood was coming. He completely misjudged things. He thought they'd be pleased. But he had no idea the toes he was stepping on."

I stared out the window. "Killed for big talk."

He sighed deeply. "Looks like it. Although it was money that was at the heart of this one. Ruthless pursuit of money. We had thought what was going on here might lead us to some bigger players, but as usual, it's the small fry that get caught." He shook his head. "The big bastards have moved on. They were quick to dispose of Fridge when they thought he was getting too much attention. Just slice that limb off and don't look back."

"But he survived," I said.

"Doesn't mean he's talking," Molloy said ruefully. "About anything other than his own involvement, anyway. He's terrified they'll hurt his family. And for Fridge, that includes all the islanders."

He was quiet for a moment, then looked out the window again. There was something about his stance. His shoulders were rigid.

"Are you okay?" I asked.

"I'm fine," he snapped. Then immediately, "Sorry."

His face was tense when he turned. I waited for him to speak.

"Look, this is stupid."

"What is?"

"I don't know what's going on with that doctor." He paused, and his features seemed to relax. "Why don't we just get married?"

My mouth fell open. "What?"

The phone rang, and automatically, I answered it. It was Leah. She sounded curious.

"There's a Mitch someone on the phone for you. He won't say who he is, but he sounds American."

Acknowledgements

Inishowen dwellers know that whilst the town of Glendara is fictitious, many of the locations I use in my books are real. This time, locals will figure out that although Inishathair does not exist, its location is similar to that of Inishtrahull, an island off Malin Head which has been uninhabited for some time. They will also work out that the fictional house of Greysbridge is probably located around Ballygorman (although the road on which it sits doesn't exist). I hope the people of Inishowen will forgive me for playing around with the topography of their peninsula (again)! Please visit. It's utterly stunning.

There were many people from whom I sought advice for this book. Thank you to Simon Mills for his medical expertise, to Donal McGuinness for his mastery of boats and sailing, and to my brother Owen Carter for his knowledge of (and rather unnerving enthusiasm for) poisons. Huge thanks are also due to Mick. All gave suggestions which made the book so much better than it would have been. All errors are of course entirely my own.

Thank you to Fidelma Tonry, Lily McGonagle, Mark Tottenham, Una ní Dhubhghaill, Henrietta McKervey, Jo Spain, Mark Thompson, Paul Gunning, Ger Biggs, Roisin Doherty, Julie Sheils and Hugh Reilly.

Thank you to my wonderful U. S. publisher, Oceanview Publishing, and to my brilliant agent, Kerry Glencorse of Susanna Lea Associates; four books later and I am so grateful for everything she has done. Thank you also to all at the Tyrone Guthrie Centre at Annaghmakerrig without whom I simply wouldn't make my deadlines!

Thank you to my parents, who both answered queries I had about old houses and gardens. I should say that I borrowed the name Belva from my mother's Welsh aunt about whom she always spoke so warmly. Belva was a large, kind lady but there the resemblance ends!

Finally, love and thanks as always to Geoff for his support (and his edits).

Publishers Note

We hope that you enjoyed *Murder at Greysbridge*, the fourth in Andrea Carter's Inishowen Mystery Series with Solicitor Ben O'Keeffe.

While the other three novels stand on their own and can be read in any order, the publication sequence is as follows:

Death at Whitewater Church
(BOOK I)

Missing groom—a deconsecrated church—a hidden crypt—a skeleton wrapped in a blanket

"Haunting, atmospheric, and gripping. One of the finest Irish mystery debuts of recent years. Tana French has some serious competition."

—John Connolly,
New York Times best-selling author

Treacherous Strand
(BOOK 2)

A woman's body washes up on a remote beach, partially clothed, with a strange tattoo on her thigh—leading to a doomsday cult—one not eager to be exposed

"*Treacherous Strand* is atmospheric, intelligent, and utterly gripping—a real treat for fans of Irish crime fiction."

—Catherine Ryan Howard,
USA Today best-selling author

The Well of Ice
(BOOK 3)

The Christmas holidays bring a gruesome discovery on Inishowen—a body lying face-down in the snow

"I adored this traditional crime novel; it's modern day Agatha Christie with Ben as Miss Marple"

—*Irish Examiner*

The Body Falls
(BOOK 5)

(Coming November 2022)